Date Due

DEC 17			
NOV 5			
NOV 2			
JAN 4			
OCT 14			
OCT 6			
SEP 27			
FE 16 '00			
MR 16 '00			
APR 17 '09			
	PRINTED IN U. S. A		

THE MACMILLAN CLASSICS

ANDERSEN'S
·FAIRY TALES·

ANDERSEN'S
·FAIRY TALES·

BY

HANS CHRISTIAN ANDERSEN

Illustrated by Lawrence Beall Smith

Afterword by Clifton Fadiman

1963

THE MACMILLAN COMPANY · NEW YORK

COLLIER-MACMILLAN LIMITED · LONDON

Afterword and Illustrations © 1963 The Macmillan Company
The text of the Andersen tales is based on the Hurd and Houghton
edition of *Andersen's Stories and Tales* and *Andersen's Wonder
Stories* (Boston, 1871, 1872), on the translations of
Mrs. E. V. Lucas and Mrs. H. B. Paull, and on the Signe
Toksvig edition, Macmillan, 1953. These translations have
been especially edited and revised for this edition.

FIRST PRINTING

The Macmillan Company, New York
Collier-Macmillan Canada, Ltd., Toronto, Ontario

Library of Congress catalog card number: 63–14840

DESIGNED BY STEFAN SALTER

Printed in the United States of America

. . . Now Ole Shut-Eye lifted little Hjalmar up to the frame, and put the boy's feet into the picture, just in the high grass. And there he stood; and the sun shone upon him through the branches of the trees. He ran to the water, and seated himself in a little boat which lay there. It was painted red and white, the sails gleamed like silver, and six swans, each with a gold circlet round its neck, and a bright blue star on its forehead, drew the boat past the great wood, where the trees tell of robbers and witches, and the flowers tell of the graceful little elves, and of what the butterflies have told them. . . .

HANS CHRISTIAN ANDERSEN

CONTENTS

LIST OF ILLUSTRATIONS

THE ROSE ELF

In the midst of the garden grew a rosebush, which was quite covered with roses. And in one of them, the most beautiful of all, there dwelt an elf. He was so tiny that no human eye could see him. Behind every leaf in the rose he had a bedroom. He was as well formed and beautiful as any child could be, and had wings that reached from his shoulders to his feet. Oh, what a fragrance there was in his rooms! and how clear and bright were the walls! They were made of the pale pink rose leaves.

The whole day long he rejoiced in the warm sunshine, flew from flower to flower, danced on the wings of the flying butterfly, and measured how many steps he would have to take to pass all the roads and crossroads that are marked out on a single hidden leaf. What we call veins on the leaf were to him highroads and crossroads. Yes, those were long roads for him! Before he had finished his journey the sun went down, for he had begun his work too late!

It became very cold, the dew fell, and the wind blew. Now the best thing to do was to go home. He hurried, but when he got there the rose had shut itself up, and he could not get in. Not a single rose stood open. The poor little elf was very much frightened. He had never been out at night before; he had always slumbered sweetly and comfortably behind the warm rose leaves. Oh, it certainly would be the death of him.

At the other end of the garden there was, he knew, an arbor of fine honeysuckle. The flowers looked like great painted horns, and he wished to go down into one of them to sleep till the next day.

He flew thither. Silence! Two people were in there—a handsome young man and a young girl. They sat side by side, and wished that they need never part. They loved each other better than a good child loves its father and mother.

"Yet we must part!" said the young man. "Your brother does not like us; therefore he sends me away on an errand far over mountains and seas. Farewell, my sweet bride, for that you shall be!"

And they kissed each other, and the young girl wept, and gave him a rose. But, before she gave it to him, she impressed a kiss so firmly and closely upon it that the flower opened. Then the little elf flew into it, and leaned his head against the delicate fragrant walls. Here he could plainly hear them say "Farewell! farewell!" and he felt that the rose was placed on the young man's heart. Oh, how that heart beat! the little elf could not go to sleep, it thumped so.

But the rose did not rest undisturbed on that breast for long. The man took it out, and as he went alone through the wood, he kissed the flower so often and so fervently that the little elf was almost crushed. He could feel through the leaf how the man's lips burned, and the rose itself had opened, as if under the hottest noonday sun.

Then came another man, gloomy and wicked. He was the bad brother of the pretty maiden. He drew out a sharp knife, and while the one kissed the rose the bad man stabbed him to death. And then, cutting off his head, buried both head and body in the soft earth under the linden tree.

"Now he's forgotten and gone!" thought the wicked brother; "he will never come back again. He was to have taken a long journey over mountains and seas. One can easily lose one's life, and he has lost his. He cannot come back again, and my sister dare not ask news of him from me."

With his feet he shuffled dry leaves over the loose earth,

and went home in the dark night. But he did not go alone, as he thought. The little elf accompanied him. The elf sat in a dry, rolled-up linden leaf that had fallen on the wicked man's hair. His hat was now placed over the leaf. It was very dark in the hat, and the elf trembled with fear and with anger at the evil deed.

In the morning hour the bad man got home; he took off his hat, and went into his sister's bedroom. There lay the beautiful blooming girl, dreaming of him whom she loved with all her heart. And she now believed that he was going across the mountains and through the forests. The wicked brother bent over her and laughed hideously, as only a fiend can laugh, and the dry leaf fell out of his hair upon the coverlet. But he did not notice it, and he went out to sleep a little himself in the morning hour. The elf slipped out of the withered leaf, placed himself in the ear of the sleeping girl, and told her, as in a dream, the dreadful history of the murder. He described to her the place where her brother had slain her lover and buried his corpse. He told her of the blooming linden tree close by it, and said:

"That you may not think it is only a dream that I have told you, you will find on your bed a withered leaf."

And when she awoke she found it. Oh, what bitter tears she wept! The window stood open the whole day: the little elf could easily get out to the roses and all the other flowers, but he could not find it in his heart to leave the afflicted maiden. In the window stood a plant, a monthly rosebush. He seated himself in one of the flowers, and looked at the poor girl. Her brother often came into the room, and, in spite of his wicked deed, he always seemed cheerful, but she dared not say a word about the grief that was in her heart.

As soon as night came, she crept out of the house, went to the wood, to the place where the linden tree stood, removed the leaves from the ground, turned up the earth, and immediately found him who had been slain. Oh, how she wept, and prayed that she might die also!

Gladly would she have taken the corpse home with her, but that she could not do. She took the pale head with the closed eyes, kissed the cold mouth, and shook the earth out of the beautiful hair. "This I will keep," she said. And when she had laid earth upon the dead body, she took the head, and a little sprig of the jasmine that bloomed in the wood where he was buried, home with her.

As soon as she came into her room, she got the biggest flowerpot she could find. In this she laid the dead man's head, strewed earth upon it, and then planted the jasmine twig in the pot.

"Farewell! farewell!" whispered the little elf. He could not endure to see all this pain, and therefore flew out to his rose in the garden. But the rose was faded; only a few pale leaves clung to the wild bush.

"Alas! how soon everything good and beautiful passes away!" sighed the elf.

At last he found another rose, and this became his house; behind its delicate fragrant leaves he could live and hide himself.

Every morning he flew to the window of the poor girl. And she was always standing weeping by the flowerpot. The bitter tears fell upon the jasmine spray, and every day, as the girl became paler and paler, the twig stood there fresher and greener, and one shoot after another sprouted forth. Little white buds burst out, and these she kissed. But the bad brother scolded his sister, and asked if she had gone mad. He could not bear it, and could not imagine why she was always weeping over the flowerpot. He did not know what closed eyes were there, what red lips had faded there into earth. And she bowed her head upon the flowerpot, and the little elf of the rosebush found her slumbering there. He seated himself in her ear, told her of the evening in the arbor, of the fragrance of the rose, and the love of the elves. And she dreamed a marvelously sweet dream, and while she dreamed her life passed away. She died a quiet death, and she was in heaven, with the one she loved.

And the jasmine opened its great white bells. They smelled peculiarly sweet; it could not weep in any other way over the dead one.

But the wicked brother looked at the beautiful blooming plant, and took it for himself as an inheritance, and put it in his bedroom, close by his bed, for it was glorious to look upon, and its fragrance was sweet and lovely. The little Rose Elf followed, and went from flower to flower—for in each dwelt a little soul—and told of the murdered young man whose head was now earth beneath the earth, and told of the evil brother and of the poor sister.

"We know it!" said each soul in the flowers; "we know it: have we not sprung from the eyes and lips of the murdered man? We know it! we know it!"

And then they nodded their heads in a strange fashion.

The Rose Elf could not at all understand how they could be so quiet. He flew out to the bees that were gathering honey, and told them the story of the wicked brother. And the bees told it to their queen, and the Queen commanded that they should all kill the murderer next morning. But in the night— it was the first night after the sister's death—when the brother was sleeping in his bed, close to the fragrant jasmine, each flower opened, and invisible, but armed with poisonous spears, the flower souls came out and seated themselves in his ear, and told him bad dreams, and flew across his lips and pricked his tongue with poisonous spears.

"Now we have avenged the dead man!" they said, and flew back into the jasmine's white bells.

When morning came and the windows of the bedchamber were opened, the Rose Elf and the Queen Bee and the whole swarm of bees rushed in to kill him.

But he was dead already. People stood around his bed, and said, "The scent of the jasmine has killed him!"

Then the Rose Elf understood the revenge of the flowers, and he told it to the Queen and to the bees, and the Queen hummed with the whole swarm around the flowerpot. The bees were not to be driven away. A man carried away the flowerpot, and one of the bees stung him in the hand, and he let the pot fall, and it broke in pieces.

Then they beheld the whitened skull, and knew that the dead man on the bed was a murderer.

And the Queen Bee hummed in the air, and sang of the revenge of the bees, and of the Rose Elf, and said that behind the smallest leaf there dwells ONE who can bring the evil to light, and repay it.

THE DROP OF WATER

SURELY you know what a microscope is—that wonderful glass which makes everything appear a hundred times larger than it really is. If you look through a microscope at a single drop of ditch water, you will see more than a thousand strange-shaped creatures, such as you never could imagine, dwelling in the water. It looks not unlike a plateful of shrimps, all jumping and crowding upon each other; and so ferocious are these little creatures, that they will tear off each other's arms and legs without mercy. And yet they are happy and merry after their fashion.

Now, there was once an old man, and all his neighbors called him Cribbley Crabbley—a curious name to be sure! He always liked to make the best of everything, and, when he could not manage it otherwise, he tried magic.

So one day he sat with his microscope held up to his eye, looking at a drop of ditch water. Oh, what a strange sight that was! All the thousand little imps in the water were jumping and springing about, and devouring each other, or pulling each other to pieces.

"Upon my word, this is too horrible!" cried old Cribbley Crabbley. "There must surely be some means of making them live in peace and quiet." And he thought and thought, but still could not hit on the right expedient. "I must give them a color," he said at last. "Then I shall be able to see them more distinctly." And accordingly he let fall into the water a tiny drop of something that looked like red wine, but in reality it was witches' blood. Whereupon all the strange little creatures immediately became red all over, not unlike the Red Indians.

The drop of water now seemed but a whole townful of naked and painted wild men.

"What have you there?" inquired another old magician, who had no name at all, which made him even more remarkable than Cribbley Crabbley.

"Well, if you can guess what it is," replied Cribbley Crabbley, "I will give it to you. But I warn you, you'll not find it out so easily."

And the magician without a name looked through the microscope. The scene now revealed to his eyes actually resembled a town where all the inhabitants were running about without any clothing. It was a horrible sight! But it was still more horrible to see how they kicked and cuffed, struggled and fought, pulled and bit at each other. All those that were lowest needed to strive to get on top, and all those that were on top must be thrust down. "Look, look!" they seemed to be crying out, "his leg is longer than mine. Pah! Off with it! And there is one who has a little lump behind his ear—an innocent enough little lump, but it pains him, and it shall pain him more!" And they hacked at it, and seized hold of him, and devoured him, merely because of this little lump. Only one of the creatures was quiet, very quiet, and still. It sat by itself, like a shy little girl, wishing for nothing but peace and rest. But the others would not have it so. They pulled the little girl forward, cuffed her, cut at her, and ate her.

"This is most uncommonly amusing," remarked the nameless magician.

"Do you think so? Well, but what is it?" asked Cribbley Crabbley. "Can you guess, or can you not? That's the question."

"To be sure I can guess," was the reply of the nameless magician, "easy enough. It is either Copenhagen or some other large city; I don't know which, for they are all alike. It is some large city."

"It is a drop of ditch water!" said Cribbley Crabbley.

THUMBELINA

ONCE upon a time there lived a young wife who longed exceedingly to possess a little child of her own, so she went to an old witch-woman and said to her, "I wish so very much to have a child—a little tiny child—won't you give me one, old mother?"

"Oh, with all my heart!" replied the witch. "Here is a barleycorn for you. It is not exactly like those that grow in the farmer's fields, or that are given to the fowls in the poultry yard, but you sow it in a flowerpot, and then you shall see what you shall see!"

"Thank you, thank you!" cried the woman. She gave the witch a silver sixpence, and then, having returned home, sowed the barleycorn, as she had been directed, whereupon a large and beautiful flower immediately shot forth from the flowerpot. It looked like a tulip, but the petals were tightly folded up—it was still in bud.

"What a lovely flower!" exclaimed the peasant woman, and she kissed the pretty red and yellow leaves, and as she kissed them the flower made a loud noise and opened. It was indeed a tulip, but on the small green pointel in the center of the flower there sat a little tiny girl, so pretty and delicate, and her whole body was scarcely bigger than the young peasant's thumb. So she called her Thumbelina.

A pretty varnished walnut shell was given her for a cradle, blue violet leaves served as her mattresses, and a rose leaf was her coverlet. Here she slept at night; but in the daytime she played on the table. The peasant wife had filled a plate with water, and laid flowers in it; their blossoms bordered the edge of the plate while the stalks lay in the water. On the surface floated a large tulip leaf, and on it Thumbelina might sit and sail from one side of the plate to the other. Two white horse-hairs were given to her for oars. That looked quite charming! And Thumbelina could sing too, and she sang in such low, sweet tones as never were heard before.

One night, while she was lying in her pretty bed, a great ugly toad came hopping in through the broken windowpane. The toad was a big creature, old and withered-looking, and wet too. She hopped at once down upon the table where Thumbelina lay sleeping under the red rose petal.

"That is just the wife for my son," said the Toad. And she seized hold of the walnut shell, with Thumbelina in it, and hopped away with her through the broken pane down into the garden.

Here flowed a broad stream. Its banks were muddy and swampy, and it was in this mud that the old Toad and her son lived.

Ugh, how hideous and deformed he was! just like his mother. "Coax, coax, brekke-ke-kex!" was all he could find to say on seeing the pretty little maiden in the walnut shell.

"Don't make such a riot, or you'll wake her," said Old Mother Toad. "She may easily run away from us, for she is as light as a swan-down feather. I'll tell you what we'll do; we'll take her out into the brook, and set her down on one of the large water-lily leaves. It will be like an island to her, who is so light and small. Then she cannot run away from us, and we can go and ready the state rooms down under the mud, where you and she are to dwell together."

Out in the brook there grew many water lilies, with their broad green leaves, each of which seemed to be floating over the water. The leaf which was the farthest from the shore was also the largest. Old Mother Toad swam to it, and on it she set the walnut shell, with Thumbelina.

The poor little tiny creature awoke quite early next morning, and, when she saw where she was, she began to weep most bitterly. There was nothing but water on all sides of the large green leaf, and she could in no way reach the land.

Old Mother Toad was down in the mud, decorating her apartment with bulrushes and yellow buttercups, to make it quite gay and tidy to receive her new daughter-in-law. At last she and her frightful son swam together to the leaf where she had left Thumbelina. They wanted to fetch her pretty cradle, and place it for her in the bridal chamber, before she herself entered in. Old Mother Toad bowed low in the water, and said to her: "Here is my son; he is to be thy husband; and you will dwell together so comfortably down in the mud!"

"Coax, coax, brekke-ke-kex!" was all that her son could say.

Then they took the neat little bed and swam away with it, while Thumbelina sat alone on the green leaf, weeping. She did not like the thought of living with the withered old Toad, and having her ugly son for a husband. The little fishes that were swimming to and fro in the water beneath had heard what Mother Toad had said, so they now put up their heads— they wanted to see the little maid. And when they saw her, they were charmed with her delicate beauty, and it vexed them that the hideous old Toad should carry her off. No, that should never be! They surrounded the green stalk in the water, whereon rested the water-lily leaf, and gnawed it in two with their teeth. The leaf floated away down the brook, with Thumbelina on it—away, far away, where the old Toad could not follow.

Thumbelina sailed past so many places, and the wild birds among the bushes saw her and sang, "Oh, what a sweet little maiden!" On and on, farther and farther, floated the leaf: Thumbelina was on her travels.

A pretty little white butterfly kept fluttering round and

round her, and at last settled down on the leaf. He loved Thumbelina very much, and she was so pleased. There was nothing to trouble her, now that she had no fear of the old Toad chasing her. Wherever she sailed everything was beautiful, and the sun shone down on the water, making it bright as liquid gold. And now she took off her sash, and tied one end of it round the Butterfly, fastening the other end firmly into the leaf. He fluttered his wings and the leaf floated on faster and faster, and Thumbelina with it.

Presently a great cockchafer came buzzing past. He caught sight of her, and immediately fastened his claw round her slender waist, and flew up into a tree with her. But the green leaf floated down the brook, and the Butterfly with it; for he was tied to the leaf, and could not get loose.

Oh, how terrified was poor Thumbelina when the Cockchafer carried her up into the tree! And how sorry she felt, too, for the darling white Butterfly which she had left tied fast to the leaf! She feared that if he could not get away, he would die of hunger. But the Cockchafer cared nothing for that. He settled with her upon the largest leaf in the tree, gave her some honey from the flowers to eat, and hummed her praises, telling her she was very pretty, although she was not at all like a Henchafer. And by-and-by all the Chafers who lived in that tree came to pay her a visit. They looked at Thumbelina, and one Miss Henchafer drew in her feelers, saying, "She has only two legs. How miserable that looks!" "She has no feelers!" cried another. "And see how thin and lean her waist is; why, she is just like a human being!" observed a third. "How very, very ugly she is!" at last cried all the Ladychafers in chorus.

The Chafer who had carried Thumbelina off still could not persuade himself that she was anything but pretty. But, as all the rest kept repeating and insisting that she was ugly, he at last began to think they must be right, and decided to have nothing more to do with her. She might go wherever she would, for the little he cared, he said. And so the whole swarm flew down from the tree with her, and set her on a daisy. Then Thumbelina wept because she was so ugly that the Ladychafers would not keep company with her. And yet she was the prettiest little creature that could be imagined, soft, and delicate, and transparent as the loveliest rose leaf.

All summer long poor Thumbelina lived alone in the wide wood. She wove herself a bed of grass-straw, and hung it under a large burdock leaf, which sheltered her from the rain. She dined off the honey from the flowers, and drank from the dew that every morning spangled the leaves and herblets around her. Thus passed the summer and autumn; but then came winter—the cold, long winter. All the birds who had sung to her so sweetly flew away, trees and flowers withered, the large burdock leaf, under which Thumbelina had lived, rolled itself up, and became a dry, yellow stalk, and Thumbelina was fearfully cold. Her clothes were wearing out, and she herself was so slight and frail; poor little thing! She was nearly frozen to death. It began to snow, and every light flake that fell upon her made her feel as we would if a whole shovelful of snow were thrown upon us. For we are giants in comparison with a little creature only an inch long. She wrapped herself up in a withered leaf, but it gave her no warmth—she shuddered with cold.

On the edge of the wood where Thumbelina had been living, lay a large cornfield. But the corn had been carried away long ago, leaving only the dry, naked stubble standing up from the hard frozen earth. It was like another forest to Thumbelina, and oh, how she shivered with cold as she made her way through it! At last she came past the Field Mouse's door; for the Field Mouse had made herself a little hole under the stubble. And there she dwelt snugly and comfortably, having a room full of corn, and a neat kitchen and store chamber besides. Thumbelina must now play the beggar girl. She stood at the door and begged for a little piece of a barleycorn, for she had had nothing to eat for two whole days.

"Thou poor little thing!" said the Field Mouse, who was indeed a thoroughly good-natured old creature. "Come into my warm room and dine with me."

She soon took a great liking to Thumbelina, and she asked her to stay. "You may dwell with me all the winter, if you will keep my room clean and neat, and tell me stories, for I love stories dearly." And Thumbelina did all that the kind old Field Mouse required of her, and was made very comfortable in her new home.

"We shall have a visitor presently," observed the Field Mouse; "my next-door neighbor comes to see me once every week. He is better off than I am. He has large rooms in his house, and wears a coat of such beautiful black velvet. It would be a wonderful thing for you if you could secure him for your husband; but unfortunately he is blind, he cannot see you. You must tell him the prettiest stories, you know."

But Thumbelina did not care at all about pleasing their neighbor, Mr. Mole. Nor did she wish to marry him. He came and paid a visit in his black velvet suit. He was so rich and so learned! And the Field Mouse declared his domestic offices were twenty times larger than hers. But he could not endure the sun and the pretty flowers. He was always abusing them, though he had never seen either. Thumbelina was called upon to sing for his amusement, and by the time she had sung "Ladybird, ladybird, fly away home!" and "The Friar of Orders Gray," the Mole had quite fallen in love with her through the charm of her sweet voice. However, he said nothing, he was such a prudent, cautious animal.

He had just been digging a long passage through the earth from their house to his, and he now gave permission to the Field Mouse and Thumbelina to walk in it as often as they liked. He told them not to be afraid of the dead bird that lay in the passage. It was a whole bird, with beak and feathers entire, and therefore he supposed it must have died quite lately, at the beginning of the winter, and had been buried just in the place where he had dug his passage.

In his mouth, the Mole took a piece of tinder, which shines like fire in the dark, and went ahead to light his friends through the long, dark passage. And when they came to the place where the dead bird lay, he thrust his broad nose up against the ceiling and pushed up the earth, and made a great hole for the light to come through. In the middle of the floor lay a swallow, his wings clinging firmly to his sides, his head and legs drawn under the feathers. The poor bird had evidently died of cold. Thumbelina felt so very sorry, for she loved all the little birds who had sung and chirped so merrily to her the whole summer long. But the Mole kicked it with his short legs, saying, "Here's a fine end to all its whistling! A miserable thing it must be to be born a bird! None of my children will be birds, that's a comfort! Such creatures have nothing but their 'Quivit,' and must be starved to death in the winter."

"Yes, indeed, a sensible animal like you may well say so," returned the Field Mouse. "What has the bird got by all his chirping and chirruping? When winter comes it must starve and freeze. And it is such a big creature too!"

Thumbelina said nothing, but when the two others had turned their backs upon the bird, she bent over it, smoothed down the feathers that covered its head, and kissed the closed eyes. "Perhaps it was this one that sang so delightfully to me in the summertime," thought she. "How much pleasure it has given me, the dear, dear bird!"

The Mole now stopped up the hole where the daylight came through, and then followed the ladies home. Thumbelina could not sleep that night. She got out of her bed and wove a carpet of hay, and then went out and spread it round the dead bird. She also fetched some soft cotton from the Field Mouse's room, which she laid over the bird, that it might be warm amid the cold earth.

"Farewell, thou dear bird!" said she, "farewell! and thanks for thy beautiful song in the summertime, when all the trees were green and the sun shone so warmly upon us!" She pressed her head against the bird's breast, and was terrified to feel something beating within it. It was the bird's heart—the bird was not dead. It had fallen in a faint, and now that it was warmer, its life returned.

Every autumn all the swallows fly away to warm countries; but if one of them lingers behind, it freezes and falls down as though dead, and the cold snow covers it.

Thumbelina trembled with fright, for the bird was very large compared with her, who was only an inch in length. However, she took courage, laid the cotton more closely round the poor Swallow, and fetching a leaf which had served as her own coverlet, spread it over the bird's head.

The next night she stole out again, and found that the bird's life had quite returned. It was still so feeble that only for one short moment could it open its eyes to look at Thumbelina, who stood by with a piece of tinder in her hand. "Thanks to thee, thou sweet little child!" said the sick Swallow. "I feel delightfully warm now. Soon I shall recover my strength, and be able to fly again, out in the warm sunshine."

"Oh, no," she replied, "it is too cold outside. It snows and freezes! You must stay in your warm bed. I will take care of you."

She brought the Swallow water in a flower petal, and he drank. Then he told her how he had torn one of his wings in a thorn bush, and therefore could not fly fast enough to keep up with the other swallows, who were all migrating to the warm countries. He had at last fallen to the earth, and more than that he could not remember. He did not know how he had got underground.

However, underground he remained all the winter long, and Thumbelina was kind to him, and loved him dearly, but she never said a word about him to the Mole or the Field Mouse. She knew they could not endure the poor Swallow.

As soon as the spring came, and the sun's warmth had penetrated the earth, the Swallow said farewell to Thumbelina, and she opened the covering of earth which the Mole had thrown back before. The sun shone in upon them so deliciously, and the Swallow asked whether she would not go with him. She could sit upon his back, and then they would fly together far out into the greenwood. But Thumbelina knew it would bother the old Field Mouse, if she were to leave her.

"No, I cannot. I must not go," said Thumbelina.

"Fare thee well, then, thou good and pretty maiden!" said the Swallow, and away he flew into the sunshine. Thumbelina looked after him, and the tears came into her eyes, for she loved the poor Swallow so much.

"Quivit, quivit," sang the bird, as he flew into the greenwood.

And Thumbelina was now sad indeed. She was not allowed to go out into the warm sunshine. The wheat that had been sown in the field above the Field Mouse's house grew up so high that it seemed a perfect forest to the poor little damsel, who was only an inch high.

"This summer you must work at getting your wedding clothes ready," said the Field Mouse. For their neighbor, the blind, dull Mole, in the black velvet suit, had now made his formal proposal to Thumbelina. "You shall have plenty of worsted and linen; you shall be well provided for with all kinds of clothes and furniture, before you become the Mole's wife."

So Thumbelina was obliged to work hard at the distaff,

and the Field Mouse hired four spiders to spin and weave night and day. Every evening the Mole came, and he always talked about the summer soon coming to an end, and that then—when the sun would no longer shine so warmly, scorching the earth till it was as dry as a stone—yes, then, his nuptials with Thumbelina should take place. This sort of conversation did not please her at all; she was thoroughly wearied of his dullness and his prating. Every morning, when the sun rose, and every evening when it set, she would steal out the door. And when the wind blew the tops of the corn aside, so that she could see the blue sky through the opening, she thought how bright and beautiful it was out there, and wished most fervently to see the dear Swallow once more. But he never came; he must have been flying far away in the beautiful greenwood.

Autumn came, and Thumbelina's wedding clothes were ready.

"Four weeks more, and you shall be married!" said the Field Mouse. But Thumbelina wept, and said she would not marry the dull Mole.

"Fiddlesticks!" exclaimed the Field Mouse. "Don't be obstinate, child, or I shall bite thee with my white teeth! Is he not handsome, pray? Why, even the Queen hasn't got such a black velvet dress as he wears! And isn't he rich—rich both in kitchens and cellars? Be thankful to get such a husband!"

So Thumbelina must be married. The set day had arrived, and the Mole had already come to fetch his bride. She must dwell with him, deep under the earth, never again to come out into the warm sunshine, which she loved so much, and which he could not endure. The poor child was in despair at the thought that she must now bid a last farewell to the beautiful sun. She had at least been allowed to catch a glimpse of it every now and then while she lived with the Field Mouse.

"Farewell, thou glorious sun!" she cried, throwing her

"Old Mother Toad bowed low in the water, and said to her: 'Here is my son; he is to be thy husband; and you will dwell together so comfortably down in the mud!'" (Page 11)

arms up into the air, and she walked on a little way beyond the Field Mouse's door. The corn had been reaped, and only the dry stubble surrounded her. "Farewell, farewell!" she repeated, and she clasped her tiny arms round a little red flower that grew there. "Greet the dear Swallow for me, if you should see him."

"Quivit! quivit!"—there was a fluttering of wings just over her head. She looked up, and behold! the little Swallow was flying past. And how pleased he was when he saw Thumbelina. She told him how she had been obliged to accept the disagreeable Mole as a husband, and that she would have to dwell deep underground, where the sun never pierced. And she could not help weeping as she spoke.

"The cold winter will soon be here," said the Swallow; "I shall fly far away to the warm countries. Will you go with me? You can sit on my back, and tie yourself firmly to me with your sash. And thus we shall fly away from the stupid Mole and his dark room, far away over the mountains, to those countries where the sun shines so brightly, where it is always summer, and flowers blossom all the year round. Come and fly with me, thou sweet little Thumbelina, who saved my life when I lay frozen in the dark cellars of the earth!"

"Yes, I will go with thee!" said Thumbelina. And she seated herself on the bird's back. Her feet rested on the outspread wings, and she tied her girdle firmly round one of the strongest feathers. And then the Swallow soared high into the air, and flew away over forest and lake—over mountains whose crests are covered with snow all the year round. How Thumbelina shivered as she breathed the keen frosty air! She soon crept down under the bird's warm feathers, with just her head peeking out, eager to behold all the glory and beauty beneath her.

At last they reached the warm countries. There the sun shone far more brightly than in her native clime. The heavens

seemed twice as high, and twice as blue. And ranged along
the sloping hills in rich luxuriance grew the loveliest green
and purple grapes. Lemons and melons were in the groves,
the fragrance of myrtles and balsams filled the air; and by
the wayside gamboled groups of pretty merry children chasing large bright-winged butterflies.

But the Swallow did not rest here. He flew on, and the
scene seemed to grow more and more beautiful. Near a calm
blue lake, overhung by lofty trees, stood a half-ruined palace
of white marble, built in times long past. Vine wreaths trailed
up the long slender pillars; and on the capitals, among the
green leaves and waving tendrils, many a swallow had built
his nest. And one of these nests belonged to the Swallow on
whose back Thumbelina was riding.

"This is my house," said the Swallow. "But if you would
rather have one of the splendid flowers growing beneath us,
I will take you there. And you shall make your home in the
loveliest of them all."

"That will be charming!" exclaimed she, clapping her tiny
hands.

On the green turf beneath, there lay the fragments of a
white marble column which had fallen to the ground, and
around these fragments twined some beautiful large white
flowers. The Swallow flew down with Thumbelina, and set
her on one of the broad petals. But what a surprise! There sitting in the very heart of the flower was a little manikin, fair
and transparent as though he were made of glass, wearing
the prettiest gold crown on his head, and the brightest, most
delicate wings on his shoulders, yet scarcely one whit larger
than Thumbelina herself. He was the Spirit of the flower. In
every blossom there dwells one such fairy youth or maiden,
but this one was the King of all the Flower Spirits.

"Oh, how handsome he is, this king!" whispered Thumbelina to the Swallow. The fairy prince was quite startled at

the sudden descent of the Swallow, who was a giant compared to him. But when he saw Thumbelina he was delighted, for she was the very loveliest maiden he had ever seen. He took his gold crown off his own head and set it upon hers. He asked her name, and whether she would be his bride and reign as queen over all the Flower Spirits. This, you see, was quite a different bridegroom from the son of the ugly old Toad, or the blind Mole with his black velvet coat. So Thumbelina replied "Yes" to the beautiful King. And the lady and gentlemen fairies came out, each from a separate flower, to pay homage to Thumbelina; so gracefully and courteously they paid their tribute! And every one of them brought her a present. The best of all the presents was a pair of transparent wings. They were fastened on Thumbelina's shoulders, and she could fly from flower to flower. That was the greatest of pleasures! And the little Swallow sat in his nest above and sang to her his sweetest song. In his heart, however, he was very sad, for he loved Thumbelina, and would have wished never to part from her.

"Thou shalt no longer be called Thumbelina," said the King of the Flowers to her, "for it is not a pretty name, and you are so lovely! We will call thee Maia."

"Farewell! farewell!" sang the Swallow, and away he flew from the warm countries far away back to Denmark. There he had a little nest just over the window of a man who writes stories for children. "Quivit! quivit! quivit!" he sang to him, and from him we have learned this story.

THE UGLY DUCKLING

Iᴛ was glorious out in the country. It was summer, and the cornfields were yellow, and the oats were green. The hay had been put up in stacks in the green meadows, and the stork went about on his long red legs, and chattered Egyptian, for this was the language he had learned from his good mother. All around the fields and meadows were great forests, and in the midst of these forests lay deep lakes.

Yes, it was really glorious out in the country. In the midst of the sunshine there lay an old farm, surrounded by deep canals, and from the wall down to the water grew great burdocks, so high that little children could stand upright under the loftiest of them. It was just as wild there as in the deepest wood. Here sat a Duck upon her nest, for she had to hatch her young ones. But she was almost tired out before the little ones came, she so seldom had visitors. The other ducks liked better to swim about in the canals than to run up to sit down under a burdock, and cackle with her.

At last one eggshell after another burst open. "Peep! peep!" they cried, and in all the eggs there were little creatures that stuck out their heads.

"Rap! rap!" they said; and they all came rapping out as fast as they could, looking all round them under the green leaves; and the mother let them look as much as they chose, for green is good for the eyes.

"How wide the world is!" said the young ones, for they certainly had much more room now than when they were in the eggs.

"Do you think this is all the world?" asked the mother. "It

extends far across the other side of the garden, clear into the parson's field, but I have never been there yet. I hope you are all together," she continued, and stood up. "No, I have not all. The largest egg still lies there. How long is that to last? I am really tired of it." And she sat down again.

"Well, how goes it?" asked an old duck who had come to pay her a visit.

"It lasts a long time with this one egg," said the Duck sitting there. "It will not burst. Now, only look at the others; aren't they the prettiest ducks one could possibly see? They are all like their father; the bad fellow never comes to see me."

"Let me see the egg which will not burst," said the old visitor. "Believe me, it is a turkey's egg. I was once cheated in that way, and had such anxiety and trouble with the young ones, for they are afraid of the water. I couldn't get them to go in. I quacked and clucked, but it was no use. Let me see the egg. Yes, that's a turkey's egg! Let it lie there, and teach the other children to swim."

"I think I will sit on it a little longer," said the Duck. "I've sat so long now that I can sit a few days more."

"Just as you please," said the old duck, and she went away.

At last the great egg burst. "Peep! peep!" said the little one, and crept forth. It was very large and very ugly. The Duck looked at it.

"It's a very large duckling," said she. "None of the others look like that. Can it really be a turkey chick? Now we shall soon find it out. It must go into the water, even if I have to thrust it in myself."

The next day the weather was splendid, and the sun shone on all the green trees. The Mother Duck went down to the water with all her little ones. Splash! she jumped into the water. "Quack! quack!" she said, and one duckling after another plunged in. The water closed over their heads, but they came up in an instant, and swam very well. Their legs went of themselves. There they were all in the water, and the ugly gray Duckling swam with them.

"No, it's not a turkey," said she. "Look how well it can use its legs, and how upright it holds itself. It is my own child! On the whole it's quite pretty, if one looks at it rightly. Quack! quack! Come with me, and I'll lead you out into the great world, and present you in the poultry yard. But keep close to me, so that no one may tread on you, and watch out for the cats!"

And so they came into the poultry yard. There was a terrible riot going on in there. Two families were quarreling about an eel's head, but the cat got it after all.

"See, that's how it goes in this world!" said the Mother Duck; and she whetted her beak, for she, too, had wanted the eel's head. "Only use your legs," she said. "See that you bustle about, and bow your heads before the old duck yonder. She's the grandest of all here. She's of Spanish blood—that's why she's so fat; and do you see, she has a red rag around her leg. That's something particularly fine, and the greatest distinction a duck can enjoy. It signifies that one does not want to lose her, and that she's to be recognized by man and beast. Shake

yourselves—don't turn in your toes. A well brought up duck turns its toes quite out, just like Father and Mother, so! Now bend your necks and say 'Rap!' "

And they did so. The other ducks round about looked at them, and said quite boldly:

"Look there! Now we're to have them hanging around, as if there were not enough of us already! And—fie!—how that Duckling yonder looks. We won't stand that!" And one duck flew up immediately, and bit him in the neck.

"Let him alone," said the mother. "He does no harm to anyone."

"Yes, but he's too large and peculiar," said the duck who had bitten him. "And therefore he must be buffeted."

"Those are pretty children that the mother has there," said the old duck with the rag round her leg. "They're all pretty but that one; that was a failure. I wish she could alter it."

"That cannot be done, my lady," replied the Mother Duck. "He is not pretty, but he really has a good disposition, and swims as well as any other. I may even say he swims better. I think he will grow up pretty, and become smaller in time. He has lain too long in the egg, and therefore is not properly shaped." And then she pinched him in the neck, and smoothed his feathers. "Moreover, he is a drake," she said, "and therefore it is not of so much consequence. I think he will be very strong; he makes his way already."

"The other ducklings are graceful enough," said the old duck. "Make yourself at home; and if you find an eel's head, you may bring it to me."

And now they were at home. But the poor Duckling which had crept out of the egg last and looked so ugly, was bitten and pushed and jeered by the other ducks and the chickens.

"He is too big!" they all said. And the turkey cock, who had been born with spurs, and therefore thought himself an emperor, blew himself up like a ship in full sail, and bore straight down upon him. Then he gobbled, and grew quite red in the face. The poor Duckling did not know where he should stand or walk. He was very melancholy because he looked so ugly, and was scoffed at by the whole yard.

So it went the first day; and afterward it got worse and worse. The poor Duckling was hounded by everyone; even his brothers and sisters were angry with him, and said, "If the cat would only catch you, you ugly creature!" And the mother said, "If you were only far away!" And the ducks bit him, and the chickens beat him, and the girl who had to feed the poultry kicked at him with her foot.

He ran and flew over the fence, and the little birds in the bushes flew up in fear.

"That is because I am so ugly!" thought the Duckling; and he shut his eyes, and flew on farther and came out into the great moor, where the wild ducks lived. Here he lay the whole night long, and was weary and downcast.

Toward morning the wild ducks flew up, and looked at their new companion.

"What sort of a one are you?" they asked. And the Duckling turned in every direction, and bowed as well as he could. "You are remarkably ugly!" said the Wild Ducks. "But that doesn't matter to us, as long as you do not marry into the family."

Poor thing! He certainly did not think of marrying. He only hoped to be able to lie among the reeds and drink some of the swamp water.

He had lain there two whole days, when two wild geese arrived, or, properly speaking, two wild ganders. It was not long since each had crept out of an egg, and that's why they were so saucy.

"Listen, comrade," said one of them. "You're so ugly that I like you. Will you go with us, and become a bird of passage? Near here, in another moor, there are a few sweet lovely wild geese, all unmarried, and all able to say 'Rap!' You've a chance of making your fortune, ugly as you are!"

"Piff! paff!" resounded through the air; and the two ganders fell down dead in the swamp, and the water became blood red. "Piff! paff!" it sounded again, and whole flocks of wild geese rose up from the reeds. And then there was another report. A great hunt was going on. The hunters were lying in wait all round the moor, and some were even sitting up in the branches of the trees, which spread far over the reeds. The blue smoke rose up like clouds among the dark trees, and was wafted far away across the water. The hunting dogs came—splash, splash!—into the swamp, and the rushes and the reeds bent down on every side. That was a fright for the poor Duckling! He turned his head, and put it under his wing; but at that moment a frightful great dog stood close by. His tongue hung far out of his mouth and his eyes gleamed horrible and ugly. He thrust out his nose close against the Duckling, showed his sharp teeth, and—splash, splash!—on he went, without seizing him.

"Oh, heaven be thanked!" sighed the Duckling. "I am so ugly that even the dog does not want to bite me!"

And so he lay quiet, while the shots rattled through the reeds and gun after gun was fired. At last, late in the day, silence was restored. But the poor Duckling did not dare rise up. He waited several hours before he looked round, and then hastened away out of the moor as fast as he could go. He ran on, over field and meadow, and there was such a storm raging that it was difficult to get from one place to another.

Toward evening the Duckling came to a miserable little peasant's hut. This hut was so dilapidated it did not know on which side to fall; and that's why it remained standing. The storm whistled round the Duckling in such a way that the poor creature was obliged to sit down, and lean against the hut. And the storm grew worse and worse. Then the Duck-

ling noticed that one of the hinges of the door had given
way, and the door hung so slanting that he could slip through
the crack into the room; and so he did.

Here lived a woman, with her tom cat and her hen. And
the Tom Cat, whom she called Sonnie, could arch his back and
purr. He could even give out sparks; but for that, one had to
stroke his fur the wrong way. The Hen had short little legs,
and therefore she was called Chickabiddy-shortshanks. She
laid good eggs, and the woman loved her as her own child.

In the morning the strange Duckling was noticed at once.
The Tom Cat began to purr, and the Hen began to cluck.

"What's this?" said the woman, and looked all round. But
she could not see well, and therefore she thought the Duckling
was a fat duck that had strayed. "This is a rare prize!" she
said. "Now I shall have duck's eggs. I hope it is not a drake.
We must try and see."

And so the Duckling was admitted on trial for three weeks;
but no eggs came. Now the Tom Cat was master of the house,
and the Hen was the lady, and they always said, "We and the
world!" for they thought they were half the world, and by far
the better half. The Duckling thought one might have a different opinion, but the Hen would not allow it.

"Can you lay eggs?" she asked.

"No."

"Then you'll have the goodness to hold your tongue."

And the Tom Cat said, "Can you curve your back, and purr,
and give out sparks?"

"No."

"Then you cannot have any opinion of your own when
sensible people are speaking."

So the Duckling sat in a corner and was melancholy. The
fresh air and the sunshine streamed in; and he was seized with
such a strange longing to swim on the water, that he could
not help telling the Hen about it.

"What are you thinking of?" cried the Hen. "You have nothing to do; that's why you have these fancies. Purr or lay eggs, and they will pass over."

"But it is so charming to swim on the water!" said the Duckling, "so refreshing to let it close above one's head, and to dive down to the bottom."

"Yes, that must be a mighty pleasure truly," quoth the Hen. "I fancy you must have gone crazy. Ask the Cat about it—he's the cleverest animal I know—ask him if he likes to swim on the water, or to dive down to the bottom. I won't speak about myself. Ask our mistress, the old woman. No one in the world is cleverer than she. Do you think she has any desire to swim, and to let the water close above her head?"

"You don't understand me," said the Duckling.

"We don't understand you? Then pray who is to understand you? You surely don't pretend to be cleverer than the Tom Cat and the woman—I won't say anything of myself. Don't be conceited, child, and be grateful for all the kindness you have received. Did you not get into a warm room, and have you not fallen into company from which you can learn something? But you are a chatterer, and it is not pleasant to associate with you. You may believe me, I speak for your good. I tell you disagreeable things, and by that one may always know one's true friends! Only take care that sometime you learn to lay eggs, or to purr and give out sparks!"

"I think I will go out into the wide world," said the Duckling.

"Yes, do go," replied the Hen.

And the Duckling went away. He swam on the water, and dived, but he was slighted by every creature because of his ugliness.

Now came the autumn. The leaves in the forest turned yellow and brown, and the wind caught them and they danced about. Up in the air it grew very cold, and the clouds hung low, heavy with hail and snowflakes. On the fence stood the Raven, crying, "Croak! croak!" for the cold.

Yes, it was enough to make one shiver. The poor little Duckling certainly did not have a good time. One evening— the sun was just setting in all its beauty—there came a flock of great handsome birds out of the bushes. They were daz- zling white, with long flexible necks—they were swans. They uttered a very peculiar cry, spread forth their glorious great wings, and flew away from that cold region to warmer lands and fair open lakes. They mounted so high, so high! and the ugly little Duckling felt quite strange as he watched them. He turned round and round in the water like a wheel, stretched out his neck toward them, and uttered such a strange loud cry that he frightened himself. Oh! He could not forget those beautiful, happy birds; and when he could see them no longer, he dived down to the very bottom, and when he came up again, was quite beside himself. He didn't know the name of those birds, and he didn't know where they were flying; but he loved them more than he had ever loved anyone. He was not at all envious of them. How could he think of even wish- ing to possess the loveliness they had? He would have been happy to have the ducks endure his company—the poor ugly creature!

The winter grew cold, very cold! The Duckling was forced to swim about in the water, to keep the surface from freezing entirely; but every night the hole in which he swam about became smaller and smaller. It froze so hard that the icy cov- ering crackled again; and the Duckling was obliged to move his legs continually to prevent the hole from freezing up. At last he became exhausted, and lay quite still, and thus froze fast into the ice.

Early in the morning a peasant came by, and when he saw what had happened, he took his wooden shoe, broke the ice crust to pieces, and carried the Duckling home to his wife.

The Duckling came to, and the children wanted to play with him. But the Duckling thought they might hurt him, and in his terror fluttered up into the milk pan, so that the milk spurted all over the room. The woman clapped her hands, and the Duckling flew down into the butter tub, and then into the meal barrel and out again. How he looked then! The woman screamed, and struck at him with the fire tongs; the children laughed and screamed and tumbled over one another in their efforts to catch the Duckling. Happily the door stood open, and the poor creature was able to slip out between the shrubs into the newly fallen snow. There he lay quite exhausted.

But it would be too sad if I were to tell you all the misery and bad times the Duckling had to endure in the hard winter. He lay out on the moor among the reeds. And then the sun began to shine again and the larks to sing; it was at last a beautiful spring.

Then all at once the Duckling could flap his wings. They beat at the air more strongly than before, and bore him strongly away. And before he knew how all this happened, he found himself in a great garden, where the elder-trees smelled sweet, and bent their long green branches down to the canal that wound through the region. Oh, here it was so beautiful, and such a happy spring! From the thicket came three glorious white swans; they rustled their wings, and swam lightly on the water. The Duckling knew the splendid creatures, and felt oppressed by a peculiar sadness.

"I will fly away to them, to the royal birds! And they will kill me, because I, who am so ugly, dare to approach them. But it is of no consequence! Better to be killed by them than to suffer hunger in winter or be pursued by ducks, and beaten by fowls, and pushed about by the girl who takes care of the poultry yard." He flew out into the water, and swam toward the beautiful swans. They looked at him, and came sailing down upon him with outspread wings. "Kill me!" said the poor creature, and bent his head down upon the water, expecting nothing but death. But what was this that he saw in the clear water? He beheld his own image; and, lo! it was no longer a clumsy, dark, gray bird, ugly and hateful to look at, but—a swan!

It does not matter if one is born in a duck yard, if one has only lain in a swan's egg.

The young Swan felt quite glad at all the need and misfortune he had suffered, for now he better realized his new happiness and all the splendor that surrounded it. And the great swans swam round him, and stroked him with their beaks.

Into the garden came little children, who threw bread and corn into the water. The youngest cried, "There is a new one!" and the other children shouted joyously, "Yes, a new one has arrived!" They clapped their hands and danced about, and ran to their father and mother; and bread and cake were thrown into the water; and they all said, "The new one is the most beautiful of all! So young and handsome!" And the old swans bowed their heads before him.

He felt quite ashamed, and hid his head under his wings, for he did not know what to do. He was very happy, and yet not at all proud. He remembered how he had been persecuted and despised; and now he heard them saying that he was the most beautiful of all birds. Even the elder-tree bent its branches straight down into the water before him, and the sun shone warm and mild. His wings rustled, he lifted his slender neck, and cried rejoicingly from the depths of his heart:

"I never dreamed it was possible to be so happy when I was the Ugly Duckling!"

GREAT CLAUS AND LITTLE CLAUS

In a village there once lived two men of the selfsame name. They were both called Claus, but one of them had four horses and the other had only one. So to distinguish them, people called the owner of the four horses "Great Claus," and he who had only one horse was called "Little Claus." Now I shall tell you what happened to them, for this is a true story.

Throughout the week Little Claus was obliged to plow for Great Claus and to lend him his one horse, but once a week —on Sunday—Great Claus lent him all his four horses. How proudly each Sunday Little Claus would smack his whip over all five, for they were as good as his own on that one day.

The sun shone brightly and the church bells rang merrily as the people passed by, dressed in their best and with their prayer books under their arms. They were going to hear the parson preach. They looked at Little Claus plowing with his five horses, and he was so proud that he smacked his whip and said, "Gee-up, my five horses."

"You mustn't say that," said Great Claus, "for only one of them is yours."

But Little Claus soon forgot what he ought not to say, and when anyone passed he would call out, "Gee-up, my five horses."

"I must really beg you not to say that again," said Great Claus. "If you do, I shall hit your horse on the head so that he will drop down dead on the spot. And that will be the end of him."

"I promise you I will not say it again," said the other. But as soon as anybody came by nodding to him and wishing him "Good day," he was so pleased and thought how grand it was to have five horses plowing in his field that he cried out again, "Gee-up, all my horses!"

"I'll gee-up your horses for you," said Great Claus. And seizing the tethering mallet he struck Little Claus's one horse on the head, and it fell down dead.

"Oh, now I have no horse at all," said Little Claus, weeping. But after a while he flayed the dead horse and hung the skin in the wind to dry.

Then he put the dried skin into a bag, hung it over his shoulder, and went off to the next town to sell it. But he had a long way to go and had to pass through a dark and gloomy forest.

Presently a storm arose and he lost his way. And before he discovered the right path, evening was drawing on, and it was still a long way to the town and too far to return home before nightfall.

Near the road stood a large farmhouse. The shutters outside the windows were closed, but lights shone through the crevices and at the top. "They might let me stay here for the night," thought Little Claus, so he went up to the door, and knocked.

The farmer's wife opened the door, but when she heard what he wanted she told him to go away. Her husband was not at home and she could not let any strangers in.

"Then I shall have to lie out here," said Little Claus to himself, as the farmer's wife shut the door in his face.

Close to the farmhouse stood a large haystack, and between it and the house there was a small shed with a thatched roof. "I can lie up there," said Little Claus, as he saw the roof. "It will make a famous bed, but I hope the stork won't fly down and bite my legs." A live stork who had his nest on the roof was standing up there.

So Little Claus climbed onto the roof of the shed. And as he turned about to make himself comfortable, he discovered that the wooden shutters did not reach to the top of the windows. He could see into the room, in which a large table was laid out with wine, roast meat, and a splendid fish. The farmer's wife and the sexton were sitting at table together. Nobody else was there. She was filling his glass and helping him plentifully to fish, which appeared to be his favorite dish.

"If only I could have some too," thought Little Claus. Then he stretched out his neck toward the window and spied a beautiful large cake. Indeed, they had a glorious feast before them.

At that moment he heard someone riding down the road toward the farm. It was the farmer coming home.

He was a good man but he had one very strange prejudice —he could not bear the sight of a sexton. If he happened to see one, he would get into a terrible rage. Because of this dislike, the sexton had gone to visit the farmer's wife during her husband's absence from home, and the good woman had put before him the best of everything she had in the house to eat.

When they heard the farmer they were dreadfully frightened, and the woman made the sexton creep into a large chest which stood in a corner. He went at once, for he was well aware of the poor man's aversion to the sight of a sexton. The woman then quickly hid all the nice things and the wine in the oven, because if her husband had seen it he would have asked why it was provided.

"Oh dear," sighed Little Claus, on the roof, when he saw the food disappearing.

"Is there anyone up there?" asked the farmer, peering up at Little Claus. "What are you doing up there? You had better come into the house."

Then Little Claus told him how he had lost his way, and asked if he might have shelter for the night.

"Certainly," said the farmer. "But the first thing is to have something to eat."

The woman received them both very kindly, laid the table, and gave them a large bowl of porridge. The farmer was hungry and ate it with a good appetite, but Little Claus could not help thinking of the good roast meat, the fish, and the cake, which he knew were hidden in the oven. He had put his sack with the hide in it under the table by his feet, for as we remember he was on his way to the town to sell it. He did not fancy the porridge, so he trod on the sack and made the dried hide squeak quite loudly.

"Hush!" said Little Claus to his sack, at the same time treading on it again so that it squeaked louder than ever.

"What on earth have you got in your sack?" asked the farmer.

"Oh, it's a goblin," said Little Claus. "He says we needn't eat the porridge, for he has charmed the oven full of roast meat and fish and cake."

"What do you say?" said the farmer, opening the oven door with all speed and seeing the nice things the woman had hidden, but which her husband thought the goblin had produced for their special benefit.

The woman dared not say anything but put the food before them, and then they both made a hearty meal of the fish, the meat, and the cake.

Then Little Claus trod on the skin and made it squeak again.

"What does he say now?" asked the farmer.

"He says," answered Little Claus, "that he has also charmed three bottles of wine into the oven for us."

So the woman had to bring out the wine too, and the farmer drank it and became very merry. Wouldn't he like to have a goblin for himself, like the one in Little Claus's sack!

"Can he charm out the devil?" asked the farmer. "I shouldn't mind seeing him, now that I am in such a merry mood."

"Oh yes!" said Little Claus. "My goblin can do everything that we ask him. Can't you?" he asked, trampling on the sack till it squeaked louder than ever. "Did you hear him say yes? But the devil is so ugly, you'd better not see him."

"Oh, I'm not a bit frightened. Whatever does he look like?"

"Well, he will show himself in the image of a sexton."

"Oh dear!" said the farmer. "That's bad! I must tell you that I can't bear to see a sexton. However, it doesn't matter. I shall know it's only the devil and then I shan't mind so much. Now my courage is up! But he mustn't come too close."

"I'll ask my goblin about it," said Little Claus, treading on the bag and putting his ear close to it.

"What does he say?"

"He says you can go along and open the chest in the corner, and there you'll see the devil moping in the dark. But hold the lid tight so that he doesn't get out."

"Will you help me to hold it?" asked the farmer, going along to the chest where the woman had hidden the real sexton, who was shivering with fright. The farmer lifted up the lid a wee little bit and peeped in.

"Ha!" he shrieked, and sprang back. "Yes, I saw him and he looked just exactly like our sexton. It was a horrible sight!" They had to have a drink after this, and there they sat drinking till far into the night.

"You must sell me that goblin," said the farmer. "You may ask what you like for him! I'll give you a bushel of money for him."

"No, I can't do that," said Little Claus. "You must remember how useful my goblin is to me."

"Oh, but I should so like to have him," said the farmer, and he went on begging for him.

"Well," said Little Claus at last, "as you have been so kind to me I shall have to give him up. You shall have him for a bushel of money, but I must have it full to the brim."

"You shall have it," said the farmer. "But you must take that chest away with you! I won't have it in the house for another hour. I'd never know whether he's there or not."

So Little Claus gave his sack with the dried hide in it to the farmer and received in return a bushel of money, and the measure was full to the brim. The farmer also gave him a large wheelbarrow to take the money and the chest away in.

"Good-by," said Little Claus, and off he went with his money and the big chest with the sexton in it.

There was a wide and deep river on the other side of the wood. The current was so strong that it was almost impossible to swim against it. A large new bridge had been built across it, and when they got into the very middle of it, Little Claus said quite loud, so that the sexton could hear him: "What am I to do with this stupid old chest? It might be full of paving stones—it's so heavy. I am quite tired of wheeling it along, so I'll just throw it into the river. If it floats down the river to my house, well and good; and if it doesn't, I shan't care."

Then he took hold of the chest and raised it up a bit, as if he were about to throw it into the river.

"No, no! Let it be!" shouted the sexton. "Let me get out!"

"Hullo!" said Little Claus, pretending to be frightened. "Why, he's still inside it! Then I must heave it into the river to drown him."

"Oh, no! Oh, no!" shouted the sexton. "I'll give you a bushel full of money if you'll let me out!"

"Oh, that's another matter," said Little Claus, opening the chest. The sexton crept out at once and pushed the empty chest into the water, and then went home and gave Little Claus a whole bushel full of money. He had already had one from the farmer, you know, so now his wheelbarrow was quite full of money.

"I got a pretty fair price for that horse, I must admit," said he to himself when he got home to his own room and turned the money out of the wheelbarrow into a heap on the floor. "What a rage Great Claus will be in when he discovers how rich I have become through my one horse. But I won't tell him the truth about it." So he sent a boy to Great Claus to borrow a bushel measure.

"What does he want that for?" thought Great Claus. And he rubbed some tallow on the bottom of the measure, so that a little of whatever was to be measured might stick to it. So it did, for when the measure came back three new silver three-penny bits were sticking to it.

"What's this?" said Great Claus, and he ran straight along to Little Claus. "Where on earth did you get all that money?"

"Oh, that was for my horse's hide which I sold last night."

"That was well paid, indeed!" said Great Claus. And he ran home, took an ax, and hit all his four horses on the head. He then flayed them and went off to the town with the hides.

"Skins! Skins! Who will buy skins?" he shouted up and down the streets.

All the shoemakers and tanners in the town came running up and asked him how much he wanted for them.

"A bushel of money for each," said Great Claus.

"Are you mad?" they all said. "Do you imagine we have money by the bushel?"

"Skins! Skins! Who will buy skins?" he shouted again.

The shoemakers took up their measures and the tanners their leather aprons, and beat Great Claus through the town. "Skins! Skins!" they mocked him. "Yes, we'll give you a raw hide. Out of the town with him!" they shouted, and Great Claus had to hurry off as fast as ever he could go. He had never had such a beating in his life.

"Little Claus shall pay for this," he said when he got home. "I'll kill him for it."

Little Claus's old grandmother had just died in his house. She certainly had been very cross and unkind to him, but now that she was dead he felt quite sorry about it. He took the dead woman and put her into his warm bed to see if he could bring her to life again. He meant her to stay there all night, and he would sit on a chair in the corner. He had slept like that before.

As he sat there in the night, the door opened and in came Great Claus with his ax. He knew where Little Claus's bed stood, and he went straight up to it and hit the dead grandmother a blow on the forehead, thinking that it was Little Claus.

"Just see if you'll cheat me again after that," he said. Then he went home again.

"What a bad, wicked man he is!" said Little Claus. "He was going to kill me there. What a good thing that poor old granny was dead already, or else he would have killed her."

He now dressed his old grandmother in her best Sunday clothes, borrowed a horse from his neighbor, harnessed it to a cart, and set his grandmother on the back seat so that she could not fall out when the cart moved. Then he started off through the wood. When the sun rose he was just outside a big inn, and Little Claus drew up his horse and went in to get something to eat. The landlord was a very, very rich man and a very good man, but he was fiery-tempered, as if he were made of pepper and tobacco.

"Good morning," said he to Little Claus. "You've got your best clothes on very early this morning!"

"Yes," said Little Claus. "I'm going to town with my old grandmother. She's sitting out there in the cart. I can't get her to come in. Won't you take her out a glass of mead? You'll have to shout at her, for she's very hard of hearing."

"Yes, she shall have it," said the innkeeper, and he poured out a large glass of mead which he took out to the dead grandmother in the cart.

"Here is a glass of mead your son has sent," said the innkeeper, but the dead woman sat quite still and never said a word. "Don't you hear?" shouted the innkeeper as loud as he could. "Here is a glass of mead from your son!"

Again he shouted and then again as loud as ever, but as she did not stir he got angry and threw the glass of mead in her face. The mead ran all over her and she fell backward out of the cart, for she was only stuck up and not tied in.

"Now," shouted Little Claus, as he rushed out of the inn and seized the landlord by the neck, "you have killed my grandmother! Just look! There's a great hole in her forehead."

"Oh, what a misfortune!" exclaimed the innkeeper, clasping his hands. "That's the consequence of my fiery temper. Good Little Claus, I will give you a bushel of money and bury your grandmother as if she had been my own, if you will only say nothing about it. Otherwise they will chop my head off, and that is so nasty."

So Little Claus had a whole bushel of money, and the innkeeper buried the old grandmother just as if she had been his own.

When Little Claus got home again with all his money, he immediately sent his boy over to Great Claus to borrow his measure.

"What?" said Great Claus. "Is he not dead? I shall have to go and see about it myself." So he took the measure over to Little Claus himself.

"I say, wherever did you get all that money?" asked he, his eyes round with amazement at what he saw.

"It was my grandmother you killed instead of me," said Little Claus. "I have sold her and got a bushel of money for her."

"That was good pay indeed!" said Great Claus, so he hurried home, took an ax, and killed his old grandmother.

He then put her in a cart and drove off to town with her

where the apothecary lived, and asked if he would buy a dead body.

"Who is it, and where did the body come from?" asked the apothecary.

"It is my grandmother, and I have killed her for a bushel of money," said Great Claus.

"Heaven preserve us!" said the apothecary. "You are talking like a madman. Pray don't say such things! You might lose your head." And he pointed out to him what a horribly wicked thing he had done and what a bad man he was, and that he deserved to be punished. Great Claus was so frightened that he rushed straight out of the shop, jumped into the cart, whipped up his horse, and galloped home. The apothecary and everyone else thought he was mad, and so they let him drive off.

"You shall be paid for this!" said Great Claus, when he got out on the highroad. "You shall pay for this, Little Claus!"

As soon as he got home, he took the biggest sack he could find, went over to Little Claus, and said: "You have deceived me again. First I killed my horses, and then my old grandmother. It's all your fault, but you shan't have the chance of cheating me again!" Then he took Little Claus by the waist and put him into the sack, put it on his back, and shouted to him, "I'm going to drown you now!"

It was a long way to go before he came to the river, and Little Claus was not so light to carry. The road passed close by a church in which the organ was playing, and the people were singing beautifully. Great Claus put down the sack with Little Claus in it close by the church door. He thought he would like to go and hear a psalm before he went any farther. As Little Claus could not get out of the bag, and all the people were in the church, Great Claus went in too.

"Oh dear, oh dear!" sighed Little Claus in the sack. He turned and twisted, but it was impossible to undo the cord.

Just then an old cattle drover with white hair and a tall stick in his hand came along. He had a whole drove of cows and bulls before him. They ran against the sack Little Claus was in and upset it.

"Oh dear," sighed Little Claus. "I am so young to be going to the kingdom of heaven!"

"And I," said the cattle drover, "am so old and cannot get there yet!"

"Open the sack!" shouted Little Claus. "Get in in place of me, and you will get to heaven directly."

"That will just suit me," said the cattle drover, undoing the sack for Little Claus, who immediately sprang out. "You must look after the cattle now," said the old man as he crept into the sack. Little Claus tied it up and walked off driving the cattle before him.

A little while afterward Great Claus came out of the church. He took the sack again on his back and he certainly thought it had grown lighter, for the old cattle drover was not more than half the weight of Little Claus.

"How light he seems to have got! That must be because I have been to church and said my prayers." Then he went on to the river, which was both wide and deep, and threw the sack with the old cattle drover in it into the water.

"Now you won't cheat me again!" he shouted, for he thought it was Little Claus.

Then he went homeward, but when he reached the crossroads he met Little Claus with his herd of cattle.

"What's the meaning of this?" exclaimed Great Claus. "Didn't I drown you?"

"Yes," said Little Claus. "It's just about half an hour since you threw me into the river."

"But where did you get all those splendid beasts?" asked Great Claus.

"They are sea cattle," said Little Claus. "I will tell you the whole story, and indeed I thank you heartily for drowning me. I'm at the top of the tree now and a very rich man, I can tell you. I was so frightened when I was in the sack! The wind whistled in my ears when you threw me over the bridge into the cold water. I immediately sank to the bottom but I was not hurt, for the grass is beautifully soft down there. The sack was opened at once by a beautiful maiden in snow-white clothes with a green wreath on her wet hair. She took my hand and said: 'Are you there, Little Claus? Here are some cattle for you, and a mile farther up the road you will come upon another herd which I will give you too!' Then I saw that the river was a great highway for the sea folk. Down at the bottom of it they walked and drove about, from the sea right up to the end of the river. The flowers were lovely and the grass was so fresh! The fishes which swam about glided close to me just like birds in the air. How nice the people were, and what a lot of cattle strolled about in the ditches!"

"But why did you come straight up here again then?" asked Great Claus. "I shouldn't have done that if it was so fine down there."

"Oh," said Little Claus, "that's just my cunning. You remember I told you the mermaid said that a mile farther up the road—and by the road she means the river, for she can't go anywhere else—I should find another herd of cattle waiting for me. Well, I know how many bends there are in the river and what a roundabout way it would be. It's ever so much shorter if you can come up on dry land and take the short cuts. You save a couple of miles by it and can get the cattle much sooner."

"Oh, you *are* a fortunate man," said Great Claus. "Do you think I should get some sea cattle if I were to go down to the bottom of the river?"

"I'm sure you would," said Little Claus. "But I can't carry you in the sack to the river. You're too heavy for me. If you'd like to walk there and then get into the sack, I'll throw you into the river with the greatest pleasure in the world."

"Thank you," said Great Claus. "But if I don't get any sea cattle when I get down there, see if I don't give you a sound thrashing."

"Oh, don't be so hard on me!" said Little Claus.

Then they walked off to the river. As soon as the cattle saw the water they rushed down to drink, for they were very thirsty. "See what a hurry they're in," said Little Claus. "They want to get down to the bottom again."

"Now, help me first," said Great Claus, "or else I'll thrash you." He then crept into a big sack which had been lying across the back of one of the cows. "Put a big stone in, or I'm afraid I shan't sink," said Great Claus.

"Oh, have no fear of that," said Little Claus, and he put a big stone into the sack and gave it a push. Plump went the sack, and Great Claus was in the river, where he sank to the bottom at once.

"I'm afraid he won't find any cattle," said Little Claus, as he drove his herd home.

THE PRINCESS AND THE PEA

THERE was once a Prince, who wished to marry a Princess, but she must be a *real* Princess. He traveled all over the world in hopes of finding such a lady, but there was always something wrong. There were plenty of Princesses, but whether they were real Princesses he had great difficulty in discovering. There was always something which was not quite right about the ladies. At last he had come home again, and he was very sad because he wanted a real Princess so badly.

One evening there was a terrible storm. It thundered and lightninged and the rain poured down in torrents. Indeed it was a fearful night.

In the middle of the storm somebody knocked at the town gate, and the old King, the Prince's father, went to open it.

A Princess stood outside, but she was in a sad condition from the rain and the storm. The water streamed out of her hair and her clothes clung to her body. It ran in at the top of her shoes and out at the heel. But she said she was a real Princess.

"Well we shall soon see if that is true," thought the old Queen, but she said nothing. She went into the bedroom, took all the bedclothes off and laid a single pea on the bedstead. Then she took twenty mattresses and piled them on top of the pea, and then piled twenty feather beds on top of the mattresses. Up on top of all these was where the Princess was to sleep that night.

In the morning they asked her, "Did you sleep well?"

"Oh, terribly badly!" said the Princess. "I hardly closed my eyes the whole night. Heaven knows what was in the bed. I seemed to be lying on something very hard, and my whole body is black and blue this morning. It was terrible!"

They saw at once that she must be a real Princess. She had been able to feel the pea through twenty mattresses and twenty feather beds. Nobody but a real Princess could have such a delicate sense of feeling.

So the Prince took her to be his wife, for now he was sure that he had found a real Princess. And the pea was put into a museum, where it may still be seen, if no one has stolen it.

Now, this is a true story.

LITTLE IDA'S FLOWERS

"My poor flowers are quite dead!" said little Ida. "They were so pretty yesterday evening, and now all the leaves droop and are withered. Why do they do that?" she asked the student, who sat on the sofa; for she liked him.

He knew the most wonderful stories, and he cut out the funniest pictures—hearts, with little ladies in them who danced, flowers, and big castles with doors that opened. He was a gay student. "Why do the flowers look so sick today?" she asked again, and showed him a whole bouquet, which had withered.

"Don't you know what's the matter with them?" said the student. "The flowers were at a ball last night, and that's why they hang their heads."

"But you know that flowers can't dance!" said little Ida.

"Oh, yes," said the student, "when it gets dark, and we are asleep, they hop around and have a good time. Almost every single night they have a ball."

"Can children go to this ball?"

"Yes," said the student, "very little daisies, and lilies of the valley."

"Where do the prettiest flowers dance?" asked little Ida.

"Haven't you often been outside the town gate, by the big castle, where the King lives in summer, and where the beautiful garden is, with all the flowers? You have seen the swans, who swim up to you when you want to give them bread crumbs? There are regular balls there, I tell you."

"I was out there in the garden yesterday, with my mother," said Ida, "but all the leaves were off the trees, and there was not one flower left. Where are they? In the summer I saw so many."

"They are inside, in the castle," said the student. "You see, as soon as the King and all the court go to town, the flowers run right away from the garden into the castle, and have fun. You ought to see it. The two most beautiful roses seat themselves on the throne, and then they are king and queen. All the red coxcombs range themselves on either side, and stand and bow; they are the chamberlains. Then all the daintiest flowers come, and there is a great ball. The blue violets stand for little naval cadets: they dance with hyacinths and crocuses, whom they call young ladies. The tulips and the great tiger lilies are old ladies who keep watch that the dancing is prettily done, and that everything is proper."

"But," asked little Ida, "does nobody do anything to the flowers, for dancing in the King's castle?"

"There is nobody who really knows about it," answered the student. "Sometimes at night, certainly, the old keeper of the castle comes, and he has a great bunch of keys with him; but as soon as the flowers hear the keys rattle they are very quiet. They hide behind the long curtains, and only poke their heads out. Then the old keeper says, 'I can smell some flowers in here,' but he can't see them."

"That's funny!" said little Ida, and clapped her hands. "But don't you think I could see the flowers?"

"Yes," said the student; "just remember to peep through the window when you go there again; then you will see them. That is what I did today. There was a long yellow lily lying on the sofa and stretching herself. She had an idea she was a court lady."

"Can the flowers from the Botanical Gardens go there? Can they come such a long way?"

"Yes, certainly," said the student, "if they want to they can fly. Haven't you seen the beautiful butterflies, red, yellow, and white? They look almost like flowers; and that is exactly what they used to be. They jumped off their stalks high in the air, and beat it with their leaves, as if the leaves were little wings, and then they flew away. And because they behaved themselves well, they were allowed to fly around in the day-time too, and didn't have to go home again and sit still on their stalks. And in that way the leaves turned into real wings. You've seen that yourself. It might be, though, that the flowers in the Botanical Garden have never been in the King's castle, or that they don't know about the good times there at night. And I'll tell you something now that will surprise the botanical professor, who lives close by here. You know him, don't you? When you come into his garden, you must tell one of the flowers that there is a big ball out at the castle. That flower will tell it to all the rest, and then they will fly away, and when the professor comes out in the garden, there won't be a single flower left. He won't be able to understand where they have gone to."

"But how can one flower tell it to another? You know flowers can't speak."

"No, that's perfectly true," said the student, "but they can play pantomime. Haven't you seen that when the wind blows a little, the flowers nod and move all their green leaves? That's just as plain as if they were talking."

"Can the professor understand pantomime?" asked Ida.

"Yes, certainly. One morning he came into his garden, and saw a large stinging nettle standing there, making pantomime with its leaves at a beautiful red carnation. It was saying, 'You are so pretty, and I am so very fond of you.' But the professor doesn't like that kind of thing, and he slapped the stinging nettle on its leaves at once, for those are its fingers. But the professor stung himself, and since that time he never dares to touch a stinging nettle."

"That was funny," cried little Ida; and she laughed.

"How can anyone put such notions into a child's head?" said the tedious privy councilor, who had come to pay a visit, and was sitting on the sofa. He didn't like the student at all, and always grumbled when he saw him cutting out those queer, funny pictures—sometimes a man hanging on a gibbet and holding a heart in his hand, to show that he stole hearts; sometimes an old witch riding on a broom, and carrying her husband on her nose. The councilor couldn't stand this, and then he said, just as he did now, "How can anyone put such notions into a child's head? What stupid ideas!"

But little Ida thought what the student told about her flowers was very funny; and she thought about it ever so much. The flowers hung their heads, for they were tired because they had danced all night; they were certainly ill. She took them to her other toys, which stood on a pretty little table. The whole drawer was full of fine things. In the doll's bed lay her doll Sophia, asleep; and little Ida said to her:

"You'll really have to get up, Sophia, and be satisfied to lie in the drawer tonight. The poor flowers are ill, and they must lie in your bed. Perhaps they will get well then."

She took the doll out; but it looked cross, and did not say a single word. It was angry because it couldn't keep its own bed.

Ida laid the flowers in the doll's bed, pulled the little coverlet up all around them, and said they were to lie still and be good, and she would make them some tea, so that they might get well again, and be able to get up tomorrow. And she pulled the curtains closely round the little bed, so the sun wouldn't shine in their eyes. The whole evening through she couldn't help thinking of what the student had told her. And when she was going to bed, she had to look behind the window curtains where her mother's beautiful flowers stood —hyacinths and tulips. And then she whispered very softly,

"I know you're going to the ball tonight!" But the flowers acted as if they didn't understand anything. They didn't move a leaf. But little Ida knew what she knew.

When she was in bed she lay for a long time thinking how nice it would be to see the beautiful flowers dancing out there in the King's castle. "I wonder if my flowers have really been there?" And then she fell asleep. In the night she woke up again. She had been dreaming of the flowers, and about the student whom the councilor had scolded for fooling her. It was very quiet in the bedroom where Ida lay; the night lamp burned on the table, and her father and mother were asleep.

"I wonder if my flowers are still lying in Sophia's bed?" she thought to herself. "How I should like to know that!" She raised herself a little, and looked at the door, which stood ajar. In there lay the flowers and all her playthings. She listened, and then it seemed to her as if she heard someone playing on the piano in the next room, but quite softly and prettily, as she had never heard it played before.

"I'm sure all the flowers are dancing in there now!" she thought. "Oh, heavens, how I should like to see it!" But she didn't dare get up, for she would have waked her father and mother.

"If they would only come in here!" she thought. But the flowers did not come. And the music kept on playing so beautifully; it was much too lovely. She couldn't help slipping out of her little bed. She went quietly to the door, and peeked into the room. And, oh, what a funny sight she saw!

There was no night lamp burning, but still it was quite light. The moon shone through the window into the middle of the floor; it was almost like day. All the hyacinths and tulips stood in two long rows on the floor; there was none left at the window. There stood the empty flowerpots. On the floor all the flowers were dancing very gracefully round each other, making a perfect chain, and holding each other by their long green leaves as they swung round. At the piano sat a big yellow lily, which little Ida had certainly seen in summer, for she remembered how the student had said, "It looks just like Miss Lina." Everybody had laughed at him; but now it seemed to little Ida as if the long yellow flower really looked like the lady. It had just her manners in playing—sometimes bending its long yellow face to one side, sometimes to the other, and nodding in tune to the lovely music! No one noticed little Ida. Then she saw a great blue crocus hop into the middle of the table, where the toys stood, and go to the doll's bed and pull the curtains aside. There lay the sick flowers. They got up right away, and nodded to the others, to say that they wanted to dance too. The old chimney-sweep doll, whose underlip was broken off, stood up and bowed to the pretty flowers; they did not look at all ill now. They jumped down among the others, and had such a good time!

Then it seemed as if something fell down from the table. It was the carnival birch rod jumping down! It had an idea that it, too, belonged to the flowers. At any rate it was very neat; and a little wax doll, with a broad hat on its head just like the councilor's, sat on top of it. The birch rod hopped about among the flowers on its three red legs, and stamped quite loud, for it was dancing the mazurka. The other flowers couldn't dance that, because they were too light, and couldn't stamp.

The wax doll on the birch rod all at once got big and long, whirled around on its paper flowers, and said, "How can one put such things in a child's head? What stupid ideas!" and then the wax doll was exactly like the councilor with the broad hat, and looked just as yellow and cross as he. But the paper flowers hit him on his thin legs, and he shrank up again, and became a tiny little wax doll. It was so funny to look at, that little Ida couldn't help laughing. The birch rod went on dancing, and the councilor had to dance too; no matter whether he made himself big and long, or stayed like the little yellow wax doll with the broad black hat. But the other flowers put in a good word for him, especially those who had been lying in the doll's bed, and then the birch rod stopped. At the same moment there was a loud knocking in the drawer, where Ida's doll, Sophia, lay with many other toys. The chimney sweep ran to the edge of the table, lay flat down on his stomach, and began to pull the drawer out a little. Then Sophia sat up, and looked around very surprised.

"There must be a ball here," she said; "why didn't somebody tell me?"

"Will you dance with me?" asked the chimney sweep.

"You'd be a nice sort of fellow to dance with!" she said sarcastically, and turned her back on him.

She sat down on the drawer again, and thought that one of the flowers would come and ask her; but not one of them came. Then she coughed, "Hem! hem! hem!" but nobody came anyway. The chimney sweep then danced all alone, and that wasn't so bad either!

As none of the flowers seemed to notice Sophia, she let herself fall down from the drawer right on the floor, with a big noise. The flowers all ran up, to ask if she had hurt herself; and they were all very polite to her, especially the flowers that had been lying in her bed. But she hadn't hurt herself at all; and Ida's flowers all thanked her for the nice bed, and liked her so much, that they took her into the middle of the floor, where the moon shone in, and danced with her. And all the other flowers made a circle around her. Now Sophia was pleased, and said they might keep her bed; she didn't at all mind lying in the drawer.

But the flowers said: "We thank you very much, but we can't live as long as that. Tomorrow we shall be quite dead.

But tell little Ida she is to bury us out in the garden, where the canary lies. Then we shall grow up again in summer, and be far more beautiful."

"No, you must not die," said Sophia; and she kissed the flowers.

At that moment the door opened, and a whole crowd of lovely flowers came dancing in. Ida couldn't imagine where they had come from. They must be flowers from the King's castle. First of all came two lovely roses, with little gold crowns on; they were a king and a queen. Then came the prettiest stocks and carnations; and they bowed in all directions. They had music with them. Large poppies and peonies blew on pea pods till they were quite red in the face. The bluebells and the little white snowdrops tinkled just as if they had bells on. That was wonderful music! Then came ever so many other flowers, and they all danced together; the blue violets and the pink primroses, the daisies and the lilies of the valley. And all the flowers kissed one another.

At last the flowers said good night. Then little Ida crept to bed, where she dreamed of all she had seen.

When she got up next morning, she went quickly to the little table, to see if the flowers were still there. She drew aside the curtains of the little bed. There they all lay, but they were quite faded, much more than yesterday. Sophia was lying in the drawer where Ida had laid her; she looked very sleepy.

"Do you remember what you had to say to me?" asked little Ida.

But Sophia looked quite stupid, and did not say a single word.

"You are not at all good!" said Ida. "And yet they all danced with you."

Then she took a little paper box, on which beautiful birds were painted. She opened it, and laid the dead flowers in it.

"This is going to be your pretty coffin," she said, "and when my Norwegian cousins come to visit me by and by, they shall help me to bury you outside in the garden, so that you will grow again in summer, and become more beautiful than ever."

The Norwegian cousins were two fine boys. Their names were Jonas and Adolph. Their father had given them two new crossbows, and they had brought them to show to Ida. She told them about the poor flowers who had died, and then they were allowed to help bury them. The two boys went first, with their crossbows on their shoulders, and little Ida followed with the dead flowers in the pretty box. Out in the garden a little grave was dug. Ida first kissed the flowers, and then she laid them in the earth in the box, and Adolph and Jonas shot their crossbows over the grave, for they had no guns nor cannons.

THE TINDERBOX

THERE came a soldier marching along the high road—*one, two!*
one, two! He had his knapsack on his back and a saber by his
side, for he had been in the wars, and now he wanted to go
home. And on the way he met with an old witch. She was very
hideous, and her lower lip hung down upon her breast. She
said, "Good evening, Soldier. What a fine sword you have,
and what a big knapsack! You're a proper soldier! Now you
shall have as much money as you would like to have."

"I thank you, you old witch!" said the soldier.

"Do you see that great tree?" quoth the witch; and she
pointed to a tree which stood beside them. "It's quite hollow
inside. You must climb to the top, and then you'll see a hole,
through which you can let yourself down and get deep into
the tree. I'll tie a rope round your body, so that I can pull
you up again when you call me."

"What am I to do down in the tree?" asked the soldier.

"Get money," replied the witch. "Listen to me. When you
come down to the earth under the tree, you will find yourself
in a great hall. It is quite light, for above three hundred lamps
are burning there. Then you will see three doors; these you
can open, for the keys are hanging there. If you go into the
first chamber, you'll see a great chest in the middle of the floor.
On this chest sits a dog, and he's got a pair of eyes as big as
two teacups. But you need not care for that. I'll give you my
blue-checked apron, and you can spread it out upon the floor.
Then go up quickly and take the dog, and set him on my
apron; then open the chest, and take as many shillings as you
like. They are of copper. If you prefer silver, you must go

into the second chamber. There sits a dog with a pair of eyes as big as mill wheels. But don't worry about that. Set him upon my apron, and take some of the money. And if you want gold, you can have that too—in fact, as much as you can carry—if you go into the third chamber. There the dog that sits on the money chest has two eyes as big as round towers. He is a fierce dog, you may be sure; but you needn't be afraid. Just set him on my apron, and he won't hurt you; and take as much gold as you like out of the chest."

"That's not so bad," said the soldier. "But what am I to give you, you old witch? For you will not do this for nothing, I fancy."

"No," replied the witch, "not a single shilling will I have. You shall only bring me an old tinderbox which my grandmother forgot when she was last down there."

"Then tie the rope round my body," cried the soldier.

"Here it is," said the witch, "and here's my blue-checked apron."

The soldier climbed up into the tree, let himself slip down into the hole, and stood, as the witch had said, in the great hall where the three hundred lamps were burning.

He opened the first door. Ugh! There sat the dog with eyes as big as teacups, staring at him. "You're a nice fellow!" exclaimed the soldier; and he set him on the witch's apron, and took as many copper shillings as his pockets would hold. Then he locked the chest, set the dog upon it, and went into the second chamber. Aha! There sat the dog with eyes as big as mill wheels.

"You should not stare so hard at me," said the soldier. "You might strain your eyes." And he set the dog upon the witch's apron. When he saw the silver money in the chest, he threw away all the copper money he had, and filled his pockets and his knapsack with silver. Then he went into the third chamber. Oh, but that was horrid! The dog there really did have eyes as big as towers, and they turned round and round in his head like wheels.

"Good evening!" said the soldier; and he touched his cap, for he had never seen such a dog as that before. When he had looked at him a little more closely, he thought, "That will do," and lifted him down to the floor, and opened his chest. Heavens! what a quantity of gold was there! He could buy the whole town with it, the sugar sucking-pigs of the cake woman, and all the tin soldiers, whips, and rocking horses in the whole world. Yes, that was a lot of money! Now the soldier threw away all the silver coins which had filled his pockets and his knapsack, and took the gold instead. Yes, all his pockets, his knapsack, his boots, and his cap were filled, so that he could scarcely walk. Now indeed he had plenty of money. He put the dog on the chest, shut the door, and then called up through the tree, "Now pull me up, you old witch."

"Have you the tinderbox?" asked the witch.

"Plague on it!" exclaimed the soldier, "I forgot." And he went back and brought the box.

The witch drew him up, and he stood on the highroad again, with pockets, boots, knapsack, and cap full of gold.

"What are you going to do with the tinderbox?" asked the soldier.

"That's nothing to you," retorted the witch. "You've got your money—just give me the tinderbox."

"Nonsense!" said the soldier. "Tell me at once what you're going to do with it, or I'll draw my sword and cut off your head."

"No!" cried the witch.

So the soldier cut off her head. There she lay! But he tied up all his money in her apron, took it on his back like a bundle, put the tinderbox in his pocket, and went straight off toward the town.

It was a splendid town! He put up at the very best inn, and asked for the finest rooms, and ordered his favorite dishes, for now he was rich. The servant who had to clean his boots certainly thought them a remarkably old pair for such a rich gentleman. But the next day he procured proper boots and handsome clothes. Now our soldier had become a fine gentleman; and the people told him of all the splendid things which were in their city, and about the King, and what a pretty Princess the King's daughter was.

"How can one get to see her?" asked the soldier.

"She is not to be seen at all," said they all together. "She lives in a great copper castle, with a great many walls and towers round about it. No one but the King may go in and out there, for it has been prophesied that she shall marry a common soldier, and the King can't bear the thought of that."

"I should like to see her," thought the soldier. But he could not get permission to do so. So he lived merrily, went to the theater, drove in the King's garden, and gave much money to the poor. For he remembered from old times how hard it is when one has not a shilling. He was rich, had fine clothes, and gained many friends, who all said he was a rare one, a true cavalier; and that pleased the soldier well. But as he spent money every day and never earned any, he had at last only two shillings left; and he was obliged to leave his fine rooms, and live in a little garret under the roof. He cleaned his boots for himself, and did his own mending with a darning needle. None of his friends came to see him, for there were too many stairs to climb.

It was very dark one evening, and he could not even buy himself a candle. Suddenly it occurred to him that there had been a candle end in the tinderbox which he had taken out of the hollow tree for the witch. He got out the tinderbox and the candle end and as soon as he struck fire, the sparks rose up from the flint, the door flew open, and the dog who had eyes as big as teacups stood before him.

"What are my lord's commands?" he said.

"What is this?" said the soldier. "That's a wonderful tinderbox, if I can get everything I want with it! Bring me some money," said he to the dog; and *whisk!* the dog was gone, and *whisk!* he was back again, with a great bag full of shillings in his mouth.

Now the soldier knew what an excellent tinderbox it was. If he struck it once, the dog came who sat upon the chest of copper money; if he struck it twice, the dog came who had the silver; and if he struck it three times, the dog who had the gold appeared. So the soldier moved back into the fine rooms, and appeared again in handsome clothes, and all his friends knew him again, and cared very much for him indeed.

Once he thought to himself: "It is a very strange thing that one cannot get to see the Princess. They all say she is very beautiful; but what is the use of that, if she has always to sit in the great copper castle with the many towers? Can't I get to see her at all? Where is my tinderbox?" And so he struck a light, and *whisk!* came the dog with eyes as big as teacups.

"It is midnight, certainly," said the soldier, "I should very much like to see the Princess, if only for one little moment."

The dog was outside the door at once, and, before the soldier could think twice, came back with the Princess. She sat upon the dog's back sound asleep. Anyone could see she was a real Princess, she was so lovely. The soldier could not refrain from kissing her, for he was a thorough soldier. Then the dog whisked the Princess back again. When morning came, and the King and Queen were drinking tea, the Princess said she had had a strange dream the night before, about a dog and a soldier—that she had ridden upon the dog, and the soldier had kissed her.

"A pretty sort of dream indeed!" said the Queen.

And she insisted that one of the old court ladies watch the next night by the Princess's bed, to see what sort of dream this might be.

The soldier had a great longing to see the lovely Princess again. So the dog came in the night, took her away, and ran as fast as he could. But the old lady put on water boots, and ran just as fast after him. When she saw them enter a great house, she thought, "Now I know where it is," and with a bit of chalk she drew a great cross on the door. Then she went home and lay down. The dog came out with the Princess; but when he saw that there was a cross drawn on the soldier's door he took a piece of chalk and drew crosses on all the doors in the town. Now that was cleverly done, for the lady would certainly be confused the next day.

In the morning early came the King and Queen, the old court lady, and all the officers, to see where it was the Princess had been. "Here it is!" said the King, when he saw the first door with a cross upon it. "No, my dear husband, it is there!" said the Queen, seeing another door with a cross. "And there is one, and there is one!" said all, for wherever they looked there were crosses on the doors. They soon saw that it would do them no good to search further.

But the Queen was an exceedingly clever woman, who could do more than ride in a coach. She took her great gold scissors, cut a piece of silk into pieces, and made a neat little bag. She filled this bag with fine wheat flour, and tied it on the Princess's back; and when that was done, she cut a little hole in the bag, so that the flour would be scattered along the way where the Princess was taken.

In the night the dog came again, took the Princess on his back, and ran with her to the soldier, who by this time loved her very much. He would gladly have been a prince, so that he might have her for his wife. The dog did not notice how the flour ran out in a white stream from the castle to the windows of the soldier's house, where he ran up the wall with the Princess. In the morning the King and the Queen saw well enough where their daughter had been, and they took the soldier and put him in prison.

There he sat. Oh, but it was dark and disagreeable there! And they said to him, "Tomorrow you shall be hanged." That was not amusing to hear, and he had left his tinderbox at the inn. In the morning he could see, through the iron grating of the little window, how the people were hurrying out of the town to see him hanged. He heard the drums beat and saw the soldiers marching. All the people were running out, and among them was a shoemaker's boy with leather apron and slippers, and he galloped so fast that one of his slippers flew off, and came right against the wall where the soldier sat looking through the iron grating.

"Hallo, you shoemaker's boy! You needn't be in such a hurry," cried the soldier to him. "It will not begin till I come. But if you will run to where I live, and bring me my tinderbox, you shall have four shillings; but you must hurry."

The shoemaker's boy wanted the four shillings, so he went and brought the tinderbox, and—well, we shall hear what happened now!

Outside the town a great gallows had been built, and round

it stood the soldiers and many thousands of people. The King and Queen sat on a splendid throne, opposite the judges and the Council, and the soldier already stood upon the ladder. But just as they were about to put the rope round his neck, he said that before a poor criminal suffered his punishment an innocent request was always granted to him. He wanted very much to smoke a pipe of tobacco. And it would be the last pipe he should smoke in this world. The King could not say "No" to this. And so the soldier took his tinderbox, and struck fire. One—two—three!—and there suddenly stood all the dogs—the one with eyes as big as teacups, the one with eyes as large as mill wheels, and the one whose eyes were as big as round towers.

"Help me now, so that I will not be hanged," said the soldier.

And the dogs fell upon the judges and all the Council. They seized one by the leg and another by the nose, and tossed them all high into the air, and they fell down and were broken into many pieces.

"I won't!" cried the King. But the biggest dog took him and the Queen, and threw them after the others. Then the soldiers were afraid, and the people cried, "Little soldier, you shall be our King! And you shall marry the beautiful Princess!"

They put the soldier into the King's coach, and the three dogs darted on in front and cried, "Hurrah!" And the boys whistled through their fingers, and the soldiers presented arms.

The Princess came out of her copper castle, and became Queen. She liked that well enough. The wedding lasted a week, and the three magic dogs sat at the table too. And their eyes opened wider than ever at all they saw.

THE WILD SWANS

FAR away, where the swallows take refuge in winter, lived a King who had eleven sons and one daughter, Elise. The eleven brothers—they were all princes—used to go to school with stars on their breasts and swords at their sides. They wrote upon golden slates with diamond pencils, and could read just as well without a book as with one, so there was no mistake about their being real princes. Their sister Elise sat upon a little footstool of looking glass, and she had a picture book which had cost the half of a kingdom. Oh, these children were very happy, but it was not to last forever.

Their father, who was King over all the land, married a wicked Queen who was not at all kind to the poor children. They found that out on the first day. All was festive at the castle, but when the children wanted to play at having company, instead of letting them have all the cakes and baked apples they wanted, she would only let them have some sand in a teacup, and said they must make-believe.

In the following week she sent little Elise into the country to board with some peasants, and it did not take her long to make the King believe so many bad things about the boys that he cared no more about them.

"Fly out into the world and look after yourselves," said the wicked Queen. "You shall fly about like birds without voices."

But she could not make things as bad for them as she would have liked: they turned into eleven beautiful wild swans. They flew out the palace window with a weird scream, right across the park and the woods.

It was very early in the morning when they came to the place where their sister Elise was sleeping in the peasant's house. They hovered over the roof of the house, turning and twisting their long necks and flapping their wings, but no one heard or saw them. They had to fly away again, and they soared up toward the clouds, far out into the wide world, and they settled in a big dark wood which stretched down to the shore.

Poor little Elise stood in the peasant's room playing with a green leaf, for she had no other toys. She made a little hole in it and looked through at the sun, and it seemed to her as if she saw her brothers' bright eyes. Every time the warm sunbeams shone upon her cheek it reminded her of their kisses.

One day passed just like another. When the wind whistled through the rose hedges outside the house, it whispered to the roses, "Who can be prettier than you are?" But the roses shook their heads and answered, "Elise." And when the old woman sat in the doorway reading her psalms, the wind turned over the leaves and said to the book, "Who can be more pious than you?" "Elise," answered the book. Both the roses and the book of psalms spoke only the truth.

She was to go home when she was fifteen, but when the Queen saw how pretty she was, she got very angry and her heart was filled with hatred. She would willingly have turned her into a wild swan like her brothers, but she did not dare to do it at once, because the King wanted to see his daughter.

The Queen always went to the bath in the early morning. It was built of marble and adorned with soft cushions and beautiful carpets.

She took three toads, kissed them, and said to the first, "Sit upon Elise's head when she comes to the bath, so that she may become sluggish like yourself. Sit upon her forehead," she said to the second, "that she may become ugly like you, and then her father won't know her. Rest upon her heart," she whispered to the third. "Let an evil spirit come over her which may be a burden to her."

Then she put the toads into the clean water, and a green tinge immediately came over it. She called Elise, undressed her, and made her go into the bath. When she ducked under the water, one of the toads got among her hair, the other got onto her forehead, and the third onto her bosom. Elise seemed unaware of it and when she stood up, three scarlet poppies floated on the water! Had the creatures not been poisonous, and been kisssed by the sorceress, they would have been changed into crimson roses, while they still rested on Elise's head and heart. She was far too good and innocent for the sorcery to have any power over her.

When the wicked Queen saw this, she rubbed her over with walnut juice and smeared her face with some evil-smelling salve. She also matted up her beautiful hair. It would have been impossible to recognize pretty Elise. When her father saw her, he was quite horrified and said that she could not be his daughter. Nobody would have anything to say to her, except the yard dog and the swallows, but they were poor dumb animals whose opinions meant nothing.

Poor Elise wept and thought of her eleven brothers who were all lost. She crept sadly out of the palace and wandered about all day, over meadows and marshes and into a big forest. She had no idea where she wanted to go. She felt very sad and longed for her brothers, and so determined to find them.

She had only been in the wood for a short time when night fell. She had quite lost her way, so she lay down upon the soft moss, said her evening prayer, and rested her head on a little hillock. It was very still and the air was mild. Hundreds of glowworms shone around her on the grass and in the marsh like green fire. When she gently moved one of the branches over her head, the little shining insects fell over her like a shower of stars.

She dreamed about her brothers all night long. Again they

were children playing together. They wrote upon the golden slates with their diamond pencils, and she looked at the picture book which had cost half a kingdom. But they no longer wrote X and O upon their slates as they used to do. No, they wrote down all their boldest exploits and everything that they had seen and experienced. Everything in the picture book was alive. The birds sang, and the people walked out of the book and spoke to Elise and her brothers. When she turned over a page they skipped back into their places again, so that there should be no confusion among the pictures.

When she woke the sun was already high. It is true she could not see it very well through the thick branches of the lofty forest trees, but the sunbeams cast a golden shimmer around beyond the forest. There was a fresh delicious scent of grass and herbs in the air, and the birds were almost ready to perch upon her shoulders. She could hear the splashing of water, for there were many springs around. They all flowed into a pond with a lovely sandy bottom. It was surrounded with thick bushes but there was one place which the stags had trampled down, and Elise passed through the opening to the waterside. It was so transparent that, if the branches hadn't been moved by the breeze, she might have thought they were painted on the bottom—every leaf was reflected so plainly, both those on which the sun played and those which were in shade.

When she saw her own face, she was quite frightened to see it so stained and ugly. But when she wet her hand and rubbed her eyes and forehead, her white skin shone through again. Then she took off all her clothes and went into the fresh water. A more beautiful royal child than she could not be found in all the world.

When she had put on her clothes again and plaited her long hair, she went to a sparkling spring and drank some of the water out of the hollow of her hand. Then she wandered farther into the wood, though she had not the least idea where she was going. She thought of her brothers, and she thought of a merciful God who would not forsake her. He lets the wild crab apples grow to feed the hungry, and He showed her a tree with its branches bending beneath their weight of fruit. Here she made her midday meal. Then, having put props under the branches, she walked on into the thickest part of the forest. It was so quiet that she could hear her own footsteps. She heard every little withered leaf which bent under her foot. Not a bird was to be seen. Not a ray of sunlight pierced the leafy branches, and the tall trunks were so close together that when she looked before her it seemed as if a thick fence of heavy beams hemmed her in on every side. Such solitude she had never known before.

It was a very dark night. Not a single glowworm sparkled in the marsh. Sadly she lay down to sleep, and it seemed to her as if the branches above her parted asunder, and that the Saviour looked down upon her with His loving eyes and that little angels' heads peeped out above His head and under His arms.

When she woke in the morning, she was not sure if she had dreamed this or whether it was really true.

She walked a little farther when she met an old woman with a basket full of berries, and she gave her some. Elise asked if she had seen eleven princes ride through the wood.

"No," said the old woman. "But yesterday I saw eleven swans with golden crowns upon their heads, swimming in the stream close by there."

She led Elise a little farther to a slope, at the foot of which the stream meandered. The trees on either bank stretched out their rich leafy branches toward each other; and where their natural growth did not let them reach each other, they had torn their roots out of the ground and leaned over the water in order to interlace their branches.

Elise said good-by to the old woman and walked along by the river till it flowed out into the great open sea.

The beautiful open sea lay before the maiden, but not a sail was to be seen on it, nor a single boat. How was she ever to go any farther? She looked at the millions of little pebbles on the beach. They were all worn quite round by the water. Glass, iron, stone—whatever was washed up—had taken their shapes from the water, and yet it was much softer than her little hand.

"With all its rolling, it is untiring, and everything hard is smoothed down," she said. "I will be just as untiring. Thank you for your lesson, you clear rolling waves! Sometime, so my heart tells me, you will bear me to my beloved brothers."

Eleven white swans' feathers were lying on the seaweed. She picked them up and made a bunch of them. There were still drops of water on them, but whether these were dew or tears no one could tell. It was very lonely there by the shore, but she did not feel it, for the sea was ever-changing. There were more changes on it in the course of a few hours than could be seen on an inland fresh-water lake in a year. If a big black cloud arose, it was just as if the sea wanted to say, "I can look black too." And then the wind blew up and the waves showed their white crests. But if the clouds were red and the wind dropped, the sea looked like a rose leaf, now white, now green. But no matter how still it was, there was always a little gentle motion just by the shore. The water rose and fell softly like the bosom of a sleeping child.

When the sun was about to go down, Elise saw eleven wild swans with golden crowns upon their heads flying toward the shore. They flew in a swaying line one behind the other, like a white ribbon streamer. Elise climbed up onto the bank and hid behind a bush. The swans settled close by her and flapped their great white wings.

As soon as the sun had sunk beneath the water the swans

shed their feathers and became eleven handsome princes. They were Elise's brothers. Although they had altered a good deal, she knew them at once. They must be her brothers and she sprang into their arms, calling them by name. They were delighted when they recognized their little sister who had grown so big and beautiful. They laughed and cried and told each other how wickedly their stepmother had treated them all.

"We brothers," said the eldest, "have to fly about in the guise of swans as long as the sun is above the horizon. When it goes down we regain our human shapes. So we always have to watch for a resting place near sunset, for should we happen to be flying up among the clouds when the sun goes down, we would be hurled to the depths below. We do not live here. There is another land just as beautiful as this, beyond the sea, but the way to it is very long and we have to cross the mighty ocean to get to it. There is not a single island on the way where we can spend the night. Only one solitary little rock rises just above the water midway. It is only just big enough for us to stand upon close together, and if there is a heavy sea the water splashes over us. Yet we thank our God for it. We stay there overnight in our human forms, and without it we could never come back here to our beloved fatherland, for our flight takes two of the longest days in the year. We are permitted to visit the home of our fathers only once a year, and we dare stay for only eleven days. We hover over this big forest and we can catch a glimpse of the palace where we were born, and where our father lives. Beyond it we can see the high church towers where our mother is buried. We fancy that the trees and bushes here are related to us. The wild horses still gallop over the moors as we used to see them in our childhood. The charcoal burners still sing the old songs we used to dance to when we were children. This is our fatherland. We are drawn toward it and here we have found you again, dear little sister. We may stay here two days longer,

and then we must fly away again across the ocean, to a lovely
country indeed, but it is not our own. How shall we ever
take you with us? We have neither ship nor boat."

"How can I deliver you?" said their sister, and they went
on talking to each other nearly all night. They dozed for only
a few hours.

Elise was awakened in the morning by the rustling of the
swans' wings above her. Her brothers were again transformed
and were wheeling round in great circles, till she lost sight of
them in the distance. One of them, the youngest, stayed behind. He laid his head against her bosom and she caressed it
with her fingers. They remained together all day. Toward
evening the others came back, and as soon as the sun went
down they took their natural forms.

"Tomorrow we must fly away and we dare not come back
for a whole year, but we can't leave you like this. Have you
courage to go with us? My arm is strong enough to bear you
through the forest, so we should have sufficient strength in
our wings to carry you over the ocean."

"Oh, yes! Take me with you," said Elise.

They spent the whole night weaving a kind of net from
the elastic bark of the willow. They bound it together with
tough rushes, and made it both large and strong. Elise lay
down upon it, and when the sun rose and the brothers became
swans again, they took up the net in their bills and flew high
up among the clouds with their precious sister, who was fast
asleep. As the sunbeams fell straight onto her face, one of the
swans flew over her head so that his broad wings would shade
her.

They were far from land when Elise woke. She thought
she must still be dreaming—it seemed so strange to be carried
through the air so high up above the sea. By her side lay a
branch of beautiful ripe berries and a bundle of savory roots,
which her youngest brother had collected for her and for
which she gave him a grateful smile. She knew it was he who

flew above her head, shading her from the sun. They were so high up that the first ship they saw looked like a gull floating on the water. A great cloud came up behind them like a mountain, and Elise saw the shadow of herself on it, and those of the eleven swans looked like giants. It was a more beautiful picture than any she had ever seen before, but as the sun rose higher, the cloud fell behind and the shadow picture disappeared.

They flew on and on all day like arrows whizzing through the air, and yet they went slower than usual for now they had their sister to carry. A storm came up, and night was drawing on. With terror in her heart Elise saw the sun sinking, and the solitary rock was nowhere to be seen. The swans seemed to be taking stronger strokes than ever. Alas, she was the cause of their not being able to go faster. As soon as the sun went down they would become men, and they would be hurled into the sea and drowned. She prayed to God from the bottom of her heart, but still no rock was to be seen. Black clouds gathered and strong gusts of wind announced a storm. The clouds looked like a great threatening leaden wave, and the flashes of lightning followed each other rapidly.

The sun was now at the edge of the sea. Elise's heart quaked, when suddenly the swans shot downward so suddenly that she thought they were falling. Then they hovered again. Half of the sun was below the horizon, and there for the first time she saw the little rock below. It looked no bigger than the head of a seal above the water. The sun sank very quickly. It was no bigger than a star, and then her foot touched solid earth. The sun went out like the last sparks of a bit of burning paper. Her brothers stood arm in arm around her. There was just enough room for them. The waves beat upon the rock and washed over them like drenching rain. The heaven shone with continuous fire and the thunder rolled, peal upon peal. But the sister and brothers held each other's hands and sang a psalm which gave them comfort and courage.

The air was pure and still at dawn. As soon as the sun rose, the swans flew off with Elise away from the islet. The sea still ran high. It looked from where they were as if the white foam on the dark green water were millions of swans floating on the waves.

When the sun rose higher, Elise saw before her, half floating in the air, great masses of ice with shining glaciers on the heights. Midway was perched a palace, a mile in length, with one bold colonnade built above another. Below swayed palm trees and gorgeous blossoms as big as mill wheels. She asked if this was the land to which she was going, but the swans shook their heads because what she saw was a mirage. It was the beautiful and ever-changing palace of Fata Morgana. No mortal dared enter it. Elise gazed at it, but as she gazed the palace, gardens, and mountains melted away. And in their place stood twenty proud churches with their high towers and pointed windows. She seemed to hear the notes of the organ, but it was the sea she heard. When she got close to the churches, they changed to a great navy sailing beneath her. It was all only a sea mist floating over the waters.

Yes, she saw constant changes passing before her eyes, but now she saw the real land she was bound for. Beautiful blue mountains rose before her with their cedar woods and palaces. Long before the sun went down, she sat among the hills in front of a big cave covered with delicate green creepers. It looked like a piece of embroidery.

"Now we shall see what you will dream here tonight," said the youngest brother, as he showed her where she was to sleep.

"If only I might dream how I could deliver you!" she said, and this thought filled her mind entirely. She prayed earnestly to God for His help, and even in her sleep she continued her prayer. It seemed to her that she was flying up to Fata Morgana in her castle in the air. The fairy came toward her. She was charming and brilliant, and yet she was very like the old woman who had given her the berries in the wood and told her about the swans with the golden crowns.

"Your brothers can be delivered," she said. "But have you courage and endurance enough for it? The sea is indeed softer than your hands, and it molds the hardest stones, but it does not feel the pain your fingers will feel. It has no heart and does not suffer the pain and anguish you must feel. Do you see the stinging nettle I hold in my hand? Many of this kind grow round the cave where you sleep. Only these and the ones which grow in the churchyards may be used. Mark that! Those you may pluck, although they will burn and blister your hands. Crush the nettles with your feet and you will have flax, and of this you must weave eleven coats of mail with long sleeves. Throw these over the eleven wild swans and the charm is broken. But remember, from the moment you begin this work till it is finished, even if it takes years, you must not utter a word. The first word you say will fall like a murderer's dagger into the hearts of your brothers. Their lives hang on your tongue. Mark this well."

She touched her hand at the same moment. The touch was like burning fire and it woke Elise. It was bright daylight, and close to where she slept lay a nettle like those in her dream. She fell upon her knees with thanks to God and left the cave to begin her work.

She seized the horrid nettles with her delicate hands, and they burned like fire. Great blisters rose on her hands and arms, but she suffered it willingly if only it would deliver her beloved brothers. She crushed every nettle with her bare feet and twisted it into green flax.

When the sun went down and the brothers came back, they were alarmed at finding her mute. They thought it was some new witchcraft exercised by their wicked stepmother. But when they saw her hands, they understood that it was for their sakes. The youngest brother wept, and wherever his tears fell she felt no more pain and the blisters disappeared.

She spent the whole night at her work, for she could not rest till she had delivered her dear brothers. All the following day, while her brothers were away, she sat solitary, but never had the time flown so fast. One coat of mail was finished and she began the next. Then a hunting horn sounded among the mountains. She was frightened. The sound came nearer and she heard dogs barking. In terror she rushed into the cave and tied the nettles she had collected and woven into a bundle and sat down upon it.

At this moment a big dog bounded forward from the thicket, and another and another. They barked loudly and ran backward and forward. In a few minutes all the huntsmen were standing outside the cave. The handsomest of them was the King of the country, and he stepped up to Elise. Never had he seen so lovely a girl.

"How came you here, beautiful child?" he said.

Elise shook her head. She dared not speak. The salvation and the lives of her brothers depended upon her silence. She hid her hands under her apron so that the King should not see what she suffered.

"Come with me," he said. "You cannot stay here. If you are as good as you are beautiful, I will dress you in silks and velvets, put a golden crown upon your head, and you shall live with me and have your home in my richest palace." Then he lifted her upon his horse. She wept and wrung her hands, but the King said, "I think only of your happiness. You will thank me one day for what I am doing." Then he darted off across the mountains, holding her before him on his horse, and the huntsmen followed.

When the sun went down, the royal city with churches and cupolas lay before them, and the King led her into the palace. Here great fountains played in the marble halls and the walls and ceilings were adorned with paintings, but she had no eyes for them. She only wept and sorrowed. Passively she allowed the women to dress her in royal robes, to twist pearls into her hair, and to draw gloves onto her blistered hands.

She was dazzlingly lovely as she stood there in all her magnificence. The courtiers bent low before her and the King wooed her as his bride, although the archbishop shook his head and whispered that he feared the beautiful wood maiden was a witch, who had dazzled their eyes and infatuated the King.

The King refused to listen to him. He ordered the music to play, the richest food to be brought, and the loveliest girls to dance before her. She was led through scented gardens into gorgeous apartments, but nothing brought a smile to her lips or into her eyes. Sorrow sat there like a heritage and a possession for all time. Last of all, the King opened the door of a little chamber close by the room where she was to sleep. It was adorned with costly green carpets and made to resemble exactly the cave where he found her. On the floor lay the bundle of flax she had spun from the nettles, and from the ceiling hung the shirt of mail which was already finished. One of the huntsmen had brought all these things away as curiosities.

"Here you may dream that you are back in your former home," said the King. "Here is the work upon which you were engaged. In the midst of your splendor it may amuse you to think of those times."

When Elise saw all these things so dear to her heart, a smile for the first time played upon her lips and the blood rushed back to her cheeks. She thought of the deliverance of her brothers and she kissed the King's hand. He pressed her to his heart and ordered all the church bells to ring marriage peals. The lovely dumb girl from the woods was to be Queen of the country.

The archbishop whispered evil words into the ear of the

King, but they did not reach his heart. The wedding was to take place and the archbishop himself had to put the crown upon her head. In his anger he pressed the golden circlet so tightly upon her head that it gave her pain. But a heavier circlet pressed upon her heart, her grief for her brothers. She thought nothing of the bodily pain. Her lips were sealed. A single word from her mouth would cost her brothers their lives, but her eyes were full of love for the good and handsome King, who did everything he could to please her.

Every day she grew more and more attached to him. She longed to confide in him and tell him her sufferings, but dumb she must remain and in silence bring her labor to completion. Therefore at night she stole away from his side into her secret chamber, which was decorated like a cave, and here she knitted one shirt after another. When she came to the seventh, all her flax was used up. She knew that these nettles grew in the churchyard, but she had to pluck them herself. How was she to get there?

"Oh, what is the pain of my fingers compared with the anguish of my heart?" she thought. "I must venture out. The good God will not desert me."

With as much terror in her heart as if she were doing some evil deed, she stole down one night into the moonlit garden and through the long alleys out into the silent streets to the churchyard. It was very dark and lonely, but she picked the stinging nettles and hurried back to the palace with them. Only one person saw her, and that was the archbishop, who watched while others slept. Surely now all his bad opinions of the Queen were justified. All was not as it should be with her. She must be a witch, and therefore she had bewitched the King and all the people.

He told the King in the confessional what he had seen and what he feared. When those bad words passed his lips, the pictures of the saints shook their heads as if to say, "It is not so. Elise is innocent." The archbishop, however, took it differently. He thought they were bearing witness against her and shaking their heads at her sin.

Two big tears rolled down the King's cheeks, and he went home with doubt in his heart. He pretended to sleep at night, but no quiet sleep came to his eyes. He saw how Elise got up and went to her private closet. Day by day his face grew darker. Elise saw it but could not imagine what was the cause of it. It alarmed her, and what was she not already suffering in her heart because of her brothers? Her salt tears ran down upon the royal purple velvet and lay there like sparkling diamonds, and all who saw their splendor wished to be Queen.

She had, however, almost reached the end of her labors. Only one shirt of mail was wanting, but again she had no more flax and not a single nettle was left. Once more, for the last time, she must go to the churchyard to pluck a few handfuls. She thought with dread of the solitary walk and the darkness, but her will was as strong as her trust in God.

Elise went, but the King and the archbishop followed her. They saw her disappear within the grated gateway of the churchyard. The King was very sorrowful, because he thought she must surely be a witch.

"The people must judge her," he groaned. And the people judged: "Let her be consumed in the glowing flames."

She was led from her beautiful royal apartments to a dark damp dungeon, where the wind whistled through the grated window. Instead of velvet and silk they gave her the bundle of nettles she had gathered to lay her head upon. The hard burning shirts of mail were to be her covering. But they could have given her nothing more precious.

She set to work again with many prayers to God. Outside her prison the street boys sang derisive songs about her, and not a soul comforted her with a kind word.

Toward evening she heard the rustle of swans' wings close to her window. It was her youngest brother, who at last had found her. He sobbed aloud with joy although he knew that the coming night might be her last. But then her work was almost done and her brothers were there.

The archbishop came to stay with her during her last hours, as he had promised the King. She shook her head at him and by looks and gestures begged him to leave her. She had only this night in which to finish her work, or else all would be wasted—all her pain, her tears, and her sleepless nights. The archbishop went away with bitter words against her, but poor Elise knew that she was innocent, and she went on with her work.

The little mice ran about the floor, bringing nettles to her feet so as to give what help they could, and a thrush sat on the grating of the window, where he sang all night as merrily as he could to keep up her courage.

It was still only dawn, and the sun would not rise for an hour, when the eleven brothers stood at the gate of the palace, begging to be taken to the King. This could not be done, they were told, for it was still night. The King was asleep and no one dared wake him. All their entreaties and threats were useless. The watch turned out and even the King himself came to see what was the matter. But just then the sun rose, and no more brothers were to be seen—only eleven wild swans hovering over the palace.

The whole populace streamed out of the town gates. They were all anxious to see the witch burned. A miserable horse drew the cart in which Elise was seated. They had put upon her a smock of green sacking, and all her beautiful long hair hung loose from the lovely head. Her cheeks were deathly pale and her lips moved softly, while her fingers unceasingly twisted the green yarn. Even on the way to her death she could not abandon her unfinished work. Ten shirts lay completed at her feet. She labored away at the eleventh amid the scoffing insults of the populace.

"Look at the witch! How she mutters! She has no book of psalms in her hands. There she sits with her loathsome sorcery. Tear it away from her and into a thousand bits!"

The crowd pressed around her to destroy her work. But just then eleven wild swans flew down and perched upon the cart, flapping their wings. The crowd gave way before them in terror.

"It is a sign from heaven! She is innocent," they whispered. But they dared not say it aloud.

The executioner seized her by the hand, but she hastily threw the eleven shirts over the swans, who were immediately transformed to eleven handsome princes. But the youngest had a swan's wing in place of an arm, for one sleeve was missing in his shirt of mail. She had not been able to finish it.

"Now I may speak! I am innocent."

The populace who saw what had happened bowed down before her as if she had been a saint, but she sank lifeless in her brothers' arms. So great had been the strain, the terror, and the suffering she had endured.

"Yes, innocent she is indeed," said the eldest brother, and he told them all that had happened.

While he spoke a wonderful fragrance spread around, like millions of roses. Every faggot in the pile had taken root and shot out branches, and a great high hedge of red roses had arisen. At the very top was one pure white blossom. It shone like a star, and the King broke it off and laid it on Elise's bosom, and she woke with joy and peace in her heart.

All the church bells began to ring of their own accord, and the singing birds flocked around them. Surely such a procession went back to the palace as no king had ever seen before!

THE EMPEROR'S NEW CLOTHES

MANY years ago there was an Emperor who was so excessively fond of new clothes that he spent all his money on them. He cared nothing about his soldiers, or the theater, or for driving in the woods—except for the sake of showing off his new clothes. He had a costume for every hour in the day. Instead of saying as one does about any other king or emperor, "He is in his council chamber," the people here always said, "The Emperor is in his dressing room."

Life was very gay in the great town where he lived. Hosts of strangers came to visit it every day, and among them one day were two swindlers. They pretended to be weavers and said that they knew how to weave the most beautiful fabrics imaginable. Not only were the colors and patterns unusually fine, but clothes made of this cloth had the peculiar quality of becoming invisible to any person who was impossibly dull or who was not fit for the office he held.

"Those must be splendid clothes," thought the Emperor. "By wearing them I should be able to discover which men in my kingdom are unfitted for their posts. I shall distinguish the wise men from the fools. Yes, I certainly must order some of that stuff woven for me."

The Emperor paid the two swindlers a lot of money in advance, so they could begin their work at once.

They put up two looms and pretended to weave, but they had nothing whatever upon their shuttles. At the beginning they asked for a quantity of the finest silk and the purest gold thread, all of which they put into their own bags while they worked away at the empty looms far into the night.

"I should like to know how those weavers are getting on

with their cloth," thought the Emperor, but he felt a little queer when he reflected that anyone who was stupid or unfit for his post would not be able to see it being made. He certainly thought that he need have no fears for himself, but still he thought it might be best to send somebody else first to see how things were getting on. Everybody in the town knew what wonderful power the stuff possessed, and everyone of course was anxious to see how stupid or wise his neighbor might be.

"I will send my faithful old minister to the weavers," thought the Emperor. "He will be best able to see how the cloth looks, for he is a clever man and no one fulfills his duties better than he does.

So the good old minister went into the room where the two swindlers sat working at the empty loom.

"Heaven help us," thought the old minister, opening his eyes very wide. "Why, I can't see a thing!" But he took great care not to say so.

The swindlers begged him to be good enough to step a little nearer, and asked if he did not think it a good pattern and beautiful coloring. They pointed to the empty loom. The poor old minister stared as hard as he could, but he could not see anything, and for a very good reason, there was nothing there.

"Good heavens," thought he. "Is it possible that I am a fool? I have never thought so, and if I am, nobody must know it. Am I not fit for my post? It will never do to say that I cannot see the stuff."

"Well, sir, you don't say anything about the cloth," said the one who was pretending to weave.

"Oh, it is beautiful—quite charming," said the minister, looking through his spectacles. "Such a pattern and such colors! I will certainly tell the Emperor that the cloth pleases me very much."

"We are delighted to hear you say so," said the swindlers,

and they named all the colors and described the peculiar pattern. The old minister paid great attention to what they said, so he could repeat it when he got home to the Emperor.

Then the swindlers asked for more money, and more silk, and more gold, so they could proceed with the weaving. But they put it all into their own pockets. Not a single strand was ever put into the loom, and they went on as before, weaving diligently away at the empty loom.

The Emperor soon sent another faithful official to see how the stuff was getting on and if it would soon be ready. The same thing happened to him as to the minister. He looked and looked, but as there was nothing there he could see nothing but the frames of the loom.

"Isn't this a beautiful piece of stuff?" said both the swindlers, showing and explaining the beautiful pattern and colors which were not there.

"I know I am no fool," thought the man, "so it must be that I am unfit for my good post. It is very strange, though. However, one must not let it be known." So he praised the cloth he did not see, and assured them of his delight in the beautiful colors and the originality of the design.

"It is absolutely charming," he said to the Emperor. Everybody in town was talking about the splendor of the cloth.

Now the Emperor decided that he would like to see it while it was still on the loom. So, accompanied by a number of selected courtiers, among whom were the two faithful officials who had already seen the imaginary stuff, he went to visit the crafty impostors. They were working away as hard as ever at the empty loom.

"It is magnificent," said both the honest officials. "Only see, Your Majesty, what a design! What colors!" And they pointed to the empty loom, for they each thought no doubt that the others could see the stuff.

"What?" thought the Emperor. "I see nothing at all. This

is terrible! Am I a fool? Am I fit to be Emperor? Why, nothing worse could happen to me!"

"Oh, it is beautiful," said the Emperor. "It has my highest approval." And he nodded his satisfaction as he gazed at the empty loom. Nothing could induce him to say that he saw nothing.

The whole troupe gazed and gazed and strained their eyes, hoping to see what they thought the others saw, but nobody saw anything. However, they all exclaimed with His Majesty, "It is very beautiful." And they advised him to wear a suit made of this wonderful cloth on the occasion of a great procession which would soon take place. "Magnificent! Gorgeous! Excellent!" The words went from mouth to mouth. They were all equally delighted with what they did not see. The Emperor gave each of the swindlers an order of knighthood to be worn in their buttonholes and the title of "Gentleman Weaver."

The swindlers sat up the whole night before the day of the great procession. They burned sixteen candles, to show the people how anxious they were to get the Emperor's new clothes ready. They pretended to take the cloth off the loom. They cut it out in the air with a huge pair of scissors, and they stitched away with needles that had no thread in them.

At last they said, "Now the Emperor's new clothes are ready."

The Emperor took his grandest courtiers and went to the weavers himself, and the swindlers raised their arms in the air, as if they were holding something up and said, "See, here are the trousers! This is the coat! Here is the mantle! The whole suit is as light as a cobweb. One might think that one had nothing on at all. But that is the very beauty of it."

"Yes," said all the courtiers, but they saw nothing, for there was nothing to see.

"Will Your Imperial Majesty be so good as to take off your

clothes?" said the impostors. "Then we can fit the new ones, here before the great mirror."

The Emperor took off all his clothes, and the impostors pretended to hand him one article of clothing after the other. They pretended to fasten something around his waist and to tie on something at his neck. This was the train, they said, and the Emperor turned round and round in front of the mirror.

"How well His Majesty looks in the new clothes! How becoming they are!" cried all his followers. "What a design, and what colors! They are most gorgeous robes."

"The canopy which is to be carried over Your Majesty in

the procession is waiting outside," said the master of the ceremonies.

"Well, I am quite ready," said the Emperor. "Don't the clothes fit well?" Then he turned around again in front of the mirror, so that he should appear to be examining his handsome new suit.

The chamberlains who were to carry the train stooped, felt about on the ground and pretended to lift it with both hands. They walked along behind with their hands in the air, for they dared not let it seem that they did not see anything.

Then the Emperor walked along in the procession under the gorgeous canopy, and everybody in the streets and at the windows exclaimed: "How beautiful the Emperor's new clothes are! What a splendid train! They fit to perfection!" Nobody let on that he saw nothing, for then he would not be fit for his post, or else he was a fool.

Never before had the Emperor's clothes been so successful!

"But he hasn't got anything on," said a little child.

"Oh, listen to the innocent," said his father. And what the child had said was whispered from one person to the other. "He has nothing on—a child says he has nothing on!"

"But he has nothing on!" cried all the people at last.

The Emperor writhed, for he knew that it was true. But he thought, "The procession must go on now." So he held himself stiffer than ever, and the chamberlains fussed and straightened the invisible train.

And the procession goes on still!

THE DARNING NEEDLE

THERE was once a darning needle, who thought herself so fine she imagined she was an embroidering needle.

"Take care, and mind you hold me tight!" she said to the fingers that took her out. "Don't let me fall! If I fall on the ground I shall certainly never be found again, for I am so fine!"

"That's as it may be," said the fingers; and they grasped her round the body.

"See, I'm coming with a train!" said the darning needle, and she drew a long thread after her, but there was no knot in the thread.

The fingers pointed the needle at the cook's slipper, in which the upper leather had burst, and had to be sewn together.

"That's vulgar work," said the darning needle. "I shall never get through. I'm breaking! I'm breaking!" And she really did break. "Did I not say so?" said the darning needle. "I'm too fine!"

"Now she's quite useless," said the fingers; but they were obliged to keep her, all the same. For the cook dropped some sealing wax upon the needle, and pinned her handkerchief together with it in the front.

"So, now I'm a breastpin!" said the darning needle. "I knew very well that I should come to honor: when one is something, one comes to something!"

And she laughed quietly to herself—for one can never see when a darning needle laughs. There she sat, and looked all about her, as proud as if she was in a state coach.

"May I be permitted to ask if you are of gold?" she inquired of the pin, her neighbor. "You have a very pretty appearance, and a peculiar head, but it is very little. You must take pains to grow, for it's not every one that has sealing wax dropped upon him."

And the darning needle drew herself up so proudly that she fell out of the handkerchief right into the sink, which the cook was rinsing out.

"Now we're going on a journey," said the darning needle. "If I only don't get lost!"

But she really was lost.

"I'm too fine for this world," she observed, as she lay in the gutter. "But I know who I am, and there's always something in that!"

So the darning needle kept her proud behavior, and did not lose her good humor. And many kinds of things swam over her, chips and straws and pieces of old newspapers.

"Only look how they sail!" said the darning needle. "They don't know what is under them! I'm here, I remain firmly here. See, there goes a chip thinking of nothing in the world but of himself—of a chip! There's a straw going by now. How he turns! how he twirls about! Don't think only of yourself, you might easily run up against a stone. There swims a bit of newspaper. What's written upon it has long been forgotten, and yet it gives itself airs. I sit quietly and patiently here. I know who I am, and I shall remain what I am."

One day something lay close beside her that glittered splendidly. The darning needle believed that it was a diamond; but it was only a bit of broken bottle. Because it shone, the darning needle spoke to it, introducing herself as a breastpin.

"I suppose you are a diamond?" she observed.

"Why, yes, something of that kind."

And then each believed the other to be a very valuable thing. And they began speaking about the world, and how very conceited it was.

"I have been in a lady's box," said the darning needle, "and this lady was a cook. She had five fingers on each hand, and I never saw anything so conceited as those five fingers. And yet they were only there that they might take me out of the box and put me back in again."

"Were they of good birth?" asked the bit of bottle.

"No, indeed," replied the darning needle, "but very haughty. There were five brothers, all of the finger family. They kept very proudly together, though they were of different lengths: the outermost, the thumbling, was short and fat; he walked out in front of the ranks, and only had one joint in his back, and could only make a single bow. He said that if he were hacked off a man, that man was useless for service in war. Daintymouth, the second finger, thrust himself into sweet and sour, pointed to sun and moon, and made the impression when they wrote. Longman, the third, looked at all the others over his shoulder. Goldborder, the fourth, went about with a golden belt round his waist; and little Playman did nothing at all, and was proud of it. There was nothing but bragging among them, and therefore I went away."

"And now we sit here and glitter!" said the bit of bottle.

At that moment more water came into the gutter. It overflowed, and the bit of bottle was carried away.

"So he is disposed of," observed the darning needle. "I remain here. I am too fine. But that's my pride, and my pride is honorable." And proudly she sat there, and had many great thoughts. "I could almost believe I had been born of a sunbeam, I'm so fine! It really appears as if the sunbeams were always seeking for me under the water. Ah! I'm so fine that my mother cannot find me. If I had my old eye, which broke off, I think I should cry. But, no, I could not do that. It's not genteel to cry."

One day a couple of street boys were grubbing in the gutter, where they sometimes found old nails, farthings, and similar treasures. It was dirty work, but they took great delight in it.

"Oh," cried one, who had pricked himself with the darning needle, "there's a fellow for you!"

"I'm not a fellow. I'm a young lady!" said the darning needle.

But nobody listened to her. The sealing wax had come off, and she had turned black. But black makes one look slender, and she thought herself finer even than before.

"Here comes an eggshell sailing along!" said the boys; and they stuck the darning needle fast in the eggshell.

"White walls, and black myself! That looks good," remarked the darning needle. "Now one can see me. I only hope I shall not be seasick!" But she was not seasick at all. "It is good against seasickness, if one steel's one's stomach, and remembers that one is a little better than the ordinary person! Now my seasickness is over. The finer one is, the more one can bear."

"Crack!" went the eggshell, for a wagon went over her.

"Good heavens, what pressure!" said the darning needle. "Now I shall break! I shall break! I shall be seasick after all."

But she did not break, though the wagon went over her. She lay there at full length. And long did she lie there—and there let her lie!

PEITER, PETER, AND PEER

WHAT children know nowadays is past belief. In fact it is hard
to say what they do not know. That the stork came and
fetched them out of the well or the milldam, when they were
tiny little things, and brought them to Father and Mother is
now such an old story that they no longer believe it, and yet
it is the real truth.

But how comes it that the little ones are down in the milldam
or the well? Ah! not everyone knows that, but there are some
few who do. Have you ever looked at the sky, on a clear,
starlight night, and watched the many shooting stars? It is as
if they were stars that fell from the sky and disappeared in the
darkness. Even the most learned cannot explain what they do
not know themselves. Nevertheless, when one knows it, one
can explain it. It is like a little candle from a Christmas tree,
that drops from the deep blue sky, and is blown out by the
evening wind. It is a soul spark from our Lord, that flies down
toward the earth, and when it comes into our thick, heavy air,
loses its brilliancy. And there only remains something that our
eyes cannot see—for it is something much finer and more delicate than our air—a little child from heaven; a little angel,
without wings, for it has to be a human child, and then what
would it do with wings, if it had them anyway?

Softly it glides through the air, and the wind wafts it into
a flower—a dandelion maybe, or a rose, or cowslip—and there
it lies and waits. It is so light and airy that a fly could carry it
off, and a bee could do it very easily. But when they come to
hunt for their sweetness in the flower, and find the little air-
child lying there in the way, they do not whisk it out. Oh, no!

they would never do that. They take it and carry it to a water-lily leaf, where they lay it down in the warm sunshine, and from the leaf the air-child creeps and scrambles into the water, where it remains, sleeping and growing till it is big enough for the stork to see it. Then he picks it up and carries it to some kind family where they very much wish for such a sweet little one. But how sweet or not it becomes depends on whether the little one has drunk pure, clear water, or whether it has swallowed mud and duckweed the wrong way: that can make one so earthy!

The stork never chooses, but takes the first one he happens to see. One comes into a pleasant house to kind and loving parents; another comes to poor people in great sorrow and misery: it would have been much better to remain in the mill-dam!

The little ones never can remember afterward what they dreamed while they lay in the water, under the water-lily leaf, where, when evening came, they heard the frogs sing "Co-ax, co-ax, gwax"; and that means, in human language, "Make haste to go to sleep and dream." Nor can they remember in what flower they lay at first, or how it smelled. And yet there is always something within them, when they are grown men and women, which makes them feel, "This flower I like best." That is because it is the one they were laid in by the wind, when they were air-children.

The stork lives to a good old age, and always takes an interest in the little ones whom he has brought out into the world. He takes note of how they get on, and if they behave well. To be sure, he cannot do much for them, or in any way change anything in their lives, for he has his own large family to attend to, but at least he never lets them go quite out of his thoughts.

I know an old and very worthy, honest Stork, who has had much experience, and has fetched many little ones out of the

water, and knows their histories—in which there is always a
little mud and duckweed from the milldam. I begged him to
tell me the history of one of them and he said I should have
three instead of one, out of the Peitersens' house.

That was a remarkably nice family, the Peitersens. The
father was a member of the common council, and that was a
great distinction. To this home the stork brought a little fellow who was called Peiter; and the year after he brought
another, and they called him Peter. And when the third one
came he got the name of Peer; because the names Peiter, Peter,
Peer are all contained in that of Peitersen. Here then were
three brothers—three shooting stars—each rocked in a flower,
then laid under the water-lily leaf in the milldam, and fetched
from there by the Stork and brought to the Peitersen family,
who live in the corner house that you have so often seen.

They grew in body and in mind, and wanted to be something more than common councilmen. Peiter said he wanted
to be a robber. He had seen the play of *Fra Diavolo,* and after
that decided upon the robber business, as the most delightful
in the world.

Peter said he would be a soap-fat man, and carry a rattle
that makes a dreadful noise—like the ones he had heard that
soap-fat men in other countries have. And Peer, who was such
a good, sweet boy, round and plump, but who used to bite his
nails—that was his only fault—Peer wanted to be "Papa." And
this was what each said he wanted to be, when people asked
them about it.

And then they were sent to school. One was first and
the other last of his class, and one came just in between. But
for all that they were each just as good and clever as the
other—and so they were—at least so said their fond and very
clear-sighted parents.

They went to children's parties, and they smoked cigars

when nobody was looking, and they made great progress in knowledge and insight.

Peiter, from the time he was quite small, was quarrelsome and fierce, just as a robber ought to be. He was a very naughty boy, but that came, his mother said, from worms—naughty children always have something the matter with them—that is mud in the stomach—from the milldam. But one day his mother's new silk gown was the worse for his obstinacy and naughtiness.

"Don't push the tea table, my sweet lamb," said his mother. "You might upset the cream pitcher, and then I should get spots on my silk gown." And the "sweet lamb," with a firm hand, took the cream pitcher, and with a firm hand poured all the cream into Mamma's lap—and Mamma could not help saying "Oh, lamb, lamb, that was careless of you, lamb!" But he had a will of his own—that she could not deny—and a strong will shows character, and that is so pleasant for a mother to see.

He might undoubtedly have become a robber, but he didn't after all; he only came to look like one—with a slouched hat, bare throat, and long, lank hair. He was to have been an artist, but only got as far as the clothes, and looked like a hollyhock, and all the people he drew looked like hollyhocks, too—they were so lanky. He was very fond of that flower, and the stork said he had lain in it when he was an air-child.

Peter must have lain in a buttercup: he looked so buttery around the corners of his mouth, and had such a yellow skin. One could not help but wonder if he were cut in the skin, butter would come out. He ought to have been a butter dealer, and he could have been his own sign. But the inner man, in him, was a soap-fat man with a rattle. He was the musical member of the Peitersen family—"musical enough for all of them," said the neighbors. He composed seventeen new polkas in one week, and then put them all together and made an opera of them, with accompaniment of drum and rattle. Ugh! how fine that was!

Peer was small, red, and white, and quite ordinary. He had lain in a daisy. He never defended himself when the other boys tried to fight him: he said he was the most reasonable, and the most reasonable always gives way.

He made collections; first of slate pencils, and after that of the seals from letters; and then he got a little cabinet of Natural History curiosities, in which there was the skeleton of a stickle-back, three blind baby rats in alcohol, and a stuffed mole. Peer had a great taste for science and an eye for the beauties of nature—and that was very satisfactory for his parents, and for Peer too.

His brothers were both engaged to be married, while he still thought of nothing but completing his collection of water-fowl's eggs. He knew a great deal more about animals than about human beings. He even thought that we never could be as great as animals in the feeling which we consider the highest of all, and that is—love. He saw that when Mrs. Nightingale was on her nest, setting, Mr. Nightingale sat on a branch close by and sang all night to his little wife, "Kluck-kluck-zi-zi-lo-lo-li!" Peer felt that he never could do that, and that it would be impossible for him to sacrifice his night's rest in that way. When Madame Stork had the baby storks in the nest, Mr. Stork stood all night on one leg on the edge of the roof, to watch. Peer could not have stood so for an hour!

And when one day he closely inspected a spider's web, and saw what it contained, he utterly renounced all ideas of marriage. Mr. Spider weaves his web that he may catch thoughtless flies, no matter how old or young, fat or lean; he lives only for the support of his family. But Mrs. Spider lives only for him. She eats him up out of sheer love. She eats his heart, his head, his stomach, and nothing but his long, thin legs remain in the web, in the place where he sat with his heart full of anxiety for the welfare of his family. And this is the real, pure truth—right straight out of the Natural History book. Peer saw all this and grew thoughtful: to be so dearly loved by one's wife, that she eats one up out of love! No, that is too much—no human being could do as much as that, and after all would it be desirable?

And then Peer resolved never to marry, never to give or take a kiss; that might look like the first step toward marriage. But he got a kiss, anyhow—the same that we must all get someday —the great kiss that Death gives.

When we have lived long enough, then Death is ordered to "kiss him away," and away we go. There comes a ray of sunshine, straight from our Lord, so bright and dazzling it almost blinds us. And then the soul which came from heaven as a shooting star, goes back like a shooting star, but not to sleep in a flower, or to dream under the leaf of the water lily. Oh, no! it has much more important things to do. It goes into the great land of eternity and there it stays, but what that land is like, no one can say and no one knows. No one has peeped into it, not even the Stork, although he knows and has seen more than almost anyone else.

He knew nothing more of Peer after he had gone to that strange land than what I have told you, though about Peiter and Peter he said he could tell much more. But I thought I had heard enough of them, and I suppose you have too, and so I thanked him and bade him good-by for this once. But now he wants his payment for this commonplace little story— three frogs and a little snake—he takes his pay in creature comforts, you see. Will you pay him? I will not. I have neither frogs nor snakes.

THE GREENIES

A ROSE tree stood in the window. Only a short time ago it was green and fresh, and now it looked sickly—no doubt it was in poor health. A whole regiment was quartered on it and was eating it up. But notwithstanding this greediness, the regiment was a very decent and respectable one. It wore bright green uniforms. I spoke to one of the "Greenies." He was only three days old, and yet he was already a grandfather! Do you know what he said? It is all true—he spoke of himself and of the rest of the regiment. Listen!

"We are the most wonderful creatures in the world. We are engaged at a very early age, and immediately have the wedding. When the cold weather comes, we lay our eggs; the little ones lie snug and warm. The wisest of creatures, the ant (we have the greatest respect for him!) understands us. He appreciates us, you may be sure. He does not eat us up at once. He takes our eggs, lays them in the family anthill, on the ground floor—lays them, labeled and numbered, side by side, layer on layer, so that each day a new one may creep out of the egg. Then he puts us in a stable, pinches our hind legs, and milks us till we die. He has given us the prettiest name—'Little milch-cow!'

"All creatures, who, like the ant, are gifted with common sense, call us this. It is only human beings who do not. They give us another name, and that we feel to be a great affront—great enough to embitter our whole life. Would you write a protest against it for us? Would you rouse these human beings to a sense of the wrong they do us? They look at us so stupidly at times, with such envious eyes, just because we eat a rose leaf, while they eat every created thing—all that is green and grows. Oh, they give us the most humiliating name! I will not even mention it. Ugh! I feel it in my stomach; I cannot even pronounce it—at least not when I have my uniform on, and I always wear that.

"I was born on a rose leaf. And the whole regiment lives on the rose tree. We live off it, in fact; but then it lives again in us, who belong to the higher order of created beings. The human beings do not like us. They come and murder us with soapsuds—it is a horrid drink! I seem to smell it even now. It is dreadful to be washed when one was not made to be washed. Man! you who look at us with your severe soapsud eyes, think what our place in nature is: we are born on roses, we die in roses—our whole life is a poem. Do not give us the name which you yourself think most despicable, the name that I cannot bear to pronounce. Call us the ants' milch-cows—the rose-tree regiment—the little green things."

And I—the man—stood looking at the tree, and at the little greenies—whose name I shall not mention, for I should not like to wound the feelings of one of the citizens of the rose tree, a large family with eggs and young ones—and at the soapsuds that I was going to wash them in, for I had come with soap and water, and murderous intentions. But now I will use it for soap bubbles. Look! How beautiful! Perhaps there lies a fairy tale in each, and the bubble grows so large and radiant, it looks as if there were a pearl lying inside of it!

The bubble swayed and swung, and flew to the door and then burst. But the door opened wide, and there stood Dame Fairy Tale herself! And now she will tell you better than I can about—I won't say the name—the little green things.

"Tree lice!" said Dame Fairy Tale. "One must call things by their right names; and if one cannot always do so, one must at least have the privilege of doing so in fairy tales!"

THE STORKS

A STORK had built his nest on the roof of a house at the very edge of a little town. The mother stork was sitting on the nest with her little ones, who stuck out their little black beaks, which had not yet turned red. The father stork stood erect and stiff a little way off on the ridge of the roof with one leg drawn up under him, as he was tired of standing on two. He stood so still that he seemed to be carved out of wood.

"It will look so grand for my wife to have a sentry on guard by the nest," he thought. "People won't know that I am her husband. I daresay they think I have orders to stand there. It looks smart!" And so he remained standing on one leg.

A party of children were playing in the street, and when they saw the stork, one of the boldest boys, followed by the others, sang what he could remember of the old song about the storks.

> *"Oh, father stork, father stork, fly to your nest;*
> *Three featherless fledglings await your return.*
> *The first of your chicks shall be stuck through the breast,*
> *The second shall hang, and the third shall burn."*

"Listen! What are the boys singing?" asked the little storks. "Did they say we are to be hanged and burned?"

"Don't bother your heads about them!" said the mother stork. "Don't listen to them. They can't do you any harm."

" 'Listen! What are the boys singing?' asked the little storks. 'Did they say we are to be hanged and burned?' "

But the boys went on singing and pointing their fingers at the storks. Only one boy, whose name was Peter, said that it was a shame to make fun of creatures and he would take no part in it.

The mother bird comforted her little ones, saying: "Do not trouble yourselves about it. Look at your father. See how quietly he stands, and on one leg too!"

"But we are frightened," said the young ones, burying their heads in the nest.

The next day when the children came back to play and saw the storks, they began their old song:

"The first of your chicks shall be stuck through the breast,
The second shall hang, and the third shall burn."

"Are we to be hanged and burned?" asked the little storks.

"No, certainly not," said the mother. "You are going to learn to fly. See if I don't drill you! Then we will go into the fields and visit the frogs. They curtsy in the water to us and sing 'Koax, Koax,' and then we gobble them up. That's a treat if you like one!"

"And what next?" asked the young ones.

"Oh, then all the storks in the country assemble for the autumn maneuvers. You will have to fly your very best, for the one who cannot fly will be run through the body by the general's beak. So you must take good care to learn everything when the drills begin."

"After all then we may be stuck through just as the boys said—listen, they are singing it again!"

"Listen to me and not to them," said the mother stork. "After the grand maneuvers we shall fly away to the warm countries, a very long way off, over the woods and mountains. We shall go to Egypt where they have houses with three-cornered sides, which reach above the clouds. They are called pyramids, and they are older than any stork can remember.

There is a river there which overflows its banks and all the land round it turns to mud, and then you walk about in mud eating frogs!"

"Oh!" said all the young ones.

"Yes, it is splendid; you do nothing but eat all day. And while we are so well off there, there is not a leaf on the trees in this country. It is so cold here that the clouds freeze and crack into pieces and fall down in little bits."

She meant snow, but did not know how to describe it any better.

"Do the naughty boys freeze to pieces?" asked the young storks.

"No, they don't freeze to pieces, but they come very near to it and have to sit moping in dark rooms. You, on the other hand, fly about in strange countries, in the warm sunshine among flowers."

Some time passed, and the little ones were big enough to stand up in the nest and look about them. The father stork flew back and forth every day with nice frogs and little snakes, and every kind of delicacy he could find. It was so funny to see the tricks he did to amuse them. He would turn his head right around onto his tail, and he would clatter with his beak as if it were a rattle. And then he would tell them all the stories he had heard in the swamps.

"Well, now you must learn to fly," said the mother stork one day. And all the young ones had to stand on the ridge of the roof. Oh, how they wobbled, trying to keep their balance with their wings. They came very close to falling off.

"Now look at me!" said the mother. "This is how you must hold your heads. And move your legs so: one, two; one, two. This will help you get on in the world."

She flew a little way, and the young ones made a clumsy little hop. But down they came with a bump, for their bodies were too heavy.

"I don't want to fly," said one of the young ones, creeping back into the nest again. "I don't care about going to the warm countries."

"Do you want to freeze to death here when the winter comes? Shall I have the boys come and hang or burn or stake you? I will soon call them!"

"No, no!" said the young one, hopping out upon the roof again with the others.

By the third day they could all fly fairly well. Then they thought they could hover in the air too, and they tried it. But flop!—they soon found they had to keep moving their wings.

Then the boys began their song again:

"Oh, father stork, father stork, fly to your nest."

"Shall we fly down and pick their eyes out?" asked the young ones.

"No, leave them alone," said their mother. "Pay attention only to me—that is much more important. One, two, three! Now we fly to the right. One, two, three! Now to the left and round the chimney. That was good! That last stroke of the wings was so pretty and the flap so well done that I will allow you to go to the swamp with me tomorrow. Several nice storks go there with their children, and just let me see that mine are the nicest. Don't forget to carry your heads high. It looks well, and gives you an air of importance."

"But are we not to have our revenge on the naughty boys?" asked the young storks.

"Let them scream as much as they like! You will fly away with the clouds to the land of the pyramids, while they will perhaps be freezing. There won't be a green leaf or a sweet apple here then!"

"We *will* have our revenge!" they whispered to each other, and then they began their drilling again.

Of all the boys in the street, none was worse at making

fun of the storks than the one who first began the derisive song. He was a tiny little fellow, not more than six years old. It is true that the young storks thought he was at least a hundred, for he was so much bigger than their father and mother, and they had no idea how old children and grown-up people could be. They reserved all their vengeance for the boy who first began to tease them, and who never would leave off. The young storks were frightfully irritated by the teasing, and the older they grew, the less they could stand it. At last their mother was obliged to promise that they should have their revenge, but not till the last day before they left.

"First we shall have to see how you behave at the maneuvers. If you come to grief and the general has to run you through the breast with his beak, the boys will be right after all, at least in one way! Now we shall see!"

"That you shall!" said the young ones. And what pains they took! They practiced every day, till they could fly as lightly as any feather. It was quite a pleasure to watch them.

Then came the autumn. All the storks began to assemble, before they started on their flight to the warm countries where they spent their winters.

Those were indeed maneuvers! They had to fly over woods and towns to try their wings, because they had such a long journey before them. The young storks did everything so well that they were pronounced worthy of frogs and snakes. This was the highest character they could obtain. Now they were allowed to eat the frogs and snakes, which you may be sure they did.

"Now we shall have our revenge!" they said.

"Yes, certainly," said the mother stork. "My plan is this—and I think it is the right one. I know the pond where all the little human babies lie, till the storks fetch them and give them to their parents. The pretty little creatures lie there asleep, dreaming sweet dreams, sweeter than any they ever dream afterward. Every parent wishes for such a little baby, and every child wants a baby brother or sister. Now we shall fly to the pond and fetch a little brother or sister for each of those children who did not join in singing that horrid song, or in making fun of the storks. But those who sang it shall not have one."

"But what about that bad wicked boy who first began the song?" shrieked the young storks. "What is to be done to him?"

"In the pond there is a little dead baby—it has dreamed itself to death. We will take it to him, and then he will cry because we have brought him a little dead brother. But you have surely not forgotten the good boy who said, 'It is a shame to make fun of the creatures!' We will take him both a brother and a sister, and, because his name is Peter, you shall all be called Peter too."

It happened just as she said, and all the storks are called Peter to this day.

THE GIRL WHO TROD
ON A LOAF

I DARESAY you have heard of the girl who stepped on a loaf so as not to soil her shoes, and all the misfortunes that befell her in consequence. At any rate the story has been written and printed too.

She was a poor child of a proud and arrogant nature, and her disposition was bad from the beginning. When she was quite tiny, her greatest delight was to catch flies and pull their wings off, to make creeping insects of them. Then she would catch chafers and beetles and stick them on a pin, after which she would push a leaf or a bit of paper close enough for them to seize with their feet, for the pleasure of seeing them writhe and wriggle in their efforts to free themselves from the pins.

"The chafer is reading now," said little Inger. "Look at it turning over the page!"

She got worse rather than better as she grew older. But she was very pretty, and that no doubt was her misfortune, or she might have had many a beating which she never got.

"It will take a heavy blow to bend that head," said her own mother. "As a child you have often trampled on my apron. I fear when you are grown up you will trample on my heart."

This she did and with a vengeance.

She was sent into service in the country with some rich people. They treated her as if she had been their own child and dressed her in the same style. She grew prettier and prettier, but her pride grew too.

When she had been with them a year, her employers said to her, "You ought to go home to see your parents, little Inger."

So she went, but she went only to show herself, so that they might see how grand she was. When she got to the town gates, and saw the young men and maids gossiping round the pond, and her mother sitting among them with a bundle of sticks she had picked up in the woods, Inger turned away. She was ashamed that one so fine as herself should have such a ragged old woman for her mother, one who picked up sticks. She was not a bit sorry that she had turned back, only angry.

Another half year passed.

"Little Inger, you really ought to go and see your old parents," said her mistress. "Here is a large loaf of wheaten bread that you may take to them. They will be pleased to see you."

Inger put on all her best clothes and her fine new shoes. She held up her skirts and picked her steps carefully so as to keep her shoes nice and clean. Now no one could blame her for this. But when she came to the path through the marsh a great part of it was wet and muddy, and she threw the loaf into the mud for a steppingstone. She stood there with one foot on the loaf and was lifting up the other for the next step, when the loaf sank deeper and deeper with her until she entirely disappeared. Nothing was to be seen but a black bubbling pool.

Now this is the story.

What had become of her? She went down to the Marsh Wife who has a brewery down there. The Marsh Wife is sister to the Elf King, and aunt to the Elf maidens who are well enough known. They have had verses written about them and pictures painted. But all that people know about the Marsh Wife is that when the mist rises over the meadows in the summer, she is at her brewing. It was into this brewery that little Inger fell, and no one can stand being there long. A scavenger's cart is sweet compared to the Marsh Wife's brewery. The smell from the barrels is enough to make people faint, and the barrels are so close together that no one can pass between them, and wherever there is a little chink it is filled up with stinking toads and slimy snakes. Little Inger fell among all this horrid living filth. It was so icy cold that she shuddered from head to foot and her limbs grew quite stiff. The loaf stuck fast to her feet and it drew her down just as an amber button draws a bit of straw.

The Marsh Wife was at home. Old Bogey and his great-grandmother were paying her a visit. The great-grandmother is a very venomous old woman, and she is never idle. She never goes out without her work, and she had it with her today too. She was busily making gadabout leather to put into people's shoes so that the wearer might have no rest. She embroidered lies and strung together all the idle words that fell to the ground, to make mischief of them. Oh, yes, old great-grandmother can knit and embroider in fine style.

As soon as she saw little Inger, she put up her eyeglass and looked at her through it. "That girl has got something in her," she said. "I should like to have her as a remembrance of my visit. She would make a very good statue in my great-grand-son's outer corridor."

So Inger was given to her and this was how she got to Bogeyland. People don't always get there by such a direct route, though it is easy enough to get there in more rounda-bout ways.

What a never-ending corridor that was, to be sure. It made one giddy to look either backward or forward. Here stood an ignominious crew waiting for the door of mercy to be opened, but long might they wait. Great, fat, sprawling spiders spun webs of a thousand years, round and round their feet. And these webs were like foot screws and held them as in a vice, or as though bound with a copper chain. Besides, there was such everlasting unrest in every soul—the unrest of torment. The miser had forgotten the key of his money chest. He knew he had left it sticking in the lock. But it would take far too long to enumerate all the various tortures here. Inger experienced the torture of standing like a statue with a loaf tied to her feet.

"This is what comes of trying to keep one's feet clean," said she to herself. "Look how they stare at me!" They did indeed stare at her. All their evil passions shone out of their eyes and spoke without words from their lips. They were a terrible sight. "It must be a pleasure to look at me!" thought Inger, "for I have a pretty face and nice clothes." And then she turned her eyes to look at them; her neck was too stiff to turn.

But oh, how dirty she had got in the Marsh Wife's brewery. She had never thought of that. Her clothes were covered with slime. A snake had got among her hair and hung dangling down her back. A toad looked out of every fold of her dress, croaking like an asthmatic pug dog. It was most unpleasant. "But all the others down here look frightful too," was her consolation.

Worse than anything was the terrible hunger she felt, and she could not stoop down to break a bit of bread off the loaf she was standing on. No, her back had stiffened, her arms and hands had stiffened, and her whole body was like a pillar of stone. She could turn her eyes, but she could only turn them entirely around, so as to look backward—and a horrible sight that was. And then came the flies! They crept upon her eyes, and however much she winked they would not fly away. They could not, for she had pulled off their wings and made creeping insects of them. That was indeed a torment added to her gnawing hunger. She seemed at last to be absolutely empty.

"If this is to go on long, I shan't be able to bear it," said she. But it did go on, and bear it she must.

Then a scalding tear fell upon her forehead. It trickled over her face and bosom right down to the loaf. Then another fell, and another, till there was a perfect shower.

Who was crying for little Inger? Had she not a mother on

earth? Tears of sorrow shed by a mother for her child will always reach it, but they do not bring healing. They burn and make the torment fifty times worse. Then this terrible hunger again, and she not able to get at the bread under her feet. She felt at last as if she had been feeding upon herself, and had become a mere hollow reed which conducts every sound. She distinctly heard everything that was said on earth about herself, and she heard nothing but hard words.

Certainly her mother wept bitterly and sorrowfully, but at the same time she said, "Pride goes before a fall. There was your misfortune, Inger. How you have grieved your mother!" Her mother and everyone on earth knew all about her sin: how she had stepped upon the loaf and sunk down under the earth, and so was lost. The cowherd had told them so much. He had seen it himself from the hillock where he was standing.

"How you have grieved your mother, Inger," said the poor woman. "But then I always said you would."

"Oh, that I had never been born!" thought Inger then. "I should have been much better off. My mother's tears are no good now."

She heard the good people her employers, who had been like parents to her, talking about her. "She was a sinful child," they said. "She did not value the gifts of God but trod them underfoot. She will find it hard to open the door of mercy."

"They ought to have brought me up better," thought Inger. "They should have knocked the nonsense out of me if it was there."

She heard that a song had been written about her and sung all over the country: "The arrogant girl who trod on a loaf to keep her shoes clean."

"That I should hear that old song so often and have to suffer so much for it!" thought Inger.

"The others ought to be punished for their sins, too," said

Inger. "There would be plenty to punish. Oh, how I am being tormented!"

And her heart grew harder than her outer shell.

"Nobody will ever get any better in this company, and I won't be any better. See how they are all staring at me!"

Her heart was full of anger and malice toward everybody.

"Now they have got something to talk about up there! Oh, this torture!"

She heard people telling her story to children, and the little one always called her "wicked Inger"—"she was so naughty that she had to be tormented." She heard nothing but hard words from the children's mouths.

But one day when anger and hunger were gnawing at her hollow shell, she heard her name mentioned and her story being told to an innocent child, a little girl, and the little creature burst into tears at the story of proud, vain Inger.

"But will she never come up here again?" asked the child. And the answer was, "She will never come up again."

"But if she were to ask pardon and promise never to do it again?"

"She won't ask pardon," they said.

"But I want her to do it," said the little girl, who refused to be comforted. "I will give my doll's house if she may only come up again. It is so dreadful for poor Inger."

These words reached down into Inger's heart and they seemed to do her good. It was the first time that anyone had said, "Poor Inger," without adding anything about her misdeeds. A little innocent child was weeping and praying for her, and it made her feel quite odd. She would have liked to cry herself, but she could not shed a tear, and this was a further torment.

As the years passed above, so they went on below without any change. She less often heard sounds from above, and she was less talked about. But one day she was aware of a sigh.

"Inger, Inger, what a grief you have been to me, but I always knew you would be." It was her mother who was dying. Occasionally she heard her name mentioned by her old employers, and the gentlest words her mistress used were, "Shall I ever see you again, Inger? One never knows whither one may go."

But Inger knew very well that her good kindly mistress could never come to the place where she was.

Again a long bitter period passed. Then Inger again heard her name pronounced, and saw above her head what seemed to be two bright stars. They were in fact two kind eyes which were closing on earth. So many years had gone by since the little girl had cried so bitterly at the story of "Poor Inger," that the child had grown to be an old woman whom the Lord was now calling to Himself. In the last hour when one's whole life comes back to one, she remembered how as a little child she had wept bitter tears at the story of Inger. The impression was so clear to the old woman in the hour of death that she exclaimed aloud, "O Lord, may I not, like Inger, have trodden on Thy blessed gifts without thinking? And may I not also have nourished pride in my heart? But in Thy mercy Thou didst not let me fall! Forsake me not now in my last hour!"

The old woman's eyes closed and the eyes of her soul were opened to see the hidden things, and as Inger had been so vividly present in her last thoughts, she saw now how deep she had sunk. And at the sight she burst into tears. Then she stood in the kingdom of heaven, as a child, weeping for poor Inger. Her tears and prayers echoed into the hollow, empty shell which surrounded the imprisoned, tortured soul, and it was quite overwhelmed by all this unexpected love from above. An angel of God weeping over her! Why was this vouchsafed to her? The tortured soul recalled every earthly action it had ever performed, and at last it melted into tears, in a way Inger had never done.

She was filled with grief for herself. It seemed as though the gate of mercy could never be opened to her. But as in humble contrition she acknowledged this, a ray of light shone into the gulf of destruction. The strength of the ray was far greater than that of the sunbeam which melts the snowman built up by the boys in the garden. And sooner, much sooner, than a snowflake melts on the warm lips of a child, did Inger's stony form dissolve before it. And a little bird with lightning speed winged its way to the upper world. It was terribly shy and afraid of everything. It was ashamed of itself and afraid to meet the eye of any living being, so it hastily sought shelter in a chink in the wall. There it cowered, shuddering in every limb. It could not utter a sound, for it had no voice. It sat for a long time before it could survey calmly all the wonders around. Yes, they were wonders indeed! The air was so sweet and fresh, the moon shone so brightly, the trees and bushes were so fragrant. And then the comfort of it all; its feathers were so clean and dainty.

How all creation spoke of love and beauty! The bird would gladly have sung aloud all these thoughts stirring in its breast, but it had not the power. Gladly would it have caroled as do the cuckoos and nightingales in summer. The good God, who hears the voiceless hymn of praise even of a worm, was also aware of this psalm of thanksgiving trembling in the breast of the bird, as the psalms of David echoed in his heart before they shaped themselves into words and melody. These thoughts and these voiceless songs grew and swelled for weeks. They must have an outlet, and at the first attempt at a good deed this would be found.

Then came the holy Christmas feast. The peasants raised a pole against a wall, and tied a sheaf of oats onto the top so that the little birds might have a good meal on the happy Christmas Day.

The sun rose bright and shone upon the sheaf of oats, and

the twittering birds surrounded the pole. Then from the chink in the wall came a feeble tweet-tweet. The swelling thoughts of the bird had found a voice, and this faint twitter was its hymn of praise. The thought of a good deed was awakened, and the bird flew out of its hiding place. In the kingdom of heaven this bird was well known.

It was a very hard winter and all the water had thick ice over it. The birds and wild creatures had great difficulty in finding food. The little bird flew along the highways, finding here and there in the tracks of the sleighs a grain of corn. At the baiting places it also found a few morsels of bread, of which it would eat only a crumb, giving the rest to the other starving sparrows which it called up. Then it flew into the town and peeped about. Wherever a loving hand had strewn bread crumbs for the birds, it ate only one crumb and gave the rest away.

In the course of the winter the bird had collected and given away so many crumbs of bread that they equaled in weight the whole loaf which little Inger had stepped upon to keep her shoes clean. When the last crumbs were found and given away, the bird's gray wings became white and spread themselves wide.

"A tern is flying away over the sea," said the children who saw the white bird. Now it dived into the sea, and now it soared up into the bright sunshine. It gleamed so brightly that it was not possible to see what became of it. They said it flew right into the sun.

THE ELDER-TREE MOTHER

THERE was once a little boy who had taken cold by going out and getting his feet wet. No one could think how he managed to do so, for the weather was quite dry. His mother undressed him and put him to bed. Then she brought in the teapot to make him a good cup of elder tea, which is so warming. At the same time, the friendly old man who lived all alone at the top of the house came in at the door. He had neither wife nor child, but he was very fond of children, and he knew so many fairy tales and stories that it was a pleasure to hear him talk.

"Now, if you drink your tea," said the mother, "very likely you will have a story in the meantime."

"Yes, if I can only think of a new one to tell," said the old man. "But how did the little fellow get his feet wet?" asked he.

"Ah," said the mother, "that we cannot find out."

"Will you tell me a story?" asked the little boy.

"Yes, if you can tell me exactly how deep the gutter is in the little street through which you go to school."

"Just halfway up to my knee," said the boy. "That is, if I stand in the deepest part."

"It is easy to see how we got our feet wet," said the old man. "Well, now I suppose I ought to tell a story, but I don't know any more."

"You can make up one, I know," said the boy. "Mother says that you can turn everything you look at into a story, and even everything you touch."

"Ah, but that kind of tale and story is worth nothing. The real ones come of themselves. They knock at my forehead and say, 'Here we are!' "

"Won't there be a knock soon?" said the boy. And his mother laughed, while she put elder flowers in the teapot and poured boiling water over them. "Oh, do tell me a story!"

"Yes, I will if a story comes by itself. But tales and stories are very grand—they come only when it pleases them. Stop!" he cried all at once. "Here we have it. Look! There is a story in the teapot now."

The little boy looked at the teapot and saw the lid gradually raise itself. Long branches sprouted out from the spout in all directions. They became larger and larger, and there appeared a large elder tree, covered with flowers white and fresh. It spread itself out to the bed and pushed the curtains aside. And oh, how fragrant the blossoms smelled!

In the midst of the tree sat a pleasant-looking old woman, in a very strange dress. The dress was green like the leaves of the elder tree, and was decorated with large white elder blossoms. It was not easy to tell whether the border was made of some kind of cloth or of real flowers.

"What is that woman's name?" asked the boy.

"The Romans and Greeks called her a dryad," said the old man, "but we do not understand that name. In the quarter of the town where the sailors live, they call her Elder-Tree Mother, and you must pay attention to her now and listen while you look at the beautiful tree.

"Just such a large blooming tree as this stands in the corner of a poor little yard. And under this tree, one bright sunny afternoon, sat two old people—a sailor and his wife. They had great-grandchildren and would soon celebrate their golden wedding, which is the fiftieth anniversary of the wedding day, as I suppose you know, and the Elder-Tree Mother sat in the tree and looked just as pleased as she does now.

" 'I know when the golden wedding is to be,' said she, but they did not hear her. They were talking of olden times.

" 'Do you remember,' said the old sailor, 'when we were

quite little and used to run about and play in the very same
yard where we are now sitting, and how we planted little
twigs in one corner and made a garden?'

" 'Yes,' said the old woman. 'I remember it quite well; and
how we watered the twigs, and one of them was a sprig of
elder that took root and put forth green shoots, until it became in time the great tree under which we old people are
now seated.'

" 'To be sure,' he replied. 'And in that corner yonder stands
the water butt in which I used to sail my boat that I had cut
out all myself. And it sailed well, too! But since then I have
learned a very different kind of sailing.'

" 'Yes, but before that we went to school,' said she. 'And
then we were prepared for confirmation. How we both cried
on that day! But in the afternoon we went hand in hand up
to the round tower, and saw the view over Copenhagen and
across the water. Then we went to Fredericksburg, where the
King and Queen were sailing in their beautiful boat on the river.'

" 'But I had to sail on a very different voyage elsewhere and
be away from home for years on long voyages,' said the old
sailor.

" 'Ah yes, and I used to cry about you,' said she, 'for I
thought you must be dead, and lying drowned at the bottom
of the sea with the waves sweeping over you. And many a
time have I got up in the night to see if the weathercock had
turned. It turned often enough, but you came not. How well
I remember one day. The rain was pouring down from the
skies and the man came to the house where I was in service,
to fetch away the dust. I went down to him with the dustbox
and stood for a moment at the door. What shocking weather
it was! And while I stood there, the postman came up and
brought me a letter from you. How that letter had traveled
about! I tore it open and read it. I laughed and wept at the
same time—I was so happy. It said that you were in warm

countries where the coffee berries grew, and you told what a beautiful country it was and described many other wonderful things. So I stood reading by the dustbin, with the rain pouring down, when all at once somebody came and clasped me round the waist.'

" 'Yes, and you gave me such a box on the ears that they tingled,' said the old man.

" 'I did not know that it was you,' she replied, 'but you had arrived as quickly as your letter, and you looked so handsome, and indeed so you are still. You had a large yellow silk handkerchief in your pocket and a shiny hat on your head. You looked quite fine. And all the time what weather it was and how dismal the street looked!'

" 'And then do you remember,' said he, 'when we were married, and our first boy came, and then Marie, and Niels, and Peter, and Hans Christian?'

" 'Indeed, I do,' she replied. 'And they are all grown-up respectable men and women whom everyone likes.'

" 'And now their children have little ones,' said the old sailor. 'There are great-grandchildren for us, strong and healthy too.'

" 'Was it not about this time of the year that we were married?'

" 'Yes. And today is the golden wedding day,' said Elder-Tree Mother, popping her head out between the two old people, and they thought it was a neighbor nodding to them.

"Then they looked at each other and clasped their hands together. Presently their children and grandchildren came. They knew very well that it was the golden wedding day. They had already wished them joy on that very morning, but the old people had forgotten it, although they remembered so well all that had happened many years before. And the elder tree smelled sweetly, and the setting sun shone upon the faces of the old people till they looked quite ruddy. And the youngest of their grandchildren danced round them joyfully and said they were going to have a feast in the evening, and there were to be hot potatoes.

"Then the Elder-Tree Mother nodded in the tree and cried, 'Hurrah,' with all the rest."

"But that is not a story," said the little boy, who had been listening.

"Not till you understand it," said the old man. "But let us ask the Elder-Tree Mother to explain it."

"It was not exactly a story," said the Elder-Tree Mother, "but the story is coming now, and it is a true one. For out of truth grow the most wonderful stories, just as my beautiful elder bush has sprung out of the teapot."

And then she took the little boy out of bed and laid him on her bosom. And the blooming branches of elder closed over them so that they sat, as it were, in a leafy bower. And the bower flew with them through the air in the most delightful manner.

At once the Elder-Tree Mother changed to a beautiful young maiden. Her dress was still of the same green stuff, ornamented with a border of white elder blossoms, just like those the Elder-Tree Mother had worn. In her bosom she wore an elder flower. A wreath of the same was entwined in her golden ringlets. Her large blue eyes were very beautiful to look at. She was the same age as the boy, and they kissed each other and felt very happy. They left the arbor together hand in hand and found themselves in a beautiful flower garden which belonged to their home. On the green lawn their father's stick was tied up. There was life in this stick for the little ones, for no sooner did they place themselves upon it than the white knob changed into a pretty neighing head with a black flowing mane, and four long slim legs sprang forth. The creature was strong and spirited, and galloped with them round the grass plot.

"Hurrah! Now we will ride many miles away," said the boy. "We'll ride to the nobleman's estate where we went last year."

Then they rode round the grass plot again, and the little maiden, who, we know, was Elder-Tree Mother, kept crying out, "Now we are in the country. Do you see the farmhouse with a great baking oven which sticks out from the wall by the roadside like a gigantic egg? There is an elder spreading its branches over it, and a cock is marching about and scratching for the chickens. See how he struts! Now we are near the church. There it stands on the hill, shaded by the great oak trees, one of which is half dead. See, here we are at the blacksmith's forge. How the fire burns! And the half-clad men are striking the hot iron with the hammer, so that the sparks fly about. Now then, away to the nobleman's beautiful estate!"

And the boy saw all that the little girl spoke of as she sat behind him on the stick. It all passed before him, although they were only galloping round the grass plot.

Then they played together on a sidewalk, and raked up the earth to make a little garden. She took elder flowers out of her hair and planted them, and they grew just like those which he had heard the old people talking about, and which they had planted in their young days. They walked about hand in hand too, just as the old people had done when they were children, but they did not go up the round tower nor to Fredericksburg garden. No. But the little girl seized the boy round the waist and they rode all over the whole country. Sometimes it was spring, then summer, then autumn, and then winter followed, while thousands of images were presented to the boy's eyes and heart. And the little girl constantly sang to him, "You must never forget all this."

And through their whole flight the elder tree sent forth the sweetest fragrance. They passed roses and fresh beech trees, but the perfume of the elder tree was stronger than all, for its flowers hung round the little maiden's heart, against which the boy so often leaned his head during their flight.

"It is beautiful here in the spring," said the maiden, as they stood in a grove of beech trees covered with fresh green leaves. At their feet the sweet-scented thyme and blushing anemone lay spread amid the green grass in delicate bloom. "Oh, that it were always spring in the fragrant beech groves!"

"Here it is delightful in summer," said the maiden, as they passed the old knights' castles, telling of days gone by. They saw the high walls and pointed gables mirrored in the rivers beneath, where swans were sailing about and peeping into the cool green avenues. In the fields the corn waved to and fro like the sea. Red and yellow flowers grew among the ruins, and the hedges were covered with wild hops and blooming convolvulus. In the evening the moon rose round and full, and the haystacks in the meadows filled the air with their sweet scent. These were scenes never to be forgotten.

"It is lovely here also in autumn," said the little maiden, and then the scene changed.

The sky appeared higher and more beautifully blue, while the forest glowed with colors of red, green, and gold. The hounds were off to the chase. Large flocks of wild birds flew screaming over the Huns' graves, where the blackberry bushes twined around the old ruins. The dark blue sea was dotted with white sails, and in the barns sat old women, maidens, and children, picking hops into a large tub. The young ones sang songs and the old ones told fairy tales of wizards and witches. There could be nothing more pleasant than all this.

"Again," said the maiden, "it is beautiful here in winter." Then in a moment all the trees were covered with hoarfrost and they looked like white coral. The snow crackled beneath the feet as if everyone had on new boots, and one shooting star after another fell from the sky. In warm rooms there could be seen the Christmas trees decked out with presents and lighted up by festivity and joy. In the country farmhouses the sound of the violin could be heard. And there were games for apples, and even the poorest child could say, "It is beautiful in winter."

Beautiful indeed were all the scenes which the maiden showed to the little boy. And always around them floated the fragrance of the elder blossom, and ever above them waved the red flag with the white cross under which the old seaman had sailed. The boy, who had become a youth and had gone as a sailor out into the wide world and sailed to warm countries where the coffee grew, and to whom the little girl had given an elder blossom from her bosom for a keepsake when she took leave of him, placed the flower in his hymnbook. And when he opened it in foreign lands, he always turned to the spot where this flower of remembrance lay. The more he looked at it, the fresher it appeared. He could, as it were, breathe the homelike fragrance of the woods and see the little girl looking at him with her clear blue eyes from between the petals of the flower, and hear her whispering, "It is beautiful here at home in spring and summer, in autumn and winter," while hundreds of these home scenes passed through his memory.

Many years passed, and he was now an old man seated with his old wife under an elder tree in full blossom. They were holding each other's hands just as the great-grandfather and grandmother had done. They spoke, as they did, of olden times and of the golden wedding.

The little maiden with the blue eyes and the elder blossoms in her hair sat in the tree and nodded to them and said, "Today is the golden wedding." And then she took two flowers out of her wreath and kissed them, and they shone first like silver and then like gold. And as she placed them on the heads of the old people, each flower became a golden crown. And there they sat like a king and queen under the sweetly scented tree, which still looked like an elder bush.

Then he told his old wife the story of the Elder-Tree Mother, just as he had heard it told when he was a little boy. And they both fancied it as much like their own story, especially in some parts, and those they liked the best.

"Well, and so it is," said the little maiden. "Some call me Elder-Tree Mother, others call me a dryad, but my real name is 'Memory.' It is I who sit in the tree as it grows and grows, and I can think of the past and relate many things. Let me see if you have still preserved the flower."

Then the old man opened his hymnbook, and there lay the elder flower as fresh as if it had only just been placed there. And "Memory" nodded, and the two old people with the golden crowns on their heads sat in the red glow of the evening sunlight, and closed their eyes, and—and—the story was ended.

The little boy lay in his bed and did not quite know whether he had been dreaming or listening to a story. The teapot stood on the table, but no elder bush grew out of it, and the old man who had really told the tale was on the threshold and just going out the door.

"How beautiful it was!" said the little boy. "Mother, I have been to warm countries."

"I can quite believe it," said his mother. "When anyone drinks two full cups of elder-flower tea, he may well get into warm countries!" And then she covered him up so he should not take cold. "You have slept well while I have been disputing with the old man as to whether it was a real story or a fairy legend."

"And where is the Elder-Tree Mother?" asked the boy.

"She is in the teapot," said the mother. "And there she may stay."

THE STEADFAST TIN SOLDIER

THERE were once five and twenty tin soldiers; they were all brothers, for they had all been born of one old tin spoon. They shouldered their muskets, they looked straight in front of them, their uniforms were red and blue, and very splendid. The first thing they heard in the world, when the lid was taken off their box, were the words "Tin soldiers!" It was shouted by a little boy who laughed and clapped his hands; for the soldiers had been given to him for his birthday. And now he put them on the table. Every soldier was the living image of all the rest, only one of them was a little different, and he had but one leg. He had been cast last of all, and there hadn't been enough tin to finish him. But he stood as firmly on his one leg as the others did on their two; and it was just this soldier who amounted to something.

On the table where they had been placed stood many other playthings, but the toy that struck the eye most was a lovely castle of cardboard. Through the little windows one could see straight into the rooms. Outside the castle some little trees stood around a little looking glass, which made believe it was a lake. Wax swans swam on this lake, and were mirrored in it. This was all very lovely; but the loveliest thing of all was a little lady, who stood at the open door of the castle. She was also cut out in paper, but she had a dress of the clearest gauze, and a little narrow blue ribbon over her shoulders, that looked like a scarf; and in the middle of this ribbon was a shining spangle as big as her whole face.

The little lady stretched out both her arms, for she was a dancer; and then she lifted one leg so high that the tin soldier couldn't see it at all, and thought that, like himself, she had only one leg.

"That would be the wife for me," he thought, "but she is very grand. She lives in a castle, and I have only a box, and there are five and twenty of us in that already. It is no place for her. But anyway I must try to get acquainted with her."

And then he lay down at full length behind a snuffbox which was on the table where he could easily watch the little dainty lady, who continued to stand on one leg without losing her balance.

When the evening came, all the other tin soldiers were put into their box, and the people in the house went to bed. Now the toys began to play at "visiting," and at "war," and "giving balls." The tin soldiers rattled in their box, for they wanted to join too, but couldn't lift the lid.

The nutcracker threw somersaults, and the pencil danced on the slate; there was so much noise that the canary woke, and began to talk too, and even in verse. The only two who did not stir from their places were the tin soldier and the little dancer. She stood straight up on the point of one of her toes, and stretched out both her arms; and he was just as steadfast on his one leg. And he never turned his eyes away from her.

Now the clock struck twelve—and, bounce!—the lid flew off the snuffbox! There was no snuff in it, but instead a little black goblin; it was a trick, you see.

"Tin soldier!" said the goblin, "will you keep your eyes to yourself?"

But the tin soldier pretended not to hear him.

"Just you wait till tomorrow!" said the goblin.

When the morning came, and the children got up, the tin soldier was placed in the window; and whether it was the goblin or the draft that did it, all at once the window flew open, and the soldier fell head over heels out of the third story. It was a terrible trip! He turned his leg straight up, and stuck with his cap down and his bayonet between the paving stones.

The servant and the little boy came down right away to look for him, and though they almost stepped on him they couldn't see him. If the soldier had cried out, "Here I am!" they would have found him; but he didn't think it was proper to scream when he was in uniform.

Now it began to rain; one drop bigger than the next. It was a regular downpour! When the rain was over, two street boys came along.

"Pipe that!" said one of them, "there's a tin soldier. He'll go for a sail."

And they made a boat out of a newspaper, and put the tin soldier in the middle of it; and so he sailed down the gutter, and the two boys ran beside him and clapped their hands. Mercy on us! how the waves rose in that gutter, and what a current! But then it had been a downpour. The paper boat rocked up and down, and sometimes turned around so quickly that the tin soldier trembled; but he remained steadfast. He never moved a muscle, but looked straight before him, and shouldered his musket.

All at once the boat went under a long board laid across the gutter, and it was as dark as if he had been in his box.

"Where am I going now?" he thought. "Well, I suppose that's the goblin's fault. Ah! if the little lady only sat here with me in the boat, it might be twice as dark for all I'd care."

Suddenly there appeared a big water rat, who lived under the drain.

"Have you a passport?" said the rat. "Give me your passport."

But the tin soldier kept still and held his musket tighter than ever.

The boat rushed on, and the rat after it. Ugh! how he gnashed his teeth, and shouted at the sticks and straws.

"Stop him! Stop him! He hasn't paid toll—he hasn't shown his passport!"

But the current went faster and faster. The tin soldier could see the bright daylight where the board ended; and he heard a roaring noise, which might well have frightened the boldest man. Just think, where the board ended the gutter plunged right down into a big canal. And for him this was as dangerous as it would be for us to sail over a big waterfall.

Now he was already so near that he couldn't stop. The boat was darted forward, the poor tin soldier stiffened himself as much as he could; no one could say that he even blinked an eye. The boat whirled round three or four times, and was filled with water to the very edge—it must sink. The tin soldier stood up to his neck in water, and the boat sank

deeper and deeper. The paper was going to pieces more and more; and now the water closed over the soldier's head. Then he thought of the pretty little dancer, and how he should never see her again; and these words rang in his ears:

Danger, danger, warrior,
Death you must suffer.

And now the paper parted, and the tin soldier fell out; and in the same moment he was swallowed by a big fish.

Oh, how dark it was in there! It was even worse than under the gutter board; and then it was very narrow too. But the tin soldier was steadfast, and lay at full length shouldering his musket.

The fish rushed around and went through the most terrible motions! At last he became very quiet, and something flashed through him like lightning. The daylight shone quite clear, and there was a loud shout, "The tin soldier!" The fish had been caught, carried to market, bought, and taken into the kitchen, where the cook cut him open with a large knife. She seized the soldier round the body with two fingers, and carried him into the room, where everyone was anxious to see the remarkable man who had traveled around in the stomach of a fish. However, our tin soldier wasn't at all proud. They placed him on the table, and there—well, what strange things do happen in the world! The tin soldier was in the very room where he had been before! He saw the same children, and the same toys stood on the table; and there was the pretty castle with the graceful little dancer. She was still standing on one foot with the other in the air. She was steadfast, too. That moved the tin soldier; he was very nearly weeping tin tears, but that wouldn't have been proper. He looked at her and she looked at him, but they didn't say a word.

And now one of the little boys took the soldier and threw

him right into the stove. He didn't say why he did it at all; but no doubt the goblin in the snuffbox had a hand in it.

The tin soldier stood there in a blaze of red light. He felt a heat that was terrible; but whether this heat was from the real fire or from the flames of love he did not know. The colors had entirely worn off him; but whether this was from the journey or from sorrow, nobody could tell. He looked at the little lady; she looked at him, and he was moved. He was melting; but he still stood steadfast, shouldering his musket. Then suddenly the door flew open, and the draft of air caught the dancer, and she flew like a sylph right into the stove to the tin soldier, and flashed up in a flame, and was gone.

The tin soldier melted down into a lump, and when the servant took the ashes out next day, she found him there in the shape of a little tin heart. But of the dancer there was only the spangle left, and that was burned as black as coal.

THE SHEPHERDESS AND
THE CHIMNEY SWEEP

HAVE you ever seen a very, very old clothespress, quite black with age, on which all sorts of flowers and leaves are carved?

Just such a one stood in a certain room. It was a legacy from a grandmother, and it was carved from top to bottom with roses and tulips. The most curious flourishes were to be seen on it, and between them little stags popped out their heads with zigzag antlers. And on the top a whole man was carved out. True, he was funny to look at; for he showed his teeth—laughing one could not call it—had goat's legs, little horns on his head, and a long beard.

The children in the room always called him General-clothespress-inspector-head-superintendent Goatslegs, for this was a name difficult to pronounce, and there are very few who receive this title. And to cut him out in wood—that was no trifle. However, there he was. He looked down upon the table and toward the mirror, for there a charming little porcelain Shepherdess was standing. Her shoes were gilded, her gown was tastefully looped up with a red rose, and she had a golden hat and cloak; in short, she was most exquisite. Close by stood a little Chimney Sweep, made of porcelain too. Except for a smudge of black on his clothes he was just as clean and pretty as another. As to his being a sweep, that was only what he represented. The porcelain manufacturer could just as well have made a prince of him as a chimney sweep. One was as easy as the other.

There he stood so prettily with his ladder, and with a little round face as fair and as rosy as that of the Shepherdess. In reality this was a fault; for a little black he certainly ought to have been. He was quite close to the Shepherdess. Both stood where they had been placed. As soon as they were put there, they had promised each other eternal fidelity. For they suited each other exactly—they were young, they were of the same porcelain, and both equally fragile.

Close to them stood another figure three times as large as they were. It was an old Chinese, that could nod his head. He was of porcelain too, and said that he was the grandfather of the little Shepherdess; but this he could not prove. He asserted, moreover, that he had authority over her, and that was the reason he had nodded his Yes to the General-clothespress-in-spector-head-superintendent Goatslegs, who also paid his attentions to the Shepherdess.

"In him," said the old Chinese, "you will have a husband who, I verily believe, is of mahogany. You will be Mrs. Goatslegs, the wife of a General-clothespress-inspector-head-super-intendent, who has his shelves full of plates besides what is hidden in his secret drawers and recesses."

"I will not go into the dark cupboard," said the little Shepherdess. "I have heard that he already has eleven wives of porcelain in there."

"Then you may be the twelfth," said the Chinese. "Tonight, as soon as the old clothespress cracks, and as sure as I am a Chinese, we will have the wedding." And then he nodded his head, and fell asleep.

But the little Shepherdess wept, and looked at her beloved —at the porcelain Chimney Sweep.

"I implore you," said she, "fly away with me. It is impossible for us to remain here."

"I will do all you ask," said the little Chimney Sweep. "Let us leave this place. I think my trade will enable me to support you."

"If we were only down from this table," said she. "I shall not be happy till we are far from here, and free."

He consoled her, and showed her how to set her little foot on the carved border and on the gilded foliage which twined around the leg of the table. He brought his ladder to her assistance, and at last both were on the floor. But when they looked toward the old clothespress, they observed a great commotion. All the carved stags stretched their heads out farther, raised their antlers, and turned round their heads. The General-clothespress-inspector-head-superintendent gave a jump, and called to the old Chinese, "They are eloping! They are eloping!"

At this the Shepherdess grew a little frightened, and jumped quickly over the ridge into an open drawer.

Here lay three or four packs of cards, which were not complete, and a little puppet show, which was set up as well as it was possible to do. A play was being performed, and all the ladies, Diamonds as well as Hearts, Clubs, and Spades, sat in the front row, and fanned themselves with the tulips they held in their hands, and behind them stood the knaves. The play was about two persons who could not have each other. At this the Shepherdess wept, for it was her own history.

"I cannot bear it longer," said she. "I must get out of this drawer."

But when she had reached the floor again, and looked up at the table, she saw that the old Chinese was awake, and that his whole body was rocking.

"The old Chinese is coming!" cried the little Shepherdess; and down she fell on her porcelain knee. She was so frightened!

"A thought has struck me," said the Chimney Sweep. "Let us creep into the great Potpourri Jar that stands in the corner. There we can lie on roses and lavender, and if he comes after us, throw dust in his eyes."

" 'Tis of no use," said she. "Besides, I know that the old Chinese and the Potpourri Jar were once betrothed; and when one has once been on such terms, a little regard always lingers behind. No; for us there is nothing left but to wander forth into the wide world."

"Have you really courage to go forth with me into the wide world?" asked the Chimney Sweep tenderly. "Have you considered how large it is, and that we can never come back here again?"

"I have," said she.

And the Sweep gazed upon her, and then said, "My way lies up the chimney. Have you really courage to go with me through the stove, and then creep through all the flues? After we get into the main flue, I am not at a loss about what to do. Up we mount! So high, that they can never reach us; and at the top is an opening that leads out into the world."

And he led her toward the door of the stove.

"It looks quite black," said she; but she still went with him, on through all the intricacies of the interior, and through the flues, where a pitchy darkness reigned.

"We are now in the chimney," said she; "and behold, behold, above us is shining the loveliest star!"

It was a real star in the sky that shone straight down upon them, as if to show them the way. They climbed and they crept higher and higher. It was a long way. But he lifted her up, he held her, and showed her the best places on which to put her little porcelain feet; and thus they reached the top of the chimney. They seated themselves on the edge of it; for they were tired, which is not surprising.

The heaven and all its stars were above them, and all the roofs of the town below them. They could see far around, far away into the world. The poor Shepherdess had never pictured it to herself this way. She leaned her little head on

her Sweep, and wept so bitterly that all the gilding came off
her girdle.

"Oh, this is too much!" said she. "I cannot bear it. The
world is too large. Oh, were I but again on the little table
under the looking glass! I shall never be happy till I am there
again. I have followed you into the wide world; and now, if
you really love me, you will follow me home again."

Now the Chimney Sweep spoke sensibly to her; he spoke
about the old Chinese and the General-clothespress-inspector-
head-superintendent. But she sobbed so violently, and kissed
her little Sweep so passionately, that he was obliged to give
in, although it was not right to do so.

So down they climbed again with great difficulty, crept
through the flue, and into the stove. They listened behind the
door, to discover if anybody was in the room. It was quite
still; they peeped, and there, on the floor, in the middle of
the room, lay the old Chinese. In trying to follow the fugi-
tives he had fallen from the table, and was broken in three
pieces. His whole back was but a stump, and his head had
rolled into a corner, while General-clothespress-inspector-
head-superintendent Goatslegs was standing just where he
had always stood, absorbed in thought.

"How dreadful!" said the little Shepherdess. "My old
grandfather is dashed to pieces, and we are the cause. I never
can survive the accident." And she wrung her little hands in
agony.

"He can be mended," said the Chimney Sweep. "He can
easily be mended. Only do not be so hasty. If we glue his back
together, and rivet his neck well, he will be as good as new,
and will be able to say enough disagreeable things to us
yet."

"Do you think so?" said she; and then they clambered up
again to the table on which they had stood before.

"You see," said the Sweep, "we might have spared ourselves these disagreeables, after all."

"If we had only mended my old grandfather!" said the Shepherdess. "Does it cost much?"

And mended he was. The family had his back glued, and his neck riveted, so that he was as good as new, except that he could not nod.

"It seems to me that you have grown haughty since you were dashed to pieces," said the General-clothespress-inspector-head-superintendent Goatslegs. "However, I don't think there is so very much to be proud of. Am I to have her, or am I not?"

The Chimney Sweep and the little Shepherdess looked so touchingly at the old Chinese! They feared he would nod, but he could not. It was disagreeable to him to have to tell a stranger that he had a rivet in his neck. So the little porcelain people remained together. They blessed the old grandfather's rivet, and loved each other till they fell to pieces.

AUNTY

You should have known Aunty. She was so charming. Yes; that is to say, not at all charming in the usual sense of charming, but sweet and quaint, and funny in her own way. Just the thing, in short, to chat about, when one feels in the mood for gossiping and laughing. She was fit to be put in a play. And simply and solely because she herself lived for the theater, and all that goes on in it. She was far above any scandal; and even Commercial Agent Bigg (or Pig, as Aunty called him) could only say she was stage-struck.

"The theater is my schoolroom," said she. "My fountain of knowledge! There I have rubbed up my old Bible history. Take 'Moses,' for instance, or 'Joseph and his Brethren,' they are operas now. It is there that I have studied my General History, my Geography, and foreign Manners and Customs. From French pieces I have learned Paris life—rather naughty, but highly interesting. How I have cried over the 'Riguebourg Family'! To think that the husband must drink himself to death, and all to allow his wife to get her young sweetheart. Aye, many and many's the tear I've shed, for all those fifty years of playgoing."

Aunty knew every piece, every bit of scenery, every actor that came on, or ever had come on. She could hardly be said to live, except in the nine theatrical months. A summer without a summer spectacle was enough to age her; while a play night that lasted till morning was a prolongation of life. She did not say like other people, "We shall soon have spring: the stork is come!" or, "There is news in the paper of the early strawberries!" No; the autumn was what she announced.

"Have you seen the box office is open; they'll soon begin the performances."

She reckoned the worth of a house and its situation by its distance from the theater. It was grief to her to leave the narrow court behind the theater, and flit to the wide street a little farther off, and live there without any close neighbors.

"At home my windows were my theater box. One can't sit there in the dumps, never seeing a soul. But where I live now I seem to be clean out in the country; not a living creature in sight unless I go into the back kitchen, and clamber up on the sink. That's the only way of getting at my neighbors. Now, in that old court of mine, I could look right into the flax dealer's; and I had only three hundred steps to take to the theater. Now it takes me three thousand steps, and trooper's steps too."

Aunty might sometimes be out of sorts; but, well or ill, she never neglected the theater. Her doctor ordered her, one evening, to put her feet in poultices. She did as he told her; but rode off to the theater, and sat there with her feet in poultices. If she had died there, she would have been contented. Thorwaldsen died in the theater; and this she called "a blessed death."

She could not form any notion of heaven if there was to be no theater there. It was not exactly promised us; but just think of all the great actors and actresses who have gone before. Surely they must find some fresh scene of action.

Aunty had her own electric wire from the theater to her room; and the telegram came every Sunday to coffee. Her electric wire was "Mr. Sivertsen of the stage machinery department." It was he who gave the signals for up or down, on or off, with the curtain and the scenery.

From him she received a brief and businesslike report of the coming pieces. Shakespeare's *Tempest* he called "wretched stuff! There is so much to set up! Why, it begins with water to back-scene No. 1." That was to say, that the rolling billows stretched so far backward. On the other hand, if a play could get through five acts without a single change of sets, he pronounced it sensible and well constructed; a steady-going piece that could play itself, without any pushing or pulling.

Aunty used to like to talk about "a goodish time back," meaning some thirty and odds years, when she and Mr. Sivertsen were both younger. How he was already in the machinery department, and how he became her "benefactor." In those days it was the custom, at the great and only theater of the town, to admit spectators into the cockloft; every carpenter could dispose of one or two places. It was soon chock-full; and the company was very select. The wives of generals and aldermen had been there, it was said. It was so interesting to look down behind the scenes, and observe how the performers behaved, when the curtain was down.

Aunty had been there many times, especially to tragedies and ballets. For the pieces that required the largest *personale* were the most interesting to see from the cockloft. One sat up there in darkness pretty nearly. Most people brought their suppers with them. Once three apples, a slice of bread and butter, and a sausage roll came straight down into the prison where *Ugolino* and his sons were just about to die of hunger. This sausage roll produced a great effect. It was cheered by the public; but it made the managing committee decide to shut up the cockloft.

"But still, I have been there seven-and-thirty times," said Aunty. "And that I shall always remember of Mr. Sivertsen."

On the very last evening that the cockloft was open to the public, the *Judgment of Solomon* was played. Aunty could remember it so well. From her benefactor, Mr. Sivertsen, she had obtained a ticket for Agent Bigg. Not that he deserved one; he was always flouting and jeering at the theater, and quizzing her about it. Still, she got him a place in the cockloft. He wanted to look at the playhouse articles wrong side uppermost: "These were his very words, and just like him," said Aunty.

So he saw the *Judgment of Solomon* from above, and fell asleep. It was easy to guess that he had been dining out and had a few drinks. He slept till he was locked in, and sat the whole dark night in the theater loft. He had a story to tell of his waking up; but Aunty did not believe a bit of it. The play was over, the lamps and lights were all out, and all the people were gone, above and beneath. Then began the after-piece, the real comedy, the best of all, said the agent. The properties came to life! It was not *Solomon's Judgment* that was given now, but *Judgment Day at the Theater*. And all this Agent Bigg, in his impudence, tried to cram into Aunty. That was her thanks for getting him into the cockloft.

What the agent went on to tell might be comical enough, but there were mockery and spite at the bottom of it.

"It was dark up there," said the agent. "But then the demon-show began, the grand spectacle, *Judgment Day at the Theater*. Check takers stood at the doors, and every spectator had to show his spiritual testimonial, to settle whether he was to enter freehanded or handcuffed, and with or without a gag in his mouth. Fine gentlefolk, who came too late, when the performance had already begun, and young fellows given to losing their time were tethered outside. They were gagged and then shod with felt, so they could creep in gently before the next act. And so began *Judgment Day at the Theater*."

"Mere spite," said Aunty; "which our Lord knows nothing of."

The scene painter, if he wished to get into heaven, had to clamber up some stairs which he had painted himself, but which were too high for the longest pair of legs. That, to be sure, was only a sin against perspective. All the trees, flowers, and buildings, which the machinist had taken such pains to plant in lands quite foreign to them, the poor wretch had to transplant into their proper homes, and all before cockcrow, if he looked for any chance at heaven. Mr. Bigg had better mind his own chances of getting there!

And then to hear what he told of the performers, both in tragedy and comedy, in song and in dance—why, it was shameful of Mr. Bigg! Mr. *Pig* indeed! He never deserved his place in the cockloft. Aunty would not believe him on his oath. It was all written out, he said. And he swore (the pig!) it would be printed when he was dead and buried—not before. He had no wish to be flayed alive.

Aunty had once been in terror and anguish in her own temple of happiness, the theater. It was a winter day. One of those days when we have just two hours of foggy daylight. It was bleak and snowy; but Aunty was bound for the theater. They were to give *Herman von Unna*, besides a little opera and a great ballet, a prologue and an epilogue. It would last the night. Aunty hurried off. Her lodger had lent her a pair of winter boots, shaggy outside and inside; and they reached all the way up her legs.

She came to the theater and went into her box. The boots were warm, so she kept them on. Suddenly there arose a cry of "Fire!" Smoke came from one of the wings, smoke came from the cockloft! There was a frightful uproar. People stormed out. Aunty sat farthest from the door. "Second tier, lefthand side; the decorations look best there," she used to say. "They are always arranged to look prettiest from the King's side of the house." Now Aunty wished to get out of it, but those before her, in their blundering excitement, had slammed the door fast. There stood Aunty. There was no way out, and no way in, for the next box had too high a partition. She called; nobody heard her. She looked over at the tier underneath; it was empty. But the balustrade was low; there was not far to drop. In her fright she felt young and active. She prepared for a jump. She got one foot on the bench, the other over the balustrade; and there she sat astride, well draped in her flowered skirt, with a long leg dangling below it, displaying an enormous boot. That was a sight to see! Seen it was, and Aunty was heard at last. She was easily saved, for there was no real fire to speak of.

That was the most memorable evening in her life, she used to say. And she thanked heaven she had not seen herself, or she would have died of shame.

Her benefactor in the machinery department, Mr. Sivertsen, came to her regularly every Sunday. But it was a long time from Sunday to Sunday. Lately, therefore, in the middle of the week, a small child came up for "the leavings"; that is to say, to make a supper off the remains of Aunty's dinner.

This child was a young member of the ballet, only too happy to get a meal. She used to tread the boards as a page or a fairy. Her hardest part was that of hind legs for the lion in Mozart's *Magic Flute*. She grew up in time to be forelegs. For this she was only paid three marks, though she had been paid a rix-dollar when she was hind legs. But then she had had to creep about stooping, and panting for want of fresh air. This was very interesting to know, observed Aunty.

If everyone got his deserts, Aunty would have lasted as long as the theater. But she could not hold out so long. She didn't die there, but quietly and decently in her own bed. Her dying words were full of meaning; she asked, "What are they going to play tomorrow?"

She left behind her about five hundred rix-dollars—so at least we conclude from the yearly income, which amounts to twenty dollars. The money was left as a legacy to some one or other deserving old spinster, living alone in the world. It was to be used for taking a place on the second tier, left side, every Saturday; for on that day they gave the best pieces. Only one condition was imposed on the legatee. As she sat in the theater, every Saturday, she was to think of Aunty who lay in her grave.

This was Aunty's Religious Foundation.

THE BUTTERFLY

THE Butterfly wanted a sweetheart, and of course he would choose a pretty little darling, one of the dear little flowers. He inspected them and saw each one sitting on her stalk, quiet and modest, as a maiden should be. But there were so many to choose from that he was quite puzzled.

So the Butterfly flew down to the Daisy. The French call her *Marguerite*, for they know that she can tell fortunes. It is done in this fashion: One by one you pluck off the dainty little florets that form the petals, and each time you ask a question about your sweetheart. "Does he love me from his heart?—or does he play a part?—love me little?—love me much? —love me not at all?" This is the way it goes on. And so the Butterfly had come to ask the Daisy to tell his fortune. But he would not bite off the leaves; he would kiss every one in turn, thinking this would please the fortuneteller.

"Sweet Miss Margaret Daisy," he began, "you are the wisest woman among all the flowers! You can tell fortunes! Tell me, what shall I do? Shall I choose this one or that one? When you have told me which to woo, I will fly straight to her and begin."

But Marguerite wouldn't answer him. She did not enjoy his calling her "a woman." Its sound made her old, and she was unmarried, and still young. He put his question to her a second time, and a third time, and as he still could not get a single word out of her, he gave up, and flew away, anxious to speed his wooing.

It was early spring; hyacinths and crocuses grew in abundance. "Really very charming!" pronounced the Butterfly.

"Neat little schoolgirls! but somewhat prim." For, like most very young bachelors, he preferred older maidens. So he flew down to the anemones, but they were too shy. The violets were a little too dreamy, the tulips much too dashing, the lime blossoms too small and were too close and exclusive in their family life. The apple blossoms were, he must admit, like roses to look at, but then they opened one day, and, if the wind blew, fell to pieces the next. Surely a union with one of them would be too brief. The Sweet Pea pleased him the most. She was red and white, dainty and piquant. She belonged to that class of comely domestic girls who are good-looking and yet useful in the kitchen. He was on the point of paying his addresses to her, when he noticed a pea pod hanging close by, with a withered flower clinging to it. "Who is that?" he asked.

"My sister," replied the Sweet Pea.

"Goodness! Think of you ever coming to look like that!" The Butterfly was horrified, and flew away, warned just in time.

Honeysuckles clung to the hedge. He looked full at these young ladies, with their long faces and yellow complexions. No, he did not like that kind of article at all. But what did he like?

Spring passed away, summer passed away, and autumn came, and he was no nearer to making up his mind. Flowers now wore handsome and gorgeous dresses, but where was the good? Fresh, fragrant youth was past, and fragrance becomes so precious to the heart as one grows older. And no one can say that dahlias and hollyhocks have any particular perfume. So the Butterfly sought out the Balm Mint.

"It is not exactly a flower—it is rather all flower! It is fragrant from the root upward, with sweet scent in every leaf. Yes, I will take her!"

So, at last, he began his love-making.

But the Balm Mint stood stiff and silent, and at last replied, "Friendship, if you will, but nothing more! I am old, and you are old. We may very well live for each other, but marriage— no! Let us not make fools of ourselves in our old age."

So the Butterfly got no sweetheart at all. He had looked about him too long, which is a mistake. He became an old bachelor.

It was late autumn, windy and wet. Cold blew the blast down the backs of the poor shaky old willow trees. In such weather it is not pleasant to fly about in summer clothing, out of doors, getting one's self chilled through and through. But the Butterfly was spared that discomfort. He happened to fly into a room where there was a fire in the stove and the atmosphere was warm as summer. Here, he could exist; "but mere existence is not enough," he sighed. "To live, one must have sunshine, freedom, and a little flower!"

He flew to the windowpane, to take a last look at the flowers; and there he was noticed, admired, captured, and set upon a needle to be stored in a museum of curiosities. More than this could not be done for him.

"Well, now I sit upon a stalk, like the flowers," quoth the Butterfly. "It is not exactly pleasant; it is very like being married, one is kept so tight!" and he comforted himself with this reflection.

"A miserable consolation, truly!" said the flowers that lived in the pots in the room.

"But one cannot quite trust the word of potted flowers," thought the Butterfly. "They have too much to do with men."

PEN AND INKSTAND

THE following remark was made in a poet's room, as the speaker looked at the inkstand that stood upon his table:

"It is marvelous, all that comes out of that inkstand! What will it produce next? Yes, it is marvelous!"

"So it is!" exclaimed the inkstand. "It is incomprehensible! That is what I always say." And so it was that the inkstand addressed itself to the pen, and to everything else on the table that could hear it.

"It is really astonishing all that can come from me! It is almost incredible! I positively do not know myself what the next thing may be, when a person begins to dip into me. One drop of me serves for half a side of paper; and who knows what may appear upon it? I am certainly something extraordinary. From me proceed all the works of the poets. These animated beings, whom people think they recognize—these deep feelings, that gay humor, these charming descriptions of nature—I do not understand them myself, for I know nothing about nature; but still it is all in me. From me have gone forth, and still go forth, these warrior hosts, these lovely maidens, these bold knights on snorting steeds, those droll characters in humbler life. The fact is, however, that I do not know anything about them myself. I assure you they are not my ideas."

"You are right there," replied the pen. "You have few ideas, and do not trouble yourself much with thinking. If you *did* exert yourself to think, you would see that all you have to give is something that is not dry. You supply me with the means of committing to paper what I have in me. I write with that. It is the pen that writes. Mankind does not doubt that; and most men have about as much genius for poetry as an old inkstand."

"You have very little experience," said the inkstand. "You have scarcely been in use a week, and you are already half worn out. Do you fancy that you are a poet? You are only a servant. I have had many of your kind before you came—many of the goose family, and of English manufacture. I know both quill pens and steel pens. I have had a great many in my service. And I shall have many more still, when he, the man who stirs me up, comes and puts down what he takes from me. I should very much like to know what the next thing will be."

"Ink tub!" said the pen.

Late in the evening the poet returned home. He had been at a concert, had heard a celebrated violin player, and was quite enchanted with his wonderful performance. It had been a complete gush of melody that the artist had drawn from the instrument. Sometimes it seemed like the gentle murmur of a rippling stream, sometimes like the singing of birds, sometimes like the tempest sweeping through the mighty pine forests. He fancied he heard his own heart weep, but in the sweet tones that can only be heard in a woman's charming voice. It seemed as if not only the strings of the violin made music, but its bridge, its pegs, and its sounding board. It was astonishing! The piece had been a most difficult one; but it seemed like play—as if the bow were but wandering capriciously over the strings. It seemed so easy that anyone might have supposed he could do it. The violin seemed to sound by itself, the bow to play by itself. These two seemed to do it all. One forgot the master who guided them, who gave them life and soul. Yes, and they forgot the master; but the poet thought of him. He named him, and wrote down his thoughts as follows:

"How foolish it would be of the violin and the bow, were

they to be vain about their performance! And yet this is what
we of the human species so often do. Poets, artists, and those
who make discoveries in science, and the military—we are all
proud of ourselves; and yet we are all only instruments in
our Lord's hands. To Him alone be the glory! We have
nothing to claim for ourselves."

This was what the poet wrote; and he headed it with, "The
Master and the Instruments."

"Well, madam," said the pen to the inkstand when they
were again alone, "you heard him read aloud what I had
written."

"Yes, what I gave you to write," corrected the inkstand. "It
was a snipe at you for your conceit. Strange that you cannot
see that people make a fool of you! I gave you that dig pretty
cleverly. Though, I confess, it was rather malicious."

"Ink holder!" cried the pen.

"Writing stick!" cried the inkstand.

They both felt assured that they had answered well. For
it is a pleasant reflection when one has made a smart reply—
one sleeps comfortably afterward. And, they both went to
sleep.

But the poet could not sleep. His thoughts welled forth
like the tones from the violin, trilling like pearls, rushing like
a storm through the forest. He recognized the feelings of his
own heart—he saw the gleam from the everlasting Master.

To Him alone be the glory!

THE SNOW QUEEN

IN SEVEN STORIES

FIRST STORY

Which Treats of the Mirror and the Pieces of It

WELL, now we're going to begin. And when we are at the end of the story we shall know more than we do now, for he was a bad troll. He was one of the very worst. He was the devil himself. One day he was in very good humor, for he had made a mirror which had this peculiarity: everything good and beautiful which was mirrored in it shrank into almost nothing, but whatever was worthless and ugly became very distinct and looked worse than ever. The most lovely landscapes when seen in this mirror looked like boiled spinach, and the nicest people were hideous, or stood on their heads and had no stomachs; their faces were so twisted you wouldn't know them, and anybody who had a freckle could be sure it would cover both his nose and mouth. This was very amusing, the devil said. When a good, pious thought passed through the person's mind, a sneer came in the mirror. And the devil chuckled at his artistic invention.

Those who went to the troll school—for he kept a troll school—declared everywhere that a miracle had happened. For now, they said, one could see, for the first time, how the world and the people in it really looked. They ran about with the mirror, and at last there was not a single country or person that hadn't been twisted in it.

Now they wanted to fly up to heaven, to sneer and scoff at
the angels and our Lord himself. The higher they flew with
the mirror, the more it grinned. They could scarcely hold on
to it. They flew higher and higher, and the mirror trembled
so terribly with its grinning that it fell down out of their hands
to the earth, where it was shattered into a hundred million
billion and more pieces.

And now this mirror made much more unhappiness than
before; for some of the pieces were hardly as large as a grain
of sand, and they flew around in the wide world, and whenever they flew into anyone's eye they stuck there. Those
people saw everything wrongly, or only had eyes for the bad
side of a thing, for every little piece of the mirror had kept
the same power which the whole glass had had. A few persons
even got a piece of the mirror into their hearts, and this was
really awful; for that heart got to be like a lump of ice. Some
of the pieces were so large that they were used as windowpanes, but it was a bad thing to look at one's friends through

these panes. Other pieces were made into spectacles, and then things certainly went wrong when people put those spectacles on and wanted to see very clearly and be very just. The Evil One laughed then till his stomach cracked, it tickled him so nicely.

Out in the world some little pieces of glass were still flying around in the air. And we'll hear about that now!

SECOND STORY

A Little Boy and a Little Girl

IN the big city, where there are so many houses and so many people that there isn't room enough for everyone to have a little garden, and where therefore most people have to be satisfied with some flowers in flowerpots, there were two poor children who had a real little garden but not much bigger than a flowerpot. They were not brother and sister, but they loved each other just as much as if they had been. Their parents lived right close to each other in two garrets, and there where the roof of the one house joined that of the other, and where the gutter ran along the eaves, were two little windows. And one had only to step across the gutter to get from one window to the other.

Each family had a big window box outside, and in them they grew herbs for the kitchen, and a little rosebush. There was a rosebush in each box, and they both grew beautifully. Now, the parents thought of placing the boxes across the gutter, so that they would reach from one window to another, and look like two banks of flowers. The pea vines hung down over the boxes, and the rosebushes grew their long branches, and clustered around the windows and bent down toward each other. It was almost like an honor gate of flowers and leaves.

The boxes were very high, and the children knew they mustn't climb up on them. But they were often allowed to come out between the boxes, and sit on their little benches under the roses, and there they had a wonderful time playing.

In the winter that fun stopped. Sometimes the windows were frozen all over, and then they warmed copper pennies on the stove, and held the hot coins against the frozen pane; and this made a lovely peephole, so round, so round! Behind it peeped a pretty, mild eye, one from each window. And it was the little boy and the little girl. His name was Kay, and her name was Gerda.

In the summer they could get over to each other with one jump, but in the winter they had to go down the many stairs and up the many stairs, while the snow was drifting, drifting outside.

"Those are the white bees swarming," said the old grandmother.

"Do they have a queen bee, too?" asked the little boy, for he knew that the real bees have one.

"Yes, they have one," said the grandmother. "She always flies where they swarm thickest. She is the largest of them all, and she never stays quietly on the earth; she flies back again to the black sky. Many a winter night she flies through the streets of the town, and looks in at the windows. And then the windows freeze in such a strange way, and they begin to look like flowers."

"Yes, I've seen that!" said both the children. Now they knew that it was true.

"Can the Snow Queen come in here?" asked the little girl.

"Just let her try," said the boy. "I'll put her on the warm stove, and then she'll melt."

But the grandmother smoothed his hair, and told some other stories.

In the evening, when little Kay was at home and half undressed, he climbed up on the chair by the window, and peeped through the little penny hole. A few flakes of snow were falling outside, and one of them, the largest of all, stayed on the edge of one of the flower boxes. The snowflakes grew larger and larger, and at last the largest turned into a whole woman clothed in the finest white gauze, made out of millions of starlike snowflakes. She was beautiful and delicate, but of ice—of dazzling, glittering ice. Still she was alive; her eyes looked like two clear stars, but there was no peace or rest in them. She nodded toward the window, and beckoned with her hand. The little boy was frightened and jumped down from the chair; and it seemed as if a large bird flew by outside, past the window.

Next day there was a clear frost, then there was a thaw, and then the spring came. The sun shone, the green peeped out, the swallows built nests, the windows were opened, and the little children sat again in their garden high up in the gutter, above all the floors.

The roses had never bloomed so wonderfully as that summer. The little girl had learned a hymn, and there was something in it about roses. And, in speaking of roses, she thought of her own, so she sang it to the little boy, and he sang, too:

> *Our roses bloom and fade away,*
> *Our Infant Lord abides alway!*
> *May we be blessed His face to see,*
> *And ever little children be!*

They held each other by the hand, kissed the roses, looked at God's bright sunshine, and spoke to it, as if the Christ-child were there. What beautiful summer days those were, and how lovely it was to be outside, among the fresh rosebushes, which seemed as if they would never stop blooming.

One day Kay and Gerda were sitting and looking at the picture book with animals and birds, when the clock was just striking five on the church tower. "Ouch! there is a sting in my heart!" Kay cried. "And now I have something in my eye!"

The little girl put her arm around his neck; he blinked his eyes. No, there was nothing at all to be seen.

"I think it is gone," he said. But it was not gone. It was one of those grains of glass which sprang from the mirror—the troll mirror that I told you about, the nasty glass that makes everything great and good seem small and mean, but in which the mean and the wicked things are brought out in relief, and every fault is noticeable at once.

Poor little Kay also had a splinter right in his heart, and it would soon make his heart like a lump of ice. It didn't hurt him now; but it was there.

"What are you crying for?" he asked Gerda. "You look ugly like that. There's nothing the matter with me. Oh, look!" he suddenly shouted, "that rose is worm-eaten, and this one is all crooked. They're disgusting roses. Just like the box they stand in."

And then he kicked the box hard with his foot, and tore both the roses off.

"Kay, what are you doing?" cried the little girl.

And when he saw she was scared, he tore off another rose, and then ran in at his own window, away from darling little Gerda.

Later when she came with her picture book, he said it was only fit for babies. When the grandmother told stories he always butted in; and when he could manage it, he would get behind her, put on a pair of spectacles, and mimic her. He was very good, and the people had to laugh at him. Soon he could imitate the way everybody in the street talked and walked. Everything that was peculiar or ugly about them Kay could imitate. And the people said, "That boy must certainly have a remarkable head." But it was really that glass he had in his eye, and the glass that stuck in his heart, that made him such a tease. He even teased little Gerda, who loved him with all her heart.

Now his games were quite different from what they were before. They were very sensible. One winter day when it snowed he came out with a big magnifying glass, held up a corner of his blue coat, and let the snowflakes fall on it.

"Now, look at the glass, Gerda," he said.

And every flake of snow was much larger, and looked like a splendid flower, or a star with ten points. It was beautiful to look at.

"See how clever that is," said Kay. "That's much more interesting than real flowers. There is not a single fault in them—they're quite regular until they begin to melt."

Soon after Kay came over wearing thick gloves, with his sled on his back. He shouted right into Gerda's ear, "They said I could go to the big square, where the other boys play," and away he went.

Over on the square the boldest boys often tied their sleds to the country people's carts, and rode with them a good way. It was fine! When they were in the midst of their playing a big sleigh arrived. It was painted all white, and in it sat somebody wrapped in woolly white fur, with a woolly white cap. The sleigh drove twice around the square. Kay quickly tied his little sled to it, and drove on with it. It went faster and faster, straight into the next street. The one who was driving turned around and nodded in a friendly way to Kay; it was as if they knew each other. Each time Kay tried to untie his little sled, the stranger nodded again, and Kay stayed where he was, and they drove right out through the town gate. The snow began to fall so fast that the boy couldn't see his own hand as he rushed along. He quickly dropped the rope to get loose from the big sleigh, but that didn't help. His little sled was tied tight to the other, and they went like the wind. Then he shouted very loudly, but nobody heard him; and the snow whirled and the sleigh flew along. Every now and then it gave a jump, and they seemed to be flying over hedges and ditches. He was very frightened. He wanted to say his prayers, but he could only remember the multiplication table.

The snowflakes got larger and larger. At last they looked like big white hens. All at once they jumped aside, the big sleigh stopped, and the person who had driven it rose up. The fur and the cap were all made of snow. It was a lady, tall and straight and dazzling white; it was the Snow Queen.

"We came a good, long way," she said. "But what are you cold for? Crawl into my bearskin."

And she seated him beside her in her own sleigh, and wrapped the fur around him. He felt as if he were sinking into a snowdrift.

"Are you still cold?" she asked, and then she kissed him on the forehead.

Oh, it was colder than ice! It went right to his heart, and half of that was already a lump of ice. He felt as if he were going to die; but only for a moment, then something helped him and he didn't notice the cold.

"My sled! Don't forget my sled!" That was the first thing he thought of. It was tied to one of the white hens, and the hen flew behind him with the sled on its back. The Snow Queen kissed Kay again, and then he forgot little Gerda, his grandmother, and everyone at home.

"Now you won't get any more kisses," said she, "for if you did I should kiss you to death."

Kay looked at her. She was so beautiful, he couldn't imagine a wiser or more lovely face. She didn't seem to be made of ice as she had when she sat at the window and beckoned to him. In his eyes she was perfect; he didn't feel scared at all. He told her that he could do mental arithmetic even with fractions, that he knew how many square miles in a country and how many inhabitants. And she always smiled, and then it seemed to him that what he knew was not enough. And he looked up into the big, big dome of the air and she flew with him, flew high up on the black clouds, and the storm was whistling and roaring; it was like the singing of ancient ballads. They flew over forests and lakes, over land and sea. Below them the cold wind went whistling, the wolves howled, the snow sparkled; over it flew the black, screaming crows; but above the moon was shining, large and clear, and Kay looked at it in the long, long winter night; and in the daytime he slept at the feet of the Snow Queen.

THIRD STORY

The Flower Garden of the Woman Who Could Conjure

BUT how did little Gerda get along when Kay didn't come any more? Where could he be? No one knew, no one could tell her. The boys could tell only that they had seen him tie his little sleigh to a fine large sleigh, which had driven along the street and out at the town gate. Nobody knew what had become of him. Many tears flowed, and little Gerda wept long and bitterly. Then they said he was dead—he had been drowned in the river that ran close by their town. Oh, those were very long dark winter days! But now spring came, with warmer sunshine.

"Kay is dead and gone," said little Gerda.

"I don't believe it," said the Sunshine.

"He is dead and gone," she said to the Swallows.

"We don't believe it," they answered; and at last little Gerda did not believe it herself.

"I will put on my new red shoes," she said one morning, "the ones that Kay never has seen; and then I will go down and ask the river about him."

It was still very early. She kissed the old grandmother, who was still sound asleep, put on her new red shoes, and went all alone out of the town gate toward the river.

"Is it true that you have taken my little playmate? I will give you my red shoes if you will give him back to me!" she said.

And it seemed to her as if the waves nodded quite strangely; and so she took her red shoes, that she liked best of anything she had, and threw them into the river. They fell close to the shore, and the little wavelets carried them back to her. It seemed as if the river would not take from her the dearest things she owned, since, of course, it hadn't really taken little Kay. But Gerda thought she hadn't thrown the shoes out far enough; so she climbed into the far end of a boat that lay among the reeds, and threw the shoes out; but the boat was not bound fast, and, at the movement she made, it glided away from the shore. She noticed this, and hurried to get back, but before she could reach the other end the boat was a yard from the bank, and now it drifted faster away.

Little Gerda was very much frightened, and began to cry; but no one heard her except the Sparrows, and they couldn't carry her ashore. They flew along the edge and sang, as if to cheer her up, "Here are we! Here are we!" The boat drifted along with the current, and little Gerda sat quite still, with only her stockings on her feet. Her little red shoes floated along behind her, but they couldn't catch up with the boat, which went much faster.

It was very pretty on both shores—lovely flowers, old trees, and slopes with sheep and cows; but not a human being in sight.

"Perhaps the river will carry me to little Kay," thought Gerda, and then she became more cheerful, and stood up, and for many hours she watched the beautiful green banks. She came to a big cherry orchard, in which stood a little house with queer red and blue windows. It had a thatched roof, and outside stood two wooden soldiers, who presented arms to those who sailed past.

Gerda called to them, for she thought they were alive, but of course they didn't answer. She came quite close to them, and the river carried the boat toward the shore.

Gerda called still louder, and out of the house came an old, old woman leaning on a hooked stick. She had on a large sunbonnet, painted over with the loveliest flowers.

"You poor little child!" said the old woman, "how did you ever come out on the big fast river and float so far out into the wide world?"

And then the old woman stepped right into the water, hooked the boat with her stick, drew it to land, and lifted little Gerda out. And Gerda was glad to be on dry land again, though she felt a little afraid of the strange old woman.

"Come and tell me who you are, and how you came here," she said. And Gerda told her everything. And the old woman shook her head, and said, "Hem! hem!" And when Gerda had told everything, and asked if she had not seen little Kay, the woman said that he had not yet come by, but that he probably would very soon. Gerda mustn't be sad, but must taste her cherries and look at her flowers; they were prettier than any picture book, for each one of them could tell a story. She took Gerda by the hand and they went into the little house, and the old woman locked the door.

The windows were up very high, and the panes were red, blue, and yellow. The daylight shone through strangely there and in all colors. On the table stood the finest cherries, and Gerda ate as many of them as she liked, for she wasn't afraid of that. While she was eating them, the old lady combed her hair with a golden comb. Her hair curled and shone so nice and yellow around her friendly little face that was so round and looked like a rose.

"I've been wanting a sweet little girl like you for a long

time," said the old woman. "Now you shall see how well we two are going to get along."

And while she was combing her hair, Gerda forgot about her adopted brother Kay more and more. For this old woman knew something about witchcraft. She wasn't a wicked witch, she only witched a little for her own amusement, and now she wanted to keep little Gerda. Therefore she went into the garden, stretched out her stick toward all the rosebushes, and no matter how beautifully they were blooming they all sank into the earth, and no one could tell where they had been. The old woman was afraid that if the little girl saw roses, she would think of her own rosebush, and remember little Kay, and run away.

Now she took Gerda out into the flower garden. What a fragrance and what loveliness! Every conceivable flower was there in full bloom. There were some for every season. No picture book could be gayer or prettier! Gerda jumped high for joy, and played till the sun went down behind the high cherry trees; then she was put into a lovely bed with red silk pillows stuffed with blue violets. And she slept there, and dreamed as wonderfully as any queen on her wedding day.

The next day she played again with the flowers in the warm sunshine. And in this way many days went by. Gerda knew every flower; but, as many as there were, it still seemed to her that one was missing. But which one she did not know. Then one day she happened to be sitting and looking at the old woman's sunbonnet with the painted flowers. The prettiest one there was a rose. The old woman had forgotten to get that one off her hat when she put the others down in the earth. But that's how it is when you don't stop to think!

"What, aren't there any roses here?" said Gerda.

And she jumped in among the flower beds, and searched and searched, but there was not one to be found. Then she sat down and cried. Her hot tears fell just on the spot where a rosebush lay buried, and when the warm tears moistened the earth the bush at once grew up as blooming as when it had sunk. And Gerda hugged it, and kissed the roses, and thought of the beautiful roses at home, and with them she thought of little Kay.

"Oh, I've been made to be so late!" said the little girl. "I was looking for Kay! Don't you know where he is?" she asked the Roses. "Do you think that he is dead and gone?"

"He is not dead," the Roses answered. "We have been in the ground. All the dead people are there, but Kay is not there."

"Thank you," said little Gerda; and she went over to the other flowers, looked into their cups, and asked, "Don't you know where little Kay is?"

But every flower stood in the sun thinking only of its own story or fairy tale. Gerda heard many, many of them; but not one knew anything of Kay.

And what did the Tiger Lily say?

"Do you hear the drum 'Tom-tom'? There are only two notes, always 'tom-tom!' Hear the mourning song of the women, hear the call of the priests. The Hindoo widow stands in her long red mantle on the funeral pile; the flames rise up around her and her dead husband; but the Hindoo woman is thinking of the living one here in the circle, of him whose eyes burn hotter than flames, whose fiery glances reach her heart more than the flames, which are soon to burn her body to ashes. Can the flame of the heart die in the flame of the funeral pile?"

"I don't understand that at all!" said little Gerda.

"That's my story," said the Lily.

What does the Convolvulus say?

"Above the narrow rock road towers an old baronial castle, the ivy grows thickly over the old red walls, leaf by leaf around the balcony, and there stands a beautiful girl; she bends over the balustrade and looks down at the road. No rose is fresher on its stem than she; no apple blossom borne by the wind from its tree floats more lightly along. How her costly silks rustle! 'Is he never coming?' "

"Do you mean Kay?" asked little Gerda.

"I'm only speaking of my own story—my dream," replied the Convolvulus.

What does the little Snowdrop say?

"Between the trees ropes hold a long board; that is a swing. Two pretty little girls, in dresses white as snow, and long, green silk ribbons flying from their hats, are sitting on it, swinging. Their brother, who is bigger than they, stands in the swing, and he has put his arm around the rope to hold himself, for in one hand he has a little saucer, and in the other a clay pipe; he is blowing bubbles. The swing flies, and the bubbles rise with beautiful changing colors; the last still hangs from the pipe bowl, swaying in the wind. The swing flies on: the little black dog, light as the bubbles, stands up on his hind legs and wants to be taken into the swing; it flies on, and the dog falls, barks, and is angry; they fooled it, and the bubble bursts. A swinging board and a bursting foam picture—that is my song."

"It may be very pretty, what you're telling, but you're so sad about it, and you don't mention little Kay at all."

What do the Hyacinths say?

"There were three beautiful sisters, so clear and delicate. The dress of one was red, that of the second blue, and that of the third all white; hand in hand they danced by the calm lake in the bright moonlight. They were not elves; they were daughters of men. The scents were so sweet and the girls were lost in the forest; the scents grew stronger, three coffins, with the three beautiful maidens lying in them, glided from the wood thicket across the lake; the glowworms flew gleaming about them like little hovering lights. Are the dancing girls sleeping, or are they dead? The flower scent says they are corpses and the evening bell tolls over the dead."

"You make me very sad," said little Gerda. "Your scent is so strong, I can't help thinking of the dead girls. Ah! is little

Kay really dead? The Roses have been down in the earth, and they say no."

"Ding! Dong!" rang the Hyacinth bells. "We are not tolling for little Kay—we don't know him; we only sing our song, the only one we know."

And Gerda went to the Buttercup, that was shining among its glistening green leaves.

"You are a little bright sun," said Gerda. "Tell me, if you know, where I can find my play brother."

And the Buttercup shone so gaily, and looked back at Gerda. What song might the Buttercup sing? It wasn't about Kay either.

"In a little yard the clear sun shone warm on the first day of spring. The sunbeams glided down the white wall of the neighboring house; close by grew the first yellow flowers, glittering gold in the warm sun's rays. The old grandmother sat out of doors in her chair; her granddaughter, the poor, pretty servant, was coming home for a short visit; she kissed her grandmother. There was gold, heart's gold, in that blessed kiss, gold in the mouth, gold in the eyes, gold up there in the bright sunrise. Well, that's my little story," said the Buttercup.

"My poor old grandmother!" sighed Gerda. "She must be lonesome for me and sad about me, just as she was about little Kay. But I shall soon go home and bring Kay with me. There is no use in my asking the flowers, they only know their own song; they can't tell me anything." And then she pinned her little dress so that she could run faster; but the Jonquil struck against her leg as she sprang over it. She stopped to look at the tall yellow flower, and asked, "Perhaps you know something?"

She bent down close to the flower, and what did it say?

"I can see myself! I can see myself!" said the Jonquil. "Oh! oh! what a smell I have! Up in the little room in the gable stands a little half-dressed dancing girl; she stands sometimes on one leg, sometimes on two; she kicks at the whole world; she's nothing but a snare for the eyes; she pours water out of a teapot on a bit of stuff—it is her bodice. Cleanliness is a good thing! Her white frock hangs on a hook; it has been washed in the teapot too, and dried on the roof; she puts it on and ties her saffron handkerchief around her neck, and the dress looks all the whiter. Kick high! Look how she struts on one stem! I can see myself! I can see myself!"

"I don't care at all about that," said Gerda. "That's nothing to tell me!"

She ran to the end of the garden. The door was locked, but she pulled at the rusty catch until it came loose and the door sprang open. And little Gerda ran in her bare feet out into the wide world. She looked back three times, but no one came after her. At last she could run no longer, and she sat down on a big stone, and when she looked around the summer was over—it was late in autumn. Nobody would ever know that back in the beautiful garden, where there was always sunshine, and the flowers of every season always bloomed together.

"Oh, dear, how late I am!" said little Gerda. "It's already autumn. I mustn't rest again!"

And she got up to go on. How sore and tired her little feet were! All around it looked cold and bleak. The long willow leaves were quite yellow, and the mist dropped from them like water; one leaf after another dropped off. Only the sloe thorn still bore fruit, but it was so sour it puckered the mouth all up. Oh! the wide world was a gray and gloomy place.

FOURTH STORY

The Prince and Princess

GERDA had to stop and rest again, and a big Crow came hopping across the snow, just opposite the spot where she was sitting. This Crow sat and looked at her for a long time, then

he wagged his head and said, "Caw, caw, how do, how do!"
He couldn't say it any better, but he felt very friendly toward
the little girl, and wanted to know where she was going all
alone. The word "alone" Gerda understood. She felt the sadness of what it meant; and she told the Crow the whole story
of her life, and asked if he had seen Kay.

The Crow nodded very thoughtfully and said:

"It might be! It might be!"

"What, do you think so?" cried the little girl. She nearly
squeezed the Crow to death, she kissed him so.

"Gently, gently!" said the Crow. "I think I know; I think
it might be little Kay, but he has probably forgotten you, with
the Princess."

"Does he live with a Princess?" asked Gerda.

"Yes, listen," said the Crow. "But it's so hard for me to
speak your language. Do you know Ravenish? I can talk it
much better."

"No, I never learned it," said Gerda; "but my grandmother
understood it, and could speak the Pye-language too. I only
wish I had learned it."

"That doesn't matter," said the Crow. "I shall tell you as
well as I can, and that won't be very well."

And then the Crow told what he knew.

"In the kingdom where we're sitting now, lives a Princess
who is marvelously clever. She has read all the newspapers in
the world, and has forgotten them again, she is so clever. The
other day she was sitting on the throne—and they say that isn't
so much fun, either—and she happened to hum a song, and it
was this, 'Why shouldn't I get married?' 'Well, there's something in that,' she said, and so she decided to marry. But she
wanted a husband who could answer sensibly when he was
spoken to, not one who only stood and looked haughty, for
that can be so tiresome. And so she had all her maids of honor
drummed together, and when they heard what she wanted

they were very glad. 'I like that,' they said. 'That's what I was thinking myself only the other day.'

"You may be sure that every word I am telling you is true," said the Crow. "I have a tame sweetheart who goes around freely in the castle, and she told me everything."

Of course the sweetheart was a crow, for birds of a feather flock together and one crow always finds another crow.

"The newspapers were published at once, with a border of hearts and the Princess's initials. One could read in them that every young man who was good-looking might come to the castle and speak with the Princess, and he who spoke best and as if he belonged there, would be chosen by the Princess for her husband. Yes, indeed," the Crow said, "you can believe me. It's as true as I sit here. People came flocking in. There was a pushing and running to and fro, but nobody had any luck the first and second days. They could all talk well enough when they were out in the street, but when they entered at the palace gates, and saw the guards in silver and went up the staircase and saw the lackeys in gold, and the big lighted halls, they were staggered. And when they stood before the throne, on which the Princess sat, they could say nothing except the last word she had said, and she certainly didn't want to hear that again. It was as if the people there had swallowed snuff and fallen into a trance, for when they got on the street again, they could talk fast enough. There was a whole row of them, from the town gate to the palace gate. I went in myself to see it," said the Crow. "They got hungry and thirsty waiting so long, but in the palace they didn't get as much as a glass of lukewarm water. A few of the wisest had brought bread and butter with them, but they wouldn't share it with their neighbor, for they thought 'Let him look hungry, and then Princess won't have him.' "

"But Kay, little Kay?" asked Gerda. "When did he come? Was he among the crowd?"

"Wait, wait! We're just coming to him. On the third day a small person, without horse or carriage, came marching cheerfully right up to the castle. His eyes sparkled like yours, and he had fine long hair, but his clothes were shabby."

"That was Kay!" cried Gerda rejoicingly. "Oh, then I have found him!" And she clapped her hands.

"He had a little knapsack on his back," said the Crow.

"No, that must have been his sled," said Gerda, "for he went away with a sled."

"That may well be," said the Crow, "for I did not look very closely. But this much I do know from my tame sweetheart, that when he came in the palace gate and saw the Life Guards in silver, and went up the staircase and saw the lackeys in gold, he wasn't the least little bit put out. He nodded, and said to them, 'It must be tedious to stand on the stairs—I'd rather go inside.' Inside, the rooms were bright with candles. Privy councilors and Excellencies went barefooted and carried gold dishes; anybody might have been impressed! His boots creaked perfectly terribly, and still he wasn't scared."

"I'm sure it's Kay," said Gerda, "I know he had new boots on; I've heard them creak in Grandmother's room."

"Yes, they certainly creaked," said the Crow. "And he went boldly in to the Princess herself, who sat on a pearl that was as big as a spinning wheel; and all the court ladies with their maids and their maids' maids, and all the cavaliers with their valets and all the valets' valets, and the valets' valets' boys were standing around. And the nearer they stood to the door, the prouder they looked. You can hardly look at the slippered valets' valet's boy, he stands so haughtily in the doorway!"

"It must be awful!" said little Gerda. "And Kay got the Princess anyway?"

"If I hadn't been a crow, I would have married her myself, although I'm engaged. They say he spoke as well as I can when I speak Ravenish. I heard that from my tame sweetheart.

He was cheerful and agreeable; he had not come to woo, but only to hear the wisdom of the Princess; and he liked it, and then she liked him."

"Yes, that was certainly Kay!" said Gerda. "He was so clever, he could do mental arithmetic up to fractions. Oh! won't you lead me to the castle too?"

"That's easily said," said the Crow. "But how are we to manage it? I'll talk it over with my tame sweetheart; she can probably advise us; because I must tell you that a little girl like you will never be let in in the regular way."

"Oh, yes, I will!" said Gerda. "When Kay hears that I'm there he'll come out right away, and bring me in."

"Wait for me at the stile over there," said the Crow; and he wagged his head and flew away.

It was late in the evening when the Crow came back.

"Caw, caw!" he said. "She wants to be remembered to you many times! And here's a little loaf for you. She took it from the kitchen. There's plenty of bread there, and you must be hungry. You can't possibly get into the palace, your feet are bare, you know, and the guards in silver and the lackeys in gold would not allow it. But don't cry; you'll get there anyway. My sweetheart knows a little back staircase that leads up to the bedroom, and she knows where she can get the key."

And they went into the garden, into the great avenue, where the leaves were falling one after the other; and where they could see lights go out one at a time in the palace. Then the Crow led Gerda to a back door, which stood ajar.

Oh, how Gerda's heart beat with fear and longing! It was just as if she had been going to do something wicked. And yet she only wanted to know if it was little Kay.

Yes, it must be he, she thought. His thoughtful eyes and his long hair were so clear in her memory, she could almost see him smile as he had smiled at home when they sat among the roses. He would certainly be glad to see her; to hear what a long distance she had come for his sake; to know how sorry they had all been at home when he did not come back. Oh, what fear and joy she felt!

Now they were on the staircase. A little lamp was burning on a cupboard, and in the middle of the floor stood the tame sweetheart, turning her black head in every direction and looking at Gerda, who curtsied to her as her grandmother had taught her to do.

"My betrothed has spoken to me very favorably of you, my little lady," said the tame Crow. "Your *Vita*, as they call it, is very moving. Will you take the lamp? then I will precede you. We will go straight up; in that way we shan't meet anybody."

"I feel as if someone were coming after us," said Gerda, and something rushed by her; it seemed like shadows on the wall; horses with flying manes and thin legs, hunters, and ladies and gentlemen on horseback.

"These are only dreams," said the Crow. "They are coming to take the thoughts of our noble masters out hunting. That's all the better, because then you can look at them more closely in their beds. But I hope that when you come to honor and dignity, you will have a grateful heart."

"I wouldn't talk about that," said the wild Crow from the wood.

Now they came into the first large room: it was hung with rose-colored satin, and artificial flowers were worked on the walls. And here the dreams already came flitting by them, but they moved so quickly that Gerda could not see the high-born lords and ladies. Each room was more splendid than the last; one might well be taken aback! Now they were in the bedroom. Here the ceiling was like a large palm tree with leaves of glass, of costly glass, and in the middle of the floor two beds hung on a thick stalk of gold, and each of them looked like a lily. One of them was white, and in that lay the Princess; the other was red, and in that Gerda was going to look for little Kay. She bent one of the red leaves aside, and then she saw a brown neck. Oh, it was Kay! She called out his name, and held the lamp toward him. The dreams rushed into the room again on horseback—he woke up, turned his head, and—it was not little Kay!

Only the Prince's neck was like his; but he was young and good-looking. The Princess peered out from the white lily, and asked who was there. Then little Gerda wept, and told her whole story, and all that the Crows had done for her.

"You poor child!" said the Prince and Princess.

They praised the Crows, and though they were not angry with them this time, they told the Crows they were not to do it again. This time, they would be rewarded.

"Do you want to be free?" asked the Princess, "or will you have fixed appointments as court crows, with all the kitchen leftovers?"

And the two Crows bowed, and begged for fixed appointments, for they thought of their old age, and said, "It is a good thing to have something for the old man," for that was what they called him.

And the Prince got up and gave his bed to Gerda. He couldn't do more than that. She folded her little hands, and thought, "How good men and animals are!" and then she shut her eyes and went quietly to sleep. All the dreams came flying in again, looking like angels, and they drew a little sled, on which Kay sat nodding; but all this was only a dream, and was gone again as soon as she woke up.

The next day she was dressed from head to foot in silk and velvet and was asked to stay in the castle and have a good time. But Gerda only wanted a little carriage, a horse to draw it, and a pair of little boots; then she would drive out again into the wide world and find her Kay.

She not only got boots but a muff; she was dressed so prettily; and when she was ready to go a coach made of pure gold stopped before her door. Upon it the coat of arms of the Prince and Princess shone like a star. Coachman, footmen, and outriders—for there were outriders, too—sat on horseback with gold crowns on their heads. The Prince and Princess themselves helped her into the carriage, and wished her all good fortune. The forest Crow, who was now married, went with her the first three miles. He sat by Gerda's side, for he could not stand riding backward. His wife stood in the doorway flapping her wings. She didn't come with them, for she had had a fixed appointment with too much to eat, for too long and she suffered from headache. Inside the coach was lined with sugar biscuits, and in the seat there were gingerbread nuts and fruit.

"Good-by, good-by!" cried the Prince and Princess; and little Gerda wept, and the Crow wept too. So they went on for the first three miles; and then the Crow said good-by. And that was the saddest good-by of all. The Crow flew up on a tree. He beat his black wings as long as he could see Gerda's coach, shining like the bright sunshine.

FIFTH STORY

The Little Robber Girl

THEY drove through the dark forest, and the coach gleamed like a torch, dazzling the eyes of the robbers, so that they couldn't bear it.

"That is gold! That is gold!" they shouted, and rushed forward. They seized the horses, killed the postilions, the coachman, and the footmen, and then pulled little Gerda out of the carriage.

"She is fat—she is pretty—she has been fattened with nut kernels!" said the old robber woman, who had a long stiff beard, and eyebrows that hung down over her eyes. "She's as good as a little pet lamb; my, how good she'll taste!"

And she drew out her shining knife, that gleamed in a horrible way.

"Ouch!" screamed the old woman at the same moment; for her own daughter who hung behind her had bit her in the ear. She was a wonder, she was so wild and rough. "You nasty brat!" screamed the old woman; and she didn't have time to butcher little Gerda.

"I want her to play with me!" said the little robber girl. "She shall give me her muff and her pretty dress, and sleep with me in my bed!"

And then she bit her mother again so that the robber woman jumped high in the air and turned right around, and all the robbers laughed and said:

"Watch her, she's dancing with her brat!"

"I want to get into the carriage," said the little robber girl.

Because she was so spoiled and so stubborn she must and would have her own way. She and Gerda sat in the carriage, and drove over stock and stone deep into the forest. The little robber girl was as big as Gerda, but stronger and more broad-shouldered. She had brown skin, and her eyes were quite black. They looked almost mournful. She put her arms around Gerda, and said:

"They shan't kill you as long as I am not angry with you. I suppose you are a Princess?"

"No," said little Gerda. And she told about everything that had happened to her, and how fond she was of little Kay.

The robber girl looked at her seriously, nodded slightly, and said:

"They shan't kill you even if I do get angry with you. For then I will do it myself!"

And then she dried Gerda's eyes, and put her two hands into the beautiful muff that was so soft and warm.

The coach stopped in the courtyard of a robber castle. It was cracked from top to bottom. Ravens and crows flew out of the open holes, and big bulldogs—each of whom looked as if he could swallow a man—jumped up high. But they didn't bark, for that was forbidden.

In the large old smoky hall a bright fire burned on the stone floor; the smoke drifted along under the ceiling and tried to find a way out. A big caldron of soup was boiling, and hares and rabbits were roasting on the spit.

"You shall sleep tonight with me and all my little animals," said the robber girl.

They got something to eat and drink, and then went to a corner, where straw and rugs were spread out. Above these more than a hundred pigeons sat on laths and perches. They all seemed asleep, but they turned a little when the two girls came in.

"They all belong to me," said the little robber girl; and she quickly seized one of the nearest, held it by the legs, and shook it so that it flapped its wings. "Kiss it!" she cried, and beat it in Gerda's face. "Here are my wood rascals," she kept on, pointing to a number of laths that had been nailed over a hole in the wall. "Those are wood rascals, those two; they fly away at once if one doesn't keep them well locked up. And here's my old sweetheart 'Ba.'" And she pulled a Reindeer out by his horn. He was tied up, and had a polished copper ring around his neck. "We have to keep him tight too, or he'd run away from us. Every evening I tickle his neck with a sharp knife, and he's very frightened at that."

And the little girl pulled a long knife from a cleft in the wall, and let it glide over the Reindeer's neck. The poor creature kicked out its legs, and the little robber girl laughed, and pulled Gerda into bed with her.

"Do you want to take the knife to bed with you?" asked Gerda, looking at it in a rather frightened way.

"I always sleep with a knife," said the robber girl. "You never can tell what's going to happen. But now tell me again what you told me just now about little Kay, and why you went out into the wide world."

And Gerda told it again from the beginning; and the Wood Pigeons cooed above them in their cage, and the other pigeons slept. The little robber girl put her arm around Gerda's neck, held her knife in the other hand, and slept so deeply that one could hear her heavy breathing. But Gerda couldn't close her eyes at all—she didn't know whether she was going to live or die. The robbers sat around the fire, singing and drinking, and the old robber woman turned somersaults. It was an awful sight for the little girl.

Then the Wood Pigeons said, "Coo, coo! We have seen little Kay. A white hen was carrying his sled. He sat in the Snow Queen's carriage, which drove low over the forest as we lay in our nests. She blew upon us young pigeons, and all died except us two. Coo! coo!"

"What are you saying up there?" asked Gerda. "Where was the Snow Queen traveling? Do you know anything about it?"

"She was probably traveling to Lapland, for there they always have ice and snow. Ask the Reindeer who is tied up with the cord."

"There are ice and snow there, and it is a lovely place," said the Reindeer. "There you run free in great, glittering valleys! There the Snow Queen has her summer tent; but her strong castle is up toward the North Pole, on the island that's called Spitzbergen."

"Oh, Kay, little Kay!" sighed Gerda.

"Now you be quiet," said the robber girl, "or you'll get my knife in your stomach."

In the morning Gerda told her all that the Wood Pigeons had said, and the robber girl looked quite serious, and nodded her head and said:

"It doesn't matter! It doesn't matter!"

"Do you know where Lapland is?" she asked the Reindeer.

"Who should know better than I?" said the animal, and his eyes sparkled in his head. "I was born and bred there; I played in the snowfields there."

"Listen!" said the robber girl to Gerda. "You see all our men have gone away. Only Mother is still here, and will remain; but toward noon she drinks out of the big bottle, and then she takes a little nap. That's when I'll do something for you."

Then she jumped out of bed, rushed over to her mother and pulled her beard, crying:

"Good morning, my own, sweet, nanny goat." And her mother tweaked her nose till it was red and blue; but it was all done for pure love.

When the mother had drunk out of her bottle and was taking a little nap, the robber girl went to the Reindeer, and said:

"I have a queer feeling that I'd like to tickle you a few times more with the knife, for you are very funny then; but it doesn't matter. I'll untie your rope and help you out, so that you can run to Lapland. You must use your legs well, and carry this little girl to the palace of the Snow Queen, where her playfellow is. You've heard what she told me, for she spoke loud enough, and you are always listening."

The Reindeer jumped for joy. The robber girl lifted little Gerda on his back, and had the forethought to tie her on, and even to give her a little cushion as a saddle.

"And here," she said, "are your fur boots. You'll need them in that cold country. The muff I'm going to keep myself; it's much too pretty to part with! You're not going to be cold. Here's my mother's big mittens, they'll reach right up to your elbows. Now your hands look as clumsy as my ugly mother's."

And Gerda wept for joy.

"I can't bear to see you whimper," said the little robber girl. "You ought to look very happy. See, here are two loaves of bread and a ham for you, so you won't be hungry."

These were tied on the Reindeer's back. Then the little robber girl opened the door, called away all the big dogs, cut the rope with her sharp knife, and said to the Reindeer:

"Run now, but take good care of the little girl."

And Gerda stretched out her hands with the big mittens toward the little robber girl, and said, "Good-by"; and the Reindeer ran over stock and stone, away through the great forest, over marshes and steppes, as fast as he could go. The wolves howled and the ravens screamed. "Whizz! whizz!" a red light flashed, and the sky looked as if it had sneezed red.

"Those are my dear old Northern Lights," said the Reindeer. "Look how they glow!" And then he ran on faster than ever, day and night he ran.

The loaves were eaten, and the ham too, and at last they were in Lapland.

SIXTH STORY

The Lapp Woman and the Finn Woman

THEY stopped at a little hut. It was a pitiful place; the roof sloped down to the ground, and the door was so low that the family had to creep on their stomachs when they wanted to go in or out. Nobody was home except an old Lapp woman, cooking fish on a fish-oil lamp. The Reindeer told Gerda's whole history, but told his own first, for this seemed to the Reindeer the more important of the two. Meanwhile, poor Gerda was so overcome with the cold that she could not speak.

"Oh, you poor things," said the Lapp woman, "you've a

long way to run yet! You must go more than a hundred miles before you arrive in Finmark. The Snow Queen lives there, and burns blue lights every evening. I'll write a few words on a dried codfish, for I have no paper, and you can take that to the Finn woman. She can give you better information than I."

And when Gerda had been warmed and refreshed with food and drink, the Lapp woman wrote a few words on a dried codfish, and telling Gerda to take care of it, tied her again on the Reindeer's back, and the Reindeer galloped away. Whizz! whizz! something said high in the air; the whole night long the most beautiful blue Northern Lights shone over the sky.

And then they arrived in Finmark. They knocked at the chimney of the Finn woman, for she didn't have a door.

In here it was so hot that the woman herself went around almost naked. She was low in stature and very dirty. She at once loosened little Gerda's dress and took off the mittens and boots; otherwise it would have been too hot for her to bear. Then she laid a piece of ice on the Reindeer's head, and read what was written on the codfish. She read it three times, for then she knew it by heart, and put the fish into the kettle, for it was eatable, and she never wasted anything.

Now the Reindeer told his own history first, and then little Gerda's; and the Finn woman blinked with her clever eyes, but said nothing.

"You are very clever," said the Reindeer. "I know you can tie all the winds of the world together with a bit of thread: if the seaman unties one knot, he has a good wind; if he unties the second, it blows hard; but if he unties the third and the fourth the wind tears the trees in the forest up by their roots. Won't you give the little girl a draught, which will give her the strength of twelve men and enable her to overcome the Snow Queen?"

"The strength of twelve men," said the Finn woman; "that would help a lot!"

And she went to a shelf, and took down a big parchment and unrolled it; strange letters were written on it, and the Finn woman read so intently that the perspiration streamed down her forehead.

But the Reindeer begged so hard for little Gerda, and Gerda looked at the Finn woman with such beseeching eyes full of tears, that the woman began to blink again with her own, and drew the Reindeer into a corner, and whispered to him, while she laid fresh ice on his head.

"Little Kay is certainly with the Snow Queen, and finds everything there to his taste and liking, and thinks it the best place in the world; but that is because he has a splinter of glass in his eye, and a little grain of glass in his heart. They must be got out, or he will never be a human being again, and the Snow Queen will be able to keep her power over him."

"But can't you give something to little Gerda, so that she will have power over all this?"

"I can give her no greater power than she has already; don't you see how great that is? Don't you see how men and animals have to serve her—a poor little girl wandering barefoot through the world. Her power is greater than ours. We mustn't tell her about her power, it is in her heart; it is in her being a sweet and innocent child. If she can't reach the Snow Queen herself and get the glass out of little Kay's eye and heart, we can be of no use! Two miles from here the Snow Queen's garden begins. You can carry the little girl there. Set her down by the big bush that stands with red berries in the snow. And no gossiping but hurry up and get back here!"

And then the wise Finn woman lifted little Gerda on the Reindeer, and away they went.

"Oh, I didn't get my boots! I didn't get my mittens!" cried little Gerda.

It was piercing cold; but the Reindeer didn't dare to stop. He ran till he came to the big bush with the red berries, and there he set Gerda down. He kissed her on the mouth, and big bright tears rolled down the creature's cheeks; and then he ran back, as fast as he could. And there stood poor Gerda, without shoes, without gloves, alone in that barren region— the terrible ice-cold Finmark.

She ran on as fast as she could; and a whole regiment of snowflakes came to meet her. But they didn't fall down from the sky, which was quite bright and shining with Northern Lights; they ran along the ground, and the nearer they came the larger they grew. Gerda still remembered how large and strange they had seemed when she had looked at them through the magnifying glass. But here they were certainly much bigger and much more terrible—they were alive. They were the guards of the Snow Queen, and had the strangest shapes. A few looked like ugly large porcupines; others like whole knots of snakes sticking out their heads; and others like little fat bears with bristling hair. All were brilliantly white, all were living snowflakes.

Then little Gerda began to say the Lord's Prayer. The cold was so intense that she could see her own breath, it came out of her mouth like smoke. Her breath got thicker and thicker, and shaped itself into bright little angels, who grew and grew whenever they touched the earth. They wore helmets on their heads and had shields and spears in their hands; their number increased more and more, and when Gerda had finished her prayer a whole legion stood around her. They thrust their spears against the awful snowflakes, and they shattered into a thousand pieces. And little Gerda went forward safe and undaunted. The angels stroked her hands and feet, and then she scarcely felt the cold and walked quickly on to the Snow Queen's palace.

But before we accompany her, let us see what Kay is doing. He certainly isn't thinking of little Gerda, and least of all that she is standing in front of the castle.

SEVENTH STORY

*What Happened in the Snow Queen's Castle
and What Happened Afterward*

THE walls of the castle were the drifting snow, and the windows and doors were the cutting winds. There were more than a hundred halls, as the snow drifted; the largest stretched for many miles; the strong Northern Lights illumined them all, and they were so big, so empty, so icily cold, and so dazzling! No fun was ever here, not as much as a little bear dance where one could imagine the wind blowing a trumpet and the polar bears walking on their hind legs with elegant manners; never even a little card party with slaps on the jaw and give-me-your-paw; never any little coffee gossip among the white-fox ladies. Empty, vast, and cold were the halls of the Snow Queen. The Northern Lights flamed so punctually that one could figure out exactly when they were going to be highest and lowest.

In the middle of this empty, endless snow hall was a frozen lake. It had cracked into a thousand pieces, but each piece was so accurately like the rest that it was a perfect work of art; and when the Snow Queen was at home she always sat in the middle of this lake. Then she said that she sat on the mirror of reason, and that this was the only one, and the best in the world.

Little Kay was quite blue with cold—indeed, almost black,

but he didn't notice it, for she had kissed the cold shivers away from him; and his heart was almost like a lump of ice. He was busy with the sharp icy fragments, joining them together in all kinds of ways—the way we do with what we call the Chinese puzzle. Kay was also making figures, the cleverest of all; it was the ice game of reason. In his eyes these figures were very remarkable and of the highest importance; that was because of the piece of glass sticking in his eye. He made figures that spelled out a whole written word —but he could never manage to spell out the one word he wanted most—the word "Eternity." And the Snow Queen had said:

"If you can puzzle out this figure, you shall be your own master, and I will give you the whole world and a new pair of skates." But he could not.

"Now I'll fly away to the hot countries," said the Snow Queen. "I will go and look into the black pots." These were the volcanoes, Etna and Vesuvius, as they are called. "I'm going to whiten them a little! That will be good for the lemons and grapes."

So the Snow Queen flew away, and Kay sat all alone in the large, empty hall that stretched for miles. He looked at his pieces of ice, and thought so hard that he creaked inside. He sat so stiff and still, one would have thought that he was frozen to death.

Then it was that little Gerda stepped into the castle through the gate of cutting winds, but she said an evening prayer and the winds lay down as if to sleep. And she stepped into the big, empty, cold halls—and there she saw Kay! She recognized him, she fell on his neck, hugged him tight, and called out:

"Kay, dear little Kay! at last I have found you!"

But he sat quite still, stiff and cold. Then little Gerda wept hot tears; they fell on his breast; they pressed into his heart, they thawed the lump of ice, and consumed the little piece of glass in it. He looked at her, and she sang the hymn:

> *Our roses bloom and fade away,*
> *Our Infant Lord abides alway!*
> *May we be blessed His face to see,*
> *And ever little children be!*

Then Kay burst into tears, and he wept until the splinter of glass rolled out of his eye. Now he recognized her, and cried with joy:

"Gerda, dear little Gerda! where have you been all this time? And where have I been?" He looked all around him. "How cold it is here! how large and empty!"

And he clung to Gerda, and she laughed and wept for joy. It was so wonderful that even the pieces of ice around them danced for joy; and when they were tired and lay down, they formed themselves into the mystical letters which the Snow Queen had said he must discover to be his own master, and to get the whole world and a new pair of skates.

Gerda kissed his cheeks, and they bloomed pink; she kissed his eyes, and they shone like her own; she kissed his hands and feet, and he was well and strong. The Snow Queen might come home now; his letter of liberty stood written on the mirror with shining pieces of ice.

They took one another by the hand, and wandered out of the big castle. They talked about the grandmother, and of the roses on their roofs. And where they went the winds rested and the sun burst forth from the dark storm clouds. When they arrived at the bush with the red berries, the Reindeer was standing there waiting. He had brought another young reindeer, whose udder was full and who gave the children warm milk, and kissed them. Then they carried Kay and Gerda to the wise Finn woman, where they warmed themselves in the hot room, and found out how to go home, and then to the Lapp woman, who had made new clothes for them and gave them a sled.

The Reindeer and the young Hind sprang at their side, and followed them as far as the boundary of the country. There the first green leaves peeped out, and there they left the two reindeer and the Lapp woman. "Farewell! Farewell!" they said. And the first little birds began to twitter, the woods burst forth with new green foliage. Suddenly the branches parted, and a spirited horse galloped out. Gerda knew it well, for it was the one that had drawn her golden coach. And on it sat a young girl with a shining red cap on her head and a pair of pistols in the holsters. It was the little robber girl, who had grown tired of staying at home, and was going on her travels, first to the north, and if that did not suit her, in some other direction. She knew Gerda at once, and there was great joy.

"You're a great one to traipse around!" she said to little Kay. "I'd like to know if you're so good that people ought to run to the end of the world for your sake!"

But Gerda patted her cheeks, and asked about the Prince and Princess.

"They've gone to foreign countries," said the robber girl.

"But the Crow?" said Gerda.

"Why, the Crow is dead," answered the other. "The tame beloved one has become a widow, and goes around with a piece of black worsted thread around her leg. But now tell me what happened to you, and how you caught him."

And Gerda and Kay told their story.

"Snip-snap-snurre-basslurre!" said the robber girl.

And she took them both by the hand, and promised that if she ever came through their town, she would come and pay them a visit. And then she rode away into the wide world.

Gerda and Kay walked hand in hand, and wherever they went it was lovely spring, with green things and flowers.

Then the church bells rang and they knew the high steeples and the great town; it was the one in which they lived. And they went to Grandmother's door, and up the stairs, and into the room, where everything stood right in the same place. The big clock was going "Tick! tock!" and the hands were turning. The only change they could find was in themselves; they had become grown-up people. The roses out on the roof gutter were blooming into the open windows, and there stood the little children's chairs. Kay and Gerda went and sat upon them still holding each other by the hand. They had forgotten the cold, empty splendor of the Snow Queen like a bad dream. The grandmother was sitting in God's bright sunshine, and reading aloud from the Bible, "Except ye become as little children, ye shall in no wise enter into the kingdom of God."

And Kay and Gerda looked into each other's eyes, and all at once they understood the old hymn:

> *Our roses bloom and fade away,*
> *Our Infant Lord abides alway!*
> *May we be blessed His face to see,*
> *And ever little children be!*

There they sat, those two happy ones, grown up, and yet children—children in their hearts, while all around them bright summer shone warm and glorious.

THE SWINEHERD

THERE was once a poor prince who had a very tiny kingdom, but it was big enough to allow him to marry, and he was
bent upon marrying.

Now it certainly was nervy of him to say to the Emperor's
daughter, "Will you have me?" He did, however, venture to
say so, for his name was known far and wide. And there
were hundreds of princesses who would have said "Yes," and
"Thank you, kindly." But see if *she* would!

Let us hear about it.

A rose tree grew on the grave of the Prince's father. It was
such a beautiful rose tree. But it bloomed only every fifth
year, and then bore only one blossom. What a rose that was!
By merely smelling it one forgot all of one's cares and sorrows.

The Prince also had a nightingale which sang as if every
lovely melody in the world dwelt in her little throat. This
rose and this nightingale were to be given to the Emperor's
daughter, so they were put into great silver caskets and sent
to her.

The Emperor had them carried before him into the great
hall where the Princess was playing at "visiting" with her
ladies-in-waiting—they had nothing else to do. When she saw
the caskets with the gifts, she clapped her hands with delight.

"If it were only a little pussy cat!" said she. But then the
rose tree with its beautiful rose came into view.

"Oh, how exquisitely it is made!" said all the ladies-in-
waiting.

"It is more than beautiful," said the Emperor. "It is made

with charm." But the Princess touched it, and was almost ready to cry.

"Fie, Papa!" she said. "It is not made. It is a real one."

"Fie," said all the ladies-in-waiting. "It is a real one."

"Well, let us see what there is in the other casket, before we get angry," said the Emperor, and out came the nightingale. It sang so beautifully that at first no one could find anything to say against it.

"*Superbe! Charmant!*" said the ladies-in-waiting, for they all had a smattering of French; one spoke it worse than the other.

"How that bird reminds me of our lamented Empress's musical box," said an old courtier. "Ah, yes, they are the same tunes and the same beautiful execution."

"So they are," said the Emperor, crying like a little child.

"I hardly think it could be a real one," said the Princess.

"Yes, it is a real one," said those who had brought it in.

"Oh, let that bird fly away then," said the Princess, and she would not hear of allowing the Prince to come.

But he was not discouraged. He stained his face brown and black, and pressing his cap over his eyes he knocked at the door.

"Good morning, Emperor," said he. "Can I be taken into service in the palace?"

"Well, there are so many wishing to do that," said the Emperor. "But let me see. Yes, I need somebody to look after the pigs. We have so many of them."

So the Prince was made imperial swineherd. A horrid little room was given him near the pigsties, and here he had to live. He sat busily at work all day, and by the evening he had made a beautiful little cooking pot. It had bells all round it, and when the pot boiled, they tinkled delightfully and played the old tune:

Ach du lieber Augustin,
Alles ist weg, weg, weg! *

But the greatest of all its charms was that by holding one's finger in the steam one could immediately smell all the dinners that were being cooked at every stove in the town. Now, this was something quite different from the rose.

The Princess came walking along with all her ladies-in-waiting, and when she heard the tune she stopped and looked pleased, for she could play "Ach du lieber Augustin" herself. It was her only tune, and she played it with one finger.

"Why, that is my tune," she said. "This must be a cultivated swineherd. Ask him what the instrument costs."

So one of the ladies-in-waiting had to go into his room, but before she entered she put on wooden clog shoes.

"How much do you want for the pot?" she asked.

"I must have ten kisses from the Princess," said the swineherd.

"Heaven preserve us!" said the lady.

"I won't take less," said the swineherd.

"Well, what does he say?" asked the Princess.

"I really cannot tell you," said the lady-in-waiting. "It is so shocking."

"Then you must whisper it." And she whispered it.

"He is a wretch!" said the Princess and went away at once. But she had gone only a little way when she heard the bells tinkling beautifully:

"Ach du lieber Augustin."

"Go and ask him if he will take ten kisses from the ladies-in-waiting."

* Alas, dear Augustin,
  All is lost, lost, lost!

"No, thank you," said the swineherd. "Ten kisses from the Princess, or I keep my pot."

"How tiresome it is," said the Princess. "Then you will have to stand round me, so that no one may see."

So the ladies-in-waiting stood round her and spread out their skirts while the swineherd took his ten kisses, and then the pot was hers.

What a delight it was to them! The pot was kept on the boil day and night. They knew what was cooking on every stove in the town, from the chamberlain's to the shoemaker's. The ladies-in-waiting danced about and clapped their hands.

"We know who has sweet soup and pancakes for dinner, and who has cutlets. How amusing it is!"

"Highly interesting," said the mistress of the robes.

"Yes, but hold your tongues, for I am the Emperor's daughter."

"Heaven preserve us!" they all said.

The swineherd—that is to say, the Prince, only nobody knew that he was not a real swineherd—did not let his day pass in idleness. He now made a rattle. When it was swung round it played all the waltzes, galops, and jig tunes ever heard since the creation of the world.

"But this is *superbe!*" said the Princess, as she walked by. "I have never heard finer compositions. Go and ask him what the instrument costs, but let us have no more kissing."

"He wants a hundred kisses from the Princess," said the lady-in-waiting.

"I think he is mad!" said the Princess, and she went away, but she had not gone far when she stopped.

"One must encourage art," she said. "I am the Emperor's daughter. Tell him he can have ten kisses, the same as yesterday, and he can take the others from the ladies-in-waiting."

"But we don't like that at all," said the ladies.

"Oh, nonsense! If I can kiss him you can do the same. Remember that I pay you wages as well as give you board and lodging." So the lady-in-waiting had to go again.

"A hundred kisses from the Princess, or let each keep his own," he said.

"Stand in front of me," said she, and all the ladies stood round while he kissed her.

"Whatever is the meaning of that crowd round the pigsties?" said the Emperor as he stepped out onto the veranda. He rubbed his eyes and put on his spectacles. "Why, it is the ladies-in-waiting. What game are they up to? I must go and see!" So he pulled up the heels of his slippers, for they were shoes which he had trodden down, and was off.

Bless us, what a hurry he was in! When he got into the yard he walked very softly. The ladies were so busy counting the kisses, so that there should be fair play, and neither too few nor too many kisses, that they never heard the Emperor. He stood on tiptoe.

"What is all this?" he said when he saw what was going on, and he hit the Princess on the head with his slipper just as the swineherd was taking his eighty-sixth kiss.

"Out you go!" said the Emperor. He was very furious, and he put both the Princess and the swineherd out of his realm.

There she stood crying, and the swineherd scolded, and the rain poured down in torrents.

"Oh, miserable creature that I am!" said the Princess. "If only I had accepted the handsome Prince. Oh, how unhappy I am!"

The swineherd went behind a tree, wiped the black and brown stain from his face, and threw away his ugly clothes. When he stepped out dressed as a prince, he looked so noble the Princess could not help curtsying to him.

"I have come to despise thee," he said. "Thou wouldst not have an honorable prince. Thou couldst not prize the rose or the nightingale. But thou wouldst kiss the swineherd for a trumpery musical box! You have made your bed; now go lie upon it!"

He went back into his own little kingdom and shut and locked the door in her face. She stood outside and sang in earnest:

> *"Ach du lieber Augustin,*
> *Alles ist weg, weg, weg!"*

THE FLYING TRUNK

THERE was once a merchant so rich that he could have
paved the whole street where he lived, and an alley besides,
with pieces of silver. But this he did not do—he knew another
way of using his money, and whenever he laid out a shilling,
he gained a crown in return. A merchant he lived, and a
merchant he died.

All his money went to his son. But the son lived merrily,
and spent all his time in pleasures. He went to masquerades
every evening, made bank notes into paper kites, and played
at ducks and drakes in the pond with gold pieces instead of
stones. In this manner his money soon vanished, until at last
he had only a few pennies left. His wardrobe was reduced
to a pair of slippers and an old dressing gown. His friends
cared no more about him, now that they could no longer be
seen with him in public. One of them, however, more good-
natured than the rest, sent him an old trunk, with this advice,
"Pack up, and be off!"

This was all very fine, but he had nothing that he could
pack up. So he put himself into the trunk.

It was a funny trunk. When the lock was pressed closed, it
could fly. The merchant's son pressed the lock. And lo! Up
he flew with the trunk, through the chimney, high into the
clouds, on and on, higher and higher. The lower part cracked,
which rather frightened him; for, if it had broken in two,
a long fall he would have had!

However, it descended safely, and he found himself in
Turkey. He hid the trunk under a heap of dry leaves in a
wood, and walked into the next town. He could do so very

easily, for, among the Turks, everybody goes about clad as
he was, in dressing gown and slippers. He met a nurse, carrying
a little child in her arms. "Hark ye, Turkish nurse," said he.
"What palace is that with the high windows close by the
town?"

"The King's daughter dwells there," replied the nurse. "It
has been prophesied of her that she shall be made very unhappy by a lover, and therefore no one may visit her except
when the King and Queen are with her."

"Thank you," said the merchant's son. He immediately
went back into the wood, sat down in his trunk, flew up
to the roof of the palace, and crept through the window
into the Princess's apartment.

She was lying asleep on the sofa. She was so beautiful that the merchant's son could not help kneeling down to kiss her hand. Whereupon she awoke, and was frightened at the sight of this unexpected visitor. But he told her that he was the Turkish Prophet, and had come down from the sky on purpose to woo her. And on hearing this she was very pleased.

So they sat down side by side, and he talked to her about her eyes, how that they were beautiful dark-blue seas, and that thoughts and feelings floated like mermaidens therein. He spoke of her brow, how it was a fair, snowy mountain, with splendid halls and pictures. And he told her many other suchlike things.

Oh, these were charming stories! And thus he wooed the Princess, and she immediately said "Yes!"

"But you must come here on Saturday," said she. "The King and Queen have promised to drink tea with me that evening. They will be so proud and so pleased when they hear that I am to marry the Turkish Prophet! And mind you tell them a very pretty story, for they are exceedingly fond of stories; my mother likes them to be very moral and aristocratic, and my father likes them to be funny, so he can laugh."

"Yes, I shall bring no other bridal present than a tale," replied the merchant's son. And here they parted, but not before the Princess had given her lover a saber all covered with gold. He knew very well what use to make of this present.

He flew away, bought a new dressing gown, and then sat down in the wood to compose the tale which was to be ready by Saturday. And, certainly composition was not the easiest thing in the world for him.

At last he was ready, and, at last, Saturday came.

The King, the Queen, and the whole Court were waiting

tea for him at the Princess's palace. The suitor was received with much ceremony.

"Will you not tell us a story?" asked the Queen, "a story that is instructive and full of deep meaning."

"But let it make us laugh," said the King.

"With pleasure," replied the merchant's son. And now you must hear his story:

"There was once a bundle of Matches, who were all extremely proud of their high descent, for their genealogical tree—that is to say, the tall fir tree, from which each of them was a splinter—had been a tree of great antiquity, and distinguished by its height from all the other trees of the forest. The Matches were now lying on the mantelpiece, between a Tinderbox and an old iron Saucepan, and to these two they often talked about their youth.

" 'Ah, when we were upon the green branches,' said they; 'when we really lived upon green branches—that was a happy time! Every morning and evening we had diamond tea—that is, dew. The whole day long we had sunshine, at least whenever the sun shone, and all the little birds used to tell stories to us. It might easily be seen, too, that we were rich, for other trees were clothed with leaves only during the summer; whereas, our family could afford to wear green clothes both summer and winter. But at last came the woodcutters, then there was the great revolution, and our family was dispersed. The paternal trunk obtained a situation as mainmast to a magnificent ship, which could sail round the world if it chose, the boughs were transported to various places, and our vocation was henceforth to kindle lights for low, common people. Now you will understand how it came to pass that persons of our high descent should be living in a kitchen.'

" 'To be sure, mine is a very different history,' remarked the iron Saucepan, near which the Matches were lying. 'From the moment I came into the world, until now, I have been rubbed and scrubbed and boiled over and over again—oh, how many times! I love to have something to do with what is solid and good, and am really of the first importance in this house. My only recreation is to stand clean and bright upon this mantelpiece after dinner, and hold some rational conversation with my companions. However, excepting the Water-pail, who now and then goes into the court, we all of us lead a very quiet, domestic life here. Our only news-monger is the Turf-basket, but he talks in such a democratic way about "government" and "the people"—why, I assure you, not long ago, there was an old Jar standing here, who was so shocked by what he heard, that he fell down from the mantelpiece, and broke into a thousand pieces! That Turf-basket is a Liberal, that's a fact—'

" 'Now you talk too much,' interrupted the Tinderbox, and steel struck flint, and the sparks flew out! 'Why should we not spend a pleasant evening?'

" 'Yes, let us settle who is of highest rank among us!' proposed the Matches.

" 'Oh, no, for my part, I would rather not speak of myself,' objected the Earthenware Pitcher. 'Suppose we have an intellectual entertainment? I will begin, I will tell of something in everyday life, such as we have all experienced. One can easily transport oneself into it, and that is so interesting! Near the Baltic, among the Danish beech groves—'

" 'That is an excellent beginning!' cried all the Plates at once. 'It will certainly be just the sort of story for us!'

" 'Yes, there I spent my youth in a very quiet family. The furniture was rubbed, the floors were washed, clean curtains were hung up every fortnight.'

" 'How very interesting! what a charming way you have of describing things!' said the Hair-broom. 'Anyone might guess immediately that it is a lady who is speaking. The tale breathes such a spirit of cleanliness!'

" 'Very true! So it does!' exclaimed the Water-pail, and in an excess of delight he gave a little jump, so that some of the water splashed upon the floor.

"The Pitcher went on with her tale, and the end proved as good as the beginning.

"All the Plates clattered applause, and the Hair-broom took some green parsley out of the sand hole and crowned the Pitcher. For he knew that this would vex the others, and thought he, 'If I crown her today, she will crown me tomorrow.'

" 'Now I will dance,' said the Fire-tongs, and accordingly she did dance. And oh! it was wonderful to see how high she threw one of her legs up into the air. The old Chair-cover in the corner tore with horror at seeing her. 'Am not I to be crowned too?' asked the Tongs. And she was crowned forthwith.

" 'This is a vulgar rabble!' thought the Matches.

"The Tea-urn was now called upon to sing, but she had a cold, she said, and could only sing when she was boiling. However, this was all pride and affectation, the real fact was that she never cared to sing except when she was standing on the parlor table before company.

"On the window ledge lay an old Quill-pen, with which the maids used to write. There was nothing remarkable about her, except that she had been dipped too low in the ink; and she was proud of that. 'If the Tea-urn does not choose to sing,' said she, 'she may let it alone. There is a Nightingale in the cage hung just outside, he can sing. To be sure, he has never learned the notes—but never mind, we will not speak evil of anyone this evening!'

" 'I think it highly indecorous,' observed the Tea-kettle,

who was the vocalist of the kitchen, and a half-brother of the Tea-urn's, 'that a foreign bird should be listened to. Is it patriotic? I appeal to the Turf-basket.'

" 'I am only vexed,' said the Turf-basket, 'I am vexed from my inmost soul that such things are thought of at all. Is it a pleasant way to spend the evening? Wouldn't it be much more rational to reform the whole house, and establish a totally new order of things, according to nature? Then everyone would get into his right place, and I would undertake and direct the revolution. What say you to it? That would be something worth doing!'

" 'Oh, yes, we will make a grand commotion!' they all cried. Just then the door opened—it was the servant-maid. They all stood perfectly still, not one dared stir. There was not a single kitchen utensil among them that was not thinking about the wonderful things he could have done, and how great his superiority over the others was. 'Ah, if I had chosen to,' thought each of them, 'what a merry evening we might have had!'

"The maid took the Matches and struck a light—oh, how they sputtered and blazed up!

" 'Now everyone may see,' thought they, 'that we are of highest rank. What a splendid, dazzling light we give, how glorious!' And in another moment they were burned out."

"That is a capital story," said the Queen. "I felt myself transported into the kitchen—yes, thou shalt have our daughter!"

"With all my heart," said the King. "On Monday thou shalt marry our daughter." They said "Thou" to him now, since he was soon to become one of the family. The wedding was a settled thing; and on the evening preceding, the whole city was lit up. Cakes, buns, and sugar plums were thrown out among the people. All the little boys in the streets stood upon tiptoes, shouting "Hurrah!" and whistling through their fingers—it was fabulous!

"Well, I suppose I ought to do my part too," thought the merchant's son. So he went and bought skyrockets, squibs, Catherine wheels, Roman candles, and every kind of conceivable fireworks. He put them all into his trunk, and flew up into the air, and let them go off as he flew.

Hurrah! What a glorious skyrocket he was!

All the Turks jumped up so hastily that their slippers flew about their ears. They had never seen such a meteor before. Now they were sure that it was indeed the Prophet who was going to marry their Princess.

As soon as the merchant's son had returned in his trunk to the wood, he said to himself, "I will now go into the city and hear what people say about me, and see what sort of figure I made in the air." And, certainly, this was a very natural reaction.

Oh, what strange accounts were given! Everyone he ran into had beheld the bright vision in a way that was peculiar to himself. But all agreed that it was marvelously beautiful.

"I saw the great Prophet with my own eyes," declared one. "He had eyes like sparkling stars, and a beard like foaming water."

"He flew enveloped in a mantle of fire," said another. "The prettiest little cherubs were peeping forth from under his folds."

Yes, he heard of many beautiful things, and the morrow was to be his wedding day.

He went back to the wood, intending to get into his trunk again, but where was it?

Alas! the trunk was burned. One spark had been left from the fireworks and had set the trunk on fire. The trunk lay in ashes. The poor merchant's son could never fly again, could never again visit his bride.

She sat the livelong day upon the roof of her palace expecting him. She expects him still. He, in the meantime, goes about the world telling stories, but none of his stories are so pleasant as that one which he told in the Princess's palace about the Brimstone Matches.

SUNSHINE STORIES

"Now I am going to tell a story," said the Wind.

"Excuse me," said the Rain, "but now it is my turn. You have been howling round the corner as hard as ever you could, this long time past."

"Is that your gratitude toward me?" said the Wind. "I who, in honor of you, turn inside out—yes, even break—all the umbrellas, when people won't have anything to do with you."

"I am going to speak!" said the Sunshine. "Silence!" And the Sunshine said it with such glory and majesty, that the long, weary Wind fell prostrate, and the Rain beat against him, and shook him, and said—"We won't stand for it! She always breaks through, that Madam Sunshine; we won't listen to her. What she says is not worth hearing."

But the Sunshine said—"A beautiful swan flew over the rolling, tumbling waves of the ocean. Every one of its feathers shone like gold. One feather drifted down on the great merchant vessel that was sailing away with all sails set. The feather dropped on the curly light hair of a young man, whose business it was to take care of the goods—supercargo they called him. The bird of Fortune's feather touched his forehead, became a pen in his hand, and brought him such luck, that very soon he became a wealthy merchant—rich enough to buy spurs of gold for himself; rich enough to change a golden dish into a nobleman's shield; and I shone on it," said the Sunshine.

"The swan flew farther, away over the bright green meadow, where the little shepherd boy, only seven years old, had lain down in the shadow of the old and only tree there was. The swan, in its flight, kissed one of the leaves of the tree. The leaf fell into the boy's hand, and it was changed to three leaves, to ten—yes, to a whole book—and in it he read about all the wonders of nature, about his native language, about faith and knowledge. At night he laid the book under his head, that he might not forget what he had been reading. The wonderful book led him to the school bench, and from there in search of knowledge. I have read his name among the names of learned men," said the Sunshine.

"The swan flew into the quiet, lonely forest, rested awhile on the dark, deep lake, where the water lilies grow; where the wild apples are to be found on the shore; where the cuckoo and wild pigeon have their homes.

"A poor woman was in the wood, gathering firewood—branches and dry sticks that had fallen down; she carried them in a bundle on her back, and in her arms she held her little child. She saw the golden swan, the bird of Fortune, rise from among the reeds on the shore. What was that that glittered? A golden egg, still quite warm. She laid it in her bosom, and the warmth remained in it. Surely there was life in the egg! She heard a gentle picking inside the shell, but mistook the sound, and thought it was her own heart that she heard beating.

"At home, in the poor cottage, she took out the egg. 'Tick, tick,' it said, as if it had been a valuable gold watch. But that it was not—it was only an egg—a real, living egg. The egg cracked and opened, and a dear little baby swan, all feathered as if with purest gold, put out its little head. Round its neck it had four rings, and as the poor woman had four boys—three at home, and the little one that she had had with her in the lonely wood—she understood at once that here was a ring for each boy. And just as she thought of that, the little gold bird took flight. She kissed each ring, and made each of the children kiss one of them, and laid it next to the child's heart. Then she put it on his finger. I saw it all," said the Sunshine, "and I saw what followed.

"One of the boys was playing in a ditch. He took a lump of clay in his hand, turned and twisted and pressed it between his fingers, till it took shape, and was like *Jason*, who went in search of and found the golden fleece.

"The second boy ran out on the meadow, where the flowers stood—flowers of all imaginable colors. He gathered a handful, and squeezed them so tight that all the juice spurted into his eyes, and some of it wetted the ring. It cribbled and crawled in his thoughts, and in his hands, and after many a day, and many a year, people in the big city talked of the great painter.

"The third child held the ring so tight in his teeth, that it gave forth sound, an echo of the song in the depth of his heart. Thoughts and feelings rose in beautiful sounds; rose like singing swans; plunged, like swans, into the deep, deep sea. He became a great master, a great composer, of whom every country has the right to say, 'He was mine!'

"And the fourth little one was—yes, he was—the 'ugly duck' of the family. They said he had the pip, and must have pepper and butter, like the little sick chickens. And that's what he got. But of me he got a warm, sunny kiss," said the Sunshine. "He got ten kisses for one; he was a poet, and was buffeted and kissed, alternately, all his life. But he had what no one could take from him—the ring of Fortune, from Dame Fortune's golden swan. His thoughts took wings, and flew up and away, like singing butterflies—the emblem of immortality!"

"That was a dreadfully long story," said the Wind.

"And oh, how stupid and tiresome!" said the Rain. "Blow on me, please, that I may revive a little."

And the Wind blew, and the Sunshine said—"The swan

of Fortune flew over the beautiful bay, where the fishermen had set their nets. The poorest of them wanted to get married, and marry he did. To him the swan brought a piece of amber; amber draws things toward it, and it drew hearts to the house. Amber is the most wonderful incense, and there came a soft perfume, as from a church; there came a sweet breath from out of the beautiful nature, that God has made. They were so happy and grateful for their peaceful home, and content even in their poverty. Their life became a real Sunshine story!"

"I think we had better stop now," said the Wind, "the Sunshine has talked long enough, and I am dreadfully bored."

"And I also," said the Rain.

And what do we others, who have heard the story, say? We say, "Now my story's done."

THE GARDEN OF PARADISE

ONCE there was a king's son. No one had so many beautiful books as he. Everything that had happened in this world he could find and read there, and he could see pictures of it in all the lovely copper plates. Of every people and of every land he could get intelligence. But there was not a word that told where the Garden of Paradise could be found, and it was just this which he thought about the most.

His grandmother had told him, when he was very little and just about to go to school, that every flower in this Paradise Garden was a delicate cake, and the pistils contained the choicest wine. On one of the flowers history was written, and on another geography or mathematics, so that you had only to eat cake, and you learned a lesson. And the more one ate, the more history, geography, or mathematics one learned. At that time he believed this. But when he became a bigger boy, and learned more and became wiser, he understood well that the splendor in the Garden of Paradise must be of a very different kind.

"Oh, why did Eve pluck from the Tree of Knowledge? Why did Adam eat the forbidden fruit? If I had been he it would never have happened—then sin would never have come into the world."

He said that then, and he still said it now, when he was seventeen years old. The Garden of Paradise filled all his thoughts.

One day he walked in the wood. He was walking alone, for that was his greatest pleasure. The evening came, and the clouds gathered together; rain streamed down as if the sky

were one single river from which the water poured out. It
was as dark as it is at night in the deepest well. Often he
slipped on the smooth grass; often he fell over the smooth
stones which peered up out of the wet rocky ground. Everything was soaked with water, and there was not a dry thread
on the poor Prince. He was obliged to climb over great
blocks of stone, where the water spurted from the thick moss.
He was nearly fainting. Then he heard a strange rushing,
and saw before him a great illuminated cave. In the midst of
it burned a fire, so large that a stag might have been roasted in
it. And this was in fact being done.

A glorious deer had been stuck, horns and all, upon a
spit, and was turning slowly between two felled pine trunks.
An elderly woman, large and strongly built, looking like a
disguised man, sat by the fire, into which she threw one piece
of wood after another.

"Come nearer!" said she. "Sit down by the fire and dry
your clothes."

"There's a great draft here!" said the Prince, as he sat down
on the ground.

"It will be worse when my sons come home," replied the
woman. "You are here in the Cavern of the Winds, and my
sons are the Four Winds of the world. Can you understand
that?"

"Where are your sons?" asked the Prince.

"It is difficult to answer when stupid questions are asked,"
said the woman. "My sons do business on their own account.
They play at shuttlecock with the clouds up yonder in the
King's hall."

And she pointed upward.

"Oh, indeed!" said the Prince. "But you speak rather gruffly,
by the way, and are not so mild as the women I generally see
about me."

"Yes, they have most likely nothing else to do! I must be

hard, if I want to keep my sons in order. But I can do it, though they are obstinate fellows. Do you see the four sacks hanging there by the wall? They are just as frightened of those as you used to be of the rod stuck behind the glass. I can bend the lads together, I tell you, and then I pop them into the bag: we don't make any ceremony. There they sit, and may not wander about again until I think fit to allow them. Here comes one of them now!"

It was the North Wind. He rushed in with piercing cold. Great hailstones skipped about on the floor, and snowflakes fluttered about. He was dressed in a jacket and trousers of bearskin. A sealskin cap was drawn down over his ears; long icicles hung on his beard, and one hailstone after another rolled from the collar of his jacket.

"Do not go near the fire so quickly," said the Prince, "you might get your hands and face frostbitten."

"Frostbitten?" repeated the North Wind, and he laughed aloud. "Cold is exactly what rejoices me most! But what kind of little tailor art thou? How did you find your way into the Cavern of the Winds?"

"He is my guest," interposed the old woman, "and if you're not satisfied with this explanation you may go into the sack. Do you understand me?"

You see, that was the right way; and now the North Wind politely told where he came from and where he had been for almost a month.

"I come from the Polar Sea," said he. "I have been in the bears' icy land with the walrus hunters. I sat and slept on the helm when they went away from the North Cape, and when I awoke now and then, the storm bird flew round my legs. That's a comical bird! He gives a sharp clap with his wings, and then holds them quite still and shoots along in full career."

"Don't be too long-winded," said the mother of the Winds. "And so you came to the Bears' Island?"

"It is very beautiful there! There's a floor for dancing that is as flat as a plate. Half-thawed snow, with a little moss, sharp stones, and skeletons of walruses and polar bears lay around, and likewise gigantic arms and legs of a rusty green color. One would have thought the sun had never shone there. I blew a little upon the mist, so that one could see the hut. It was a house built of wreck-wood and covered with walrus skins—the fleshy side turned outward. It was full of green and red, and on the roof sat a live polar bear who was growling. I went to the shore to look after the birds' nests, and saw the unfledged nestlings screaming and opening their beaks. I blew down into their thousand throats, and taught them to shut their mouths. Farther on, the huge walruses were splashing like great maggots with pigs' heads and teeth an ell long!"

"You tell your story well, my son," said the old lady. "My mouth waters when I hear you!"

"Then the hunting began! The harpoon was hurled into the walrus's breast, so that a smoking stream of blood spurted like a fountain over the ice. When I thought of my sport, I blew, and let my sailing ships, the big icebergs, crush the boats between them. Oh, how the people whistled and how they cried! But I whistled louder than they. They were obliged to throw the dead walruses and their chests and tackle out upon the ice. I shook the snowflakes over them, and let them drive south in their crushed boats with their booty to taste salt water. They'll never come to Bears' Island again!"

"Then you have done a wicked thing!" said the mother of the Winds.

"The good I have done others will tell," replied he. "But here comes a brother from the west. I like him best of all. He tastes of the sea and brings a delicious coolness with him."

"Is that little Zephyr?" asked the Prince.

"Yes, certainly, that is Zephyr," replied the old woman.

"But he is not little. Years ago he was a pretty boy, but that's past now."

He looked like a wild man, and he had a broad-brimmed hat on, to protect his face. In his hand he held a club of mahogany, hewn in the American mahogany forest. It was no trifle.

"Where do you come from?" said his mother.

"Out of the forest wilderness," said he, "where the water snake lies in the wet grass, and people don't seem to be wanted."

"What were you doing there?"

"I looked into the deepest river, and watched how it rushed down from the rocks, and turned to spray, and shot up toward the clouds to carry the rainbow. I saw the wild buffalo swimming in the stream, but the stream carried him away. He drifted with the flock of wild ducks that flew up where the water fell down in a cataract. The buffalo had to go down it! That pleased me, and I blew a storm, so that ancient trees were split up into splinters!"

"And have you done nothing else?" asked the old dame.

"I have thrown somersaults in the savannahs. I have stroked the wild horses and shaken the coconut palms. Yes, yes, I have stories to tell! But one must not tell all one knows. You know that, old lady."

And he kissed his mother so roughly that she almost tumbled over. He was a terribly wild young fellow!

Now came the South Wind, with a turban on and a flying Bedouin's cloak.

"It's terribly cold out here!" cried he, and threw some more wood on the fire. "One can feel that the North Wind came first."

"It's so hot that one could roast a polar bear here," said the North Wind.

"You're a polar bear yourself," reported the South Wind.

"Do you want to be put in the sack?" asked the old dame. "Sit upon the stone yonder and tell me where you have been."

"In Africa, Mother," he answered. "I was out hunting the lion with the Hottentots in the land of the Kaffirs. Grass grows there in the plains, green as an olive. There the ostrich ran races with me, but I am swifter than he. I came into the desert where the yellow sand lies: it looks there like the bottom of the sea. I met a caravan. The people were killing their last camel to get water to drink, but it was very little they got. The sun burned above and the sand below. The outspread deserts had no bounds. Then I rolled in the fine loose sand, and whirled it up in great pillars. That was a dance! You should have seen how the dromedary stood there terrified, and the merchant drew the caftan over his head. He threw himself down before me, as before Allah, his God. Now they are buried—a pyramid of sand covers them all. When I someday blow that away, the sun will bleach the white bones; then travelers may see that men have been there before them. Otherwise, one would not believe that, in the desert!"

"So you have done nothing but evil!" exclaimed the mother. "March into the sack!"

And before he was aware, she had seized the South Wind round the body, and popped him into the bag. He rolled about on the floor. But she sat down on the sack, and then he had to keep quiet.

"Those are lively boys of yours," said the Prince.

"Yes," she replied, "and I know how to punish them! Here comes the fourth!"

That was the East Wind, who came dressed like a Chinaman.

"Oh! do you come from that region?" said his mother. "I thought you had been in the Garden of Paradise."

"I don't fly there till tomorrow," said the East Wind. "It will be a hundred years tomorrow since I was there. I come from China now, where I danced around the porcelain tower till all the bells jingled again! In the streets the officials were being thrashed: the bamboos were broken upon their shoulders, yet they were high people, from the first to the ninth level. They cried, 'Many thanks, my paternal benefactor!' but it didn't come from their hearts. And I rang the bells and sang, 'Tsing, tsang, tsu!' "

"You are foolish," said the old dame. "It is a good thing that you are going into the Garden of Paradise tomorrow. That always helps with your education. Drink bravely out of the spring of Wisdom, and bring home a little bottleful for me."

"That I will do," said the East Wind. "But why have you clapped my brother South in the bag? Out with him! He shall tell me about the Phœnix bird, for about that bird the Princess in the Garden of Paradise always wants to hear, when I pay my visit every hundredth year. Open the sack, and you shall be my sweetest of mothers, and I will give you two pocketfuls of tea, green and fresh as I plucked it at the place where it grew!"

"Well, for the sake of the tea, and because you are my darling boy, I will open the sack."

She did so, and the South Wind crept out. He looked very downcast, because the strange Prince had seen his disgrace.

"There you have a palm leaf for the Princess," said the South Wind. "This palm leaf was given me by the Phœnix bird, the only one left in the world. With his beak he has scratched upon it a description of all the hundred years he has lived. Now she may read herself how the Phœnix bird set fire to her nest, and sat upon it, and was burned to death like a Hindu's widow. How the dry branches crackled! What a smoke and a steam there was! At last everything burst into flame, and the old Phœnix turned to ashes, but her egg lay red hot in the fire. It burst with a great bang, and the young one flew out. Now this young one is ruler over all the birds, and the only Phœnix in the world. It has bitten a hole in the palm leaf I have given you, and that is a greeting to the Princess."

"Let us have something to eat," said the mother of the Winds.

And now they all sat down to eat of the roasted deer. The Prince sat beside the East Wind, and they soon became good friends.

"Just tell me," said the Prince, "who is this Princess that you talk so much about? And where does the Garden of Paradise lie?"

"Ho, ho!" said the East Wind, "do you want to go there? Well, then, fly tomorrow with me! But I must tell you, that no man has been there since the time of Adam and Eve. You have read of them in your Bible histories?"

"Yes," said the Prince.

"When they were driven away, the Garden of Paradise sank into the earth; but it kept its warm sunshine, its mild air, and all its splendor. The Queen of the Fairies lives there, and there lies the Island of Happiness, where death never comes, and where it is beautiful. Sit upon my back tomorrow, and I will take you with me: I think it can very well be done. But now stop talking, for I want to sleep."

And then they all went to rest.

In the early morning the Prince awoke, and was a little astonished to find himself high above the clouds. He was sitting on the back of the East Wind, who was holding him faithfully. They were so high in the air that the woods and fields, rivers and lakes below them looked as if they were painted on a map.

"Good morning!" said the East Wind. "You might very well sleep a little longer, for there is not much to be seen on the flat country under us, unless you care to count the churches. They stand out like dots of chalk on the green carpet."

What he called green carpet was field and meadow.

"It was rude of me not to say good-by to your mother and your brothers," said the Prince.

"When one is asleep one must be excused," replied the East Wind.

And they flew on faster than ever. One could hear it in the tops of the trees. When they passed over them the leaves and twigs rustled, and one could hear it on the sea and on the lakes, for when they flew by the water rose higher, and the great ships bowed themselves toward the water like swimming swans.

Toward evening, when it became dark, the great towns looked charming, for lights were burning below, here and there. It was the same as when one has lighted a piece of paper, and sees all the little sparks vanish one after another. And the Prince clapped his hands; but the East Wind begged him to stop and to hold fast instead, otherwise he might fall down and land on a church spire.

The eagle in the dark woods flew lightly, but the East Wind flew more lightly still. The Cossack on his little horse skimmed swiftly over the surface of the earth, but the Prince skimmed more swiftly still.

"Now you can see the Himalayas," said the East Wind. "That is the highest mountain range in Asia. Now we shall soon get to the Garden of Paradise."

They turned more to the south, and soon the air was fragrant with flowers and spices. Figs and pomegranates grew wild, and the wild vine bore clusters of red and purple grapes. Here they landed and stretched themselves on the soft grass, where the flowers nodded to the wind, as though they said "Welcome!"

"Are we now in the Garden of Paradise?" asked the Prince.

"Not at all," replied the East Wind. "But we shall soon get there. Do you see the rocky wall yonder, and the great cave,

"In the early morning the Prince awoke, and was a little astonished to find himself high above the clouds. He was sitting on the back of the East Wind." (Page 211)

where the vines cluster like a broad green curtain? Through that we shall pass. Wrap yourself in your cloak. Here the sun scorches you, but a step farther it will be icy cold. The bird which hovers past the cave has one wing in the region of summer and the other in the wintry cold."

"So this is the way to the Garden of Paradise?" observed the Prince.

They went into the cave. Ugh! it was icy cold there, but this did not last long. The East Wind spread out his wings, and they gleamed like the brightest fire. What a cave it was! The water dripped down from great blocks of stone, which hung over them in the strangest shapes. Sometimes it was so narrow they had to creep on their hands and knees, sometimes it was as lofty and broad as the open air. The place looked like a number of mortuary chapels, with dumb organ pipes, and the organs themselves were petrified.

"We are going through the way of death to the Garden of Paradise, are we not?" inquired the Prince.

The East Wind answered not a syllable, but pointed forward to a lovely blue light that gleamed upon them. The stone blocks over their heads became more and more like a mist, and at last looked like a white cloud in the moonlight. Now they were in a deliciously mild air, fresh as on the hills, fragrant as among the roses of the valley. There ran a river, clear as the air itself, and the fishes were like silver and gold. Purple eels, flashing out blue sparks at every moment, played in the water below; and the broad water-plant leaves shone in all the colors of the rainbow; the flower itself was an orange-colored burning flame, to which the water gave nourishment, as the oil to the burning lamp. A bridge of marble, strong, indeed, but so lightly built that it looked as if made of lace and glass beads, led them across the water to the Island of Happiness, where the Garden of Paradise bloomed.

Were these palm trees that grew here, or gigantic water

plants? Such verdant mighty trees the Prince had never seen before. The most wonderful climbing plants hung in long festoons. They were like the vines one sees illuminated in gold and bright colors on the margins of gold missal books or twined among the initial letters. Here were the strangest groupings of birds, flowers, and twining lines. Close by, in the grass, stood a flock of peacocks with their shining starry trains outspread.

Yes, it was really so! But when the Prince touched them, he found they were not birds, but plants; they were great burdocks, which shone like the peacock's gorgeous train. The lion and the tiger sprang to and fro like agile cats among the green bushes, which were fragrant as the blossom of the olive tree; and the lion and the tiger were tame. The wild wood pigeon shone like the most beautiful pearl, and beat her wings against the lion's mane; and the antelope, usually so timid, stood by nodding its head, as if it wished to play too.

Now came the Fairy of Paradise. Her garment shone like the sun, and her countenance was as cheerful as that of a happy mother when she is well pleased with her child. She was young and beautiful, and was followed by a number of pretty maidens, each with a gleaming star in her hair. The East Wind gave her the written leaf from the Phœnix bird, and her eyes shone with pleasure.

She took the Prince by the hand and led him into her palace, where the walls had the color of a splendid tulip leaf when it is held up in the sunlight. The ceiling was a great sparkling flower, and the more one looked up at it, the deeper its cup appeared. The Prince stepped to the window and looked through one of the panes. Here he saw the Tree of Knowledge, with the serpent, and Adam and Eve were standing close by.

"Were they not driven out?" he asked.

And the Fairy smiled, and explained to him that Time had

burned in the picture upon that pane, but not as people are accustomed to seeing pictures. No, there was life in it. The leaves of the trees moved; men came and went as in a dissolving view. And he looked through another pane, and there was Jacob's dream, with the ladder reaching up into Heaven, and the angels with great wings were ascending and descending. Yes, everything that had happened in the world lived and moved in the glass panes. Only Time could burn in such cunning pictures.

The Fairy smiled, and led him into a great lofty hall, whose walls appeared transparent. Here there were portraits, and each face looked fairer than the last. They were millions of blessed spirits who smiled and sang, and it flowed together into a melody; the uppermost were so small that they looked like the smallest rosebud when it is drawn as a point upon paper. And in the middle of the hall stood a great tree with rich pendant boughs. Golden apples, great and small, hung like oranges among the leaves. That was the Tree of Knowledge, of whose fruit Adam and Eve had eaten. From each leaf a shining red dewdrop fell, and it was as though the tree wept tears of blood.

"Let us get into the boat," said the Fairy. "We will find it so refreshing. The boat rocks without moving from its place, and all the lands of the earth will appear to glide past us."

And it was wonderful to behold how the whole coast moved. First came the lofty snow-covered Alps, with clouds and black pine trees; the horn sounded its melancholy note, and the shepherd trolled his merry song in the valley. Then the banana trees bent their long hanging branches over the boat; coal-black swans swam on the water, and the strangest animals and flowers showed themselves upon the shore. That was New Holland, the fifth great division of the world. It glided past with a background of blue hills. They heard the song of the priests, and saw the savages dancing to the sound of drums and bone trumpets. Egypt's pyramids, towering aloft to the clouds, overturned pillars and sphinxes, half buried in the sand—all sailed past. The Northern Lights shone over the extinct volcanoes of the Pole—they were fireworks that no one could imitate. The Prince was so happy! He saw a hundred times more than we can relate here.

"And may I always stay here?" asked he.

"That depends upon yourself," answered the Fairy. "If you do not, like Adam, yield to the temptation to do what is forbidden, you may always remain here."

"I shall not touch the apples on the Tree of Knowledge!" said the Prince. "There are thousands of fruits here just as beautiful as those."

"Search your own heart, and if you are not strong enough, go away with the East Wind who brought you. He is going to fly back, and will not show himself here again for a hundred years. Time will pass for you in this place as if it were only a hundred hours. But it is a long time for the temptation of sin. Every evening, when I leave you, I shall have to call to you, 'Come with me!' and I shall have to beckon to you with my hand. But stay where you are. Do not go with me, or your longing will become greater with every step. You will then come into the hall where the Tree of Knowledge grows. I sleep under its fragrant pendant boughs. You will bend over me, and I must smile; but if you press a kiss upon my mouth, the Paradise will sink deep into the earth and be lost to you. The keen wind of the desert will rush around you, the cold rain drop upon your head, and sorrow and woe will be your portion."

"I shall stay here!" said the Prince.

And the East Wind kissed him on the forehead, and said:

"Be strong, and we shall meet here again in a hundred years. Farewell! farewell!"

And the East Wind spread out his broad wings, and they

flashed like sheet lightning in harvesttime, or like the Northern Lights in cold winter.

"Farewell! farewell!" sounded the flowers and the trees. Storks and pelicans flew away in rows like fluttering ribbons, and bore him company to the boundary of the garden.

"Now we will begin our dances!" cried the Fairy. "At the end, when the sun goes down, I will dance with you. You will see me beckon to you. You will hear me call to you, 'Come with me'; but do not obey. For a hundred years I must repeat this every evening. Every time, when the trial is over, you will gain more strength. At last you will not think of it at all. This evening is the first time. Now I have warned you."

And the Fairy led him into a great hall of white transparent lilies. The yellow stamens in each flower formed a little golden harp, which sounded like a stringed instrument and flute. The most beautiful maidens, floating and slender, clad in gauzy mist, glided by in the dance, and sang of the happiness of living. They declared that they would never die, and that the Garden of Paradise would bloom for ever.

And the sun went down, and the whole sky shone like gold, giving the lilies the hue of the most glorious roses; and the Prince drank of the foaming wine which the maidens poured out for him, and felt a happiness he had never known before. He saw how the background of the hall opened, and the Tree of Knowledge stood in a glory that blinded his eyes. The singing there was as soft and lovely as the voice of his dear mother, and it was as though she sang, "My child! my beloved child!"

Then the Fairy beckoned to him, and called out persuasively:

"Come with me! Come with me!"

He rushed toward her, forgetting his promise, forgetting it on the very first evening. And still she beckoned and smiled. The fragrance, the delicious fragrance around him became stronger, the harps sounded far more lovely, and it seemed as though the millions of smiling heads in the hall, where the tree grew, nodded and sang, "One must know everything— man is the lord of the earth." And they were no longer drops of blood that the Tree of Knowledge wept. They were red shining stars which he seemed to see.

"Come! come!" the quivering voice still cried, and at every step the Prince's cheeks burned more hotly and his blood flowed more rapidly.

"I must!" said he. "It is no sin, it cannot be one. Why not follow beauty and joy? I only want to see her asleep. There will be nothing lost if I don't kiss her. And I will not kiss her; I am strong and have a resolute will!"

The Fairy threw off her shining cloak and bent back the branches, and in another moment she was hidden among them.

"I have not yet sinned," said the Prince, "and I will not."

And he pushed the boughs aside. There she slept already, beautiful as only a fairy in the Garden of Paradise can be. She smiled in her dreams, and he bent over her, and saw tears quivering beneath her eyelids!

"Do you weep for me?" he whispered. "Weep not, thou glorious woman! Now I understand the bliss of Paradise! It streams through my blood, through my thoughts; I feel the power of the angel and of increasing life in my mortal body! Let what will happen to me now. One moment like this is wealth enough!"

And he kissed the tears from her eyes—his mouth touched hers.

Then there resounded a clap of thunder so loud and dreadful that no one had ever heard the like. And everything was wild confusion. The beautiful Fairy and the blooming Paradise sank down, deeper and deeper. The Prince saw it vanish into the black night; like a little bright star it gleamed out of the far distance. A deadly chill ran through his frame, and he closed his eyes and lay for a long time, apparently dead.

The cold rain fell upon his face, the keen wind roared round his head, and then his senses returned to him.

"What have I done?" he sighed. "I have sinned like Adam —sinned so that Paradise has sunk low beneath the earth!"

And he opened his eyes, and he saw a star in the distance— the star that gleamed like the Paradise that had fallen. It was the morning star in heaven.

He stood up, and found himself in the great forest, near the Cave of the Winds. And the mother of the Winds sat by his side. She looked angry, and raised her arm in the air.

"The very first evening!" said she. "I thought it would be so! Yes, if you were my son, you would have to go into the sack!"

"Yes, he shall go in there!" said Death. He was a strong old man, with a scythe in his hand, and with great black wings. "Yes, he shall be laid in his coffin, but not yet. I shall only register him now, and let him wander awhile in the world to expiate his sins. He may improve. He may get better. But one day I shall come. When he least expects it, I shall clap him in the black coffin, put him on my head, and fly up toward the star. The Garden of Paradise blooms there too. And if he is good and pious he will go in. But if his thoughts are evil, and his heart still full of sin, he will sink with his coffin deeper than Paradise sank. And once every thousandth year I shall fetch him, so that he may sink deeper, or reach for the star—the shining star up yonder!"

THE TOAD

THE well was deep, and so the rope was long, and the wheel went heavily round, before one could hoist the bucket over the side of the well. The sun could not see its face in the water, no matter how brightly it shone. But as far down as it could shine there were green weeds growing between the stones.

A family of the toad race dwelt here. They were emigrants. Indeed, they had all come plump down in the person of the old toad mother, who was still alive. The green frogs who swam in the water had been at home here ever so much longer, but they acknowledged their cousins, and called them the "well guests." The latter, however, had no thoughts of ever flitting. They made themselves very comfortable here on the dry land, as they called the wet stones.

Dame Toad had once traveled, riding in the bucket as it went up; but the light was too much for her, and gave her a spasm in the eyes. Luckily she got out of the bucket. She fell with a frightful splash in the water, and was laid up for three days with a backache. She didn't have much to tell about the upper world, but one thing she did know, and so did all the others now—that the well was not the whole world. Dame Toad might have told them a thing or two more, but since she never answered any questions, they stopped asking.

"Nasty, ugly, squat, and fat she is!" said the young green frogs. "And her brats are getting just like her."

"Maybe so!" said Dame Toad, "but one of them has a jewel in its head, or else I have it myself."

The green frogs listened and stared and, as they did not

like hearing this, they made faces and went to the bottom. But the young toads stretched their hind legs out of sheer pride. Each of them thought it had the jewel, and so they all kept their heads quite still. At last they grew curious and began to ask what sort of a thing they had to be proud of, and what was a jewel exactly.

"It is something so splendid and so precious," said Dame Toad, "that I cannot describe it. It is something that one wears to please one's self, and that others fret to death after. But don't ask any more questions; I shan't answer them."

"Well, I have not got the jewel," said the smallest toad, who was as ugly as ugly could be. "How could I have anything so splendid? And if it vexes others, why, how can it please me? No; all I want is to get up to the well side, and have one peep out. That would be glorious!"

"Better stay where you are," said the old one. "Here you are at home, and you know what it's like. Keep clear of the bucket, or it may squash you. And even if you get safely into it, you may fall out again, and it is not every one that can fall so luckily as I did, and keep legs and eggs all safe and sound."

"Quack!" said the little one, which has the same meaning as when we men say "Alack!"

It did so long to get up to the well side, and look out. It felt quite a yearning for the green things up yonder. And so, next morning, as the bucket was going up, it happened to stop for an instant by the stone where the toad sat, and the little creature quivered through and through, and edged into the bucket. It sank to the bottom of the water, which was presently drawn up and poured out.

"Phuh, botheration!" said the man, when he saw it. "It is the ugliest I have ever seen." He kicked with his wooden shoe at the toad, which was close to being crippled, but managed to escape into the middle of some tall stinging nettles. It saw stalks side by side around it. And it looked upward too. The sun shone on the leaves; they were quite transparent. For the toad it was the same as it is for us men when we come all at once into a great forest, where the sun is shining between leaves and branches.

"It is much prettier here than down in the well! One might well stop here for a whole lifetime," said the little toad. It lay there one hour; it lay there two. "Now, I wonder what there is outside. Since I have gone so far, I may as well go farther." And it crawled as fast as it could crawl, till it came out into the full sunshine, and got powdered with dust as it marched across a high road.

"This is something like being on dry land," said the toad. "I am getting almost too much of a good thing. It tickles right into me."

Now it came to a ditch; the forget-me-not grew here, and the meadow-sweet; beyond it was a hedge of whitethorn and elder bushes, and the convolvulus crept and hung about. There were fine colors to be seen! And yonder flew a butterfly. The toad thought that it was a flower which had broken loose, in order to look about in the world. It really seemed very natural.

"If one could only get along like that!" said the toad. "Quack—alack. Oh, how glorious!"

For eight days and nights it lingered by the ditch, and felt no need of food. The ninth day it thought, "Farther—forward!" But was there anything more beautiful to be found then? perhaps a little toad, or some green frogs. There had been a sound in the wind last night, as if there were "cousins" in the neighborhood.

"It is a fine thing to live! To come up out of the well; to lie in stinging nettles; to creep along a dusty road; and to rest in a wet ditch! But forward still! Let us find frogs or a little toad. One cannot do without them, after all. Nature, by itself, is not enough for me!" And so the little toad set out again on its wanderings.

It came to a field and a large pond, with rushes round it; it took a look inside.

"It is too wet for you here, isn't it?" said the frogs. "But you are quite welcome. Are you a he or a she?—not that it matters, you are welcome all the same."

And so it was invited to a concert in the evening—a family concert, great excitement and thin voices! We all know that sort of thing. There were no refreshments, except drink. But that was free to all—the whole pond, if they pleased.

"Now I shall travel farther," said the little toad. It was always craving after something better.

It saw the stars twinkle, so large and so clear. It saw the new moon shine. It saw the sun rise higher and higher.

"I think I am still in the well, in a larger well. I must get higher up! I feel a restlessness, a longing!" And when the moon had grown full and round, the poor creature thought, "Can *that* be the bucket which is being let down, and which I must pop into if I wish to get higher up? Or is the sun the great bucket? How great it is and how beaming! It could hold all of us together. I must watch for my opportunity. What a brightness in my head! I do not believe that the jewel could shine any better. The jewel! I don't have it, and shall not cry after it. No; higher still in glitter and gladness! I feel an assurance, and yet a fear. It is a hard step to take, but it must be taken. Forward! Right on along the highroad!"

And it stepped out as well as such a crawling creature can, till it came to the great thoroughfare, where the men lived. Here there were flower gardens and cabbage gardens. It turned aside to rest in a cabbage garden.

"What a number of different beings there are, which I

know nothing about! And how great and blessed is the world! One must keep looking about one, instead of sitting always in the same corner." And so the toad sidled on into the cabbage garden. "How green it is here! How pretty it is here!"

"That I know well enough," said the caterpillar, on the leaf. "My leaf is the largest here. It covers half the world—but as for the world, I can do without it."

"Cluck! cluck!" said somebody, and fowls came tripping into the cabbage garden. The first hen was farsighted; she spied the worm on the curly leaf, and pecked at it, so that it fell to the ground, where it lay twisting and turning. The hen looked first with one eye and then with the other, for she could not make out what the end of all this wriggling was to be.

"It does not do this of its own accord," thought the hen, and lifted her head for a finishing stroke. The toad grew so frightened, that it crawled right up against the hen.

"So it has friends to fight for it," said she. "Just look at the crawler!" and the hen turned tail. "I shan't trouble myself about the little green mouthful; it only gives one a tickling in the throat." The other fowls were of the same opinion, and away they went.

"I have wriggled away from her," said the caterpillar. "It is good to have presence of mind, but the hardest task remains, to get back up on my cabbage leaf. Where is it?"

And the little toad came forward and expressed its sympathies. It was glad of its own ugliness, and that it had frightened away the hen.

"What do you mean by that?" asked the caterpillar. "I got rid of her myself, I tell you. You are very unpleasant to look at! Mayn't I be allowed to get back on my own? Now I smell cabbage. Now I am near my leaf. There is nothing so beautiful as what is one's own. I must go higher up still."

"Yes, higher up!" said the little toad, "higher up! It feels just like I feel. But it is not in good humor today; that comes of the fright. We all wish to get higher up." And the toad looked up as high as it could.

The stork sat in his nest on the farmer's roof; he clattered, and the stork mother clattered.

"How high they live," thought the toad. "Pity that one can't get up there!"

There were two young students lodging in the farmhouse; one of them was a poet, the other a naturalist. The one sang and wrote in gladness of all that God had created, even as its image was reflected in his heart. He sang it out short and clear, and rich in resounding verses. The other took hold of the thing itself; aye, and split it up, if necessary. He treated our Lord's creation like some vast piece of arithmetic; subtracted, multiplied, wished to know it outside and inside, to talk of it with reason; nothing but reason. But he talked of it in gladness too, and cleverly. They were good, glad-hearted men, both of them.

"Yonder sits a fine specimen of a toad," said the naturalist. "I must have it in spirits."

"You have two already," said the poet. "Let it sit in peace, and enjoy itself."

"But it is so beautifully ugly!" said the other.

"Yes, if we could find the jewel in its head," said the poet, "then I myself might lend a hand in splitting it up."

"The jewel!" said the other. "Much you know about natural history!"

"But is there not something very fine, at least, in the popular belief that the toad, the ugliest of creatures, often hides in its head the most precious of all jewels? Is it not the same with men? Was there not such a jewel hidden in Æsop, and Socrates too?"

The toad heard nothing more; and it couldn't even understand half of what it had heard. The two friends went on talking, and the toad escaped being put into spirits.

"They were talking about the jewel, too," said the toad. "I am just as well off without it; otherwise I should have been in trouble."

There was a clattering upon the farmer's roof. Father Stork was delivering a lecture to his family, while they all looked down askance at the two young men in the cabbage garden.

"Man is the most conceited of creatures," said the stork. "Hark, how they are going on—clatter, clatter—and yet they cannot rattle off a regular tattoo. They puff themselves up with notions of their eloquence—their language. A rare language indeed; it shifts from one jabber to another, at every day's journey. We can talk our language the whole world over, whether in Denmark or in Egypt. As for flying, they can't manage it at all. They push along by means of a contrivance which they call a 'railway,' but there they often get their necks broken. It gives me the shivers in my bill when I think of it. The world can exist without men. What good are they to us? All we want are frogs and earthworms."

"That was a grand speech now," thought the little toad. "What a great man he is, and how high he sits. Higher than I have ever seen any one before; and how well he can swim," it exclaimed, as the stork took flight through the air with outstretched wings.

And Mother Stork talked in the nest. She told of the land of Egypt, of the water of the Nile, and of the first-rate mud that was to be found in foreign parts. It sounded fresh and charming to the ears of the little toad.

"I must go to Egypt," it said. "Oh, if the stork would only give me a lift; or one of the young ones might take me. I would do the youngster some service in my turn, on his wedding day. I am sure I shall get to Egypt, for I am so lucky; and all the longing and the yearning which I feel; surely, this is better than having a jewel in one's head."

But the toad had it—the true jewel; the eternal longing and yearning to go upward, ever upward. This was the jewel, and it shone within it, shone with gladness and beamed with desire.

At that very moment the stork came. He had seen the toad in the grass, and he swooped down and took hold of the little creature, not very tenderly. The bill pinched; the wind whistled; it was not very comfortable. But still it was going upward, and away to Egypt, it knew. And that was why its eyes glittered, till it seemed as if a spark flew out of them.

"Quack—ack!"

The body was dead, the toad was killed. And the spark from its eyes, what became of *that?*

The sunbeam took it; the sunbeam bore away the jewel from the head of the toad. Whither?

You must not ask the naturalist; instead ask the poet. He will tell it to you as a fairy tale. And the caterpillar will take a part in it, and the stork family will take a part too. Think, the caterpillar will be changed, and become a beautiful butterfly! The stork family will fly over mountains and seas far away to Africa, and yet find the shortest way home again to the Danish land, to the same spot, to the same roof! Yes, it is all nearly too much like a fairy tale—and yet it is true. You may fairly ask the naturalist about the truth of it. He will admit *that*, and, indeed, you know it yourself, for you have seen it.

But the jewel in the toad's head? Look for it in the sun! Look *at* it if you can.

The splendor is too strong. We haven't eyes yet that can look into all the glories which God hath revealed. But someday we shall have them, and that will be the most beautiful fairy tale of all, for we ourselves shall take a part in it.

THE OLD STREET LAMP

Did you ever hear the story of the old Street Lamp? It is not very remarkable, but it may be listened to once in a while.

It was a very honest old Lamp, that had done its work for many, many years, but it was now to be pensioned off. It hung for the last time on its post, and gave light to the street. It felt as an old dancer at the theater, who is dancing for the last time, and who tomorrow will sit forgotten in her garret. The Lamp was in great fear about the morrow, for it knew that it was to appear in the council house, and to be inspected by the mayor and the council, to see if it were fit for further service or not.

And then it was to be decided whether in the future it was to show its light for the inhabitants of some suburb, or in the country in some factory. Perhaps it would have to go at once into an iron foundry to be melted down. In this last case anything might be made of it. But the question whether it would remember, in its new state, that it had been a Street Lamp, troubled it terribly. Whatever might happen, this much was certain, that it would be separated from the watchman and his wife, whom it had come to look upon as part of its family.

When the Lamp had been hung up for the first time the watchman was a young, sturdy man: it happened to be the very evening on which he entered his office. Yes, that was certainly a long time ago, when it first became a Lamp and he a watchman. The wife was a little proud in those days. Only in the evening, when she went by, did she bother to glance at the Lamp; in the daytime never. But now, in these latter years, when all three, the watchman, his wife, and the

Lamp, had grown old, the wife had also tended it, cleaned it, and provided it with oil. The two old people were thoroughly honest; never had they cheated the Lamp of a single drop of the oil provided for it.

It was the Lamp's last night in the street, and tomorrow it was to go to the council house—those were two dark thoughts! No wonder it did not burn brightly. But many other thoughts passed through its brain. What a number of events it had shone on—how much it had seen! Perhaps as much as the mayor and the whole council had beheld. But it did not give utterance to these thoughts, for it was a good honest old Lamp, that would not willingly hurt anyone, least of all those in authority. Many things passed through its mind, and at times its light flashed up. In such moments it had a feeling that it, too, would be remembered.

"There was that handsome young man—it is certainly a long while ago—he had a letter on pink paper with a gilt edge. It was so prettily written, as if by a lady's hand. Twice he read it, and kissed it, and looked up to me with eyes which said plainly, 'I am the happiest of men!' Only he and I know what was written in this first letter from his true love. Yes, I remember another pair of eyes. It is wonderful how our thoughts fly about! There was a funeral procession in the street. The young beautiful lady lay in the decorated hearse, in a coffin adorned with flowers and wreaths. And a number of torches darkened my light. The people stood in crowds by the houses, and all followed the procession. But when the torches had passed from before my face, and I looked round, a single person stood leaning against my post, weeping. I shall never forget the mournful eyes that looked up to me!"

These and similar thoughts occupied the old Street Lantern, as it shone tonight for the last time.

The sentry relieved from his post, at least knows who is to succeed him, and may whisper a few words to him; but the

Lamp did not know its successor. And yet it might have given a few useful hints with respect to rain and fog, and some information as to how far the rays of the moon lit up the pavement, and from what direction the wind usually came, and much more of the same.

On the bridge of the gutter stood three persons who wished to introduce themselves to the Lamp, for they thought the Lamp itself should appoint its successor. The first was a herring's head, that could gleam with light in the darkness. He thought it would be a great saving of oil if they put him up on the post. Number two was a piece of rotten wood, which also glimmered in the dark. He thought himself descended from an old stem, once the pride of the forest. The third person was a glowworm. Where this one had come from the Lamp could not imagine; but there it was, and it could give light. But the rotten wood and the herring's head swore by all that was good that it gave light only at certain times, and could not be brought into competition with themselves.

The old Lamp declared that not one of them gave sufficient light to fill the office of a street lamp; but not one of them would believe this. When they heard that the Lamp didn't have the authority to give the office away, they were very glad of it, and declared that the Lamp was too decrepit to make a good choice anyway.

At the same moment the Wind came careening around the corner of the street, and blew through the air holes of the old Street Lamp.

"What's this I hear?" he asked. "Are you to go away tomorrow? Do I see you for the last time? Then I must make you a present in parting. I will blow into your brainbox in such a way that you shall be able in the future not only to remember everything you have seen and heard, but you shall have a light within you to enable you to see all that is read or spoken in your presence."

"Yes, that is really much, very much!" said the old Lamp. "I thank you heartily. I only hope I shall not be melted down."

"That is not likely to happen at once," said the Wind. "Now I will blow a memory into you. If you receive several presents of this kind, you may pass your old days very agreeably."

"If I am only not melted down!" said the Lamp again. "Or shall I retain my memory even in that case?"

"Be sensible, old Lamp," said the Wind. And he blew, and at that moment the Moon stepped forth from behind the clouds.

"What will you give the old Lamp?" asked the Wind.

"I'll give nothing," replied the Moon. "I am on the wane. The lamps never lighted me; but, on the contrary, I've often given light for the lamps."

And with these words the Moon hid herself again behind the clouds, to be safe from further importunity.

A drop now fell upon the Lamp, as if from the roof; but the drop explained that it came from the clouds, and was a present—perhaps the best present possible.

"I shall penetrate you so completely that you shall, if you wish, receive the faculty to turn into rust in one night, and crumble into dust."

The Lamp considered this a bad present, and the Wind thought so too.

"Does no one give more? Does no one give more?" The Wind blew as loud as he could.

Then a bright shooting star fell down, forming a long bright stripe.

"What was that?" cried the herring's head. "Didn't a star fall? I really think it went into the Lamp! Certainly if such high-born personages try for this office, we may say good night and go home."

And so they did, all three. But the old Lamp shed a marvelous strong light around.

"That was a glorious present," it said. "The bright stars which I have always admired, and which shine as I could never shine though I shone with all my might, have noticed me, a poor old lamp, and have sent me a present. They give me the faculty that all I remember and see as clearly as if it stood before me shall also be seen by all whom I love. And in this lies the true pleasure; for joy that we cannot share with others is only half enjoyed."

"That sentiment does honor to your heart," said the Wind. "But for that wax lights are necessary. If these are not lit up in you, your rare faculties will be of no use to others. Look you, the stars did not think of that. They take you and every other light for wax. But I will go down." And he went down.

"Good heavens! wax lights!" exclaimed the Lamp. "I never had those till now, nor am I likely to get them! If I am only not melted down!"

The next day—yes, it will be best that we pass over the next day. The next evening the Lamp was resting in a grandfather's chair. And guess where! In the watchman's dwelling. He had begged as a favor of the mayor and the council that he might keep the Street Lamp, in consideration of his long and faithful service, for he himself had put up and lit the lantern for the first time on the first day of entering his duties four and twenty years ago. He looked upon it as his child, for he had no other. And the Lamp was given to him.

Now it lay in the great armchair by the warm stove. It seemed as if the Lamp had grown bigger, now that it occupied the chair all alone.

The old people sat at supper, and looked kindly at the old Lamp, to whom they would willingly have granted a place at their table.

Their dwelling was certainly only a cellar two yards below the footpath, and one had to cross a stone passage to get into the room. But within, it was very comfortable and warm, and strips of list had been nailed to the door. Everything looked clean and neat, and there were curtains round the bed and the little windows. On the windowsill stood two curious flower-pots, which sailor Christian had brought home from the East or West Indies. They were only of clay, and represented two elephants. The backs of these creatures had been cut off; and instead of them there bloomed from within the earth with which one elephant was filled, some very excellent chives, and that was the kitchen garden. Out of the other grew a great geranium, and that was the flower garden. On the wall hung a great colored print representing the Congress of Vienna. There you had all the Kings and Emperors at once. A clock with heavy weights went "tick! tick!" and in fact it always went too fast. But the old people declared this was far better than if it went too slow.

They ate their supper, and the Street Lamp lay, as I have said, in the armchair close beside the stove. It seemed to the Lamp as if the whole world had been turned round. But when the old watchman looked at it, and spoke of all that they two had gone through in rain and in fog, in the bright short nights of summer and in the long winter nights, when the snow beat down, and when one longed to be at home in the cellar, then the old Lamp found its wits again. It saw everything as clearly as if it was happening then. Yes, the Wind had kindled an excellent light inside it.

The old people were very active and industrious. Not a single hour was wasted in idleness. On Sunday afternoon some book or other was brought out; generally a book of travels. And the old man read aloud about Africa, about the great woods, with elephants running about wild. The old woman listened intently, and looked furtively at the clay elephants which served for flowerpots.

"I can almost imagine it to myself!" said she.

And the Lamp wished particularly that a wax candle had

been there, and could be lighted up in it. For then the old woman would be able to see everything in the smallest detail, just as the Lamp saw it—the tall trees with great branches all entwined, the naked black men on horseback, and whole droves of elephants crashing through the reeds with their broad clumsy feet.

"Of what use are all my faculties if I can't obtain a wax light?" sighed the Lamp. "They have only oil and tallow candles, and that's not enough."

One day a great number of wax candle ends came down into the cellar. The larger pieces were burned, and the smaller ones the old woman used for waxing her thread. So there were wax candles enough; but no one thought of putting a little piece into the Lamp.

"Here I stand with my rare faculties!" thought the Lamp. "I carry everything within me, and cannot let them partake of it. They don't know that I am able to cover these white walls with the most gorgeous tapestry, to change them into noble forests, and all that they can possibly wish."

The Lamp was kept neat and clean, and stood all shining in a corner, where it caught the eyes of all. Strangers considered it a bit of old rubbish; but the old people did not care for that. They loved the Lamp.

One day—it was the old watchman's birthday—the old woman approached the Lamp, smiling to herself, and said—

"I'll make an illumination today, in honor of my old man!"

And the Lamp rattled its metal cover, for it thought, "Well, at last there will be a light within me." But only oil was produced, and no wax light appeared. The Lamp burned throughout the whole evening, but now understood, only too well, that the gift of the stars would be a hidden treasure for all its life. Then it had a dream. For one possessing its rare faculties dreaming was not difficult. It seemed as if the old people were dead, and that it had been taken to the iron foundry to be melted down. It felt as much alarmed as on that day when it was to appear in the council house to be inspected by the mayor and council. But though the power had been given to it to fall into rust and dust at will, it did not use this power. It was put into the furnace, and turned into an iron candlestick, as fair a candlestick as you would desire—one on which wax lights were to be burned. It had received the form of an angel holding a great nosegay; and the wax light was to be placed in the middle of the nosegay.

The candlestick had a place assigned to it on a green writing table. The room was very comfortable. Many books stood round about the walls, which were hung with beautiful pictures. It belonged to a poet. Everything that he wrote or composed showed itself round about him. Nature appeared sometimes in thick dark forests, sometimes in beautiful meadows, where the storks strutted about; sometimes again in a ship sailing on the foaming ocean, or in the blue sky with all its stars.

"What faculties lie hidden in me!" said the old Lamp, when it awoke. "I could almost wish to be melted down! But, no! that must not be so as long as the old people live. They love me for myself; they have cleaned me and brought me oil. I am as well off now as the whole Congress, in looking at which they also take pleasure."

And from that time it enjoyed more inward peace. And the honest old Street Lamp had well deserved to enjoy it.

THE SWANS' NEST

BETWEEN the Baltic and the North Sea lies an old Swans' Nest
—it is called Denmark. In it have been born, and will be born
hereafter, Swans whose names shall never die.

In the olden time, a flock of Swans flew over the Alps to
Milan's lovely green plains. There they lighted down and
dwelt, for it was right pleasant to dwell there. These Swans
were called Lombards.

Another flock, with bright shining plumage, and clear,
truthful eyes, lighted down at Byzantium, nestled round the
Emperor's throne, and spread out their broad white wings as
shields to protect him. These were known as Varangians.

From the coasts of France a cry of anguish and terror arose
—terror at the bloody Swans who, with fire under their wings,
flew thither from the North. Loud was the prayer of village
and town, "God save us from the wild Normans!"

On England's fresh meadow turf, near the shore, wearing a
triple crown on his kingly head, his golden scepter stretching
far over the land, stood the royal Swan, Canute the Dane.

And on Pomerania's shores the heathens bowed the knee,
for there, too, with drawn swords, and bearing the standard
of the cross, the Danish Swans had flown.

"But this was in the days of old."

In times nearer our own, mighty Swans have been seen to
fly out from the Nest. A flash of lightning cleft the air—lightning that shone over all Europe—for a Swan had flapped his
strong wings and scattered the twilight mist, and the starry
heavens became more visible—were brought, as it were, nearer
the earth. The Swan's name was Tycho Brahe.

"Yes, just that once," it will be granted. "But now, in our own generation?" they ask.

Well, in our own generation we have beheld Swans soaring in a high and glorious flight.

One we saw gently sweep his wings over the golden chords of the harp, whereupon sweet music thrilled through the northern lands. The wild Norwegian mountains lifted their proud crests higher in the full sunlight of the olden time, pine and birch bowed their heads and rustled their leaves, the "Gods of the North"—the heroes and noble women of Scandinavian history—lived and breathed again, their tall, stately figures standing out from the dark background of deep forests.

We saw a second Swan strike his pinions upon the hard marble rock till it cleft asunder, and new forms of beauty, hitherto shut up in the stone, were revealed to the light of day. And the nations of Europe gazed in wonder and admiration at the glorious statuary.

A third Swan we have seen weaving threads of thoughts that spun and spread around the earth, so that words flew with lightning speed from land to land.

Dear to the protecting heavens above is the old Swans' Nest between the Baltic and the North Sea. Let mighty birds of prey, if they will, speed there to tear it down. It shall not be! Even the unfledged, unplumed young ones will press forward to the margin of the Nest—we have seen it—they will fight desperately with beak and claw, will offer their bleeding breast in defense of their home.

Centuries will pass away, and Swans will still fly forth from the Nest, and make themselves seen and heard far over the world. Long will it be before the time shall come when in sad truth it may be said, "Behold the last Swan! Listen to the last sweet song from the Swans' Nest!"

THE SNOW MAN

"I⊤ is so wonderfully cold that my whole body crackles!" said the Snow Man. "This is a kind of wind that can blow life into one; and how the gleaming one up yonder is staring at me." That was the sun he meant, which was just about to set. "It shall not make *me* wink—I shall manage to keep my pieces."

He had two triangular pieces of tile in his head instead of eyes. His mouth was made of an old rake, and consequently was furnished with teeth.

He had been born amid the joyous shouts of the boys, and welcomed by the sound of sleigh bells and the slashing of whips.

The sun went down, and the full moon rose, round, large, clear, and beautiful in the blue air.

"There it comes again from the other side," said the Snow Man. He intended to say the sun is showing himself again. "Ah! I have cured him of staring. Now let him hang up there and shine, that I may see myself. If I only knew how I could manage to move from this place. I should like so much to move. If I could, I would slide along on the ice, just as I see the boys slide. But I don't understand it; I don't know how to run."

"Away! away!" barked the old Yard Dog. He was quite hoarse, and could not pronounce a genuine "bow, wow." He had got the hoarseness from the time when he was an indoor dog, and lay by the fire. "The sun will teach you to run! I saw that last winter in your predecessor, and before that in *his* predecessor. Away! away! and away they all go."

"I don't understand you, comrade," said the Snow Man.

"That thing up yonder is to teach me to run?" He meant the moon. "Yes, it was running itself, when I saw it a little while ago, and now it comes creeping from the other side."

"You know nothing at all," retorted the Yard Dog. "But then you've only just been patched up. What you see up there is the moon, and the one that went before was the sun. It will come again tomorrow, and it will teach you to run down into the ditch by the wall. We shall soon have a change of weather. I can feel that in my left hind leg, for it pricks and pains me. The weather is going to change."

"I don't understand him," said the Snow Man. "But I have a feeling that he's talking about something disagreeable. The one who stared so just now, and whom he called the sun, is not my friend. I can feel that."

"Away! away!" barked the Yard Dog. And he turned round three times, and crept into his kennel to sleep.

The weather really changed. Toward morning a thick, damp fog lay over the whole region. Later there came a wind, an icy wind. The cold seemed to seize upon one; but when the sun rose, what splendor! Trees and bushes were covered with hoarfrost, and looked like a complete forest of coral, and every twig seemed covered with gleaming white buds. The many delicate ramifications, concealed in summer by the wreath of leaves, now made their appearance. It seemed like a lacework, gleaming white. A snowy radiance sprang from every twig. The birch waved in the wind—it had life, like the rest of the trees in summer. It was wonderfully beautiful. And when the sun shone, how it all gleamed and sparkled, as if diamond dust had been strewn everywhere, and big diamonds had been dropped on the snowy carpet of the earth! Or one could imagine that countless little lights were gleaming, whiter than the snow itself.

"That is wonderfully beautiful," said a young girl, who came with a young man into the garden. They both stood still near the Snow Man, and contemplated the glittering trees. "Summer cannot display a more beautiful sight," said she. And her eyes sparkled.

"And we can't have such a fellow as this in summertime," replied the young man, and he pointed to the Snow Man. "He is great."

The girl laughed, nodded to the Snow Man, and then danced away over the snow with her friend—over the snow that cracked and crackled under her tread as if she were walking on starch.

"Who were those two?" the Snow Man inquired of the Yard Dog. "You've been longer in the yard than I. Do you know them?"

"Of course I know them," replied the Yard Dog. "She has stroked me, and he has thrown me a meat bone. I don't bite those two."

"But what are they?" asked the Snow Man.

"Lovers!" replied the Yard Dog. "They will go to live in the same kennel, and gnaw at the same bone. Away! away!"

"Are they the same kind of beings as you and I?" asked the Snow Man.

"Why, they belong to the master," retorted the Yard Dog. "People certainly know very little who were only born yesterday. I can see that in you. I have age and information. I know everyone here in the house, and I know a time when I did not lie out here in the cold, fastened to a chain. Away! away!"

"The cold is charming," said the Snow Man. "Tell me, tell me. But you must not clank with your chain, for it jars within me when you do that."

"Away! away!" barked the Yard Dog. "They told me I was a pretty little fellow then. I used to lie in a chair covered with velvet, up in Master's house, and sit in the lap of the mistress. They used to kiss my nose, and wipe my paws with an embroidered handkerchief. I was called 'Ami—dear Ami—sweet Ami.' But afterward I grew too big for them, and they gave me away to the housekeeper. So I came to live in the basement. You can look into that from where you are standing, and you can see into the room where I was master; for I was master at the housekeeper's. It was certainly a smaller place than upstairs, but I was more comfortable, and was not continually poked and pulled about by children as I had been. I received just as much good food as ever, and even better. I had my own cushion, and there was a stove, the finest thing in the world at this season. I went under the stove, and could lie down beneath it. Ah! I still sometimes dream of that stove. Away! away!"

"Does a stove look so beautiful?" asked the Snow Man. "Is it at all like me?"

"It's just the reverse of you. It's as black as a crow, and has a long neck and a brazen drum. It eats firewood, so that the fire spurts out of its mouth. One must keep at its side or under it, and there one is very comfortable. You can see it through the window from where you stand."

And the Snow Man looked and saw a bright, polished thing with a brazen drum, and the fire gleamed from the lower part of it. The Snow Man felt very strange. An odd emotion came over him; he didn't know what it meant, and could not account for it. But people who are not snow men know the feeling.

"And why did you leave her?" asked the Snow Man, for it seemed to him that the stove must be of the female sex. "How could you leave such a comfortable place?"

"I was obliged," replied the Yard Dog. "They turned me out of doors, and chained me up here. I had bitten the youngest young master in the leg, because he kicked away the bone I was gnawing. 'Bone for bone,' I thought. They took that very badly, and from that time I have been fastened to a

chain and have lost my voice. Don't you hear how hoarse I
am? Away! away! I can't talk any more like other dogs.
Away! away! that was the end of the affair."

But the Snow Man was no longer listening to him. He was
looking in at the housekeeper's basement lodging, into the
room where the stove stood on its four iron legs, just the
same size as the Snow Man himself.

"What a strange crackling within me!" he said. "Shall I
ever get in there? It is an innocent wish, and our innocent
wishes are certain to be fulfilled. I must go in there and lean
against her, even if I have to break through the window."

"You'll never get in there," said the Yard Dog. "And if
you approach the stove you'll melt away—away!"

"I am as good as gone," replied the Snow Man. "I think I
am breaking up."

The whole day the Snow Man stood looking in through
the window. In the twilight hour the room became still more
inviting. From the stove came a mild gleam, not like the sun
nor like the moon. No, it was only as a stove can glow when
she has something to eat. When the room door opened the
flame started out of her mouth; this was a habit the stove had.
The flame fell distinctly on the white face of the Snow Man,
and gleamed red upon his bosom.

"I can endure it no longer," said he. "How beautiful she
looks when she stretches out her tongue!"

The night was long; but it did not seem long to the Snow
Man, who stood there lost in his own charming reflections,
crackling with the cold.

In the morning the windowpanes of the basement lodging
were covered with ice. They bore the most beautiful ice
flowers that any snow man could desire; but they concealed
the stove. The windowpanes would not thaw. He could not
see the stove, which he pictured to himself as a lovely female.
It crackled and whistled in him and around him; it was just

the kind of frosty weather a snow man must thoroughly enjoy.

But he did not enjoy it. And, indeed, how could he enjoy himself when he was stove-sick?

"That's a terrible disease for a Snow Man," said the Yard Dog. "I have suffered from it myself, but I got over it. Away! away!" he barked; and he added, "the weather is going to change."

And the weather did change; it began to thaw. The warmth increased, and the Snow Man decreased. He made no complaint—and that's an infallible sign.

One morning he broke down. And, behold, where he had stood, something like a broomstick remained sticking up out of the ground. It was the pole around which the boys had built him up.

"Ah! now I can understand why he had such an intense longing," said the Yard Dog. "Why, there's the shovel for cleaning out the stove fastened to the pole. The Snow Man had a stove-rake in his body, and that's what moved within him. Now he has got over that, too. Away! away!"

And soon they got over the winter.

"Away! away!" barked the hoarse Yard Dog: but the girls in the house sang:

> *Green thyme! from your house come out;*
> *Willow, your woolly fingers stretch out;.*
> *Lark and cuckoo, cheerfully sing,*
> *For in February is coming the spring;*
> *And with the cuckoo I'll sing too,*
> *Come thou, dear sun, come out, cuckoo!*

And nobody thought any more of the Snow Man.

THE RED SHOES

THERE was once a little girl. She was a tiny, delicate, little thing, but she always had to go about barefoot in summer, because she was very poor. In winter she had only a pair of heavy wooden shoes, and her ankles were terribly chafed.

An old mother shoemaker lived in the middle of the village, and she made a pair of little shoes out of some strips of red cloth. They were very clumsy, but they were made with the best intention, for the little girl was to have them. Her name was Karen.

These shoes were given to her, and she wore them for the first time on the day her mother was buried. They were certainly not mourning-shoes, but she had no others, and so she walked barelegged in them behind the poor pine coffin.

Just then a big old carriage drove by, and a big old lady was seated in it. She looked at the little girl and felt very, very sorry for her, and said to the parson, "Give the little girl to me and I will look after her and be kind to her." Karen thought it was all because of the red shoes, but the old lady said they were hideous, and they were burned. Karen was well and neatly dressed, and had to learn reading and sewing. People said she was pretty, but her mirror said, "You are more than pretty. You are lovely!"

At this time the Queen was taking a journey through the country, and she had her little daughter the Princess with her. The people, and among them Karen, crowded round the palace where they were staying, to see them. The little Princess stood at a window to show herself. She wore neither a train nor a golden crown, but she was dressed all in white

"Away she danced, and away she had to dance, right away into the dark forest. Something shone up above the trees and she thought it was the moon, for it was a face, but it was the old soldier with the red beard." (Page 247)

with a beautiful pair of red morocco shoes. They were indeed a contrast to those the poor old mother shoemaker had made for Karen. Nothing in the world could be compared to these red shoes.

The time came when Karen was old enough to be confirmed. She had new clothes and she was also to have a pair of new shoes. The rich shoemaker in the town was to take the measure of her little foot. His shop was full of glass cases of the most charming shoes and shiny leather boots. They looked beautiful but the old lady could not see very well, so it gave her no pleasure to look at them. Among all the other shoes there was one pair of red shoes like those worn by the Princess. Oh, how pretty they were! The shoemaker told them that they had been made for an earl's daughter, but they had not fitted. "I suppose they are patent leather," said the old lady. "They are so shiny."

"Yes, they do shine," said Karen, who tried them on. They fitted and were bought, but the old lady had not the least idea that they were red, or she would never have allowed Karen to wear them for her confirmation. This she did, however.

Everybody looked at her feet, and when she walked up the church to the chancel she thought that even the old pictures, those portraits of dead and gone priests and their wives, with stiff collars and long black clothes, fixed their eyes upon her shoes. She thought of nothing else when the minister laid his hand upon her head and spoke to her of holy baptism, the covenant of God, and said that henceforth she was to be a responsible Christian person. The solemn notes of the organ resounded, the children sang with their sweet voices, and the old precentor sang, but Karen thought only about her red shoes.

By the afternoon the old lady had been told on all sides that the shoes were red, and she said it was very naughty and most improper. For the future, whenever Karen went to the church she was to wear black shoes, even if they were old. Next Sunday there was holy communion, and Karen was to receive it for the first time. She looked at the black shoes and then at the red ones. Then she looked again at the red—and at last put them on.

It was beautiful sunny weather. Karen and the old lady went by the path through the cornfield, and it was rather dusty. By the church door stood an old soldier with a crutch. He had a curious long beard; it was more red than white—in fact, it was almost red. He bent down to the ground and asked the old lady if he might dust her shoes. Karen put out her little foot too. "See what beautiful dancing shoes!" said the soldier. "Mind you stick fast when you dance." And as he spoke he struck the soles with his hand. The old lady gave the soldier a copper and went into the church with Karen. All the people in the church looked at Karen's red shoes, and all the portraits looked too. When Karen knelt at the altar rails and the chalice was put to her lips, she thought only of the red shoes. She seemed to see them floating before her eyes. She forgot to join in the hymn of praise, and she forgot to say the Lord's Prayer.

Now everybody left the church, and the old lady got into her carriage. Karen lifted her foot to get in after her, but just then the old soldier, who was still standing there, said, "See what pretty dancing shoes!" Karen couldn't help it: she took a few dancing steps and, when she began, her feet continued to dance. It was just as if the shoes had a power over them. She danced right round the church. She couldn't stop. The coachman had to run after her, take hold of her, and lift her into the carriage; but her feet continued to dance, so that she kicked the poor lady horribly. At last they got the shoes off, and her feet had a little rest.

When they got home the shoes were put away in a cupboard, but Karen could not help going to look at them.

The old lady became very ill. They said she could not live. She had to be carefully nursed and tended, and no one was nearer than Karen to do this. But there was to be a grand ball in the town and Karen was invited. She looked at the old lady, who after all could not live. Then she looked at the red shoes—she thought there was no harm in doing so. She put on the red shoes—that much she thought she might do—and then she went to the ball and began to dance. The shoes would not let her do what she liked: when she wanted to go to the right, they danced to the left. When she wanted to dance up the room, the shoes danced down the room, and then down the stairs, through the streets and out of the town gate. Away she danced, and away she had to dance, right away into the dark forest. Something shone up above the trees and she thought it was the moon, for it was a face, but it was the old soldier with the red beard. He nodded and said, "See what pretty dancing shoes!"

This frightened her terribly and she wanted to throw off the red shoes, but they stuck fast. She tore off her stockings, but the shoes had grown fast to her feet. So off she danced, and off she had to dance, over fields and meadows, in rain and sunshine, by day and by night, but at night it was fearful.

She danced into the open churchyard, but the dead did not join her dance; they had something much better to do. She wanted to sit down on a pauper's grave where the bitter worm-wood grew, but there was no rest nor repose for her. When she danced toward the open church door, she saw an angel standing there in long white robes and wings which reached from his shoulders to the ground. His face was grave and stern, and in his hand he held a broad and shining sword.

"Dance you shall!" said he. "You shall dance in your red shoes till you are pale and cold. Till your skin shrivels up and you are a skeleton! You shall dance from door to door, and wherever you find proud vain children, you must knock at the door so that they may see you and fear you. Yea, you shall dance—"

"Mercy!" shrieked Karen, but she did not hear the angel's answer, for the shoes bore her through the gate into the fields, and over roadways and paths. Ever and ever she was forced to dance.

One morning she danced past a door she knew well. She heard the sound of a hymn from within, and a coffin covered with flowers was being carried out. Then she knew that the old lady was dead, and it seemed to her that she was forsaken by all the world and cursed by the holy angels of God.

On and ever on she danced. Dance she must, even through the dark nights. The shoes bore her away over briars and stubble till her feet were torn and bleeding. She danced away over the heath till she came to a little lonely house. She knew the executioner lived here, and she tapped with her fingers on the windowpane and said, "Come out! Come out! I can't come in for I am dancing!"

The executioner said, "Don't you know who I am? I chop the bad people's heads off, and I see that my ax is quivering."

"Don't chop my head off," said Karen, "for then I can never repent of my sins. But pray, pray chop off my feet with the red shoes!"

Then she confessed all her sins and the executioner chopped off her feet with the red shoes, but the shoes danced right away with the little feet into the depths of the forest.

Then he made her a pair of wooden feet and crutches, and he taught her a psalm, the one penitents always sing. And she kissed the hand which had wielded the ax and went away over the heath.

"I have suffered enough for those red shoes!" said she. "I will go to church now, so that they may see me." And she went as fast as she could to the church door. When she got there, the red shoes danced right up in front of her, and she was frightened and went home again.

She was very sad all the week and shed many bitter tears, but when Sunday came she said, "Now then, I have suffered long enough. I should think I am quite as good as many who sit holding their heads so high in church."

She went along quite boldly, but she did not get farther than the gate before she saw the red shoes dancing in front of her. She was more frightened than ever and turned back, this time with real repentance in her heart. Then she went to the parson's house and begged to be taken into service. She would be very industrious and work as hard as she could. She didn't care what wages they gave her, if only she might have a roof over her head and live among kind people. The parson's wife was sorry for her, and took her into her service. She proved to be very industrious and thoughtful. She sat very still and listened most attentively in the evening when the parson read the Bible. All the little ones were very fond of her, but when they chattered about finery and dress and about being as beautiful as a queen, she would shake her head.

Next Sunday they all went to church and they asked her if she would go with them, but she looked sadly, with tears in her eyes, at her crutches. And they went without her to hear the word of God, while she sat in her little room alone. It was only big enough for a bed and a chair. She sat there with her prayer book in her hand, and as she read it with a humble mind she heard the notes of the organ, borne from the church by the wind. She raised her tear-stained face and said, "Oh, God, help me!"

Then the sun shone brightly round her, and the angel in the white robes whom she had seen that night at the church door stood before her. He no longer held the sharp sword in his hand, but a beautiful green branch covered with roses. He touched the ceiling with it and it rose to a great height, and wherever he touched it a golden star appeared. Then he touched the walls and they spread themselves out, and she saw and heard the organ. She saw the pictures of the old parsons and their wives. The congregation were all sitting in their seats singing aloud—for the church itself had come home to the poor girl in her narrow little chamber, or else she had been taken to it. She found herself on the bench with the other people from the parsonage. And when the hymn had come to an end, they looked up and nodded to her and said, "It was a good thing you came after all, little Karen!"

"It was through God's mercy!" she said. The organ sounded and the children's voices echoed so sweetly through the choir. The warm sunshine streamed brightly in through the window, right up to the bench where Karen sat. Her heart was so over-filled with the sunshine, with peace, and with joy, that it broke. Her soul flew with the sunshine to heaven, and no one there asked about the red shoes.

THE NECK OF A BOTTLE

IN a narrow, crooked street, among many shabby dwellings, stood one very narrow, very tall house. None but poor folk lived here, but poorest looking of all was the attic. Outside the little window, an old birdcage hung in the sunshine. It could not even boast of a proper bird glass. Instead it had the neck of a bottle, placed upside down, with a cork stopping up the mouth. At the open window stood an old maid. She had just been adorning the cage with chickweed. The little canary who lived a prisoner within it hopped from perch to perch, and sang with all his might.

"Ah! you may well sing!" said the broken bottle. Truly it could not speak aloud as we speak, but within it had its own thoughts for all that. "Ah! It is easy for you to sing!— you, with your limbs whole. You should just see how it feels to have lost one's lower half—to have only a neck and a mouth left, and a cork stuffed into one. I should like to hear you sing then! But it is well that somebody is pleased. I have no cause to sing, neither can I. But I could sing, once, when I was a whole bottle—I was called a lark then. Didn't I sing that day in the wood when the furrier's daughter was be- trothed? I remember it as though it had happened yesterday. I have lived through many things—I have been through fire and water—down in the black earth and higher up than most. And now I hover amid air and sunshine outside the cage. It might be worth while to listen to my history. But I am not going to proclaim it aloud, for one good reason—I can't!"

And so it told, or rather thought over, its own history to it- self in silence, and the little bird sang merrily all the while.

And the people down below drove, or rode, or walked through the street, each thinking of his own affairs, just as the broken bottle did.

It remembered the fiery furnace in the factory, where it had been blown into being. It remembered how warm it was at first—how it had looked into the wild furnace, the home of its birth, and longed to leap into it again. But then, little by little, as it cooled, it found itself well off where it was, standing in a row with a whole regiment of brothers and sisters, all born from the same furnace. But some were blown into champagne bottles, others into bottles for ale—and this makes a difference. Certainly, in the course of time and events, an ale flask may possibly embrace the costliest Lachryma Christi, and a champagne bottle may be basely filled with blacking; but what each was born for will still be apparent by the form of each. Not even blacking can efface that patent of nobility.

All the bottles were soon packed up and off, our bottle among them. Little did it know at the time that it would end up serving as a bird glass. No matter, it is an honorable life and is thus useful to the last. It first saw daylight again, after it had been unpacked, together with its comrades, in a wine merchant's cellar, and was then, for the first time, rinsed out—which was a ridiculous performance, it thought. The bottle now lay empty and corkless—felt itself wonderfully dull, as though wanting something—it knew not what. But then it was filled with good, glorious wine, received a cork, and was sealed up, with a label pasted on it, "Best Quality." It felt it was now a first-class bottle; the wine was good, and the bottle was good. Something within it seemed to be singing of things it knew nothing whatever about. The green sunlit mountains, where the vine grows, and where fair girls and merry youths sing and dance together. Ah! there it is right pleasant to live! Something seemed to be singing about this inside the bottle, as within the hearts of young poets, who know no more about the matter than even the bottle knew.

One morning it was bought. The furrier's boy was sent to fetch a bottle of the best wine, and so it was transported into a large basket, together with ham, cheese, and sausages, the best butter, and the whitest bread. The furrier's daughter herself packed the basket. She was very young and very pretty. She had laughing brown eyes, and smiling lips, almost as expressive as the eyes. Her hands were small, soft, and white, but not so white as her forehead and her throat. She was one of the prettiest girls in the town, and not yet betrothed.

The basket lay in her lap while the party drove out into the wood. The neck of the bottle peeped forth between the folds of the white tablecloth. There was red sealing wax on the cork, and this sealing wax looked right into the young girl's face, and into the face of the young man who sat next to her. He had been her companion from childhood. He was a portrait-painter's son, and had lately passed with honorable mention through his examination for naval service. On the morrow he was to go with his ship to foreign lands. There was some talk about his voyage, and while this was talked about it was not quite so pleasant to look at the eyes and lips of the furrier's pretty daughter.

The two young people took a walk in the green forest— what did they talk about? The bottle could not hear that—it was left in the basket. It was a very long time before the basket was unpacked, but then? Why certainly some pleasant things must have happened in the meantime, for all eyes were laughing, even those of the furrier's daughter, though she talked less than before, and her cheeks blushed like two red roses.

The furrier took up the bottle, took up the corkscrew. Oh! what a strange sensation that was when, for the first time, the cork was drawn! The bottle had never been able to forget that solemn moment. And then came the gurgling noise as the wine flowed out into the glasses!

"The health of the betrothed!" cried the father, and every glass was emptied, and the young man kissed his pretty bride. Then he refilled the glasses, exclaiming: "To our joyful wedding this day next year!" And when the glasses had been emptied the second time, he took the bottle and raised it high in the air, saying, "You have served us here on the brightest day of my life, you shall never be profaned by any meaner service!"

And he flung it high into the air. It came down again—it fell softly among the thick reeds fringing the little woodland lake. The broken bottle remembered perfectly well how it had lain there, thinking: "I gave them wine, they gave me muddy water. No matter, it was well meant!" It could see no more of the happy couple and the pleased parents, but it could hear them talking and singing in the distance. And presently two peasant boys came that way. They peeped in among the reeds, spied the bottle, and took it away. Now it would be provided for.

At their home in the little woodland hut, where they lived, they had, the day before, parted from their elder brother, who was a sailor. They had been to say farewell to him before he went out on a long voyage. The mother was now packing up a few things which the father was to take to him in the town that evening—he would see him once more before his departure. A little flask full of spiced brandy had been placed in the parcel, but now the boys showed the larger and stronger bottle which they had found—it could hold more than the little one. So it was filled now, not with red wine as before, but with bitter, wholesome drops, good for the stomach. The new-found bottle was to go, the little one to stay at home.

So now the bottle went forth on its travels. It went on board ship to be Peter Jensen's property, on board the very same ship on which the young mate who had been betrothed that morning was also going. He never looked at the bottle, or if he had, it would never have occurred to him to think, "This is the same bottle from which our health was drunk."

And now it contained no wine indeed, but something as good as wine. When Peter Jensen took it out, his comrades always called it "The apothecary." It gave right good medicine, they thought, and it helped them just as long as a drop was left in it. It was a pleasant time, and the bottle sang after its fashion. And so it came to be nicknamed, "The great lark," "Peter Jensen's lark."

A long time had passed away and the bottle stood empty in a corner. It had never been ashore and so didn't know whether it was on its way out or on its way home. The night was dark as pitch, and a mighty storm arose. Great heavy black waves surged and tossed the vessel to and fro. The mast broke, the planks flew out, the pumps were of no use. The ship was sinking; but in the last minute, the young sailor wrote on a fragment of paper: "Lord Jesu, have mercy on us! we perish!" He added his bride's name, his own, and that of the ship, rolled the note into an empty bottle that came to his hand, pressed the cork down tight, and flung the bottle far into the stormy sea. Little did he know that this was the same bottle that had given him wine on the day of his happiness and hope. Now it rocked and tossed upon the billows, bearing its message, its greeting from the dead to the living.

The ship sank, the crew perished, but the bottle flew on like a bird—it bore a love letter. And the sun rose up and the sun went down—and that reminded the bottle of the hour of its birth, in the red glowing furnace. It longed to fly back into his embrace. It encountered new storms. Still it was neither swallowed up by sharks nor dashed against rocks. For more than a year and a day it drifted about, now northward, now southward, carried by the tide. Certainly it was its own master; but one may get tired of that.

The letter, the last farewell from bridegroom to bride, would bring only sorrow, if it ever fell into the right hands. But where were those hands? The hands that had gleamed so white when they spread the tablecloth over the fresh grass in the green wood, on the day of betrothal? Where was the furrier's daughter? Where, indeed? What land was nearest now? The bottle could not answer these questions. It drifted and drifted, and was at last weary of drifting—for it had never been intended for this. But it drifted on all the same, till at last it was cast ashore on a foreign land. It understood not a word of what was spoken here. It was not the language it had always heard before, and one loses much in a country where one does not understand the language.

The bottle was picked up and examined, the letter inside was noticed, taken out, turned and twisted about, but the people could not make out a word of what was written thereon. They understood, of course, that the bottle had been flung overboard, and that something was written on the paper, but that "something" was a complete mystery. And so the note was rolled up and put into the bottle again, and the bottle was placed in a large cabinet, in a large room, in a large house. Every time strangers came to the house the note was taken out, unrolled, turned and twisted about, until the writing—it was only pencil writing—became more and more illegible. At last the letters could hardly be traced at all. For a year the bottle remained in the cabinet, then it was sent up into an attic, where it got smothered up with dust and spider webs. There it lurked and thought on its better days, when it poured out red wine in the fresh wood; when it was rocked by the billows and had had a secret, a letter, a sigh of farewell, intrusted to its safekeeping.

It was left among old lumber for twenty years. It would

have been left there longer if the house had not been rebuilt. The roof was taken off, the bottle was discovered, remarks were made about it, but it could not understand. One learns nothing, banished in a lumber room—not even in twenty years. "Had I only spent that time in the parlor downstairs!" sighed the bottle, "how much I should have learned!"

It was now washed and rinsed out; and in truth, it needed washing. It felt quite clear and transparent. It had renewed its youth in its old age, but the note, the precious note, was lost in the process. It was now filled with seed corn, corked up tight, and well packed—it knew not where, but it could see neither lamp nor candle, not to speak of sun or moon. And "it is a pity to see nothing when one is traveling," thought the bottle. It saw nothing, but it did something—that was more important. It traveled, and arrived at the place for which it was destined. It was unpacked.

"What a deal of trouble those outlandish folk have taken about it!" Those were the first words it heard, and it understood them well. They were spoken in the language the bottle had heard from the first, at the factory, at the wine merchant's, in the wood, and on shipboard. The only right, good old language, made to be understood! The bottle had come home to its own country! it nearly sprang out of the hands that held it, in its joy. It was emptied of its contents, and sent down into the cellar to be out of the way; no matter! home is home, even in the cellar! There it never thought how long it lay unnoticed, for it lay comfortably. And one day, after a long interval, people came in, took this bottle and others, and went out.

The garden of the house was decked out in great magnificence; bright-colored lamps were hung in wreaths, and paper lanterns shone like large bright tulips. It was a lovely evening. The air was still and mild, the stars glittered brilliantly, and as for the new moon, why, people with good eyesight could see the whole, like a round, grayish globe, with one corner tinged with gold.

In the sidewalks there were a few lights too, though not so many as in the center of the garden. A row of bottles, each with a candle in it, was set up along the hedges. The bottle that we know was among them. It felt in a state of perfect rapture. It was now in a garden, as it had been in the wood. Again it heard festive sounds, song and music, the hum and buzz of passers-by, especially from the garden side, where the lamps were burning, and the paper lanterns displayed their varied colors. For its own part, it stood on a sidewalk—that even supplied matter for thought. The bottle stood bearing its light—stood there for use and for ornament both, and that was just right. In such an hour one forgets twenty years spent in a lumber room—and it is good to forget when memory is sadness.

Near by a pair passed, arm in arm, like the bridal pair out in the wood, like the mate and the furrier's daughter. The bottle lived it all over again. A tide of guests passed to and fro in the gardens, and among them an old maid, not friend-less, indeed—far from it! But one who had survived all her relatives. And she was thinking of the same day years ago that the bottle thought of—she thought of the greenwood and the young pair of betrothed lovers. Well might she think of them! For of those two she had been one; she was the survivor! that had been the happiest hour of her life—an hour never to be forgotten, however old an old maid may be. But she did not recognize the bottle, nor did the bottle recognize her. And so folk pass one another by in this world. But they are sure to meet again, sooner or later, as these two did. Now they were residents of the same town.

The bottle's fate took it from the garden to the wine merchant's. There it was again filled with wine, and then sold to the aeronaut, who took it with him on his next ascent in his balloon. A crowd of people came to watch, a band of musicians had been engaged, and many other preparations made. The bottle witnessed all these from a basket, wherein he kept company with a live rabbit, who was wretchedly low-spirited, because he knew he went up only to come down again with the parachute. The bottle, on the contrary, knew nothing about the matter. It saw how the balloon swelled out larger and larger, and when larger could not be, it began to lift itself higher and higher, and rolled uneasily. Then the ropes that held it down were cut, and up it flew with aeronaut, basket, rabbit, and bottle. The musicians struck up, and the people all cried, "Hurrah!"

"This is a new style of navigation," thought the bottle. "There's one good point about it; one can hardly run upon rocks this way."

And the eyes of several thousands of people looked after the balloon, and the old maid watched it too. She was standing at her open attic window, where the cage with the little canary hung. At that time the little bird did not possess a glass for his water, but had to content himself with a cup. In the window stood a flowering myrtle; the old maid had thrust it to one side while she leaned forward to look out. She could see into the balloon. She saw how the aeronaut let the rabbit fall with the parachute; how he drank to the health of the crowd down below, and then flung the bottle high into the air. But she didn't realize that she had seen this identical bottle flying in the air once before, on her day of happiness in the greenwood, in the time of her youth.

The bottle had no time to think at all, it had attained the highest point of its life so unexpectedly. Towers and roofs lay far below. Men were so tiny, they could hardly be seen at all.

And now it fell in a very different fashion from the rabbit's descent. The bottle made somersaults in the air, felt so

young, so wild! It was half filled with wine at first, but not
for long. What an air voyage! The sun shone on the bottle,
the eyes of all men followed it. The balloon was already far
away. Soon the bottle fell upon one of the roofs and dashed
in two, but such a spirit seemed to animate the fragments,
that they could not be still! They leaped and they rolled,
ever downward, downward, till they reached the courtyard,
where they broke into smaller fragments. Only the neck of
the bottle was left whole; and it looked as if it had been cut
off with a diamond.

"It is still good for a bird glass," said the man who lived
in the cellar; but he himself possessed neither bird nor cage.
And it would have been hardly worth while to procure these
because a fragment of a bottle that might be used as a glass
had fallen into his hands. But it might be useful to the old
maid in the attic, he thought; and thus the broken bottle was
taken upstairs, a cork was put in, the part that had formerly
been uppermost was set lowest, as often happens in changes,
fresh water was poured in, and it was hung on the side of the
cage for the use of the little bird who sang so merrily.

"Ah, it is easy for you to sing!" said the bird glass. It was
certainly a remarkable bird glass! It had been up in a balloon;
that, at least, was known of its history. Now, in its place by
the cage, it could hear the hum and buzz of the people in
the street below, could hear the old maid chatting in her chamber. She had a visitor just now, a friend of her own age, and
they were talking, not about the bird glass, but about the
myrtle at the window.

"Indeed, I will not let you throw away two rix-dollars for
your daughter's bridal bouquet," said the old maid. "You
shall have a charming one, full of flowers! Just look at my
beautiful myrtle! It is only an offshoot from the myrtle you
gave me the day after my betrothal—don't you remember?
I was to have made my bridal bouquet from it, when the year

was up. But my wedding day never came! Those eyes closed to this world that were to have been my light and joy through life. Down, down, low beneath the waves he sleeps sweetly, my own darling! And the myrtle and I grew old together; and when the myrtle withered, I took the last fresh bough, and set it in the mold, and now the bough is a tree, and shall serve at last at a wedding feast—shall supply your daughter's bridal bouquet!"

And there were tears in the old maid's eyes, as she remembered her betrothal in the wood, her lover's bright face, his caressing words, his first kiss—but she said no more; she was an old maid now. She thought of so many things; but she never thought that just outside her window was a memorial of that time, the neck of the bottle whence had gushed the wine from which her own and her lover's health had been drunk. The old bottle didn't recognize her either, for it didn't listen to a single word she said, partly and chiefly because it could only think of itself.

THE NIGHTINGALE

In China, as you know, the Emperor is Chinese, and all the people around him are Chinese too. It is many years since the story I am going to tell you happened, but that is all the more reason for telling it, lest it should be forgotten.

The Emperor's palace was the most beautiful thing in the world. It was made entirely of finest porcelain, which was very costly, and so brittle and fragile that it was dangerous even to touch it. The most extraordinary flowers were to be seen in the garden. The most beautiful ones had little silver bells tied to them which tinkled perpetually, so that no one could pass the flowers without looking at them. Every little detail in the garden had been most carefully thought out, and it was so big that even the gardener himself did not know where it ended.

If one went on walking, one came to beautiful woods with lofty trees and beyond that to a lake. The wood extended to the edge of the lake, which was deep and blue. Great ships could sail to and fro under the branches of the trees. Among these trees lived a nightingale, that sang so deliciously that even the poor fisherman, who had plenty of other things to do, lay still to listen to it when he was out at night drawing in his nets.

"Heavens, how beautiful it is," he said, but then he had to attended to his nets, and forgot the bird. The next night he heard it again and exclaimed, "Heavens, how beautiful it is."

Travelers came to the Emperor's capital from every country in the world. They admired everything very much, especially the palace and the gardens, but when they heard the nightingale they all said, "This is better than anything."

When they got home they described it, and learned men wrote many books about the town, the palace, and the garden. But nobody forgot the nightingale—it was always put above everything else. Those among them who were poets wrote the most beautiful poems, all about the nightingale in the woods by the deep blue sea. These books went all over the world, and in the course of time some of them reached the Emperor. He sat in his golden chair reading and reading, and nodding his head, well pleased to hear such beautiful descriptions of the town, the palace, and the garden. "But the nightingale is the best of all," he read.

"What is this?" said the Emperor. "The nightingale? Why, I know nothing about it. Is there such a bird in my kingdom, and in my own garden, and I have never heard of it? Imagine my having to discover this from a book."

Then he called his gentleman-in-waiting, who was so grand that when anyone of a lower rank dared to speak to him or to ask him a question, he would only answer, "P," which means nothing at all.

"There is said to be a very wonderful bird called a nightingale here," said the Emperor. "They say that it is better than anything else in all my great kingdom. Why have I never been told anything about it?"

"I have never heard it mentioned," said the gentleman-in-waiting. "It has never been presented at court."

"I wish it to appear here this evening to sing to me," said the Emperor. "The whole world knows what I possess, and I know nothing about it!"

"I have never heard it mentioned before," said the gentleman-in-waiting. "I will seek it, and I will find it." But where was the bird to be found? The gentleman-in-waiting ran upstairs and downstairs and in and out of all the rooms and corridors. Nobody had ever heard anything about the nightingale. So the gentleman-in-waiting ran back to the Emperor and said that it must be a myth, invented by the writers of the books. "Your Imperial Majesty must not believe everything that is written! Books are often mere inventions, even if they do not belong to what we call the black art."

"But the book in which I read it was sent to me by the powerful Emperor of Japan. Therefore it can't be untrue. I will hear this nightingale. I insist upon its being here tonight. I extend my most gracious protection to it, and if it is not forthcoming, I will have the whole court trampled upon after supper."

"Tsing-pe!" said the gentleman-in-waiting, and away he ran again, up and down all the stairs, in and out of all the rooms and corridors. Half the court ran with him, for none of them wished to be trampled on. There was much questioning about this nightingale, which was known to all the outside world but to no one at court.

At last they found a poor little maid in the kitchen, who said, "Oh, heavens! The nightingale? I know it very well. Yes indeed, it can sing. Every evening I am allowed to take broken meat to my poor sick mother who lives down by the shore. On my way back, when I am tired I rest awhile in the wood, and then I hear the nightingale. Its song brings the tears into my eyes. I feel as if my mother were kissing me."

"Little kitchenmaid," said the gentleman-in-waiting, "I will procure you a permanent position in the kitchen and permission to see the Emperor dining, if you will take us to the nightingale. It is commanded to appear at court tonight."

Then they all went out into the wood where the night-ingale usually sang. Half the court was there. As they were going along at their best pace, a cow began to bellow.

"Oh," said a young courtier, "there we have it. What won-

derful power for such a little creature. I have certainly heard
it before."

"No, those are the cows bellowing. We are a long way
from the place." Then frogs began to croak in the marsh.

"How beautiful!" said the Chinese chaplain. "It is just like
the tinkling of church bells."

"No, those are the frogs," said the little kitchenmaid. "But
I think we shall soon hear it now."

Then the nightingale began to sing.

"Listen, listen! There it sits," said the little girl. And she
pointed to a little gray bird up among the branches.

"Is it possible?" said the gentleman-in-waiting. "I should
never have thought it was like that. How common it looks.
Seeing so many grand people must have frightened all its
colors away."

"Little nightingale," called the kitchenmaid quite loud,
"Our Gracious Emperor wishes you to sing to him."

"With the greatest pleasure," said the nightingale, warbling
away in the most delightful fashion.

"It is just like crystal bells," said the gentleman-in-waiting.
"Look at its little throat, how active it is. It is extraordinary
that we have never heard it before. I am sure it will be a
great success at court."

"Shall I sing again to the Emperor?" said the nightingale,
who thought he was present.

"My precious little nightingale," said the gentleman-in-
waiting, "I have the honor to command your attendance at
a court festival tonight, where you will charm His Gracious
Majesty the Emperor with your fascinating singing."

"I sound best among the trees," said the nightingale, but
it went with them willingly when it heard that the Emperor
wished it.

The palace had been brightened up for the occasion. The
walls and the floors, which were all of china, shone by the

light of many thousand golden lamps. The most beautiful flowers, all of the tinkling kind, were arranged in the corridors. There was hurrying to and fro, and a great draft, but this was just what made the bells ring. One's ears were full of the tinkling. In the middle of the large reception room where the Emperor sat, a golden rod had been fixed, on which the nightingale was to perch. The whole court was assembled, and the little kitchenmaid had been permitted to stand behind the door, for she now had the actual title of Cook. They were all dressed in their best. Everybody's eyes were turned toward the little gray bird at which the Emperor was nodding.

The nightingale sang delightfully, and the tears came into the Emperor's eyes and rolled down his cheeks. And when the nightingale sang more beautifully than ever, its notes melted all hearts. The Emperor was so charmed that he said the nightingale should have his gold slipper to wear round its neck. But the nightingale declined with thanks—it had already been sufficiently rewarded.

"I have seen tears in the eyes of the Emperor," he said. "That is my richest reward. The tears of an Emperor have a wonderful power. God knows I am sufficiently recompensed." And it again burst into its sweet heavenly song.

"That is the most delightful coquetting I have ever seen!" said the ladies. And they took some water into their mouths to try and make the same gurgling, when anyone spoke to them, thinking they could equal the nightingale. Even the lackeys and the chambermaids announced that they were satisfied, and that is saying a great deal. They are always the most difficult people to please. Yes indeed, the nightingale had made a sensation. It was to stay at court now, and have its own cage, as well as liberty to walk out twice a day and once in the night. It always had twelve footmen, with each one holding a ribbon which was tied round its leg. There was not much pleasure in an outing of that sort.

The whole town talked about the marvelous bird. If two people met, one said to the other "Night," and the other answered "Gale." And then they sighed, perfectly understanding each other. Eleven cheesemongers' children were named after it, but not one among them could sing a note.

One day a large parcel came for the Emperor. Outside was written the word "Nightingale."

"Here we have another new book about this celebrated bird," said the Emperor. But it was not a book. It was a little work of art in a box, an artificial nightingale exactly like the living one, except that it was studded all over with diamonds, rubies, and sapphires.

When the artificial bird was wound up, it could sing one of the songs the real one sang, and it wagged its tail, which glittered with silver and gold. A ribbon was tied round its neck on which was written, "The Emperor of Japan's nightingale is very poor compared to the Emperor of China's."

Everybody said, "Oh, how beautiful!" And the person who brought the artificial bird immediately received the title of Imperial Nightingale-Carrier-in-Chief.

"Now they must sing together. What a duet that will be!"

They sang together, but they did not get along very well, for the real nightingale sang in its own way and the artificial one could sing only waltzes.

"There is no fault in that," said the music master. "It is perfectly in time and correct in every way."

Then the artificial bird had to sing alone. It was just as great a success as the real one, and it was much prettier to look at, because it glittered like bracelets and breastpins.

It sang the same tune three and thirty times over, and still it was not tired. People would willingly have heard it from the beginning again, but the Emperor said that the real one must have a turn now. But where was it? No one had noticed that it had flown out of the open window, back to its own green woods.

"What is the meaning of this?" said the Emperor.

All the courtiers railed at it and said it was a most ungrateful bird.

"We have got the best bird though," said they, and then the artificial bird had to sing again. This was the thirty-fourth time that they had heard the same tune, but they did not know it thoroughly even yet because it was so difficult.

The music master praised the bird tremendously and insisted that it was better than the real nightingale, not only on the outside with all its diamonds, but inside too.

"You see, my ladies and gentlemen, and the Emperor before all, in the real nightingale you never know what you will hear, but in the artificial one everything is decided beforehand. So it is, and so it must remain. It can't be otherwise. You can account for things: you can open it and show the human ingenuity in arranging how the waltzes go, and how one note follows upon another."

"Those are exactly my opinions," they all said, and the music master got permission to show the bird to the public next Sunday. They were also to hear it sing, said the Emperor. So they heard it, and they all became as enthusiastic over it as if they had drunk themselves merry on tea, because that is a thoroughly Chinese habit.

Then they all said, "Oh!" and stuck their forefingers in the air and nodded their heads. But the poor fisherman who had heard the real nightingale said, "It sounds very nice, and it is very nearly like the real one, but there is something wanting. I don't know what." The real nightingale was banished from the kingdom.

The artificial bird had its place on a silken cushion, close to the Emperor's bed. All the presents it had received, gold and precious jewels, were scattered round it. Its title had risen to be Chief Imperial Singer-of-the-Bed-Chamber. In rank it stood Number One on the left side, for the Emperor reckoned that side where the heart was seated was the important one. And even an Emperor's heart is on the left side.

The music master wrote five and twenty volumes about the artificial bird. The treatise was very long, and was written in all the most difficult Chinese characters. Everybody said they had read and understood it, for otherwise they would have been reckoned stupid, and then their bodies would have been trampled upon.

Things went on in this way for a whole year. The Emperor, the court, and all the other Chinamen knew every little gurgle in the song of the artificial bird by heart. And they liked it all the better for this, for they could all join in the song themselves. Even the street boys sang "Zizizi! cluck, cluck, cluck!" And the Emperor sang it too.

But one evening, when the bird was singing its best and the Emperor was lying in bed listening to it, something gave way inside the bird with a "whizz." "Whirr!" went all the wheels, and the music stopped.

The Emperor jumped out of bed and sent for his private physicians, but what good could they do? Then they sent for the watchmaker, who after a good deal of talk and examination got the works to go again somehow. But he said the bird would have to be spared as much as possible, because it was so worn out, and that he could not renew the works so as to be sure of the tune. This was a great blow! They now dared to let the artificial bird sing only once a year, and hardly that. But then the music master made a little speech using all the most difficult Chinese words. He said it was just as good as ever, and his saying it made it so.

Five years passed, and then a great grief came upon the nation. They were all very fond of their Emperor, and now he was ill and could not live, it was said. A new Emperor was already chosen, and people stood about in the street and asked the gentleman-in-waiting how the Emperor was getting on.

"P," answered he, shaking his head.

The Emperor lay pale and cold in his gorgeous bed. The courtiers thought he was dead, and they all went off to pay their respects to their new Emperor. The lackeys ran off to talk matters over, and the chambermaids gave a great coffee party. Cloth had been laid down in all the rooms and corridors to deaden the sounds of footsteps, and it was very, very quiet. But the Emperor was not dead yet. He lay stiff and pale in the gorgeous bed with velvet hangings and heavy golden tassels. There was an open window high above him, and the moon streamed in upon the Emperor and the artificial bird beside him.

The poor Emperor could hardly breathe. He seemed to have a weight on his chest. He opened his eyes and then he saw that it was Death sitting upon his chest, wearing his golden crown. In one hand he held the Emperor's golden sword, and in the other his Imperial banner. From among the folds of the velvet hangings peered many curious faces. Some were hideous, others gentle and pleasant. They were all the Emperor's good and bad deeds, which now looked him in the face as Death was weighing him down.

"Do you remember that?" whispered one after the other. "Do you remember this?" And they told him so many things that the perspiration poured down his face.

"I never knew that," said the Emperor. "Music, music! Sound the great Chinese drums," he cried, "that I may not hear what they are saying." But they went on and on, and Death sat nodding his head like a Chinaman at everything that was said. "Music, music!" shrieked the Emperor. "You precious little golden bird, sing, sing! I have loaded you with precious stones, and even hung my own golden slipper round your neck. Sing, I tell you, sing!"

But the bird stood silent. There was nobody to wind it up, so of course it could not go. Death continued to fix the great empty sockets of his eyes upon him, and all was silent, terribly silent.

Suddenly, close to the window there was a burst of lovely song. It was the living nightingale, perched on a branch outside. It had heard of the Emperor's need and had come to bring comfort and hope to him. As it sang, the faces round became fainter and fainter, and the blood coursed with fresh vigor in the Emperor's veins and through his feeble limbs. Even Death himself listened to the song and said, "Go on, little nightingale, go on!"

"Yes, if you give me the gorgeous golden sword. Yes, if you give me the Imperial banner. Yes, if you give me the Emperor's crown."

And Death gave back each of these treasures for a song, and the nightingale went on singing. It sang about the quiet churchyard where the roses bloom, where the elder flowers scent the air, and where the fresh grass is ever moistened anew by the tears of the mourners. This song brought to Death a longing for his own garden, and like a cold gray mist he passed out of the window.

"Thanks, thanks!" said the Emperor. "You heavenly little bird, I know you. I banished you from my kingdom, and yet you have charmed the evil visions away from my bed by your song, and even Death away from my heart. How can I ever repay you?"

"You have rewarded me," said the nightingale. "I brought tears to your eyes the very first time I ever sang to you, and I shall never forget it. Those are the jewels which gladden the heart of a singer. But sleep now, and wake up fresh and strong. I will sing to you."

Then it sang again, and the Emperor fell into a sweet refreshing sleep. The sun shone in at his window, and he awoke refreshed and well. None of his attendants had yet come back to him, for they thought he was dead, but the nightingale still sat there singing.

"You must always stay with me," said the Emperor. "You shall sing only when you like, and I will break the artificial bird into a thousand pieces."

"Don't do that," said the nightingale. "It did all the good it could. Keep it as you have always done. I can't build my nest and live in this palace, but let me come whenever I like. Then I will sit on the branch in the evening and sing to you. I will sing to cheer you and to make you thoughtful too. I will sing to you of the happy ones and of those that suffer.

I will sing about the good and the evil, which are kept hidden from you. The little singing bird flies far and wide, to the poor fisherman and to the peasant's home, to people who are far from you and your court. I love your heart more than your crown, and yet there is an odor of sanctity round the crown too! I will come, and I will sing to you. But you must promise me one thing."

"Everything!" said the Emperor, who stood there in his Imperial robes which he had just put on, and he held the sword heavy with gold upon his heart.

"Only one thing I ask you. Tell no one that you have a little bird who tells you everything. It will be better so."

Then the nightingale flew away. The attendants came in to look after their dead Emperor—and there he stood, bidding them "Good morning!"

THE ICE MAIDEN

Little Rudy

LET us pay a visit to Switzerland. Let us look around us in that magnificent mountainous country, where the woods creep up the sides of the precipitous walls of rock. Let us ascend to the dazzling snowfields above, and descend again to the green valleys beneath, where the rivers and the brooks foam along as if they were afraid that they should not reach the ocean fast enough to be lost in its immensity.

The sun's burning rays shine on the deep dales, and upon the heavy masses of snow above, and the ice blocks which have been accumulating there for years melt and become rolling avalanches, piled-up glaciers. Two such glaciers lie in the broad mountain clefts under Schreckhorn and Wetterhorn, near the little mountain town of Grindelwald. They are wonderful to behold, and therefore in summertime many strangers come here from foreign lands. They come over the lofty snow-covered hills; they come through the deep valleys, and from thence for hours and hours they must mount; and always, as they ascend, the valleys seem to become deeper and deeper, until they appear as if viewed from a balloon high up in the air. The clouds often hang like thick heavy curtains of smoke around the lofty mountain peaks, while down in the valley, where the many brown wooden houses lie scattered about, a bright ray of the sun may be shining, and bringing into strong relief some brilliant patch of green. The waters foam and roar as they rush along below—they murmur and tinkle above. They look like silver ribbons streaming down over the rocks.

On both sides of the ascending road lie wooden houses. Each house has its little potato garden, and this is a necessity. For within yonder doors are many mouths—the houses are crammed with children—and children often waste their food. From all the cottages they sally forth in swarms, and throng around the travelers. The troop of children are like little merchants—they offer for sale charming toy wooden houses, models of the dwellings one sees here among the mountains. Whether it be fair weather or foul, the crowds of children come out with their wares.

Some twenty years ago there occasionally stood here, but always at a short distance from the other children, a little boy who was also ready to engage in trade. He stood with an earnest, grave expression on his face and held his deal box fast with both hands, as if he were afraid of losing it. The very earnestness of his face, and his being such a little fellow, caused him to be noticed and called forward, so that he often sold the most—he did not himself know why.

Higher up among the hills lived his maternal grandfather, who cut out the neat, pretty little houses, and in a room up above was an old press full of all sorts of things—nutcrackers, knives, forks, boxes with prettily carved leafwork, and springing chamois. There was everything to please a child's eye. But little Rudy, as he was called, looked with greater interest and longing at the old firearms and other weapons which were hung up under the beams of the roof. "He will have them someday," said his grandfather. "When he is big enough and strong enough to make use of them."

Young as the boy was, he had to take care of the goats; and he who had to clamber after them was obliged to keep a good lookout and to be a good climber. And Rudy *was* an excellent climber. He went even higher than the goats, for he was fond of hunting birds' nests up among the tops of the trees. Bold and adventurous he was, but no one ever saw him smile, except when he stood near the roaring cataract or heard the thunder of a rolling avalanche. He never played with the other children—he never went near them, except when his grandfather sent him down to sell the things he made. And Rudy did not care much for that; he preferred scrambling about among the mountains, or sitting at home with his grandfather, and hearing him tell stories of olden days, and of the people near by at Meyringen, from whence he came. "This tribe had not been settled here from the earliest ages of the world," he said. "They were wanderers from afar; they came from the distant North, where their race still lives, and they were called 'Swedes.' " There was a great deal for Rudy to learn, and he learned more from other sources, too, and these were the animals that lived in the house. One was a large dog, Ajola, a legacy from Rudy's father—the other was a tomcat. Rudy had much to thank the Cat for—he had taught him to climb.

"Come out upon the roof with me!" the Cat had said, distinctly and intelligibly; for when one is a young child, and can scarcely speak, fowls and ducks, cats and dogs, are almost as easily understood as the language that fathers and mothers use. Indeed one must be very little, for it is the time when Grandpapa's stick neighs, and becomes a horse with head, legs, and tail.

Some children retain these childish thoughts longer than others; and of these it is said that they are very backward, exceedingly stupid children—people say so much!

"Come out upon the roof with me, little Rudy!" was one of the first things the Cat said, and Rudy understood him.

"It is all nonsense to think you'll fall down. You won't fall unless you are afraid. Come! Set one of your paws here, the other there, and balance yourself with the rest of your paws! Keep a sharp lookout, and be active in your limbs! If there be a hole, spring over it, and keep a firm footing as I do."

And so little Rudy did. Very often he sat on the shelving roof of the house with the Cat, often too in the tops of the trees. But he also sat higher up among the towering rocks, where the Cat did not go.

"Higher! higher!" said the trees and the bushes. "Do you not see how we climb up—to what height we go, and how fast we hold on, even among the narrowest points of rock?"

And Rudy gained the top of the hill earlier than the sun had gained it. And there he took his morning drink, the fresh invigorating mountain air—that drink which only our Lord can prepare, and which mankind pronounces to be the early fragrance from the mountain herbs and the wild thyme and mint in the valley. All that is heavy the overhanging clouds absorb within themselves, and the winds carry them over the pinewoods, while the spirit of fragrance becomes air—light and fresh; and this was Rudy's morning drink.

The sunbeams—those daughters of the sun, who bring blessings with them—kissed his cheeks; and Vertigo (Dizziness) stood near on the watch, but dared not approach him. And the swallows from his grandfather's house beneath (there were not less than seven nests) flew up to him and the goats, singing, "We and you, and you and we!" They brought him greetings from his home, even from the two hens, the only birds in the establishment, though Rudy was not intimate with them.

Young as he was, he had traveled, and traveled a good deal for such a little fellow. He was born in the Canton of Valais, and brought from there over the hills. He had visited Staubbach on foot. It seems like a silver veil to flutter before the snow-clad, glittering white mountain Jungfrau. And he had been at the great glaciers near Grindelwald, and that was connected with a sad event. His mother had died there. There, his grandfather used to say, "little Rudy got all his childish merriment knocked out of him." Before the child was a year old, "he laughed more than he cried," his mother had written;

but from the time that he fell into the crevasse in the ice, his disposition had entirely changed. The grandfather did not say much about this, but the whole hill knew the fact.

Rudy's father had been a postilion, and the large dog who now shared Rudy's home had always accompanied him in his journeys over the Simplon down to the Lake of Geneva. Rudy's kindred on his father's side lived in the valley of the Rhone, in the Canton Valais. His uncle was a celebrated chamois hunter, and a well-known Alpine guide. Rudy was not more than a year old when he lost his father; and his mother was anxious to return with her child to her own family in the Bernese Oberland. Her father lived only a few hours' journey from Grindelwald. He was a carver in wood, and he made so much by this that he was very well off.

Carrying her infant in her arms, she set out homeward in the month of June, in company with two chamois hunters, over the Gemmi to reach Grindelwald. They had accomplished the greater portion of the journey. They had crossed the highest ridges to the snowfields, and could already see her native valley with all its scattered brown cottages. They had only the labor of going over the upper part of one great glacier. The snow had recently fallen, and concealed a crevasse —not one so deep as the abyss below where the water foamed along, but deeper far than the height of any human being. The young woman who was carrying her infant slipped, sank in, and suddenly disappeared. Not a shriek, not a groan was heard—nothing but the crying of a little child. An hour elapsed before her two companions were able to obtain ropes and poles from the nearest house to help them get her out. It was with much difficulty and labor that they at last brought up from the crevasse two dead bodies. Every means of restoring breathing was employed, and they were successful in recalling the child to life, but not the mother. And so the old grandfather received into his house, not a daughter, but a daughter's son—the little one "who laughed more than he cried." But a change seemed to have come over him since he had been in the glacier crevasse—in the cold underground ice world, where the souls of the condemned are imprisoned until Doomsday, as the Swiss peasants assert.

Like a rushing stream, frozen and pressed into blocks of green crystal, lies the glacier, one great mass of ice balanced upon another. In the depths beneath, the accumulating stream of melted ice and snow tears along. Deep hollows, immense crevasses, yawn within it. A wondrous palace of crystal it is, and in it dwells the Ice Maiden—the queen of the glaciers. She, the slayer, the crusher, is half the mighty ruler of the rivers, half a child of the air. Therefore she is able to soar to the highest haunts of the chamois, to the loftiest peaks of the snow-covered hills, where the boldest mountaineer has to cut footsteps for himself in the ice. She sails on the slightest sprig of the pine tree over the raging torrents below, and bounds lightly from one mass of ice to another, with her long snow-white hair fluttering about her, and her bluish-green robe shining like the water in the deep Swiss lakes.

"To crush—to hold fast—such power is mine!" she cries; "yet a beautiful boy was snatched from me—a boy whom I had kissed, but not kissed to death. He is again among mankind; he tends the goats upon the mountain heights. He is always climbing higher and higher still, away, away from other human beings, but not from me! He is mine—I wait for him!"

And she commanded Vertigo to undertake the mission. It was in summertime; the Ice Maiden was melting in the green valley where the green mint grew, and Vertigo mounted and dived. Vertigo has several sisters, quite a flock of them, and the Ice Maiden selected the strongest among the many who exercise their power within doors and without—those who sit on the banisters of steep staircases and the outer rails of lofty towers, who bound like squirrels along the mountain ridges, and, springing thence, tread the air as the swimmer treads the water, and lure their victims onward, down to the abyss beneath.

Vertigo and the Ice Maiden both grasp after mankind, as the polypus grasps after all that comes within its reach. Vertigo was to seize Rudy.

"Seize him, indeed!" cried Vertigo. "I cannot do it! That good-for-nothing Cat has taught him its art. Yon child of the human race possesses a power within himself which keeps me at a distance. I cannot reach the little urchin when he hangs from the branches out over the depths below, or I would willingly loosen his hold, and send him whirling down through the air. But I cannot."

"We must seize him, though!" said the Ice Maiden, "either you or I! I will—I will!"

"No—no!" broke upon the air, like a mountain echo of the church bells' peal. It was a whisper, it was a song, it was the liquid tones of a chorus from other spirits of nature—mild, soft, and loving, the daughters of the rays of the sun. They station themselves every evening in a circle upon the mountain peaks, and spread out their rose-tinted wings, which, as the sun sinks, become redder and redder, until the lofty Alps seem all in a blaze. Men call this the Alpine glow. When the sun has sunk, they retire within the white snow on the crests of the hills, and sleep there until sunrise, when they come forth again. They love flowers, butterflies, and mankind very much, and among men they had taken a great fancy for little Rudy.

"You shall not imprison him—you shall not get him!" they sang.

"Greater and stronger have I seized and imprisoned," said the Ice Maiden.

Then the daughters of the sun sang about the wanderer whose hat the whirlwind tore off, and carried away in its stormy flight. The wind could take his cap, but not the man himself—no, it could make him tremble with its violence, but it could not sweep him away. "The human race is stronger and more ethereal even than we are; they alone may mount higher than even the sun, our parent. They know the magic words that can rule the wind and the waves so that they are compelled to obey and to serve them. You loosen the heavy oppressive weight, and they soar upward."

Thus sang the sweet tones of the bell-like chorus.

And every morning the sun's rays shone through the one little window in the grandfather's house upon the quiet child. The daughters of the rays of the sun kissed him—they wished to thaw, to obliterate the ice kiss that the queenly maiden of the glaciers had given him when, in his dead mother's lap, he lay in the deep crevasse of ice from which almost as by a miracle he had been rescued.

The Journey to the New Home

RUDY was now eight years of age. His father's brother, who lived in the valley of the Rhone, on the other side of the mountain, wished to have the boy, as he could be better educated there and taught to do for himself. So also thought the grandfather, and he therefore agreed to part with him.

The time for Rudy's departure drew nigh. There were many more to take leave of than his grandfather. First there was Ajola, the old dog.

"Your father was the postilion, and I was the postilion's dog," said Ajola. "We have often journeyed up and down, and I know dogs and men on both sides of the mountains. It has not been my habit to speak much, but now that we have so short a time for conversation, I will say a little more than usual, and will tell you something upon which I have ruminated a great deal. I cannot understand it, nor can you; but that is of no consequence. I have gathered this from it—that the good things of this world are not dealt out equally either to dogs or to mankind. All are not born to lie in laps or to drink milk. I have never been accustomed to such indulgences. But I have seen a whelp of a little dog traveling in the inside of a mail coach, occupying a man's or a woman's seat, and the lady to whom he belonged, or whom he governed, carried a bottle of milk, from which she fed him. She also offered him spongecakes, but he would not condescend to eat them. He only sniffed at them, so she ate them herself. I was running in the sun by the side of the carriage, as hungry as a dog could be, but all *I* had to chew was the cud of bitter reflection. Things were not so justly meted out as they might have been—but when are they? May you come to drive in carriages, and lie in Fortune's lap. But you can't bring all this about yourself. I never could, either by barking or growling."

This was Ajola's discourse; and Rudy threw his arms round his neck and kissed him on his wet mouth. And then he grabbed the Cat in his arms, but the animal was angry at this, and exclaimed, "You are getting too strong for me, but I will not use my claws on you. Scramble away over the mountains—I have taught you how to do so. Never think of falling, but hold fast, have no fear, and you will be safe enough."

And the Cat sprang down and ran off, for he did not wish Rudy to see how sorry he was.

The hens hopped upon the floor. One of them had lost her tail, to a traveler, who chose to play the sportsman, and shot off her tail, mistaking the poor fowl for a bird of prey.

"Rudy is going over the hills," murmured one of the hens.

"He is in a hurry," said the other, "and I don't like leave-takings." And they both hopped out.

The goats also bleated their farewells, and very sorry they were to see him go.

Just at that time there were two active guides about to cross the mountains. They proposed descending the other side of the Gemmi, and Rudy was to accompany them on foot. It was a long and laborious journey for such a little fellow, but he had a good deal of strength, and his courage was indomitable.

The swallows flew a little way with him, and sang to him, "We and you, and you and we!"

The travelers' path led across the rushing Lütschine, which in numerous small streams falls from the dark clefts of the Grindelwald glaciers. Here the trunks of fallen trees and fragments of rock serve as bridges. They had soon passed the thicket of alders, and began to ascend the mountain, close to where the glaciers had loosened themselves from the side of the hill. And they went upon the glacier over the blocks of ice, and round them.

Rudy crept here, and walked there; his eyes sparkling with joy, as he firmly placed his iron-tipped mountain shoe wherever he could find footing for it. The small patches of black earth, which the mountain torrents had cast upon the glacier, gave it a burned appearance, but still the bluish-green, glass-like ice shone out visibly. They had to go round the little pools which were dammed up amidst detached masses of ice. In this circuitous route they approached an immense stone, which lay rocking on the edge of a crevasse in the ice. The stone lost its balance, toppled over, and rolled down; and the echo of its thundering fall resounded faintly from the glacier's deep abyss, far—far beneath.

Upward, always upward, they journeyed on. The glacier itself stretched upward, like a continued stream of ice piled up in wild confusion, amidst bare and rugged rocks. Rudy remembered for a moment what had been told him—that he, with his mother, had lain buried in one of these cold, mysterious fissures; but he soon threw off such gloomy thoughts, and only looked upon the tale as one among the many fables he had heard. Once or twice, when the men with whom he was traveling thought that it was rather difficult for so little a boy to mount up, they held out their hands to help him. But he never needed any assistance. He stood upon the glacier as securely as if he had been a chamois itself.

Now they came upon rocky ground, now mossy stones, now low pine trees, and again out upon the green pastures—always changing, always new. Around them towered lofty snow-clad mountains. Every child in the neighborhood knows their names—Jungfrau, the Monk, and Eiger.

Rudy had never before been so far from his home—never before beheld the wide-spreading ocean of snow that lay with its immovable billows of ice, from which the wind occasionally swept little clouds of powdery snow, as it sweeps the scum from the waves of the sea. Glacier stretched close to glacier—one might have said they were hand in hand, and each a crystal palace belonging to the Ice Maiden, whose pleasure and occupation it is to seize and imprison her victims.

The sun was shining warmly, and the snow dazzled the eyes as if it had been strewn with flashing pale-blue diamond sparks. Innumerable insects, especially butterflies and bees, lay dead in masses on the snow. They had winged their way too high, or else the wind had carried them upward to the regions that meant cold and death for them. Around Wetterhorn hung a threatening cloud that might be likened to a large tuft of very fine dark wool. It sank, bulging out with what it had concealed in itself—a *Föhn*,* fearfully violent in its might when it broke loose.

The whole of this journey—the night quarters above—the wild track—the mountain clefts where the water, during an incalculably long period of time, had penetrated through the

---

* *Föhn*, a humid south wind on the Swiss mountains and lakes, the forerunner of a storm.—*Translator*.

blocks of stone—made an indelible impression upon little Rudy's mind.

A forsaken stone building, beyond the sea of snow, gave the travelers shelter for the night. Here they found some charcoal and branches of pine trees. A fire was soon kindled, couches of some kind were arranged as well as they could be, and the men placed themselves near the blazing fire, took out their tobacco, and began to drink the warm spiced beverage they had prepared for themselves, nor did they forget to give some to Rudy.

The conversation fell upon the mysterious beings who haunt the Alpine land: upon the strange gigantic snakes in the deep lakes—the night folks—the specter host, that carry sleepers off through the air to the wonderful, almost floating city of Venice—the wild herdsman, who drives his black sheep over the green pastures. If these had not been seen, the sound of their bells and the frightful noise made by the phantom herds had undoubtedly been heard.

Rudy listened with intense curiosity to these superstitious tales, but without any fear, for *that* he did not know; and while he listened, he fancied that he heard the uproar of the wild spectral herd. Yes! It became more and more distinct. The men heard it too. They were awed into silence; and as they hearkened to the unearthly noise, they whispered to Rudy that he must not sleep.

It was a *Föhn* that had burst forth—that violent tempestuous wind which issues downward from the mountains into the valley beneath, and in its fury snaps large trees as if they were but reeds, and carries the wooden houses from one bank of a river to the other as we would move men on a chessboard.

After an hour had elapsed, Rudy was told that it was all over, and he might now go to sleep safely. Weary with his long walk, he did sleep, as if duty bound to do so.

At a very early hour in the morning, the party set off again. The sun that day lighted up new mountains, new glaciers, and new snowfields for Rudy. They had entered the Canton Valais, and were upon the other side of the ridge of hills seen from Grindelwald, yet still far from his new home.

Other mountain clefts, other pastures, other woods, and other hilly paths unfolded themselves; Rudy saw other houses, and other people too. But what kind of human beings were these? The outcasts of fate they were, with frightful, disgusting, yellowish faces, and necks from which the hideous flesh hung down like bags. They were the cretins—poor diseased wretches, dragging themselves along, and looking with stupid lusterless eyes upon the strangers who crossed their path— the women were even more disgusting than the men. Were these the people who would be round his new home?

The Uncle

WHEN Rudy arrived in his uncle's house, he saw, and he thanked God for it, people such as he had been accustomed to see. There was only one cretin there, a poor idiotic lad— one of those unfortunate beings who, in their poverty—in fact, in their utter destitution—go by turns to different families and remain a month or two in each house. Poor Saperli happened to be in his uncle's house when Rudy arrived.

The uncle was a bold and experienced hunter, and was by trade a cooper. His wife was a lively little woman, with a face something like that of a bird, eyes like those of an eagle, and a long skinny throat.

Everything was new to Rudy—the dress, customs, employments—even the language itself; but his childish ear would soon learn to understand that. The difference between his grandfather's home and his uncle's home was very favorable to the latter. The house was larger; the walls were adorned by horns of the chamois and brightly polished guns. A painting of the Virgin Mary hung over the door, and fresh Alpine roses, and a lamp that was kept always burning, were placed before it.

His uncle, as has been told, was one of the most renowned chamois hunters of the district, and was also one of the best and most experienced of the guides.

Rudy became the pet of the house; but there was another pet as well—a blind, lazy old hound, who could no longer be of any use. But he *had been* useful, and the worth of the animal in his earlier days was remembered, and he therefore now lived as one of the family, and had every comfort. Rudy patted the dog, but the animal did not like strangers, and as yet Rudy was a stranger; but he soon won every heart, and became one of them.

"Things don't go so badly in Canton Valais," said his uncle. "We have plenty of chamois; they do not die off so fast as the wild he-goats. Matters are much better nowadays than in old times. A hole is burst in the bag, and we have a current of air now in our confined valley. Something better always starts up when antiquated things are done away with."

The uncle became quite chatty, and talked to the boy of the events of his own boyhood and those of his father. Valais was then, as he called it, only a receptacle for sick people— miserable cretins. "But the French soldiers came, and they made capital doctors; they soon killed the disease, and the patients with it. They know how to strike—aye, how to strike in many ways—and the girls could strike too!" The uncle nodded to his wife, who was of French descent, and laughed. "The French could split solid stones if they chose. It was they who cut out of the rocks the road over the Simplon—yes, cut such a road that I could say to a child of three, 'Go down to

Italy! You just have to keep to the highroad, and you'll find yourself there.' " The good man then sang a French *chanson*, and wound up by shouting "hurrah!" for Napoleon Bonaparte.

It was the first time that Rudy had ever heard of France, and he was interested in hearing of it, especially Lyons, that great city on the river Rhone, where his uncle had been.

The uncle prophesied that Rudy would become, in a few years, a smart chamois hunter, as he had quite a talent for it. He taught the boy to hold, load, and fire a gun. He took him up with him, in the hunting season, among the hills, and made him drink of the warm chamois' blood to ward off giddiness from the hunter. He taught him to know the time when, upon the different sides of the mountains, avalanches were about to fall, at midday or in the evening, whenever the sun's rays took effect. He taught him to notice the movements of the chamois, and learn their spring, so that he might alight on his feet and stand firmly. And he told him that if on the fissures of the rock there was no footing, he must support himself by his elbows, and exert the muscles of his thighs and the calves of his legs to hold on fast. Even the neck could be of use, if necessary.

The chamois are cunning, and place outposts on the watch; but the hunter must be more cunning, and scent them out. Sometimes he might cheat them by hanging up his hat and coat on an Alpine staff, and the chamois would mistake the coat for the man. This trick the uncle played one day when he was out hunting with Rudy.

The mountain pass was narrow. Indeed, there was scarcely a path at all, scarcely more than a slight cornice close to the yawning abyss. The snow that lay there was partially thawed, and the stones crumbled away whenever they were trod on. So the uncle laid himself down his full length, and crept forward. Every fragment of stone that broke off, fell rolling and knocking from one side of the rocky wall to another, until it sank to rest in the dark depths below. About a hundred paces behind his uncle stood Rudy, upon the verge of the last point of solid rock, and as he stood, he saw careening through the air, and hovering just over his uncle, an immense *lämmergeier*, which, with one tremendous stroke of its wing, could speedily cast the creeping worm into the abyss beneath, and there prey upon his carcass.

The uncle had eyes for nothing but the chamois, which, with its young kid, had appeared on the other side of the crevasse. Rudy was watching the bird; well did he know what its aim was. And he kept his hand on his gun ready to fire the moment it might be necessary. Just then the chamois made a bound upward. Rudy's uncle fired, and the animal was hit by the deadly bullet, but the kid escaped as cleverly as if it had had a long life's experience in danger and flight. The enormous bird, frightened by the loud report, wheeled off in another direction; and the uncle was freed from a danger of which he was quite unconscious until Rudy told him about it.

In high good humor they wended their way homeward. The uncle was humming a tune he remembered from his younger days. They suddenly heard a peculiar noise, which seemed to come from near by. They looked round on both sides —they looked upward; and there, in the heights above, on the sloping verge of the mountain, the heavy covering of snow was lifted up, and it heaved, as a sheet of linen stretched out heaves when the wind creeps under it; and the lofty mass cracked as if it had been a marble slab—it broke, and, resolving itself into a foaming cataract, came rushing down with a rumbling noise like that of distant thunder. It was an avalanche that had fallen, not indeed over Rudy and his uncle, but near them—all too near!

"Hold fast, Rudy—hold fast with all your might!" cried his uncle.

Rudy threw his arms around the trunk of a tree that was

close by, while his uncle climbed above him and held fast to the branches of the tree. The avalanche rolled past a little distance from them, but the gust of wind that swept like the tail of a hurricane after it, rattled around the trees and bushes, and snapped them asunder as if they had been but dry rushes, and cast them down in all directions. Rudy was dashed to the ground, for the trunk of the tree to which he had clung was overthrown. The upper part was flung a great distance. There, amidst the shattered branches, lay his poor uncle with his skull fractured! His hand was still warm, but it would have been impossible to recognize his face. Rudy stood pale and trembling. It was the first shock in his young life—the first moment he had ever known terror.

Late in the evening he reached his home with the fatal tidings—his home which was now to be a home of sorrow. The bereaved wife stood like a statue—she did not utter a word—she did not shed a tear; and it was not until the corpse was brought in that her grief found its natural vent. The poor cretin stole away to his bed, and nothing was seen of him during the whole of the next day. Toward evening he came to Rudy.

"Will you write a letter for me?" he asked. "Saperli cannot write—Saperli can only go down to the post office with the letter."

"A letter for you?" exclaimed Rudy. "And to whom?"

"To our Lord Christ!"

"Whom do you mean?"

And the half-idiot, as the cretin was called, looked with a most touching expression at Rudy, clasped his hands, and said solemnly and reverentially—

"Jesus Christ! Saperli would send Him a letter to pray of Him that Saperli may lie dead, and not the good master of the house here."

And Rudy took his hand and wrung it. "That letter would

not go up there—that letter would not restore him we have lost."

But Rudy found it very difficult to convince Saperli of the impossibility of his wishes.

"Now you must be the support of the house," said his aunt to him. And Rudy became this.

Babette

WHO is the best marksman in the Canton Valais? The chamois well knew. "Save yourselves from Rudy!" they might have said. And "who is the handsomest marksman?" "Oh, it is Rudy!" said the girls. But they did not add, "Save yourselves from Rudy." Neither did the sober mothers say so, for he bowed as politely to them as to the young girls. He was so brave and so joyous, his cheeks so brown, his teeth so white, his dark eyes so sparkling. A handsome young man he was, and only twenty years of age. The most ice-chill water never seemed too cold for him when he was swimming—in fact he was like a fish in the water. He could climb better than anyone else; he could cling fast, like a snail, to the wall of rock. There were good muscles and sinews in him; this was quite evident whenever he made a spring. He had learned first from the Cat how to spring, and then from the chamois. Rudy had the reputation of being the best guide on the mountain, and he could have made a great deal of money by this occupation. His uncle had also taught him the cooper's trade, but he had no inclination for that. He cared for nothing but chamois hunting. He delighted in this, and *it* also brought in money. Rudy would be an excellent match, it was said, if he only did not look too high. He was such a good dancer that the girls who were his partners often dreamed of him, and more than one let her thoughts dwell on him even after she awoke.

"He kissed me in the dance!" said Annette, the schoolmaster's daughter, to her dearest friend; but she should not have said this even to her dearest friend. Such secrets are seldom kept: like sand in a bag that has holes, they ooze out. Therefore, however well behaved Rudy might be, it was soon spread about that he kissed in the dance. And yet he had never kissed the one he would have liked to kiss.

"Take care of him!" said an old hunter. "He has kissed Annette. He has begun with A, and he will kiss through the whole alphabet."

A kiss in the dance was all that the gossips could find to bring against Rudy. He certainly had kissed Annette, and yet she was not the flower of his heart.

Below at Bex, amidst the great walnut trees, close to a small rushing mountain stream, lived the rich miller. His dwelling house was a large building three stories high, with small turrets. Its roof was composed of shavings of wood covered with tinned iron plates, which shone in sunshine and moonlight. On the highest turret was a vane, a glittering arrow passed through an apple, in allusion to Tell's celebrated arrow shot. The mill was a conspicuous object, and permitted itself to be sketched or written about; but the miller's daughter did not permit herself to be described in writing or to be sketched—so at least Rudy would have said. And yet her image was engraved on his heart. Both her eyes blazed in on it, so that it was in flames. The fire had, like other fires, come on suddenly; and the strangest part of it was, that the miller's daughter, the charming Babette, was quite ignorant of it, for she and Rudy had never so much as spoken two words to each other.

The miller was rich, and, on account of his wealth, Babette was rather high to hope for. "But nothing is so high," said Rudy to himself, "that one may not aspire to it. One must climb perseveringly, and if one has confidence one does not fall." He had received this teaching in his early home.

It so happened that Rudy had some business to transact at Bex. It was a long journey to that place, for there was then no railroad. From the glaciers of the Rhone, immediately at the foot of the Simplon, among many and often shifting mountain peaks, stretches the broad valley of the Canton Valais, with its mighty river, the Rhone, whose waters are often so swollen they overflow its banks, inundating fields and roads, and destroying all. Between the towns of Sion and St. Maurice the valley takes a turn, bending like an elbow, and below St. Maurice it becomes so narrow that there is only space for the bed of the river and the confined carriage road. An old tower, like the guardian of the Canton Valais, which ends here, stands on the side of the mountain, and commands a view over the stone bridge to the customhouse on the other side, where the Canton Vaud commences; and nearest of the not very distant towns lies Bex. In this part, at every step forward, is an increased display of fruitfulness and abundance. One enters, as if it were a grove of chestnut and walnut trees. Here and there cypresses and pomegranates peep forth. It is almost as warm there as in Italy.

Rudy reached Bex, got through his business, and looked about him; but not a soul (Babette was out of the question) from the mill did he see. This was not what he wanted.

Evening came on. The air was filled with the perfume of the wild thyme and the blossoming lime trees. There lay what seemed a shining sky-blue veil over the wooded green hills. A stillness reigned around—not the stillness of sleep, not the stillness of death—no, it was as if all nature were holding its breath, in order that its image might be photographed upon the blue surface of the heavens above. Here and there amidst the trees stood poles, or posts, which conveyed the wires of the telegraph along the silent valley. Close against one of these leaned an object, so motionless that one might have thought it was the decayed trunk of a tree; but no, it was Rudy. He was standing there as still as all that was around him. He was not sleeping, nor was he dead. But, as through the wires of the telegraph there are often transmitted the great events of the world and matters of the utmost importance to individuals, without the wires, by the slightest tremor or faintest tone, betraying them, so there passed through Rudy's mind anxious overwhelming thoughts, fraught with the happiness of his future life, and constituting, from this time forth, his one unchanging aim. His eyes were fixed on one point before him, and that was a light in the parlor of the miller's house, where Babette resided. Rudy stood so still that one might have thought he was on watch to fire at a chamois; but at that moment he was like a chamois himself. One minute he could stand as if he were chiseled out of the rock, and suddenly, if a stone rolled past, he could make a spring and leave the hunter in the lurch. And thus did Rudy, for a thought rolled through his mind.

"Never despair!" said he. "A visit to the mill, say good evening to the miller, and good day to Babette. One does not fall unless one fears to do so. If I am to be Babette's husband, she must see me someday or other."

And Rudy laughed, and made up his mind to go to the miller's. He knew what he wanted, and that was to marry Babette.

The stream, with its yellowish-white water, was dashing on. The willows and lime trees hung over it. And Rudy, as it says in the old nursery rhyme—

> *Found to the miller's house his way;*
> *But there was nobody at home,*
> *Except a pussy cat at play!*

The cat, which was standing on the steps, put up its back and mewed; but Rudy was not inclined to listen to it. He knocked at the door; no one seemed to hear him, no one answered. The cat mewed again. Had Rudy been still a little boy, he might have understood the cat's language, and heard that it said "No one is at home." But now he had to go to the mill to make the necessary inquiries, and there he was told that the master had gone on a long journey to the town of Interlaken—"Inter Lacus, amidst the lakes," as the schoolmaster, Annette's father, in his great learning had explained the name.

Ah! so far away, then, were the miller and Babette? There was a great shooting match to be held at Interlaken. It was to begin the next morning, and to last for eight days. The Swiss from all the German cantons were to assemble there.

Poor Rudy! It was not a fortunate time for him to have come to Bex. He had only to return again. He did so, taking the road over St. Maurice and Sion to his own valley, his own hills. But he was not disheartened. When the sun rose next morning, he was in high spirits, but indeed they had never really been depressed.

"Babette is at Interlaken, a journey of many days from here," he said to himself. "It is a long way off if one goes by the circuitous highroad, but not so far if one cuts across the mountains, and that way just suits a chamois hunter. I have gone that way before. Over yonder lies my early home, where, as a little boy, I lived with my grandfather. And there are shooting matches at Interlaken. I shall take my place as the first there, and there also shall I be with Babette, and become acquainted with her."

Carrying his light knapsack, with his Sunday finery in it, and his musket and game bag, Rudy went up the mountain, the shortest though still long way. The shooting matches were only to begin that day, and were to continue for a week. During all that time, he had been assured, the miller and

Babette would stay with their relatives at Interlaken. So over the Gemmi trudged Rudy. He decided to descend near Grindelwald.

In high health and spirits he set off, enjoying the fresh, pure, and invigorating mountain air. The valleys sank deeper, the horizon became more extensive; here a snow-crested summit, there another, and speedily the whole of the bright shining Alpine range became visible. Rudy knew well every ice-clad peak. He kept his course opposite to Schreckhorn, which raised its white powdered stone finger high toward the blue vault above.

At length he had crossed the loftier mountain ridge. The pasture lands sloped down toward the valley that was his former home. The air was pleasant, his thoughts were pleasant. Hill and dale were blooming with flowers and verdure, and his heart was full of the glowing dreams of youth. He felt as if old age, as if death, were never to approach him, and life, power, enjoyment were before him. Free as a bird, light as a bird was Rudy; and the swallows flew past him, and sang as in the days of his childhood, "We and you, and you and we!" All was movement and pleasure.

Beneath lay the green velvet meadows, dotted with brown wooden houses. The river Lütschine rushed foaming along. He saw the glacier with its borders like green glass edging the dirty snow, and he saw the deep chasms, while the sound of the church bells came upon his ear, as if they were ringing a welcome to his old home. His heart beat rapidly, and his mind became so full of old recollections that for a moment he almost forgot Babette.

He was again traversing the same road where, as a little boy, he had stood along with other children to sell their carved wooden toy houses. Yonder, above the pine trees, his grandfather's house still stood, but strangers dwelt there now. The children came running after him, as before. They wished to sell their little wares. One of them offered him an Alpine rose. Rudy took it as a good omen, and thought of Babette. He had soon crossed the bridge where the two Lütschines unite, and reached the smiling country where the walnut and other embowering trees afford grateful shade. He soon saw waving flags, and beheld the white cross on the red ground—the standard of the Swiss as of the Danes—and before him lay Interlaken.

Rudy thought it was certainly a splendid town—a Swiss town in its holiday dress. It was not, like other market towns, a heap of heavy stone houses, stiff, foreign-looking, and aiming at grandeur; no! it looked as if the wooden houses from the hills above had taken a start into the green valley beneath, with its clear stream whose waters rushed swiftly as an arrow, and had ranged themselves into rows—somewhat unevenly, it is true—to form the street. And that prettiest of all, the street which had been built since Rudy was a little boy—*that* seemed to be composed of all the nicest wooden houses his grandfather had cut out, and with which the cupboard at home had been filled. They seemed to have transplanted themselves there, and to have grown in size, as the old chestnut trees had done.

Almost every house was a hotel, as it was called, with carved wooden work round the windows and balconies, with smart-looking roofs. Before each house was a flower garden, between it and the wide macadamized highroad. Near these houses, but only on one side of the road, stood some other houses: had they formed a double row, they would have concealed the fresh green meadow, where the cows wandered with bells that rang as in the high Alpine pastures. The valley was encircled by lofty hills, which, about the center, seemed to retire a little to one side, so as to render visible that glittering snow-white Jungfrau, the most beautiful of all the mountains of Switzerland.

What a number of gayly dressed gentlemen and ladies from foreign lands—what crowds of Swiss from the adjacent cantons! The candidates for the prizes carried the numbers of their shots in a garland round their hats. There was music of all kinds—singing, hand organs, and wind instruments, plus the shouting and hubbub of the crowd. The houses and bridges were adorned with verses and emblems. Flags and banners waved; the firing of gun after gun was heard, and that was the best music to Rudy's ears. Amidst all this excitement he almost forgot Babette, for whose sake he had gone there.

Crowds were thronging to the target shooting. Rudy was soon among them, and he was always the luckiest—the best shot—he always struck the bull's-eye.

"Who is that young stranger—that excellent marksman?" everyone asked. "He speaks the French language as they speak it in the Canton Valais. He also expresses himself fluently in our German," said several people.

"When a child he lived here in the valley, near Grindelwald," replied someone.

The youth was full of life; his eyes sparkled, his aim was steady, his arm sure, and therefore his shots always told. Good fortune bestows courage, and Rudy always had courage. He soon had a whole circle of friends round him. Everyone noticed him. In short, he was the observed of all observers. Babette had almost vanished from his thoughts. Just then a heavy hand was laid upon his shoulder, and a rough voice accosted him in the French language with—

"You are from the Canton Valais?"

Rudy turned round, and beheld a red jolly countenance and a stout person. It was the rich miller from Bex. His broad bulk hid the slender lovely Babette, who, however, soon came forward with her dark, bright eyes. The rich miller was very proud that it was a huntsman from his own canton that had been declared the best shot, and was so distinguished and so praised. Rudy was truly the child of good fortune; what he had traveled so far to look for, but had since his arrival nearly forgotten, now found him.

When at a distance from home one meets persons from there, acquaintance is speedily made, and people speak as if they knew each other well. Rudy held first place at the shooting matches, as the miller held first place at Bex, on account of his money and his mill. So the two men shook hands, although they had never met before. Babette, too, held out her hand frankly to Rudy, and he pressed it warmly, and gazed with such admiration at her that she became scarlet.

The miller talked of the long journey they had made, and the numerous large towns they had seen, and how they had traveled both by steam and by post.

"I came the shorter way," said Rudy. "I went over the mountains. There is no road so high that one cannot venture to take it."

"Aye, at the risk of breaking one's neck!" replied the miller. "And you look like one who will some day or other break his—you are so daring!"

"One does not fall unless one has the fear of doing so," said Rudy.

And the miller's relations at Interlaken, with whom he and Babette were staying, invited Rudy to visit them, since he came from the same canton as their kindred did. It was a pleasant invitation for Rudy. Luck was with him, as it always is with those who depend upon themselves, and remember that "our Lord bestows nuts upon us, but He does not crack them for us!"

And Rudy sat, almost like one of the family, among the miller's relations, and a toast was drunk in honor of the best shot, to which Rudy returned thanks, after clinking glasses with Babette.

In the evening the whole party took a walk on the pretty

avenue past the gay-looking hotels under the walnut trees; and there was such a crowd, and so much pushing, that Rudy had to offer his arm to Babette. He told her how happy he was to have met people from the Canton Vaud, for Vaud and Valais were close neighbors. He spoke so cordially that Babette could not resist squeezing his hand a little. They seemed almost like old acquaintances, and she was very lively —that pretty little girl. Rudy was much amused at her remarks about what was absurd and overfine in the dress of the foreign ladies, and the affectation of some of them. She did not wish to ridicule them, for there might be some excellent people among them—yes, nice amiable people, Babette was sure of that, for she had a godmother who was a very superior English lady. Eighteen years before, when Babette was christened, that lady was at Bex. She had given Babette the valuable brooch she wore. Her godmother had written to her twice, and this year they were to have met her at Interlaken, where she was coming with her daughters. They were old maids, going on thirty, said Babette—she herself was only eighteen.

The tongue in her pretty little mouth was not still for a moment, and all that she said appeared to Rudy to be matters of the greatest importance. And he told her what he had to tell—told her how he had been to Bex, how well he knew the mill, and how often he had seen her, though, of course, she had never noticed him. He said he had been more distressed than he could tell, when he found that she and her father were away, far away; but still not too far to prevent one from scrambling over the wall that made the road so long.

He said all this, and he said a great deal more. He told her how much she occupied his thoughts, and that it was on her account, and not for the sake of the shooting matches, that he had come to Interlaken.

Babette became very silent—it was almost too much, all that he confided to her.

As they walked on, the sun sank behind the lofty heights, and the Jungfrau stood in strong relief, clothed in a splendor and brilliancy reflected by the green woods of the surrounding hills. Everyone stood still and gazed at it. Rudy and Babette also stood and looked at the magnificent scene.

"Nothing can be more beautiful than this!" said Babette.

"Nothing!" said Rudy, with his eyes upon Babette.

"Tomorrow I must go," he added a little later.

"Come and visit us at Bex," whispered Babette. "My father will be so glad to see you."

On the Way Home

OH! how much Rudy had to carry next day when he started on his journey homeward over the mountains! He had two handsome guns, three silver goblets, and a silver coffeepot—the latter would be of use when he set up a house. But these valuables were not the weightiest load he had to bear; a still weightier load he had to carry—or did it carry him?—over the high, high hills.

The road was rough; the weather was dismal, gloomy, and rainy; the clouds hung like a mourning veil over the summits of the mountains, and shrouded their shining peaks. From the woods had resounded the last stroke of the ax, and down the side of the hill rolled the trunks of the trees. They looked like sticks from the vast heights above, but nearer they were seen to be like the thick masts of ships. The river murmured with its monotonous sound, the wind whistled, the clouds began to sail hurriedly along.

Close to Rudy there suddenly appeared a young girl. He had not seen her until she was quite near him. She also was going to cross the mountain. Her eyes had an extraordinary power; they seemed to have a spell in them—they were so clear, so deep, so unfathomable.

"Have you a lover?" asked Rudy. All his thoughts were filled with love.

"I have none," she replied with a laugh, but it seemed as if she did not speak the truth. "Let us not go the long way round. We must keep to the left; it is shorter."

"Yes—to fall into some crevasse," said Rudy. "You would know the paths better if you took it upon yourself to be a guide."

"I know the way well," she answered, "and I have my wits about me. Your thoughts are down yonder in the valley. Up here one should think of the Ice Maiden. Mankind say that she is not friendly to their race."

"I am not in the least afraid of her," said Rudy. "She could not keep me when I was a child. And she shall not catch me now that I am a man."

It became very dark, the rain fell, and it began to snow heavily. It dazzled the eyes, and blinded them.

"Give me your hand, and I will help you to mount upward," said the girl, touching him with her ice-cold fingers.

"*You* help me!" cried Rudy. "I do not yet require a woman's help in climbing." And he walked on more briskly away from her. The snowstorm thickened like a curtain around him, the wind moaned, and behind him he heard the girl laughing and singing. It sounded so strange. It was surely Glamourie, she surely, one of the attendants of the Ice Maiden. Rudy had heard of such things when, as a little boy, he had spent a night on the mountains, on his journey over the hills.

The snow fell more thickly, the clouds lay below him. He looked back. There was no one to be seen, but he heard laughter and jeering, and it did not seem to come from a human being.

When at length Rudy had reached the highest part of the

mountain, where the path led down to the valley of the Rhone, he saw on the pale blue of the horizon, in the direction of Chamouni, two glittering stars. They shone so brightly; and Rudy thought of Babette, of himself, and of his happiness, and grew warm with these thoughts.

The Visit to the Mill

"You have really brought costly things home," said his old foster mother, and her strange, eagle eyes sparkled, while she worked her thin, wrinkled neck even more quickly than usual. "You carry good luck with you, Rudy. I must kiss you, my dear boy."

Rudy allowed himself to be kissed, but it was evident by his countenance that he did not relish this domestic greeting.

"How handsome you are, Rudy!" exclaimed the old woman.

"Oh! don't flatter me," replied Rudy, laughing; but he was pleased at the compliment nevertheless.

"I repeat it," said the old woman, "and good fortune smiles on you."

"Yes, I believe you are right there," he said, while his thoughts strayed to Babette.

Never before had he longed so much for the deep valley.

"They must have come back," he said to himself; "it is now more than two days after the time they fixed for their return. I must go to Bex."

And to Bex he went. The miller and his daughter were at home. He was well received, and many greetings were given to him from the family at Interlaken. Babette did not speak much; she had become very silent. But her eyes spoke, and that was quite enough for Rudy. The miller, who generally had enough to say, and was accustomed to joke and have all his jokes laughed at, for he was *the rich miller*, seemed to prefer listening to Rudy's stirring adventures, and hearing him tell of all the difficulties and dangers that the chamois hunter has to encounter on the mountain heights—how he has to crawl along the unsafe snowy cornice work on the edges of the hills, which is attached to the rocks by the force of the wind and weather, and tread the frail bridges the snowstorm has cast over many a deep abyss.

Rudy spoke with much spirit, and his eyes sparkled while he described the life of a hunter, the cunning of the chamois and the wonderful springs they took, the mighty *Föhn*, and the rolling avalanche. He observed that, at every new description, the miller grew more and more interested and that he was particularly interested in his account of the *lämmergeier* and the bold royal eagle.

Not far from Bex, in the Canton Valais, there was an eagle's nest, built most ingeniously under a projecting platform of rock, on the margin of the hill. There was a young one in it, which no one could take. An Englishman had, a few days before, offered Rudy a large handful of gold if he would bring him the young eagle alive.

"But there are limits even to the most reckless daring," said Rudy. "The young eagle up there is not to be got at. It would be madness to make the attempt."

And the wine circulated fast, and the conversation flowed on faster, and Rudy thought the evening was much too short, although it was past midnight when he left the miller's house after this first visit.

The lights shone for a short time through the windows, and were reflected on the green branches of the trees, while through the skylight on the roof, which was open, the parlor Cat crept out and met the kitchen Cat in the water conduit on the roof.

"Don't you see that there is something new going on here?" said the parlor Cat. "There is secret love-making in the house. The father knows nothing of it yet. Rudy and Babette have been all the evening treading on each other's toes under the table. They trod on me twice, but I did not mew, for that would have aroused suspicion."

"Well *I* would have done it," said the kitchen Cat.

"What might suit the kitchen would not do in the parlor," replied the parlor Cat. "I should like very much to know what the miller will say when he hears of this engagement."

Yes, indeed—what would the miller say? *That* Rudy also was anxious to know. He could not bring himself to wait long. Therefore, before many days had passed, when the omnibus rolled over the bridge between the Cantons Valais and Vaud, Rudy sat in it, with plenty of confidence as usual, and pleasant thoughts of the favorable answer he expected that evening.

And when the evening had come and gone, and the omnibus was returning, Rudy also sat in it, going homeward. At the miller's, the parlor Cat jumped out again.

"Look here, you from the kitchen—the miller knows everything now. There was a strange end to the affair. Rudy came here toward the afternoon, and he and Babette had a great deal to whisper about. They stood on the path a little below the miller's room. I lay at their feet, but they had neither eyes nor thoughts for me.

" 'I will go straight to your father,' said Rudy. 'My proposal is honest and honorable.'

" 'Shall I go with you,' said Babette, 'that I may give you courage?'

" 'I have plenty of courage,' replied Rudy, 'but if you are with me, he must put some control upon himself, whether he likes the matter or not.'

"So they went in. Rudy trod heavily on my tail—he is very

clumsy. I mewed, but neither he nor Babette had ears for me. They opened the door, and entered together, and I with them, but I sprang up to the back of a chair. I could scarcely hear what Rudy said, but I heard how the master blazed forth. It was a regular throwing him out of his doors, up to the mountains and the chamois. Rudy could look after these, but not after our little Babette."

"But what did they say?" asked the kitchen Cat.

"Say! they said all that is generally said under such circumstances when people go a-wooing. 'I love her, and she loves me; and when there is milk in the can for one, there is milk in the can for two.'

" 'But she is far above you,' said the miller. 'She has lots of gold, and you have none. Don't you see that you cannot aspire to her?'

" 'There is nothing or no one so high that one may not reach if one is only determined to do so,' said Rudy, getting angry.

" 'But you said not long since that you could not reach the young eagle in its nest. Babette is a still higher and more difficult prize for you to take.'

" 'I will take them both,' replied Rudy.

" 'Very well! I will give her to you when you bring me the young eaglet alive,' said the miller, and he laughed until the tears stood in his eyes. 'But now, thank you for your visit, Rudy! If you come again tomorrow, you will find no one at home. Farewell, Rudy!'

"And Babette also said farewell, in as timid and pitiable a voice as that of a little kitten which cannot find its mother."

" 'A promise is a promise, and a man is a man!' said Rudy. 'Do not weep, Babette. I shall bring the young eagle.'

" 'You will break your neck, I hope!' exclaimed the miller. 'Then we shall be free of this bad job.' I call that sending him off with a flea in his ear!

"Now Rudy is gone, and Babette sits and cries, but the miller sings German songs which he learned in his journey. I shall not distress myself about the matter. It would do no good."

"But it is all very curious," said the kitchen Cat.

The Eagle's Nest

From the mountain path came the sound of a person whistling in a strain so lively that it betokened good humor and undaunted courage. The whistler was Rudy. He was going to his friend Vesinand.

"You must help me! We shall take Ragli with us. I must carry off the young eagle up yonder under the shelving rock!"

"Had you not better try first to take down the moon? That would be about as hopeful an undertaking," said Vesinand. "You are in great spirits, I see."

"Yes, for I am thinking of my wedding. But now, to speak seriously, you shall know how matters stand with me."

And Vesinand and Ragli were soon made acquainted with what Rudy wished.

"You are a daring fellow," they said, "but you won't succeed—you will break your neck."

"One does not fall if one has no fear!" said Rudy.

About midnight they set out with alpenstocks, ladders, and ropes. The road lay through copsewood and brushwood, over rolling stones—upward, always upward, upward in the dark and gloomy night. The waters roared below, the waters murmured above, humid clouds swept heavily along. The hunters reached at last the precipitous ridge of rock. It became even darker here, for the walls of rock almost met, and light penetrated only a little way down from the open space above. Close by, under them, was a deep abyss, with its hoarse-sounding, raging water.

They all three sat quite still. They had to await the dawn of day, when the parent eagle should fly out. All they could do was fire if they had any hope of capturing the young one. Rudy sat as still as if he had been a portion of the rock on which he sat. He held his gun ready to fire, his eyes were steadily fixed on the highest part of the cleft, under a projecting rock in which the eagle's nest was concealed. The three hunters had long to wait.

At length, high above them there was a crashing, whirring noise. The air was darkened by a large object soaring in it. Two guns were ready to aim at the enormous eagle the moment it flew from its nest. A shot was fired; for an instant the outspread wings fluttered, and then the bird began to sink slowly, and it seemed as if with its size and the stretch of its wings it would fill the whole chasm, and in its fall drag the hunters down with it. The eagle disappeared in the abyss below; the cracking of the trees and bushes was heard, as they snapped and crushed in the fall of the stupendous bird.

And now began the business that had brought the hunters there. Three of the longest ladders were tied securely together. They were intended to reach the outermost and last stepping place on the margin of the abyss. But they did not get so high. Higher up the perpendicular rocky ascent was as smooth as a well built wall. And this was where the nest was hidden under the shelter of the uppermost projecting portion of rock. After some consultation the young men came to the conclusion, that there was nothing better to be done than to hoist up two more ladders tied together, and then to attach these to the three which had already been raised. With immense difficulty they pushed the two ladders up, and the ropes

"A shot was fired; for an instant the outspread wings fluttered, and then the bird began to sink slowly, and it seemed as if with its size and the stretch of its wings it would fill the whole chasm."

were made fast. The ladders shot out from over the rock, and hung there swaying in the air above the unfathomable depth beneath. Rudy had placed himself already on the lowest step. It was an ice-cold morning. The mist was rising heavily from the dark chasm below. Rudy sat as a fly upon some swinging straw which a bird in building its nest might have dropped. But the fly could fly if the straw gave way—Rudy could only break his neck. The wind was howling around him, and away in the abyss below roared the gushing water from the melting glacier—the Ice Maiden's palace.

His ascent set the ladder into tremulous motion, as the spider does as it holds fast to its long waving slender thread. When Rudy had gained the top of the fourth ladder, he felt more confidence in them. He knew that they had been bound together by sure and skillful hands, though they dangled as if they had but slight fastenings.

But there was even more dangerous work before Rudy than mounting a line of ladders that now swayed like a frame of rushes in the air, and knocked against the perpendicular rock. He had to climb as a cat climbs. But Rudy could do that, thanks to the Cat who had taught him. He did not perceive the presence of Vertigo, who trod the air behind him, and stretched forth her polypus arms after him. He gained, at length, the last step of the highest ladder, and then he observed that he had not got high enough even to see into the nest. It was only by using his hands that he could raise himself up to it. He tried to see if the lowest part of the thick interlaced underwood, which formed the base of the nest, was sufficiently strong; and when he had assured himself that the stunted trees were firm, he swung himself up by them from the ladder, until his head and breast had reached the level of the nest. Then there poured forth to him a stifling stench of carrion; for putrefied lambs, chamois, and birds lay there crowded together.

Swimming-in-the-Head, a sister to Vertigo, though she could not overpower him, puffed the disgusting almost poisonous odor into his face, that he might become faint. And down below, in the black yawning ravine, upon the dank dashing waters, sat the Ice Maiden herself, with her long pale-green hair. She gazed upward with her death-giving eyes, while she exclaimed—

"Now I will seize you!"

In a corner of the eagle's nest, Rudy beheld the eaglet sitting—a large and powerful creature, even though it could not yet fly. Rudy fixed his eyes on it, held on marvelously with one hand, and with the other hand cast a noose around the young eagle; it was captured alive, its legs were in the tightened cord, and Rudy flung the sling with the bird over his shoulder, so that the creature hung a good way down beneath him. With the help of a rope, he held on, until at last his foot touched the highest step of the ladder.

"Hold fast! don't fear to fall, and you will not do so!" Such was his early lesson, and Rudy acted on it. He held fast, crept down, and did not fall.

A shout of joy and congratulation arose, and Rudy stood safely on the rocky ground, laden with his prize, the young eagle.

What More the Parlor Cat
Had to Tell

"HERE is what you demanded!" said Rudy, as he entered the miller's house at Bex, and placed a large basket on the floor. When he took its cover off, two yellow eyes surrounded by a dark ring glared forth—eyes so flashing, so wild, that they looked as though they would burn or blast everything they saw. The short hard beak opened to bite; the neck was red and downy.

"The young eagle!" exclaimed the miller. Babette screamed, and sprang to one side, but she could not take her eyes off Rudy and the eaglet.

"You are not to be frightened!" said the miller, addressing Rudy.

"And you will keep your word," said Rudy. "Everyone has his object."

"But how is it that you did not break your neck?" asked the miller.

"Because I held fast," replied Rudy; "and so I do now—I hold fast to Babette."

"Wait till you get her!" said the miller, laughing, and Babette thought that was a good sign.

"Let us take the young eagle out of the basket. It is frightful to see how its eyes glare. How did you manage to capture it?"

Rudy had to describe his feat, and, as he spoke, the miller's eyes opened wider and wider.

"With your confidence and your good fortune, you might maintain three wives," said the miller.

"Oh, thank you!" cried Rudy.

"But you won't get Babette just yet," said the miller, slapping the young Alpine hunter on his shoulder with good humor.

"Do you know there is something going on again here!" said the parlor Cat to the kitchen Cat. "Rudy has brought us the young eagle, and takes Babette as his reward. They have kissed each other in the father's presence! That was as good as a betrothal. The old man did not storm at all. He kept in his claws, took an afternoon nap, and left the two to sit and chatter to each other. They have so much to say that they will not be tired talking till Christmas."

And they were not tired talking till Christmas. The wind whirled in eddies through the groves, and shook down the yellow leaves. The snowdrifts appeared in the valleys as well as on the lofty hills. The Ice Maiden sat in her proud palace, which she occupied during the wintertime. The upright walls of rock were covered with sleet; enormous masses of ice tapestry were to be seen where, in summer, the mountain streams came pouring down; fantastic garlands of crystal ice hung over the snow-powdered pine trees. The Ice Maiden rode on the howling wind, over the deepest dales. The carpet of snow was laid down as far as Bex. She could go there, and see Rudy in the house where he now passed so much of his time with Babette. The wedding was to take place in summer, and they heard enough of it—their friends talked so much about it.

Then came sunshine; the most beautiful Alpine roses bloomed. The lovely laughing Babette was as charming as the early spring—the spring which makes all the birds sing of summertime, when the wedding day was to be.

"How these two do sit and hang over each other!" exclaimed the parlor Cat. "I am sick of all this stuff."

The Ice Maiden's Scorn of Mankind

SPRING had unfolded her fresh green garlands of walnut and chestnut trees which were bursting into bloom, particularly in the country that extends from the bridge at St. Maurice to the Lake of Geneva and the banks of the Rhone, which, with wild speed, rushes from its source under the green glaciers—the Ice Palace where the Ice Maiden dwells—where, on the keen wind, she permits herself to be borne up to the highest fields of snow, and, in the warm sunshine, reclines on their drifting masses. Here she sat, and gazed fixedly down into the deep valley beneath, where human beings, like ants on a sunlit stone, were to be seen busily moving about.

"Beings of mental power, as the children of the sun call you," cried the Ice Maiden, "ye are but vermin! Let a snowball but roll down, and you and your houses and your villages are crushed and overwhelmed." And she raised her proud head higher, and looked with death-threatening eyes around her and below her. But from the valley arose a strange sound: it was the blasting of rocks—the work of men—the forming of roads and tunnels before the railway was laid down.

"They are working underground like moles; they are digging passages in the rock, and therefore come these sounds like the reports of guns. I shall remove my palaces, for the noise is greater than the roar of thunder itself."

There ascended from the valley a thick smoke, which seemed agitated like a fluttering veil. It came curling up from the locomotive, which upon the newly opened railway drew the train that, carriage linked to carriage, looked like a winding serpent. With an arrow's speed it shot past.

"They pretend to be the masters down yonder, these powers of mind!" exclaimed the Ice Maiden. "But the mighty powers of nature are still the rulers."

And she laughed, she sang; her voice resounded through the valley.

"An avalanche is falling!" cried the people down there.

Then the children of the sun sang in louder strains about the power of thought in mankind. It commands all, it brings the wide ocean under the yoke, levels mountains, fills up valleys. The power of thought in mankind makes them lords over the powers of nature.

Just at that moment, there came, crossing the snowfields where the Ice Maiden sat, a party of travelers. They had bound themselves fast to each other, to be as one large body upon the slippery ice, near the deep abyss.

"Vermin!" she exclaimed. "*You*, the lords of the powers of nature!" and she turned away from them, and looked scornfully toward the deep valley, where the railway train was rushing by.

"There they go, these thoughts! They are full of might; I see them everywhere. One stands alone like a king, others stand in a group, and yonder half of them are asleep. And when the steam engine stops still, they get out and go their way. The thoughts then go forth into the world." And she laughed.

"There goes another avalanche!" said the inhabitants of the valley.

"It will not reach us," cried two who sat together in the train—"two souls, but one mind," as has been said. These were Rudy and Babette; the miller accompanied them.

"Like baggage," he said, "I am with them as a sort of necessary appendage."

"There sit the two," said the Ice Maiden. "Many a chamois have I crushed; millions of Alpine roses have I snapped and broken, not a root left—I destroyed them all! Thought—power of mind, indeed!"

And she laughed again.

"There goes another avalanche!" said those down in the valley.

The Godmother

At Montreux, one of the nearest towns, which, with Clarens, Bernex, and Crin, encircle the northeast part of the Lake of Geneva, resided Babette's godmother, the distinguished English lady. Her daughters and a young relation lived with her. They had only lately arrived, yet the miller had already paid them a visit, announced Babette's engagement, and told about

Rudy and the young eagle, the visit to Interlaken—and in short, the whole story. It had highly interested his hearers, and pleased them with Rudy, Babette, and even the miller himself. They were invited all three to come to Montreux, and they went. Babette ought to see her godmother, and her godmother wished to see her.

At the little town of Villeneuve, about the end of the Lake of Geneva, lay the steamboat, that, in a voyage of half an hour, went from there to Bernex, a little way below Montreux. It is a coast which has often been celebrated in song by poets. There, under the walnut trees, on the banks of the deep bluish-green lake, Byron sat, and wrote his melodious verses about the prisoner in the gloomy mountain castle of Chillon. There, where Clarens is reflected amidst weeping willows in the clear water, Rousseau wandered, dreaming of Eloise. The river Rhone glides away under the lofty snow-clad hills of Savoy; and here there lies not far from its mouth a small island, so small that from the shore it looks as if it were but a toy islet. It is a patch of rocky ground, which about a century ago, a lady caused to be walled round and covered with earth, in which three acacia trees were planted. These trees now overshadow the whole island. Babette had always been charmed with this little islet; she thought it the loveliest spot to be seen on the whole voyage. She said she would like so much to land there—she must land there—it would be so de-lightful under these beautiful trees. But the steamer passed it by, and did not stop until it had reached Bernex.

The little party proceeded then up amidst the white sunlit walls that surrounded the vineyards in front of the little town of Montreux, where the peasants' houses are shaded by fig trees, and laurels and cypresses grow in the gardens. Halfway up the hill stood the boardinghouse where the godmother lived.

The meeting was very cordial. The godmother was a stout

pleasant-looking woman, with a round smiling face. When a child she must certainly have exhibited a Raphael-like cherub's head. It was still an angel's head, but older, and with silver-white hair clustering round it. The daughters were well dressed, elegant-looking, tall and slender. The young cousin who was with them, and who was dressed in white almost from top to toe, and had red hair and red whiskers large enough to have been divided among three gentlemen, began immediately to pay the utmost attention to little Babette.

Splendidly bound books and drawings were lying on the large table; and music books were also to be seen in the room. The balcony looked out upon the beautiful lake, which was so bright and calm that the mountains of Savoy, with their villages, woods, and snowpeaks, were clearly reflected in it.

Rudy, who was generally so lively and so undaunted, found himself not at all at his ease. He was obliged to be as much on his guard as if he were walking on peas over a slippery floor. How tediously time passed! It was like being in a treadmill. And now they were to go out to walk! This was just as tiresome. Two steps forward and one backward Rudy had to take to keep pace with the others. They went down to Chillon, the gloomy old castle on the rocky island, to look at dungeons and instruments of torture, rusty fetters attached to the rocky walls, stone pallets for those condemned to death, trap doors through which the unfortunate creatures were hurled down to fall upon iron spikes amidst burning piles. They called it a pleasure to look at all these! It was a dreadful place of execution, elevated by Byron's verse into the world of poetry. Rudy viewed it only as a place of execution. He leaned against the wide stone embrasure of the window, and gazed down on the deep blue-green of the water, and over to the little solitary island with the three acacias. How much he wished himself there—free from the whole babbling party!

But Babette felt quite happy. She had been excessively

amused, she said afterward; the cousin had "found her perfect."

"Oh, yes—mere idle talk!" replied Rudy. And this was the first time he had ever said anything that did not please her.

The Englishman had made her a present of a little book as a souvenir of Chillon. It was Byron's poem, "The Prisoner of Chillon," translated into French, so that Babette was able to read it.

"The book may be good enough," said Rudy, "but the nicely combed fop who gave it to you is no favorite of mine."

"He looks like a meal sack without meal," cried the miller, laughing at his own wit.

Rudy laughed too, and said it was an excellent remark.

The Cousin

WHEN Rudy a few days afterward went to pay a visit to the miller, he found the young Englishman there. Babette had just placed before him a plate of trout, and she had taken much pains to decorate the dish. Rudy thought that was unnecessary. What was the Englishman doing there? What did he want? Why was he served and pampered by Babette? Rudy was jealous, and that pleased Babette. It amused her to see all the feelings of his heart—the strong and the weak. As yet love was to her but a pastime, and she played with Rudy's whole heart; but nevertheless it is certain that he was the center of all her thoughts—the dearest, the most valued in this world. Still, the more gloomy he looked, the merrier her eyes laughed. She could almost have kissed the fair Englishman with the red whiskers, if she could by doing this have seen Rudy rush out in a rage. It would have shown her how greatly she was beloved by him.

This was not right, not wise in little Babette; but she was only nineteen years of age. She did not reflect on her unkindness to Rudy; still less did she think how her conduct might appear to the young Englishman; was it not lighter and more wanting in propriety than became the miller's modest, lately betrothed daughter?

Where the highway from Bex passes under the snow-clad rocky heights, which, in the language of the country, are called Diablerets, stood the mill, not far from a rapid rushing mountain stream of a grayish-white color and looking as if covered with soapsuds. It was not that which turned the mill, but a smaller stream, which on the other side of the river came tumbling down the rocks, through a circular reservoir surrounded by stones in the road beneath. With its violence and speed it forced itself up and ran into an inclosed basin, a wide dam which, above the rushing river, turned the large wheel of the mill. When the dam was full of water, it overflowed, and caused the path to be damp and slippery. It was difficult to walk on it, and there was the chance of a fall into the water, and then being carried by it more swiftly than pleasantly toward the mill. Such a mishap had nearly befallen the young Englishman. Equipped in white like a miller's man, he was climbing the path in the evening, guided by the light that shone from Babette's chamber window. He had never learned to climb, and had almost gone head foremost into the water, but escaped with wet arms and bespattered clothes. Covered with mud and dirty-looking, he arrived beneath Babette's window, clambered up the old linden tree, and there began to mimic the owl—no other bird would he attempt to imitate. Babette heard the sounds, and peeped through the thin curtains; but when she saw the man in white and felt certain who he was, her little heart beat with terror, and also with anger. She quickly extinguished her light, felt if the window were securely fastened, and then left him to screech at his leisure.

How terrible it would be if Rudy were now at the mill! But Rudy was not at the mill. No—it was much worse—he was close by outside. High words were spoken—angry words— there might be blows, there might even be murder!

Babette hastened to open her window, and, calling Rudy's name, bade him go away, adding that she could not permit him to remain there.

"You will not permit me to remain here!" he exclaimed. "Then this is an appointment! You are expecting some good friend—someone whom you prefer to me! Shame on you, Babette!"

"You are unbearable!" cried Babette; "I hate you!" and she burst into tears. "Go—go!"

"I have not deserved this," said Rudy, as he went away, his cheeks like fire, his heart like fire.

Babette threw herself weeping on her bed.

"And you can think ill of me, Rudy—of me who love you so dearly!"

She was angry—very angry, and that was good for her; she would otherwise have been deeply afflicted. As it was, she could fall asleep and slumber as only youth can do.

Evil Powers

RUDY left Bex, and took his way homeward, choosing the path up the mountains, with its cold fresh air, where amidst the deep snow the Ice Maiden holds her sway. The largest trees with their thick foliage looked so far down that they were but potato tops. The pines and the bushes became smaller; the Alpine roses were covered with snow, which lay in single patches, like linen on a bleach field. One solitary blue gentian stood in his path; he crushed it with the butt end of his gun. Higher up two chamois showed themselves. Rudy's eyes sparkled, and his thoughts took flight into another world, but he was not near enough for a sure aim. Higher still he ascended, where only a few blades of grass grew amidst the blocks of ice. The chamois passed in peace over the fields of snow. Rudy pressed angrily on. Thick mists gathered around him, and presently he found himself on the brink of the steep precipice of rock. The rain began to fall in torrents. He felt a burning thirst; his head was hot, his limbs were cold. He looked for his hunting flask, but it was empty. He had not given it a thought when he rushed up the mountains. He had never been ill in his life, but now he experienced a sensation like illness. He was very tired, and felt a strong desire to throw himself down and sleep, but water was streaming all around him. He tried to arouse himself, but every object seemed to be dancing in a strange manner before his eyes.

Suddenly he beheld what he had never before seen there— a newly built low hut that leaned against the rock, and in the doorway stood a young girl. He thought she was the schoolmaster's daughter, Annette, whom he had once kissed in the dance, but she was not Annette; yet certainly he had seen her before, perhaps near Grindelwald the evening he was returning home from the shooting matches at Interlaken.

"How did you come here?" he asked.

"I am at home," she replied. "I am watching my flocks."

"Your flocks! Where do they find grass? Here there is nothing but snow and rocks."

"You know much about it, to be sure!" she said, laughing. "Behind this, a little way down, is a very nice piece of pasture land. My goats go there. I take good care of them; I never miss one; I keep what belongs to me."

"You are stouthearted," said Rudy.

"And so are you," she answered.

"If you have any milk, pray give me some; my thirst is almost intolerable."

"I have something better than milk," she replied. "You shall have that. Today some travelers came here with their guides. They left half a flask of wine behind them. They will not return for it, and I shall not drink it, so you can have it."

She went for the wine, poured it into a wooden goblet, and gave it to Rudy.

"It is excellent," said he. "I never tasted any wine so warming, so reviving." And his eyes beamed with a wondrous brilliancy; there came a thrill of enjoyment, a glow over him, as if every sorrow and every vexation were vanishing from his mind. The free gushing feeling of man's nature awoke in him.

"But you are surely Annette, the schoolmaster's daughter," he exclaimed. "Give me a kiss."

"First give me the pretty ring you wear on your finger."

"My betrothal ring?"

"Yes, just it," said the girl; and replenishing the goblet with wine, she held it to his lips, and again he drank. A strange sense of pleasure seemed to rush into his very blood. The whole world was his, he seemed to fancy—why torment himself? Everything is given for our gratification and enjoyment. The stream of life is the stream of happiness. Flow on with it, let yourself be borne away on it—that is felicity. He gazed on the young girl. She was Annette, and yet *not* Annette; still less was she the magical phantom, whom he had met near Grindelwald. The girl up here upon the mountain was fresh as the new-fallen snow, blooming like an Alpine rose, and lively as a kid; yet still formed from Adam's rib, a human being like Rudy himself. And he flung his arms around her, and gazed into her marvelously clear eyes. It was only for a moment; and in that moment—how shall it be expressed, how described in words? Was it the life of the spirit or the life of death which took possession of him? Was he raised higher, or was he sinking down into the deep icy abyss, deeper, always deeper? He beheld the walls of ice shining like blue-green glass; endless crevasses yawned around him, and the waters dripped with a sound like the chime of bells—they were clear as a pearl lighted by pale-blue flames.

The Ice Maiden kissed him; it chilled him through his whole body. He uttered a cry of horror, broke resolutely away from her, stumbled and fell. All became dark to his eyes, but he opened them again. The evil powers had played their game.

The Alpine girl was gone, the sheltering hut was gone; water poured down the naked rocks, and snow lay all around. Rudy was shivering with cold, soaked through to the very skin, and his ring was gone—the betrothal ring Babette had given him. His gun lay on the snow close by him. He took it up, and tried to discharge it, but it misfired. Damp clouds rested like thick masses of snow on the mountain clefts. Vertigo sat there, and glared upon her powerless prey, and beneath her rang through the deep crevasse a sound as if a mass of rock had fallen down, and was crushing and carrying away everything that opposed it in its furious descent.

At the miller's, Babette sat and wept. Six days had elapsed since Rudy had been there—he who was in the wrong, he who ought to ask her forgiveness, for she loved him with her whole heart.

At the Miller's House

"How frightfully foolish mankind are!" said the parlor Cat to the kitchen Cat. "It is all broken off now between Babette and Rudy. She sits and cries, and he thinks no more about her."

"I don't like that," said the kitchen Cat.

"Nor I either," replied the parlor Cat, "but I am not going to distress myself about it. Babette can take the red whiskers for her sweetheart. He has not been here since the evening he wanted to go on the roof."

The powers of evil carry on their game without and within us. Rudy was aware of this, and he reflected on it. What had passed around him and within him up yonder on the mountain? Was it sin, or was it a fever dream? He had never known fever or illness before. While he blamed Babette, he took a retrospective glance within himself. He thought of the wild tornado in his heart, the hot whirlwind which had recently broken loose there. Could he confess all to Babette—every thought which in the hour of temptation might have been carried out? He had lost her ring, and in this very loss she had won him back. Was any confession due from her to him? He felt as if his heart were breaking when his thoughts reverted to her—so many recollections crowded on his mind. He saw in her a laughing merry child, full of life; many of the affectionate words she had addressed to him in the fullness of her heart came, like a ray of the sun, to gladden his soul, and soon it was all sunshine there for Babette.

She must, however, apologize to him, and she should do so.

He went to the miller's, and confession followed. It began with a kiss, and ended in Rudy's being the sinner. His great fault was that he could have doubted Babette's constancy— *that* was too bad of him! Such distrust, such impetuosity, might cause misery to them both. Yes, very true! and therefore Babette preached him a little sermon, which pleased herself vastly, and during which she looked very pretty. But, in one particular, Rudy was right—the godmother's nephew was a mere babbler. She would burn the book he had given her, and not keep the slightest article that would remind her of him.

"Well, it is all right again," said the parlor Cat. "Rudy has come back, they have made friends; and that is the greatest of pleasures, they say."

"I heard during the night," said the kitchen Cat, "the rats declaring that the greatest of pleasures was to eat candle grease and to banquet on tainted meat. Which of them is to be believed, the lovers or the rats?"

"Neither of them," replied the parlor Cat. "It is always safest to believe no one."

The greatest happiness for Rudy and Babette was about to take place. The auspicious day, as it is called, was approaching —their wedding day!

But not in the church at Bex, not at the miller's house, was the wedding to be solemnized. The godmother had requested that the marriage should be celebrated at her house, and that the ceremony should be performed in the pretty little church at Montreux. The miller was very urgent that this arrangement be agreed to. He alone knew what the godmother intended to bestow on the young couple. They were to receive from her a wedding gift that was well worth such a small concession to her wishes. The day was set. They were to go to Villeneuve the evening before, in order to proceed by an early steamer next morning to Montreux, so the godmother's daughters might adorn the bride.

"There ought to be a second day's wedding here in this house," said the parlor Cat. "Else I am sure I would not give a mew for the whole affair."

"There is going to be a grand feast," replied the kitchen Cat. "Ducks and pigeons have been killed, and an entire deer hangs against the wall. My mouth waters when I look at all this. Tomorrow they start their journey."

Yes, tomorrow! That evening Rudy and Babette sat as a betrothed couple for the last time at the miller's house. Outside was the Alpine glow; the evening bells were ringing; the daughters of the sun sang, "That which is best will be!"

Night Visions

THE sun had set; the clouds lay low in the valley of the Rhone amidst the lofty mountains, the wind blew from the south—an African wind. Suddenly over the high Alps there arose a *Föhn* which swept the clouds asunder; and when the wind had lulled, all became for a moment perfectly still. The scattered clouds hung in fantastic forms amidst the wooded hills that skirted the rapid Rhone. They hung in forms like those of the marine animals of the antediluvian world, like eagles hovering in the air, and like frogs springing in a marsh. They sank down over the gushing river, and seemed to sail upon it, yet they sailed in the air. The current carried with it an uprooted pine tree; the water whirled in eddies around it. It was Vertigo and some of her sisters dancing in circles upon the foaming stream. The moon shone on the snow-capped hills, on the dark woods, on the curious white clouds—those appearances of the night that seem to be the spirits of nature. The mountain peasant saw them through his little window; they sailed outside in hosts before the Ice Maiden who came from her glacier palace. She sat on a frail skiff, the uprooted pine; the water from the glaciers bore her down to the river near the lake.

"The wedding guests are coming!" the air and the waters seemed to murmur and to sing.

Warnings without, warnings within! Babette had an extraordinary dream.

It seemed to her as if she were married to Rudy, and had been so for many years; that he was out chamois hunting, but she was at home; and that the young Englishman with the red whiskers was sitting with her. His eyes were full of passion, his words had as it were a magic power in them. He held out his hand to her, and she felt compelled to go with him. They went forth from her home, and always downward. And Babette felt as if there were a weight in her heart, which was becoming heavier every moment. She was committing a sin against Rudy—a sin against God. And suddenly she found herself forsaken. Her dress was torn to pieces by thorns, her hair was gray. She looked upward in deep distress, and on the margin of a mountain ridge she beheld Rudy. She stretched her arms up toward him, but did not dare either to call to him or to pray. Neither would have been of any good, for she soon saw that it was not him, but only his shooting jacket and cap hanging on an alpenstock. Hunters sometimes place them so, to deceive the chamois. And in great misery Babette exclaimed:

"Oh, that I had died on my wedding day—the day that was the happiest of my life! O Lord my God! that would have been a mercy—a blessing! That would have been the best thing that could have happened for me and Rudy. No one knows his future fate." And in impious despair she cast herself down into the deep mountain chasm. A string seemed to have broken —a tone of sorrow was echoed around.

Babette awoke. Her vision was at an end, and what had happened in the dream world had partially vanished from her mind. She knew she had dreamed something frightful, and dreamed about the young Englishman, whom she had not seen or thought of for several months. Could he still be at Montreux? Would she see him at her wedding? A slight shade of displeasure stole around Babette's pretty mouth, and for a moment her eyebrows knitted; but a smile soon came and a gay sparkle in her eye. The sun was shining so brightly outside, and tomorrow was their wedding day!

Rudy was already in the parlor when she came down, and shortly after they set off for Villeneuve. The two were all happiness, and the miller likewise. He laughed and joked, and was in the highest spirits. A kind father, a good soul, he was.

"Now we have the house to ourselves," said the parlor Cat.

The Conclusion

It was not yet late in the day when the three happy travelers reached Villeneuve. After they had dined, the miller placed himself in a comfortable armchair with his pipe, intending, when he had finished smoking, to take a short nap. The engaged couple went arm in arm out of the town, along the highroad, under the wooded hills that bordered the blue-green lake. The gray walls and heavy towers of the melancholy-looking Chillon were reflected in the clear water. The little island with the three acacias seemed quite near. It looked like a bouquet on the calm lake.

"How charming it must be over yonder!" exclaimed Babette, who felt again the greatest desire to go to it. And this time her wish might be gratified at once, for a boat was lying close to the bank, and the rope by which it was secured was easy to undo. There was no one of whom they could ask permission, so they got into it without leave. Rudy knew very well how to row. The oars, like the fins of a fish, divided the mass of water that is so pliant and yet so potent, so strong to bear, so ready to swallow—gentle, smiling, smoothness itself, and yet terror-inspiring and mighty to destroy. A line of foam floated behind the boat, which, in a few minutes, arrived at the little island, where the happy pair immediately landed. There was just room for two to dance.

Rudy swung Babette three or four times round, and then they sat down on the little bench under the drooping acacia, and looked into each other's eyes, and held each other's hands, while around them streamed the last rays of the setting sun. The pine forests on the hills assumed a purplish red tint, resembling the hue of the blooming heather. And where the trees stopped, and the bare rocks stood forward, there was a rich luster, as if the mountain were transparent. The skies were brilliant with a crimson glow; the whole lake was covered with a tinge of pink, as if it had been thickly strewn with fresh blushing roses. As the shades of evening gathered around the snow-decked mountains of Savoy, they became a dark blue in color, but the highest peaks shone like red lava, and for a moment reflected their light on the mountain forms before these vast masses were lost in darkness. It was the Alpine glow, and Rudy and Babette thought they had never before beheld one so magnificent. The snow-bedecked Dent du Midi gleamed like the disk of the full moon when it shows itself above the horizon.

"Oh, what beauty! Oh, what pleasure!" exclaimed the lovers at the same time.

"Earth can bestow no more on me," said Rudy; "an evening like this is as a whole life. How often have I been aware of my good fortune, as I am aware of it now, and have thought that, if everything were to come at once to an end for me, I have lived a happy life? What a blessed world is this! One day ends, but another begins, and I always fancy the last is the brightest. Our Lord is infinitely good, Babette."

"I am so happy," she whispered.

"Earth can bestow no more on me," repeated Rudy. And the evening bells rang from the hills of Savoy and the mountains of Switzerland. In golden splendor toward the west stood the dark-blue Jura.

"God grant you all that is brightest and best!" exclaimed Babette fervently.

"He will," said Rudy. "Tomorrow will fulfill that wish. Tomorrow you will be wholly mine—my own little charming wife."

"The boat!" cried Babette at that moment.

The boat which was to take them across again had got loose, and was drifting away from the island.

"I will bring it back," said Rudy. He took off his coat and boots, and, springing into the lake, swam vigorously toward the boat.

Cold and deep was the clear bluish-green icy water from the glacier of the mountain. Rudy looked down into it—he took but a glance, yet he saw a gold ring trembling, glittering, and playing there. He thought of his lost betrothal ring, and the ring became larger and extended itself out into a sparkling circle, within which appeared the clear glacier. Endless deep chasms yawned around it, and the water dropped tinkling like the sound of bells, and gleaming with pale-blue flames. In a second he beheld what it will take many words to describe. Young hunters and young girls, men and women who had been lost in the crevasses of the glacier, stood there, lifelike, with open eyes and smiling lips; and far beneath them arose from buried villages the church bells' chimes. Multitudes knelt under the vaulted roofs. Ice blocks formed the organ pipes, and the mountain torrents made the music. The Ice Maiden sat on the clear transparent ground. She raised herself up toward Rudy, and kissed his feet, and there passed throughout his limbs a deathlike chill, an electric shock—ice and fire: it was impossible to distinguish one from the other in the quick touch.

"Mine! mine!" sounded around him and within him. "I kissed thee when thou wert little—kissed thee on thy mouth! Now I kiss thee on thy feet. Now thou art wholly mine!"

And he disappeared in the clear blue water.

All was still around. The church bells had stopped ringing. Their last tones had died away along with the last streak of red on the skies above.

"Thou art mine!" resounded in the depths below. "Thou art mine!" resounded from beyond the heights—from infinity!

Happy to pass from love to love, from earth to heaven!

A string seemed to have broken—a tone of sorrow was

echoed around. The ice kiss of death had triumphed over the corruptible; the prelude to the drama of life had ended before the game itself had begun. All that seemed harsh, or sounded harshly, had subsided into harmony.

Do you call this a sad story?

Poor Babette! For her it was an hour of anguish. The boat drifted farther and farther away. No one on the mainland knew that the betrothed couple had gone over to the little island. The evening advanced, the clouds gathered, darkness came. Alone, despairing, wailing, she stood there. A furious storm came up. The lightning played over the Jura Mountains, and over those of Switzerland and Savoy. From all sides flash followed flash, while the peals of thunder rolled in all directions for many minutes at a time. One moment the lightning was so vivid that all around became as bright as day— every single vine stem could be seen as distinctly as at high noon—and in another moment the blackest darkness enveloped all. The lightning darted in zigzags around the lake, and the roar of the thunder was echoed among the surrounding hills. On land the boats were drawn far up on the beach, and all that were living sought shelter. And now the rain poured down in torrents.

"Where can Rudy and Babette be in this awful weather?" said the miller.

Babette sat with folded hands, with her head in her lap, exhausted by grief, by screaming, by weeping.

"In the deep water," she sobbed to herself, "far down yonder, as under a glacier, *he* lies."

She remembered what Rudy had told her about his mother's death, and of his being saved himself when taken up apparently dead from the cleft in the glacier. "The Ice Maiden has him again!"

And there came a flash of lightning as dazzling as the sun's rays on the white snow. Babette looked up. The lake rose at that moment like a shining glacier. The Ice Maiden stood there, majestic, pale, glittering, and at her feet lay Rudy's corpse.

"Mine!" she cried, and again all around was gloom, and darkness, and torrents of rain.

"Terrible!" groaned Babette. "Why should he die just when our happy day was so close at hand? Great God, enlighten my understanding—shed light upon my heart! I comprehend not Thy ways, determined by Thine almighty power and wisdom."

And God *did* shed light on her heart. A retrospective glance —a sense of grace—her dream of the preceding night—all crowded together on her mind. She remembered the words she had spoken—a wish for that which might be best for herself and Rudy.

"Woe is me! Was it the germ of sin in my heart? Was my dream a glimpse into the future, whose course had to be so violently stopped to save me from guilt? Unhappy wretch that I am!"

She sat wailing there in the pitch-dark night. During the deep stillness Rudy's words seemed to ring around her—the last he had ever spoken—"Earth can bestow no more on me!" Their sound was filled with the fullness of joy; they were echoed amidst the depths of grief.

Some few years have elapsed since then. The lake smiles, its shores smile; the vines bear luscious grapes; steamboats with waving flags glide swiftly by; pleasure boats with their two unfurled sails skim like white butterflies over the watery mirror; the railway beyond Chillon is open, and it goes far into the valley of the Rhone. At every station strangers issue from it—they come with their red-bound guidebooks, and study therein what they ought to see. They visit Chillon, observe the lake and the little island with the three acacias, and read in the book about a bridal pair who, in the year 1856, rowed over to it one afternoon—of the bridegroom's death, and of the next morning when the bride's despairing cries were heard upon the shore.

But the guidebook gives no account of Babette's quiet life at her father's house—not at the mill (strangers now live there), but at a pretty spot where from her window she can often look beyond the chestnut trees to the snowy hills over which Rudy loved to range. She can see at the hour of evening the Alpine glow—up where the children of the sun revel, and repeat their song about the wanderer whose cap the whirlwind carried off, but it could not take himself.

There is a rosy tint upon the mountain's snow—there is a rosy tint in every heart, which admits the thought, "God ordains what is best for us!" But it is not granted to us all so fully, as it was to Babette in her dream.

THE LITTLE MATCH GIRL

It was dreadfully cold, it was snowing fast, and almost dark. The evening—the last evening of the Old Year—was drawing in. But, cold and dark as it was, a poor little girl, with bare head and feet, was still wandering about the streets. When she left her home she had slippers on, but they were much too large for her—indeed, they really belonged to her mother —and had dropped off her feet while she was running very fast across the road, to get out of the way of two carriages. One of the slippers was not to be found. The other had been snatched up by a little boy, who ran off with it, thinking it might serve him as a doll's cradle.

So now the little girl walked on, her bare feet quite red and blue with the cold. She carried a small bundle of matches in her hand, and a good many more in her tattered apron. No one had bought any of them the whole livelong day. No one had given her a single penny. Trembling with cold and hunger she crept on, the picture of sorrow. Poor little child!

The snowflakes fell on her long, fair hair, which curled in pretty ringlets over her shoulders; but she thought not of her own beauty, nor of the cold. Lights were glimmering through every window, and the savory smell of roast goose reached her from several houses. It was New Year's Eve, and it was of this that she was thinking.

In a corner formed by two houses, one of which projected beyond the other, she sat down, drawing her little feet close under her, but in vain—she could not warm them. She dared not go home; she had sold no matches, earned not a single penny, and perhaps her father would beat her. Besides, her

home was almost as cold as the street, for it was an attic. And, although the larger of the many chinks in the roof were stopped up with straw and rags, the wind and snow often came through. Her hands were nearly dead with cold. One little match from her bundle would warm them, perhaps, if she dared light it. She drew one out, and struck it against the wall. Bravo! It was a bright, warm flame, and she held her hands over it. It was quite an illumination for that poor little girl—nay, call it instead a magic taper, for it seemed to her as though she were sitting before a large iron stove with brass ornaments, so beautifully blazed the fire within! The child stretched out her feet to warm them also. But alas! In an instant the flame had died away, the stove vanished, and the little girl sat cold and comfortless, with the burned match in her hand.

A second match was struck against the wall. It kindled and blazed, and wherever its light fell the wall became transparent as a veil, and the little girl could see into the room within. She saw the table spread with a snow-white damask cloth, whereon shining china dishes were arranged. The roast goose stuffed with apples and dried plums stood at one end, smoking-hot. And what was pleasantest of all, was the goose. With knife and fork still in her breast, she jumped down from the dish, and waddled along the floor right up to the poor child. But the match burned out, and only the thick, hard wall was beside her.

She kindled a third match. Again the flame shot up. And now she was sitting under a most beautiful Christmas tree, far larger, and far more prettily decked out, than the one she had seen last Christmas Eve through the glass doors of the rich merchant's house. Hundreds of wax tapers lighted up the green branches, and tiny painted figures, like the ones she had seen in the shop windows, looked down at her from the tree. The child stretched out her hands toward them in delight, and in that moment the light of the match was quenched. Even so the Christmas candles still burned, higher and higher, and she beheld them beaming like stars in heaven. One of them fell, the lights streaming behind it like a long, fiery tail.

"Now someone is dying," said the little girl, softly, for she had been told by her old grandmother, the only person who had ever been kind to her, and who was now dead, that whenever a star falls an immortal spirit returns to the God who gave it life.

She struck another match against the wall. It flamed up, and, surrounded by its light, there appeared before her that same dear grandmother, gentle and loving as always, but bright and happy as she had never looked during her lifetime.

"Grandmother!" exclaimed the child, "oh, take me with you! I know you will leave me as soon as the match goes out—you will vanish like the warm fire in the stove, like the splendid New Year's feast, like the beautiful large Christmas tree!" And she quickly lighted all the remaining matches in the bundle, lest her grandmother should disappear. And the matches burned with such a blaze of splendor, that noonday could scarcely have been brighter. Never had the good old grandmother looked so tall and stately, so beautiful and kind. She took the little girl in her arms, and they both flew together—joyfully and gloriously they flew—higher and higher, till they were in that place where neither cold, nor hunger, nor pain, is ever known—they were in Paradise.

In the cold morning hour, crouching in the corner of the wall, the body of the poor little girl was found—her cheeks glowing, her lips smiling—frozen to death on the last night of the Old Year. The New Year's sun shone on the lifeless child. She sat there with the matches in her lap, and one bundle of them was all burned out.

"She had been trying to warm herself, poor thing!" the people said. But no one knew of the sweet visions she had beheld, or how gloriously she and her grandmother were celebrating their New Year's festival.

THE LITTLE MERMAID

FAR out at sea the water is as blue as the petals of the loveliest cornflower, and as clear as the purest glass, but it is very deep, deeper than the length of the cable of any anchor, and many church steeples would have to be put on top of each other to reach from the bottom up over the water. Down there the sea people live.

Now, you mustn't for a moment think that down there they have only the bare white sand. Oh, no, the strangest trees and plants grow there, with leaves and stems so supple that at the least stir in the water they move as if they were alive. All the fishes, big and little, dart through the branches just like the birds in the air up here. In the very deepest spot lies the castle of the Sea King. The walls are of coral and the tall, pointed windows of the clearest amber. The roof is made of mussel shells that open and close with the flow of the water. That looks lovely, for in each shell lie gleaming pearls, and just a single one of them would be the grandest thing in the crown of any queen.

The Sea King down there had been a widower for many years, and his old mother kept house for him. She was a clever woman, but proud of her royal birth, and therefore she wore twelve oysters on her tail; the other people of rank could wear only six. Otherwise she deserved only praise, especially because she was so fond of her granddaughters, the little Sea Princesses. They were six lovely children, but the youngest was the most beautiful of them all. Her skin was as clear and as fine as a rose leaf, her eyes were as blue as the deepest sea, but, like all the rest, she had no feet, for her body ended in a fishtail.

All day long they could play in the castle, down in the halls, where living flowers grew out of the walls. The large amber windows were opened, and then the fishes swam into them, just as the swallows fly in to us when we open our windows. But the fishes swam straight up to the Princesses, ate out of their hands, and let themselves be petted.

Outside the castle was a large garden with fiery red and dark blue trees. The fruits gleamed like gold, and the flowers like a burning fire, always moving their stalks and leaves. The earth itself was of the finest sand, but blue as the flame of brimstone. A strange blue light lay on everything down there. One would have thought oneself high in the air, with the sky above and below, rather than at the bottom of the sea. During a calm the sun could be seen; it seemed like a purple flower, from whose chalice all light streamed out.

Each of the little Princesses had her own little plot in the garden, where she might dig and plant whatever she wanted. One gave her flower bed the form of a whale; another thought it better to make hers like a little mermaid; but the youngest made hers quite round, like the sun, and had only flowers which shone as red as the sun itself. She was a queer child, quiet and thoughtful; and when the other sisters dressed their plots up with strange things they had got from wrecked ships, she would have nothing except the red flowers which resembled the sun, and a pretty marble statue. This was a figure of a charming boy, hewn out of white clear stone, which had sunk down to the bottom of the sea from a wreck. She planted a rose-pink weeping willow beside this statue. The tree grew splendidly; it hung its fresh branches over the statue down to the blue sandy ground, where the shadow showed violet, and moved like the branches. It seemed as if the top of the tree and the roots were playing at kissing each other.

There was no greater pleasure for her than to hear of the world of men above them. The old grandmother had to tell all she knew of ships and towns, of men and animals. She found it especially strange and lovely that the flowers on earth had fragrance—they had none at the bottom of the sea— and that the woods were green, and that the fishes which one saw there among the trees could sing so loud and clear that it was a pleasure to hear them. What the grandmother called fishes were really the little birds. Otherwise they wouldn't have understood her, for they had never seen a bird before.

"When you have completed your fifteenth year," said the grandmother, "you'll be allowed to rise up out of the sea, to sit on the rocks in the moonlight, and to see the great ships sailing by. Then you will see forests and towns!"

The next year one of the sisters was fifteen years of age, but each of the others was one year younger than the next; so that the youngest had all of five years to wait before she could come up from the bottom of the sea, and find out how our world looked. But one promised to tell the others what she had seen and what she had thought the most beautiful on the first day of her visit. For their grandmother hadn't told them enough—there were so many things they wanted to know about.

None was so full of longing as the youngest—just that one who had the longest time to wait, and who was always quiet and thoughtful. Many a night she stood by the open window, and looked up through the dark blue water at the fishes splashing with their fins and tails. Moon and stars she could see; of course they shone faintly, but through the water they looked much larger than they do to us. When something like a black cloud passed among them, she knew that it was either a whale swimming over her head, or a ship with many people: they certainly did not think that a lovely little mermaid was standing down below stretching up her white hands toward the keel of their ship.

Now the eldest Princess was fifteen years old, and was allowed to rise up to the surface of the sea.

When she came back, she had a hundred things to tell—but the nicest of all, she said, was to lie in the moonshine on a sandbank in the quiet sea, and to see the large town close to the coast, where the lights twinkled like a hundred stars, and to hear the music and the noise and clamor of carriages and men, to see the many church steeples, and to hear the ringing of the bells. Just because she couldn't get up there, she longed for them more than for anything else.

Oh, how the youngest sister listened. And afterward when she stood at the open window and looked up through the dark blue water, she thought of the great city with all its bustle and noise; and then she thought she could hear the church bells ringing, even down to the depth where she was.

In the following year, the second sister was allowed to rise up through the water and to swim wherever she pleased. She rose up just as the sun was setting; and that sight seemed to her the most beautiful. The whole sky had looked like gold, she said, and the clouds—well, their loveliness was more than she could describe. Red and violet they sailed away above her, but, far swifter than they, a flight of wild swans flew like a long white veil over the water in the path of the sun. She swam toward them; but the sun sank, and the rose light quenched on the sea and in the clouds.

In the following year the next sister went up. She was the boldest of them all, and therefore she swam up a broad stream that ran to the sea. She saw lovely green hills clothed with vines; castles and farms peeped out from fine woods; she heard how all the birds sang; and the sun shone so warm that she often had to dive under the water to cool her burning face. In a little bay she found a whole swarm of little human children. They were quite naked, and splashed about in the water. She wanted to play with them, but they ran away scared, and a little black animal came—it was a dog, but she had never seen a dog—and it barked at her so terribly that she became frightened, and took to the open sea. But she could never forget the fine woods, the green hills, and the pretty children, who could swim in the water even though they had no fishtails.

The fourth sister was not so bold: she stayed in the midst of the stormy sea, and declared that just there it was most beautiful. One could see for many miles around, and the sky above looked like a bell of glass. She had seen ships, but only in the far distance—they looked like sea gulls; and the funny dolphins had thrown somersaults, and the big whales spouted out water from their nostrils, so that it looked like hundreds of fountains all around.

Now came the turn of the fifth sister. Her birthday came in the winter, and so she saw what the others had not seen the first time. The sea looked quite green, and large icebergs floated all around. Every one looked like a pearl, she said, and they were much taller than the church steeples built by men. They came in the strangest shapes, and sparkled like diamonds. She had seated herself on one of the largest, and all the sailing ships tacked around, frightened, hurrying to get out of her way and let the wind play with her long hair. But in the evening clouds covered the sky. It thundered and lightened, and the black waves lifted the great ice blocks high up, and let them shine in the big flashes. On all the ships the sails were reefed, and there were fear and anguish. But she sat quietly on her floating iceberg, and saw the blue lightning strike zigzag into the sea.

Each of the sisters was delighted with the new and beautiful sights she saw when she first came out of the water. But now since they were allowed, as grown-up girls, to go whenever they liked, they didn't really care to. They wished themselves back again, and after about a month they said it was best of all down below, for there one felt so cozily at home.

Many an evening hour the five sisters linked arms and rose up in a row over the water. They had lovely voices, more charming than any mortal could have. And when a storm was approaching, and ships might be expected to go down, they swam in front of the ships and sang lovely songs, about how beautiful it was at the bottom of the sea, and they told the sailors not to be afraid to come down. But the sailors couldn't understand the words. And they thought it was the storm. They did not see the beauty below, for if the ships sank they were drowned, and came only as corpses to the Sea King's palace.

When the sisters rose up, arm in arm, in the evening through the water, the little sister stood all alone looking after them. She felt as if she must cry, but the mermaid has no tears, and so she suffers all the more.

"Oh, if I were only fifteen years old!" said she. "I know I shall love the world up there very much, and the people who live and dwell there."

And at last she was really fifteen years old.

"Well, now you're off our hands," said the grandmother, the old dowager Queen. "Come, let me dress you up like your sisters."

And she put a wreath of white lilies in the girl's hair, but each petal in the flower was half a pearl. And the old lady let eight big oysters pinch onto the princess's tail, in token of her high rank.

"But that hurts so!" said the little mermaid. "Well, you can't have both style and comfort," said the old lady.

Oh, how glad she would have been to shake off all the finery and to lay aside the heavy wreath! Her red flowers in the garden were much more becoming, but she was afraid to change. "Good-by!" she said, and then she rose, light and clear as a bubble, up through the water.

The sun had just set when she lifted her head above the sea, but all the clouds still shone like roses and gold, and in the pale pink sky the evening star gleamed bright and beautiful. The air was mild and fresh and the sea without a ripple. There lay a great ship with three masts; one single sail only was set, for not a breeze stirred, and around in the tackling and on the yards sat the sailors. There were music and singing, and as the evening closed in, hundreds of colored lanterns were lighted, and it looked as if the flags of every nation were waving in the air. The little mermaid swam straight to the cabin window, and each swell of the sea lifted her up and she could look through the panes. They were clear as crystal, and she could see people standing, all dressed in their best. But the handsomest of all was the young Prince with the great black eyes. He couldn't be much more than sixteen years old. It was his birthday, and therefore they were having this fine party. The sailors were dancing on deck; and when the young Prince came out, more than a hundred rockets rose into the air. They shone as bright as day, so that the little mermaid was almost frightened, and dived under the water; but soon she put out her head again, and then it seemed as if all the stars of heaven were falling down on her. She had never seen such fireworks. Big suns whirled around, splendid fire fishes swung up into the blue air, and everything was mirrored in the clear, still sea. The ship itself was so brightly lit up that every little rope could be seen, and the people even more clearly. Oh, how handsome the young Prince was! And he pressed the people's hands and smiled, while the music rang out in the lovely night.

It grew late; but the little mermaid could not turn her eyes from the ship and from the beautiful Prince. The colored lanterns were put out, rockets no longer flew into the air, and no more cannons were fired. But away down in the deep the sea murmured and muttered; and she sat on the water, swaying up and down, so that she could look into the cabin. As the ship went faster, one sail after another was spread. And now the waves rose higher, big clouds came up, and there was lightning in the distance. Oh! it was going to be terrible weather; and the sailors furled the sails. The big ship flew over the wild sea; the water rose up like great black mountains, ready to fall on the masts; but like a swan the ship ducked down among the high waves and was lifted again on the towering waters.

The little mermaid thought this was an amusing trip, but the sailors didn't think so. The ship groaned and creaked; the thick planks were bent by the heavy blows the sea struck against the ship. At last the mainmast snapped in two like a thin reed; and the ship lay over on her side, while the water rushed into the hold.

Now the little mermaid saw that the people were in danger; and she herself had to take care to avoid the beams and bits of the ship which were floating about on the water. One moment it was so pitch dark she couldn't see a thing, but when it lightened it was so bright she could see every one on board. Every one was doing the best he could for himself. She looked particularly for the young Prince, and when the ship finally collapsed she saw him sink into the deep sea. At first she was very glad, for now he would come down to her. But then she remembered that people could not live in the water, and that when he got down to her father's palace he would certainly be dead. No, he must not die. She swam around among the drifting beams and planks, quite forgetting that one of them might have crushed her. Diving down deep under the water, she again rose high up among the waves, and in this way she at last came to the Prince, who could scarcely swim any longer in that stormy sea. His arms and legs began to fail him, his beautiful eyes closed, and he would have died if the little mermaid hadn't come. She held his head up over the water, and then let the waves carry her and him wherever they wanted to.

In the morning the bad weather was over. There wasn't a stick of the ship left. The sun came up red and shining out of the water; it was as if its sunbeams brought back life to the cheeks of the Prince. But his eyes remained closed. The mermaid kissed his high fair forehead and put back his wet hair, and he seemed to her to be like the marble statue in her little garden. She kissed him again and hoped that he might live.

Now she saw dry land in front of her—high blue mountains, on whose tops the white snow gleamed as if swans were lying there. Down on the coast were lovely greenwoods, and there was a building—she could not tell whether it was a church or a convent—but a building it was. In its garden grew orange and lemon trees, and high palms waved in front of the gate. The sea formed a little bay there; it was calm, but very deep. Straight toward the rock where the fine white sand had been cast up, she swam with the handsome Prince, and laid him on the sand, taking especial care that his head was raised in the warm sunshine.

Now all the bells rang in the big white building, and many young girls came walking through the garden. Then the little mermaid swam farther out between some high stones that rose out of the water, laid some sea foam on her hair and neck, so that no one could see her little face, and watched to see who would come to help the poor Prince.

In a short time a young girl came by. She seemed to be quite frightened, but only for a moment. Then she brought more people, and the sea maid saw that the Prince came back to life and that he smiled at everybody around him. But he didn't smile in her direction; he couldn't know, of course, that she had saved him. She felt very sorrowful; and when he was taken away into the big building, she dived mournfully under the water and returned to her father's palace.

She had always been gentle and thoughtful, but now she became much more so. Her sisters asked her what she had seen for the first time up there, but she wouldn't tell them anything.

Many an evening and many a morning she went up to the place where she had left the Prince. She saw how the fruits of the garden grew ripe and were gathered; she saw how the snow melted on the high mountain; but she did not see the Prince, and so she always returned home more sorrowful still. Then her only comfort was to sit in her little garden, and to put her arms around the beautiful marble statue that looked like the Prince. She didn't take care of her flowers; they grew like a wilderness over the paths, and trailed their long leaves and stalks up into the tree branches, so that it was quite dark there.

At last she couldn't stand it any longer, and told everything to one of her sisters, and others heard of it too. And nobody knew except these and a few other mermaids who didn't say a word except to their best friends. One of these knew who the Prince was; she, too, had seen the festival on board the ship; and she knew where he came from and where his kingdom lay.

"Come, little sister!" said the other Princesses; and linking their arms together, they rose up in a long row out of the sea, at the place where they knew the Prince's palace stood.

This palace was built of a pale yellow, glistening stone, with great marble staircases, one of which went right down into the sea. Over the roof rose splendid gilt cupolas, and between the pillars which surrounded the whole building stood marble statues which looked as if they were alive.

Through the clear glass in the tall windows one looked into the most gorgeous halls, where costly silk curtains and tapestries were hung, and all the walls were decked with splendid pictures. It was a perfect delight to look at them. In the middle of the largest hall a big fountain splashed. Its jets shot high up toward the glass dome in the ceiling, and the sun shone down upon the water and on the lovely plants growing in the great basin.

Now she knew where he lived, and many an evening and many a night she spent there on the water. She swam closer to the land than any of the others would have dared. Indeed, she even went up the narrow canal under the splendid marble balcony, which threw a long shadow on the water. Here she sat and watched the young Prince, who thought himself all alone in the bright moonlight.

Many an evening she saw him sailing. There was music in his fine boat, the flags were waving! She peeped up through the green reeds, and when the wind caught her silvery-white veil, and anyone saw it, they thought it was a white swan lifting its wings.

Many a night when the fishermen lay with torches on the sea she heard them tell much good of the young Prince. And she was happy that she had saved his life when he was drifting half dead on the waves; she thought how quietly his head had rested on her bosom, and how tenderly she had kissed him. But he knew nothing of this, and could not even dream of her.

More and more she began to love human beings, and more and more she wanted to rise up among them. Their world seemed far larger than her own. For they could fly over the sea in ships, and mount up the high hills far above the clouds. And the lands they owned stretched out in woods and fields farther than her eyes could reach. There was so much she wanted to know, but her sisters couldn't answer all her questions. So she asked the old grandmother; for she was well acquainted with the "higher world" as she very rightly called the countries above the sea.

"If human beings are not drowned," asked the little mermaid, "can they live forever? Don't they die as we die down here in the sea?"

"Yes," said the old lady. "They, too, must die, and their life is even shorter than ours. We can live to be three hundred years old, but when we no longer exist here, we become only foam on the water, and have not even a grave down here among those we love. We have no immortal soul; we never receive another life; we are like the green rushes that once severed can never be green again. But human beings have a soul which lives forever, lives even after the body has turned to earth. It rises through the bright air up to all the shining stars. Just as we rise out of the water and see the human countries, so they rise up to lovely, unknown places, never to be seen by us."

"Why didn't we get an immortal soul?" asked the little mermaid sorrowfully. "I would gladly give all the hundreds of years I have to live to be a human being only for one day, and later to come to the world of heaven."

"You mustn't be thinking about that," said the old lady. "We're much happier and much better off than the people up there."

"I must die and float as foam on the sea, and not hear the music of the waves, and not see the pretty flowers and the red sun? Can I not do anything to win an immortal soul?"

"No!" answered the grandmother. "Only if a man were to love you so that you should be more to him than father or mother. If he should cling to you with his every thought and with all his love, and let the priest lay his right hand in yours with a promise of faithfulness here and in all eternity, then his soul would flow into your body, and you would receive a share of the happiness of mankind. He would give a soul to you and still keep his own. But that can never come to pass. The thing that's so nice here in the sea—the fishtail—they would consider ugly on the earth. They don't understand it. To be called beautiful there one must have two clumsy supports which they call legs."

Then the little mermaid sighed, and looked mournfully at her fishtail.

"Let's be happy!" said the old lady. "Let's skip and jump in the three hundred years we have to live. That's more than long enough, then afterward we can rest all the merrier in our graves. This evening we shall have a court ball."

Such pomp as that was never seen on earth. The walls and the ceiling of the big ballroom were of thick but transparent glass. Several hundreds of huge shells, rose pink and grass green, stood on each side in rows, filled with a blue fire which lit up the whole hall and shone through the walls, so that the sea outside was quite lit up. One could see all the innumerable fishes, big and small, swimming toward the glass walls. On some the scales gleamed purple, while in others they shone like silver and gold. Through the middle of the hall flowed a broad stream, and on this the mermen and mermaids danced to their own lovely songs. The people of the earth haven't such beautiful voices. The little mermaid sang most sweetly of all, and everybody applauded her, and for a moment she felt joy in her heart, for she knew she had the loveliest voice of all in the sea or on the earth. But soon she thought again of the world above her; she could not forget the charming Prince, or her sorrow at not having an immortal soul like his. Therefore she crept out of her father's palace, and while song and gaiety went on inside, she sat sadly in her little garden.

Suddenly she heard the bugle horn sounding through the waters, and thought, "Now he must be sailing above, he whom

I love more than father or mother, he on whom my wishes hang, and in whose hand I should like to lay my life's happiness. I will dare everything to win him and an immortal soul. While my sisters dance in there in my father's palace, I will go to the sea witch. I've always been so frightened of her, but perhaps she can counsel and help me."

Now the little mermaid went out of her garden to the roaring whirlpools behind which the sea witch lived. She had never gone that way before. No flowers grew there, no sea grass; only the bare gray sand stretched out toward the whirlpools, where the water rushed round like roaring mill wheels and tore everything it seized down into the deep. She had to walk in between these crushing whirls to get into the domain of the sea witch. And for a long way there was no other road except one which led over warm bubbling mud: this the witch called her peat bog. Behind it lay her house in the midst of a weird wood, in which all the trees and bushes were polyps—half animals, half plants. They looked like hundred-headed snakes growing up out of the earth. All the branches were long slimy arms, with fingers like supple worms, and they moved joint by joint from the root to the farthest point. All that they could seize in the water they held fast and never again let it go. The little mermaid stopped in front of them quite frightened. Her heart beat with fear, and she was nearly turning back, when she thought of the Prince and the human soul, and her courage came back again. She bound her long fluttering hair closely around her head, so that the polyps might not seize it. She put her hands together on her breast, and then shot forward as a fish shoots through the water among the hideous polyps, who stretched out their supple arms and fingers after her. She saw that each of them held something it had seized with its hundreds of little arms, like strong iron bands. People who had perished at sea and had sunk deep down peered out as white skeletons from the arms of the polyps. Ships' rudders and chests were also held fast, and skeletons of land animals, and a little mermaid whom they had caught and strangled. And this seemed to her the most terrible of all.

Now she came to a big slimy place in the wood, where fat water snakes rolled about, showing their ugly white and yellow bodies. In the middle of this place was a house built of white bones of shipwrecked men. There sat the sea witch feeding a toad out of her mouth, just as a person might feed a little canary bird with sugar. The horrid fat water snakes she called her little chickens and let them roll around on her large swampy breast.

"I know what you want," said the sea witch. "It is stupid of you, but you shall have your way, for it will get you in

trouble, my little Princess. You want to get rid of your fish-tail, and get two stumps instead in its place, like those the people of the earth walk with. Then the young Prince may fall in love with you, and you may get him and an immortal soul as well." And with this the witch laughed loudly and disagreeably, so that the toad and the water snakes tumbled down to the ground, where they crawled about. "You come just in time," said the witch; "for tomorrow at the rise of the sun I could not help you until another year had gone by. I will make you a draught, with which you must swim to land. Tomorrow before the sun rises, seat yourself there and drink it. Then your tail will part in two and shrink in and become what the people of the earth call pretty legs. But it will hurt you—it will seem as if you have been cut with a sharp sword. All who see you will say you are the loveliest daughter of man they ever saw. You will keep your graceful walk; no dancer will be able to move so lightly as you. But every step you take will be as if you walked upon sharp knives, and as if your blood must flow. If you will bear all this, I can help you."

"Yes!" said the little mermaid, with a trembling voice; and she thought of the Prince and the immortal soul.

"But, remember," said the witch, "when you have once received a human form, you can never be a mermaid again. You can never go down through the water to your sisters or to your father's palace. And if you do not win the Prince's love, so that he forgets father and mother for your sake, clings to you with every thought, and tells the priest to join your hands, you will not receive an immortal soul. On the first morning after he has married another, your heart will break and you will become foam on the water."

"I will do it," said the little mermaid; but she became as pale as death.

"You must pay me, too," said the witch; "and it is not a

trifle that I ask. You have the finest voice of all here at the bottom of the sea. With this voice you think to enchant him; but this voice you must give to me. The best thing you own I will have for my costly draught! For I must give you my own blood in it, so that the draught may be sharp as a two-edged sword."

"But if you take away my voice," said the little mermaid, "what will I have?"

"Your beautiful form," replied the witch, "your graceful walk, and your eloquent eyes. With those you can surely be-witch a human heart. Well, have you lost your courage? Put out your little tongue, and then I will cut it off for my payment, and then you shall have the strong draught."

"Let it be so," said the little mermaid.

And the witch put on her pot to brew the draught.

"Cleanliness is a good thing," said she. And she scoured out the pot with the snakes, which she tied up in a big knot; then she scratched her breast, and let her black blood drop into it. The steam rose up in the strangest forms, enough to frighten and terrify anyone. Every moment the witch threw something else into the pot; and when it boiled hard it was like the weeping of crocodiles. At last the draught was ready. It looked like the purest water.

"There you have it," said the witch.

And she cut off the little mermaid's tongue. Now she was dumb, and could neither sing nor speak.

"If the polyps should lay hold of you when you go back through my forest," said the witch, "just throw a single drop of this drink on them, and their arms and fingers will fly into a thousand pieces." But the little mermaid didn't need to do this: the polyps drew back in terror when they saw the shining drink. It gleamed in her hand as if it were a twinkling star. In this way she soon passed through the for-est, the bog, and the roaring whirlpools.

She could see her father's palace. The torches were extinguished in the big ballroom, and they were certainly sleeping inside, but she did not dare to go to them, now that she was dumb and was about to leave them forever. She felt as if her heart would break with sorrow. She crept into the garden, took a flower from each of her sisters' flower beds, blew a thousand kisses toward the palace, and rose up through the dark blue sea.

The sun had not yet risen when she saw the Prince's castle and mounted the splendid marble staircase. The moon shone beautifully clear. The little mermaid drank the sharp burning draught, and it seemed as if a two-edged sword went through her delicate body. She fainted from it, and lay as if she were dead. When the sun shone out over the sea she woke up, and felt a sharp pain. But before her stood the handsome young Prince. He fixed his coal-black eyes on her, and she cast down her own. Then she saw that her fishtail was gone, and that she had the prettiest pair of white legs a little girl could have. But she had no clothes, so she wrapped herself in her long hair.

The prince asked who she was and how she had come there; and she looked at him mildly, but very sadly, with her dark blue eyes, for she could not speak. Then he took her by the hand, and led her into the castle. Each step she took was, as the witch had told her, as if she were treading on pointed needles and sharp knives, but she bore it gladly. At the Prince's right hand she moved on, light as a bubble, and he, like all the rest, was astonished at her graceful swaying movements.

Now she got costly clothes of silk and silken muslins. In the castle she was the most beautiful of all; but she was dumb, and could neither sing nor speak. Lovely slaves, dressed in silk and gold, stepped forward and sang before the Prince and his royal parents. One sang more charmingly than all the rest, and the Prince smiled at her and clapped his hands. Then the little mermaid was sad; she knew that she herself had sung far more sweetly, and thought:

"Oh! if only he could know that I have given away my voice forever to be with him."

Now the slaves danced pretty waving dances to the loveliest music, and the little mermaid lifted her beautiful white arms, stood on the tips of her toes, and glided dancing over the floor as no one had yet danced. At each movement her beauty was seen more clearly, and her eyes spoke straighter to the heart than the songs of the slaves.

All were delighted, and especially the Prince, who called her his little foundling. She danced again and again, although every time she touched the earth it seemed as if she were treading on sharp knives. The Prince said that she should always stay with him, and she received permission to sleep on a velvet cushion before his door.

He had a page's dress made for her, so that she could follow him on horseback. They rode through the fragrant woods, where the green boughs swept their shoulders and the little birds sang in the fresh leaves. She climbed with the Prince up the high mountains, and although her delicate feet bled so that the others could see it, she laughed at it, and followed him until they saw the clouds sailing beneath them like a flock of birds traveling to distant lands.

At home in the Prince's castle, when the others slept at night, she went out on the broad marble steps. It cooled her burning feet to stand in the cold sea water. And then she thought of those in the deep.

Once, in the nighttime, her sisters came arm in arm. They sang sadly as they swam over the water; and she beckoned to them, and they recognized her, and told her how she had grieved them all. They visited her every night; and once far out she saw the Sea King with his crown on his head and her old grandmother, who had not been above the surface for many years. They stretched out their hands toward her, but did not venture near the land as her sisters did.

Day by day the Prince grew more fond of her. He loved her as one loves a dear, good child, but it never came into his head to make her his wife. And yet she must become his wife, or she would not receive an immortal soul, and would have to become foam on the sea on his wedding morning.

"Don't you like me better than anybody else?" the eyes of the little mermaid seemed to say, when he took her in his arms and kissed her fair forehead.

"Yes, you are dearest to me!" said the Prince, "for you have the best heart of them all. You are the most devoted to me, and you look like a young girl whom I once saw, but whom I certainly shall not find again. I was on board a ship which was wrecked. The waves threw me ashore near a holy temple, where several young girls performed the service. The youngest of them found me by the shore and saved my life. I only saw her twice. She was the only one in the world I could love; but you are so like her you almost take the place of her image in my soul. She belongs to the holy temple, and therefore my good fortune has sent you to me. We will never part!"

"Ah! he does not know that I saved his life," thought the little mermaid. "I carried him over the sea to the wood where the temple stands. I sat there under the foam and looked to see if anyone would come. I saw the beautiful girl whom he loves better than me." And the mermaid sighed deeply—she could not weep. "The girl belongs to the holy temple," he has said, "and will never come out into the world, they will meet no more. I am with him and see him every day. I will cherish him, love him, give up my life for him."

But now it was said that the Prince was to marry. The beautiful daughter of a neighboring King was to be his wife, and that was why so splendid a ship was being fitted out. The story was that the Prince would travel to visit the land of the neighboring King, but it was really done so he might see the King's daughter. A great company was to go with him. The little mermaid shook her head and smiled; she knew the Prince's thoughts far better than any of the others.

"I must travel," he had said to her. "I must see the beautiful Princess. My parents desire it, but they do not wish to force me to bring her home as my bride. I cannot love her. She is not like the beautiful maiden in the temple, whom you are like. If I were to choose a bride, I would rather choose you, my dumb foundling with the speaking eyes."

And he kissed her red lips and played with her long hair, and laid his head on her heart, so that it dreamed of happiness and of an immortal soul.

"You are not afraid of the sea, my dumb child?" said he when they stood on the splendid ship which was to carry him to the country of the neighboring King; and he told her of storm and calm, of strange fishes in the deep, and of what the divers had seen there. And she smiled at his tales, for she knew better than anyone what there was at the bottom of the sea.

In the moon-clear night, when all were asleep, except the steersman who stood by the helm, she sat on the side of the ship gazing down through the clear water. She thought she saw her father's palace. High on the battlements stood her old grandmother, with the silver crown on her head, and she looked through the rushing tide up at the vessel's keel. Then her sisters came up over the water, and looked mournfully at her and wrung their white hands. She waved at them, smiled, and wished to tell them that she was well and happy; but the cabin boy came near her, and her sisters dived down again, and he continued to think that the white he had seen was foam on the water.

The next morning the ship sailed into the harbor of the neighboring King's splendid city. All the church bells were ringing, and from the high towers the trumpets were blowing, while the soldiers stood with flying colors and flashing bayonets. Each day brought some festivity with it; balls and entertainments followed one another; but the Princess was still not there. People said she was being educated in a holy temple far away, where she was learning every royal virtue. At last she arrived.

The little mermaid was anxious to see the beauty of the Princess, and she had to acknowledge it. A lovelier being she had never seen. The Princess's skin was pure and clear, and behind the long dark eyelashes smiled a pair of faithful dark blue eyes.

"It is you," said the Prince, "you who saved me when I lay like a corpse on the shore!" and he folded his blushing bride to his heart. "Oh, I am too, too happy!" he said to the little mermaid. "What I never dared to hope for is fulfilled. You will rejoice at my happiness, for you are the most devoted to me of them all!"

And the little mermaid kissed his hand; and it seemed already to her as if her heart was broken, for his wedding morning was to bring death to her, and change her into foam on the sea.

All the church bells were ringing, and heralds rode about the streets announcing the betrothal. On every altar fragrant oil was burning in costly silver lamps. The priests swung their censers, and bride and bridegroom laid hand in hand, and received the bishop's blessing. In silk and gold the little mermaid held up the bride's train; but her ears heard nothing of the festive music, her eyes did not see the holy ceremony; she thought of the night of her death, and of all she had lost in this world.

On the same evening the bride and bridegroom went on

board the ship. The cannon roared, all the flags waved. In the midst of the ship a costly tent of gold and purple, with the most beautiful cushions, had been set up, and there the married pair were to sleep in the cool still night.

The sails swelled in the wind and the ship glided smoothly and lightly over the clear sea. When it grew dark, colored lamps were lighted and the sailors danced lively dances on deck. The little sea maid thought of the first time when she had risen up out of the sea, and had seen the same splendor and joy, and she whirled into the dance, hovering as the swallow hovers when it is pursued. And all shouted their admiration; never had she danced so marvelously. Her delicate feet seemed cut by sharp knives, but she did not feel it, for in her heart was a crueler cut. She knew this was the last evening on which she might see him, the man for whom she had left her people and her home, had given up her beautiful voice, and had suffered unheard-of pains every day, while he was utterly unconscious of all. It was the last evening she might breathe the same air with him, and see the starry sky and the deep sea. Everlasting night without thought or dream awaited her, for she had no soul, and could win none. And everything was merriment and gladness on the ship till past midnight, and she laughed and danced with thoughts of death in her heart. The Prince kissed his beautiful bride, and she played with his black hair, and hand in hand they went to rest in the splendid tent.

It became quiet on the ship; only the helmsman stood by the helm, and the little mermaid leaned her white arms on the bulwark and looked out toward the east for the morning dawn—the first ray, she knew, would kill her. Then she saw her sisters rising out of the sea; they were pale, like herself; their long beautiful hair no longer fluttered in the wind—it had been cut off.

"We have given it to the witch, that she might bring you

help, so that you may not die tonight. She has given us a knife; here it is—look! how sharp! Before the sun rises you must thrust it into the heart of the Prince, and when the warm blood falls on your feet they will grow together again into a fishtail, and you will become a mermaid again, and come back to us, and live for three hundred years before you become dead salt sea foam. Hurry! He or you must die before the sun rises! Our old grandmother mourns so that her white hair has fallen off, as ours did under the witch's scissors. Kill the Prince and come back! Hurry! Do you see that red streak in the sky? In a few minutes the sun will rise, and you must die!"

And they gave a strange, deep sigh, and sank into the waves.

The little mermaid drew back the purple curtain from the tent, and saw the beautiful bride sleeping with her head on the Prince's breast; and she bent down and kissed his brow, and looked up to the sky where the morning red was gleaming brighter and brighter. Then she looked at the sharp knife, and again fixed her eyes on the Prince, who in his sleep murmured his bride's name. Only she was in his thoughts, and the knife trembled in the mermaid's hands. But then she flung it far away into the waves—they gleamed red where it fell, and it seemed as if drops of blood trickled up out of the water. Once more she looked with half-extinguished eyes upon the Prince; then she threw herself from the ship into the sea, and felt her body dissolving into foam.

Now the sun rose up out of the sea. The rays fell mild and warm on the cold sea foam, and the little mermaid felt nothing of death. She saw the bright sun, and over her head hovered hundreds of lovely transparent beings. Through them she could see the white sails of the ship and the red clouds of the sky. Their speech was melody, but so spiritual that no human ear could hear it, just as no earthly eye could see them; without wings they floated through the air. The little mermaid found that she had a body like these, and was rising more and more out of the foam.

"To whom am I coming?" she asked, and her voice sounded like that of the other beings, so spiritual that no earthly music could be compared to it.

"To the daughters of the air!" answered the others. "A mermaid has no immortal soul, and can never gain one, unless she wins the love of a mortal. Her eternal existence depends on the power of another. The daughters of the air have likewise no immortal soul, but they can make themselves one through good deeds. We fly to the hot countries, where the close, pestilent air kills men, and there we bring coolness. We spread the fragrance of the flowers through the air, and send refreshment and health. After we have striven for three hundred years to do all the good we can, we receive an immortal soul and take part in the eternal happiness of men. You, poor little mermaid, have striven with your whole heart after the same things. You have suffered and endured; now you can raise yourself by good deeds to the world of the spirits of the air, and can gain an immortal soul after three hundred years."

And the little mermaid lifted her bright arms toward God's sun, and for the first time she felt tears. On the ship there were life and noise again. She saw the Prince and his lovely bride searching for her. They looked mournfully at the bubbling foam, as if they knew that she had thrown herself into the waves. Invisible, she kissed the forehead of the bride, smiled to the Prince, and mounted with the other children of the air on the rosy cloud which floated through the air.

"After three hundred years we shall thus float into paradise!"

"And we may even get there sooner," whispered one. "We float invisibly into the houses of men with children, and for every day on which we find a good child who brings joy to his parents and deserves their love, our time of trial is shortened. The child does not know when we fly through the room. And when we smile with joy over the child, a year is counted off from the three hundred. But when we see a naughty or a wicked child, we shed tears of grief, and for every tear a day is added to our time of trial."

THE MARSH KING'S DAUGHTER

THE storks have a great many stories, which they tell their little ones—all about the bogs and the marshes. They suit them to their age and capacity. The youngest ones are quite satisfied with "Kribble krabble," or some such nonsense; but the older ones want something with more meaning in it, or at any rate something about the family. We all know one of the two oldest and longest tales which have been kept up among the storks; the one about Moses, who was placed by his mother on the waters of the Nile, and found there by the King's daughter. How she brought him up and how he became a great man whose burial place nobody to this day knows. This is all common knowledge.

The other story is not known yet, because the storks have kept it among themselves. It has been handed on from one mother stork to another for more than a thousand years, and each succeeding mother has told it better and better, till we now tell it best of all.

The first pair of storks who told it, and who actually lived it, had their summer quarters on the roof of the Viking's timbered house up by "Vidmosen" (the Wild Bog) in Wendyssel. It is in the county of Hiorring, high up toward the Skaw, in the north of Jutland, if we are to describe it according to the authorities. There is still a great bog there, which we may read about in the county chronicles. This district used to be under the sea at one time but the ground has risen, and it stretches for miles. It is surrounded on every side by marshy meadows, quagmires, and peat bogs, on which grow cloud berries and stunted bushes. There is nearly always a damp mist hanging over it, and seventy years ago it was still overrun with wolves. It may well be called the Wild Bog, and one can easily imagine how desolate and dreary it was among all these swamps and pools a thousand years ago. In detail everything is much the same now as it was then. The reeds grow to the same height, and have the same kind of long purple brown leaves with feathery tips as now. The birch still grows there with its white bark and its delicate loosely hanging leaves. With regard to living creatures, the flies still wear their gauzy draperies of the same cut; and the storks now, as then, still dress in black and white, with long red stockings. The people certainly had a very different style of dressing than at the present day; but if any of them, serf or huntsman, stepped on the quagmires, the same fate befell him a thousand years ago as would overtake him now if he ventured on them—in he would go, and down he would sink to the Marsh King, as they call him. He rules down below over the whole kingdom of bogs and swamps. He might also be called King of the Quagmires, but we prefer to call him the Marsh King, as the storks did. We know very little about his rule, but that is perhaps just as well.

Near the bogs, close to the arm of the Kattegat, called the Limfiord, lay the timbered hall of the Vikings with its stone cellar, its tower and its three stories. The storks had built their nest on the top of the roof, and the mother stork was sitting on the eggs which she was quite sure would soon be successfully hatched.

One evening father stork stayed out rather late, and when he came back he looked somewhat ruffled.

"I have something terrible to tell you!" he said to the mother stork.

"Don't tell it to me then," she answered. "Remember that I am setting; it might upset me and that would be bad for the eggs!"

"You will have to know it," said he. "She has come here, the daughter of our host in Egypt. She has ventured to take the journey, and now she has disappeared."

"She who is related to the fairies! Tell me all about it. You know I can't bear to be kept waiting when I am setting."

"Look here, Mother! She must have believed what the doctor said as you told me. She believed that the marsh flowers up here would do something for her father, and she flew over here in feather plumage with the other two Princesses, who come north every year to take the baths to make themselves young. She came, and she has vanished."

"You go into too many particulars," said the mother stork; "the eggs might get a chill. I can't stand being kept in suspense."

"I have been on the outlook," said father stork, "and tonight when I was among the reeds where the quagmire will hardly hold me, I saw three swans flying along, and there was something about their flight which said to me, 'Watch them; they are not real swans! They are only in swan's plumage.' You know, Mother, as well as I, that one feels things intuitively, whether or not they are what they seem to be."

"Yes, indeed!" she said, "but tell me about the Princess; I am quite tired of hearing about swan's plumage."

"You know that in the middle of the bog there is a kind of lake," said father stork. "You can see a bit of it if you raise your head. Well there was a big alder stump between the bushes and the quagmire, and on this the three swans settled, flapping their wings and looking about them. Then one of them threw off the swan's plumage, and I at once recognized in her the Princess from Egypt. There she sat with no covering but her long black hair. I heard her beg the two others to take good care of the swan's plumage while she dived under the water to pick up the marsh flower which she thought she could see. They nodded and raised their heads, and lifted up the loose plumage. What are they going to do with it, thought I, and she no doubt asked them the same thing; and the answer came; she had ocular demonstration of it: they flew up into the air with the feathered garment! 'Just you duck down,' they cried. 'Never again will you fly about in the guise of a swan; never more will you see the land of Egypt. You may sit in your swamp.' Then they tore the feather garment into a hundred bits, scattering feathers all over the place, like a snowstorm; then away flew those two good-for-nothing Princesses."

"What a terrible thing!" said mother stork; "but I must have the end of it."

"The Princess moaned and wept! Her tears trickled down upon the alder swamp, and then it began to move, for it is the Marsh King himself, who lives in the bog. I saw the stump turn round, and saw that it was no longer a stump. It stretched out long miry branches like arms. The poor child was terrified, and she sprang away onto the shaking quagmire. It would not even bear my weight, far less hers. She sank at once and the alder stump after her. It was dragging her down. Great black bubbles rose in the slime, and then there was nothing more to be seen. Now she is buried in the Wild Bog and never will she take back the flowers she came for. You could not have endured the sight, Mother!"

"You shouldn't even tell me anything of the sort just now, it might have a bad effect upon the eggs. The Princess must look after herself! She will get help somehow; if it had been you or I now, or one of our sort, all would have been over with us!"

"I mean to keep a watch though, every day," said the stork, and he kept his word.

A long time passed, and then one day he saw that a green stem shot up from the fathomless depths, and when it reached the surface of the water, a leaf appeared at the top which grew broader and broader. Next a bud appeared close by it, and one morning at dawn, just as the stork was passing, the bud opened out in the warm rays of the sun, and in the middle of it lay a lovely baby, a little girl, looking just as fresh as if she had come out of a bath. She was so exactly like the Princess from Egypt that at first the stork thought it was she who had grown small; but when he put two and two together, he came to the conclusion that it was her child and the Marsh King's. This explained why she appeared in a water lily. "She can't stay there very long," thought the stork; "and there are too many of us in my nest as it is, but an idea has just come into my head! The Viking's wife has no child, and she has often wished for one. As I am always said to bring the babies, this time I will do so in earnest. I will fly away to the Viking's wife with the baby, and that will indeed be a joy for her."

So the stork took up the little girl and flew away with her to the timbered house. He picked a hole in the bladder skin which covered the window, and laid the baby in the arms of the Viking's wife. This done he flew home and told the mother stork all about it. And the young ones heard what he said; for they were old enough to understand it.

"So you see that the Princess is not dead. She must have sent the baby up here and I have found a home for her."

"I said so from the very first," said mother stork. "Now just give a little attention to your own children; it is almost time to start on our own journey. I feel a tingling in my wings every now and then! The cuckoo and the nightingale are already gone, and I hear from the quails that we shall soon have a good wind. Our young people will do themselves credit at the maneuvers if I know them aright!"

How delighted the Viking's wife was when she woke in the morning and found the little baby on her bosom. She kissed and caressed it; but it screamed and kicked terribly, and seemed anything but happy. At last it cried itself to sleep, and as it lay there a prettier little thing could not have been seen. The Viking's wife was delighted, body and soul were filled with joy. She was sure that now her husband and all his men would soon come back as unexpectedly as the baby had come. So she and her household busied themselves in putting the house in order for their return. The long colored tapestries which she and her handmaids had woven with pictures of their gods—Odin, Thor, and Freya as they were called—were hung up. The serfs had to scour and polish the old shields which hung round the walls. Cushions were laid on the benches, and logs upon the great hearth in the middle of the hall, so that the fire might be lighted at once. The Viking's wife helped with all this work herself and when evening came she was very tired and slept soundly. She woke toward morning and she was very alarmed to find that the little baby had disappeared. She sprang up and lighted a pine chip and looked about. There was no baby, but at the foot of the bed sat a hideous toad. She was horrified at the sight, and seized a heavy stick to kill it, but it looked at her with such curious sad eyes, that she had not the heart to strike it. Once more she looked round and the toad gave a faint pitiful croak which made her start. She jumped out of bed and threw open the window shutter. The sun was just rising and its beams fell upon the bed and the great toad. All at once the monster's wide mouth seemed to contract, and to become small and rosy, the limbs stretched and again took their lovely shapes, and it was her own dear little baby which lay there, and not a hideous toad.

"Whatever is this?" she cried. "I have had a bad dream. This is my own darling elfin child." She kissed it and pressed it to her heart, but it struggled and bit like a wild kitten.

Neither that day nor the next did the Viking lord come

home although he was on his way. The winds were against him; they were blowing southward for the storks. "It is an ill wind that blows nobody good."

In the course of a few days and nights it became clear to the Viking's wife how matters stood with her little baby. Some magic power had a terrible hold over her. In the daytime it was as beautiful as any fairy, but it had a bad wicked temper. At night on the other hand she became a hideous toad, quiet and pathetic with sad mournful eyes. There were two natures continually shifting in her both in soul and body. The reason was that the little girl brought by the stork had her mother's form and her father's evil nature by day; but at night her kinship with him appeared in outward form, and her mother's sweet nature and gentle spirit beamed out of the misshapen monster.

Who could release her from the power of this witchcraft? It caused the Viking's wife much grief and trouble, and her heart yearned over the unfortunate soul. She knew that she would never dare tell her husband the true state of affairs, because he would without doubt, according to custom, put the poor child out on the highway for any one who chose to look after it. The good woman hadn't the heart to do this, and so she determined that he should only see the child by broad daylight.

One morning there was a sound of storks' wings swishing over the roof. During the night more than a hundred pairs of storks had made it their resting place, after the great maneuvers. And now they were trying their wings before starting on their long southward flight.

"Every man ready!" they cried; "all the wives and children, too."

"How light we feel," cried the young storks. "Our legs tingle as if we were full of live frogs! How splendid it is to be traveling to foreign lands."

"Keep in line!" said the father and mother, "and don't let your beaks clatter so fast, it isn't good for the chest." Then away they flew.

At the very same moment a horn sounded over the heath. The Viking had landed with all his men. They were bringing home no end of rich booty from the Gallic coast, where the people cried in terror as did the people of Britain:

"Deliver us from the wild Northmen!"

What life and noise came to the Viking's home by the Wild Bog now. The mead cask was brought into the hall, the great fire was lighted, and horses slaughtered for the feast, which was to be an uproarious one. The priest sprinkled the thralls with the warm blood of the horses as a consecration. The fire crackled and roared, driving the smoke up under the roof, and the soot dripped down from the beams. But they were used to all that.

Guests were invited and they received handsome presents. All feuds and double dealing were forgotten. They drank deeply, and threw the knuckle bones in each other's faces after they had gnawed them, for that was a sign of affection.

The Skald—the minstrel of the times, but he was also a warrior, for he went with them on their expeditions, and he knew what he was singing about—gave them one of his ballads recounting all their warlike deeds and their prowess. After every verse came the same refrain: "Fortunes may be lost, friends may die, one dies oneself but a glorious name lives forever!" Then they banged on their shields, and hammered with their knives or the knuckle bones on the table before them. And the hall rang out.

The Viking's wife sat on the cross bench in the banqueting hall. She was dressed in silk with gold bracelets and large amber beads. The Skald brought her name into the song too. He spoke of the golden treasure she had brought to her wealthy husband, and his delight at the beautiful child which at present he had seen only under its charming daylight guise. He rather admired her passionate nature, and said she would grow into a doughty shield maiden or Valkyrie, able to hold her own in battle. She would be the kind who wouldn't blink if a practiced hand cut off her eyebrows in jest with a sharp sword.

The barrel of mead came to an end, and a new one was rolled up in its place. This one too was soon drained to the dregs, but they were a hardheaded people who could stand a great deal. They had a proverb, "The beast knows when it is time to go home from grass, but the fool never knows when he has had enough." They knew it very well, but people often know one thing and yet do another.

They also knew that "the dearest friend becomes a bore if he sits too long in one's house!" but yet they sat on. Meat and drink are such good things! They were a jovial company! At night the thralls slept among the warm ashes, and they dipped their fingers in the sooty grease and licked them. Those were rare times indeed.

The Viking went out once more that year on a raid although the autumn winds were beginning. He sailed with his men to the coast of Britain, "It was just over the water," he said. His wife remained at home with the little girl, and it was certain that the foster-mother soon grew fonder of the poor toad with the pathetic eyes and plaintive sighs than she was of the little beauty who tore and bit at the heart.

The raw, wet autumn fog, "gnaw worm," which gnaws the leaves off the trees, lay over wood and heath. And "Bird loosefeather," as they called the snow, followed closely upon it. Winter was on its way. The sparrows took the storks' nest under their protection, and discussed the absent owners in their own fashion. The stork couple and their young— where were they now?

The storks were in the land of Egypt under the kind of

"Just as the stork was passing, the bud opened out in the warm rays of the sun, and in the middle of it lay a lovely baby, a little girl, looking just as fresh as if she had come out of a bath." (Page 368)

sun we have on a warm summer's day! They were surrounded by flowering tamarinds and acacias. Mahomet's cres-
cent glittered from every cupola on the mosques, and many
a pair of storks stood on the slender towers resting after
their long journey. Whole flocks of them had their nests side
by side on the mighty pillars, or the ruined arches of the
deserted temples. The date palm lifted high its screen of
branches as if to form a sunshade. The grayish white Pyramids
stood like shadowy sketches against the clear atmosphere of
the desert where the ostrich knew it would find space for its
stride. The lion crouched gazing with his great wise eyes at
the marble Sphinx half buried in the sand. The Nile waters
had receded and the land teemed with frogs; to the stork this
was the most splendid sight in all the land. The eyes of the
young ones were quite dazzled with the sight.

"See what it is to be here, and we always have the same in
our warm country," said the mother stork, and the stomachs
of the little ones tingled.

"Is there anything more to see?" they asked. "Shall we go
any further inland?"

"There is not much more to see," said the mother stork.
"On the fertile side there are only secluded woods where
the trees are interlaced by creeping plants. The elephant,
with its strong clumsy legs, is the only creature which can
force a way through. The snakes are too big for us, and the
lizards are too nimble. If you go out into the desert you will
get sand in your eyes if the weather is good, and if it is bad
you may be buried in a sandstorm. No, we are best off here.
There are plenty of frogs and grasshoppers. Here I stay and
you too!" And so she stayed.

The old ones stayed in their nests on the slender minarets
resting themselves, but at the same time busily smoothing
their feathers and rubbing their beaks upon their red stockings. Or they would lift up their long necks and gravely bow

their heads, their brown eyes beaming wisely. The young stork "misses" walked gravely among the juicy reeds, casting glances at the young bachelor storks, or making acquaintance with them. They would swallow a frog at every third step, or walk about with a small snake dangling from their beak; it had a very good effect they thought, and besides it tasted so good!

The young he-storks engaged in many a petty quarrel, in which they flapped their wings furiously and stabbed each other with their beaks till the blood came. Then they took mates and built nests for themselves; it was what they lived for. New quarrels soon arose, for in these warm countries people are terribly passionate. All the same it was very pleasant to the old ones; nothing their young ones did could be wrong. There was sunshine every day, and plenty to eat. Nothing to think of but pleasure!

But in the great palace of their Egyptian host, as they called him, matters were not so pleasant. The rich and mighty lord lay stretched upon his couch, as stiff in every limb as if he had been a mummy. The great painted hall was as gorgeous as if he were lying within a tulip. Relatives and friends stood around him—he was not dead—yet he could hardly be called living. The healing marsh flower from the northern lands, which was to be found and plucked by the one who loved him best, would never be brought. His young and lovely daughter, who in the plumage of a swan had flown over sea and land to the far north, would never return. The two other swan Princesses had come back and this is the tale they told.

"We were flying high up in the air when a huntsman saw us and shot his arrow. It pierced our young friend to the heart and she slowly sank. As she sank she sang her farewell song and fell into the midst of a forest pool. There by the shore under a drooping birch we buried her. But we had our revenge; we bound fire under the wings of a swallow which had its nest under the eaves of his cottage. The roof took fire and the cottage blazed up and he was burned in it. The flames shone on the pool where she lay, 'earth of the earth, under the birch.' Never more will she come back to the land of Egypt."

Then they both wept, and the father stork who heard it clattered with his beak and said, "Pack of lies; I should like to drive my beak right into their breasts!"

"Where it would break off, and a nice sight you would be then," said the mother stork. "Think of yourself first and then of your family. Everything else comes second to that!"

"I will perch upon the open cupola tomorrow when all the wise and learned folk assemble to talk about the sick man. Perhaps they will get a little nearer to the truth!"

The sages met together and talked long and learnedly, but the stork could not make head or tail of it. Nothing came of it, however, for the sick man or for his daughter who was buried in the Wild Bog! But we may just as well hear what they said. And then, perhaps, we may understand the story better, or at least as well as the stork.

"Love is the food of life! The highest love nourishes the highest life! Only through love can this life be won back!" This had been said and well said, by the sages.

"It is a beautiful idea!" said father stork at once.

"I don't rightly understand it," said the mother stork. "However that is not my fault, but the fault of the idea. It really does not matter to me, though. I have other things to think about!"

The sages had talked a great deal about love, the difference between the love of lovers, and that of parent and child, light and vegetation and how the sunbeams kissed the mire and forthwith young shoots sprang into being. The whole discourse was so learned that the father stork could not understand it, far less repeat it. He became quite pensive and stood on one leg for a whole day with his eyes half shut. Learning was a heavy burden to him.

Yet one thing the stork had thoroughly comprehended. He had heard from high and low alike what a misfortune it was to thousands of people and to the whole country that this man should be lying sick without hope of recovery. It would indeed be a blessed day which would see his health restored. "But where blossoms the flower of healing for him?" they had asked of one another, and they had also consulted all their learned writings, the twinkling stars, the winds, and the waves. The only answer that the sages had been able to give was, "Love is the food of life"; but how to apply the saying they knew not.

At last all were agreed that succor must come through the Princess who loved her father with her whole heart and soul. And they at last decided what she was to do. It was more than a year and a day since they had sent her at night, when there was a new moon, out into the desert to the Sphinx. Here she had to push away the sand from the door at the base of it, and walk through the long passage which led right into the middle of the pyramid, where one of the mightiest of their ancient kings lay swathed in his mummy's bands in the midst of his wealth and glory. Here she was to bend her head to the corpse, and it would be revealed to her where she would find healing and salvation for her father.

All this she had done, and the exact spot had been shown to her in dreams, where in the depths of the morass, she would find the lotus flower that would touch her bosom beneath the water. And this she was to bring home. So she flew away in her swan's plumage to the Wild Bog in the far north.

Now all this the father and mother stork had known from the beginning, and they understood the matter better than we did.

We know that the Marsh King dragged her down to himself, and that to those at home she was dead and gone. The wisest of them said, like the mother stork, "She will look out for herself!" so they awaited her return, not knowing in fact what else to do.

"I think I will snatch away the swan's plumage from the two deceitful Princesses," said the father stork. "Then they could not go to the Wild Bog to do any more mischief. I will keep the plumages up there till we find a use for them."

"Up where will you keep them?" asked the mother stork.

"In our nest at the Wild Bog," said he. "The young ones and I can carry them between us, and if they are too cumbersome, there are places enough on the way where we can hide them till our next flight. One plumage would be enough for her, but two are better. It is a good plan to have plenty of wraps in a northern country!"

"You will get no thanks for it," said the mother stork. "But you are the master. I have nothing to say except when I am sitting."

In the meantime the little child in the Viking's hall by the Wild Bog, where the storks flew in the spring, had been given a name. It was Helga, but such a name was far too gentle for the wild spirit that dwelt within her. Month by month and year by year while the storks took the same journey—in autumn toward the Nile, and in spring toward the Wild Bog—it showed itself more plainly. The little child grew to be a big girl, and before one knew how, she was the loveliest sixteen-year-old maiden possible. The husk was lovely, but the kernel was hard and rough; wilder than most, even in those hard, wild times.

Her greatest pleasure was to dabble her white hands in the blood of the horses slaughtered for sacrifice. In her wild freaks she would bite the heads off the black cocks which the priest was about to slay, and she said in full earnest to her foster-father, "If thy foe were to come and throw a rope round the beams of thy house and pull it about thine ears, I would not wake thee if I could. I should not hear him for the tingling of the blood in my ear, that you boxed years ago! I do not forget!"

But the Viking did not believe what she said. He, like everybody else, was infatuated by her beauty, nor did he know how body and soul changed places in his little Helga in the dark hours of the night. She rode a horse bare-backed as if she were a part of it, and she didn't jump off when her steed bit and fought with the other wild horses. She would often throw herself from the cliff into the sea in all her clothes, and swim out to meet the Viking when his boat neared the shore. And she cut off the longest strand of her beautiful long hair to string her bow. "Self made is well made," said she.

The Viking's wife, though strong-willed and strong-minded after the fashion of the times, treated her daughter like any other weak anxious mother. She knew that a spell rested over the terrible child. Often when her mother stepped out on the balcony Helga, from pure love of teasing it seemed, would sit upon the edge of the well, throw up her hands and feet, and go backward plump into the dark narrow hole. Here with her toad's nature she would rise again and clamber out like a cat dripping with water, carrying a perfect stream into the banqueting hall, washing aside the green twigs strewn on the floor.

One bond, however, always held little Helga in check, and that was twilight. When it drew near, she became quiet and pensive, allowing herself to be called and directed. An inner perception as it were drew her to her mother, and when the sun sank and the transformation took place, she sat sad and quiet, shriveled up into the form of a toad. Her body was now much bigger than those creatures ever are, but for that reason all the more unsightly. She looked like a wretched dwarf with the head of a toad and webbed fingers. There was something piteous in her eyes. And voice, she had none, only a hollow croak like the smothered sobs of a dreaming child. Then the Viking's wife would take her on her knee, and looking into her eyes would forget the misshapen form, and would often say, "I could almost wish that you would always remain my dumb toad-child. You are more terrible to look at when you are clothed in beauty." Then she would write Runes against sickness and sorcery, and throw them over the miserable girl, but they did no good at all.

"One would never think that she had been small enough to lie in a water lily!" said the father stork. "Now she is grown up, and the very image of her Egyptian mother, whom we never saw again! She did not manage to take such good care of herself as you and the sages said she would. I have been flying across the marsh year in, year out, and never have I seen a trace of her. Yes, I may as well tell you that all these years when I have come on in advance of you to look after the nest and set it to rights, I have spent many a night flying about like an owl or a bat scanning the open water, but all to no purpose. Nor have we had any use for the two swan plumages which the young ones and I dragged up here with so much difficulty. It took us three journeys to get them here. They have lain for years in the bottom of the nest, and if ever a disaster happens, like a fire in the timbered house, they will be lost entirely."

"And our good nest would be lost too," said the mother stork; "but you think less of that than you do of your feather dresses and your marsh Princess. You had better go down to her one day and stay in the mire for good. You are a bad father to your own chicks and I have always said so since the first time I hatched a brood. I wouldn't be surprised if we or the young ones didn't get an arrow through our wings from that mad Viking girl. She doesn't know what she is about. We are more at home here than she is, and she ought to remember that. We never forget our obligations. Every year we pay our toll of a feather, an egg, and a young one, as it is only right we should. Do you think that while she is about I care to go down there as I used to do, and as I do in Egypt where I am 'hail fellow well met' with everybody, and where I peep into their pots and kettles if I like? No, indeed; I sit up here vexing myself about her, the vixen, and you too. You should have left her in the water lily, and that would have been an end to her."

"You are much more estimable than your words," said the father stork. "I know you better than you know yourself, my dear." Then he gave a hop and flapped his wings thrice, proudly stretched out his neck and soared away without moving his outspread wings. When he had gone some distance he made more powerful strokes, his head and neck bending proudly forward, while his plumage gleamed in the sunshine. What strength and speed there were in his flight!

"He is the handsomest of them all," said the mother stork; "but I don't tell him that."

The Viking came home early that autumn with his booty and prisoners. Among them was a young Christian priest, one of those men who persecuted the heathen gods of the north. There had often been discussions of late, both in the hall and in the women's bower, about the new faith which was spreading in all the countries to the south. Through the holy Ansgarius it had spread as far as Hedeby on the Schlei. Even little Helga had heard of the belief in the "White Christ," who out of love for man had given Himself for their salvation. As far as Helga was concerned it had all gone in one ear and out the other, as one says. The very meaning of the word "love" seemed to dawn upon her only when she was shriveled up into the form of a toad in her secret chamber, but the Viking's wife had listened to the story and had felt herself strangely moved by these tales about the Son of the only true God.

The men on their return from their raids told them all about the temples built of costly polished stone, which were raised to Him whose message was Love. Once a couple of heavy golden vessels of cunning workmanship were brought home and around them hung a peculiar spicy odor. They were censers used by the Christian priests to swing before the altars on which blood never flowed, but where the bread and wine were changed to the Body and Blood of Him who gave Himself for the yet unborn generations.

The young priest was imprisoned in the deep stone cellars of the timber house and his feet and hands were bound with strips of bark. He was as "beautiful as Baldur," said the Viking's wife, and she felt pity for him, but young Helga proposed that he should be hamstrung and then tied to the tails of wild oxen.

"Then would I let the dogs loose on him. Hie and away over the marshes and pools; that would be a merry sight, and merry it would be to follow in his course."

However, this was not the death the Viking wished him to die, but rather as a denier and the persecutor of the great gods. He should be offered up in the morning upon the blood-stone in the groves. For the first time a man was to be sacrificed here. Young Helga begged that she might sprinkle the effigies of the gods and the people with his blood. She polished her sharp knife, and when one of the great ferocious dogs, of which there were so many about the place, sprang toward her, she dug her knife into its side, "to try it," she said. The Viking's wife looked sadly at the wild, badly disposed girl. When night came and the girl's beauty of body and soul changed places, she spoke tender words of grief from her sorrowful heart. The ugly toad with its ungainly body stood fixing its sad brown eyes upon her, listening and seeming to understand with the mind of a human being.

"Never once to my husband has a word of my double grief about you passed my lips," said the Viking's wife. "My heart is full of grief for you; great is a mother's love! But love never entered your heart. It is like a lump of cold clay. How did you ever get into my house?"

Then the ungainly creature trembled, as if the words touched some invisible cord between body and soul, and great tears came into its eyes.

"A bitter time will come to you," said the Viking's wife, "and it will be a terrible one for me too! Better would it have been if as a child you had been exposed on the highway, and lulled by the cold sleep of death!" And the Viking's wife shed bitter tears, and went away in anger and sorrow, passing under the curtain of skins which hung from the beams and divided the hall.

The shriveled-up toad crouched in the corner, and a dead silence reigned. At intervals a half-stifled sigh rose within her; it was as if in anguish something came to life in her heart. She took a step forward and listened. Then she stepped forward again and grasped the heavy bar of the door with her clumsy hands. Softly she drew it back, and silently lifted the latch, and took up the lamp which stood in the anteroom. It seemed as if a strong power gave her strength. She drew out the iron bolt from the barred cellar door, and slipped in to the prisoner.

He was asleep. She touched him with her cold clammy hand, and when he awoke and saw the hideous creature, he shuddered as if he beheld an evil apparition. She drew out her knife and cut his bonds and beckoned him to follow her. He named the Holy Name and made the sign of the cross, and, as the form remained unchanged, he repeated the words of the psalmist: "Blessed is the man who hath pity on the poor and

needy; the Lord will deliver him in the time of trouble!"
Then he asked "Who art thou? whose outward appearance
is that of an animal, whilst thou willingly performest deeds
of mercy?"

The toad only beckoned to him, led him behind the
sheltering curtains down a long passage to the stable, and
pointed to a horse, onto which he sprang. And she sprang
after him. She sat in front, clutching the mane of the animal.
The prisoner understood her and they rode at a quick pace
along a path he never would have found, to the heath. He
forgot her hideous form, knowing that the mercy of the Lord
worked through the spirits of darkness. He prayed and sang
holy songs which made her tremble. Was it the power of
prayer and his singing working upon her, or was it the chill
air of the advancing dawn? What were her feelings? She
raised herself and wanted to stop and jump off the horse, but
the Christian priest held her tightly, with all his strength, and
sang aloud a psalm, as if this could lift the spell which held her.

The horse bounded on more wildly than before; the sky
grew red, and the first sunbeams pierced the clouds. As the
stream of light touched her, the transformation took place.
She was once more a lively maiden but her demoniac spirit
was the same. The priest held a blooming maiden in his arms
and he was terrified at the sight. He stopped the horse and
sprang down, thinking he had met with a new device of the
Evil One. But young Helga sprang to the ground too. The
short child's frock only reached to her knee. She tore the
sharp knife from her belt and rushed upon the startled man.
"Let me get at thee!" she cried, "let me reach you and my
knife shall pierce through you! You are ashen-pale, beardless
slave!"

She closed upon him and they wrestled together, but an
invisible power seemed to give strength to the Christian. He
held her tight, and the old oak under which they stood seemed

to help him, for the loosened roots above the ground tripped her up. Close by rose a bubbling spring, and he sprinkled her with water and commanded the unclean spirit to leave her, making the sign of the cross over her according to Christian usage. But the baptismal water has no power if the spring of faith does not flow from within. Yet even here something more than man's strength, through him, opposed itself against the evil which struggled within her.

Her arms fell, and she looked with astonishment and paling cheeks at this man who seemed to be a mighty magician skilled in secret arts. These were dark Runes he was repeating and cabalistic signs he was tracing in the air. She would not have blanched had he flourished a shining sword or a sharp ax before her face, but she trembled now as he traced the sign of the cross upon her forehead and bosom, and at last she sat before him with drooping head like a wild bird tamed.

He spoke gently to her about the deed of love she had performed for him this night—when she came in the hideous shape of a toad, cut his bonds asunder, and led him out to light and life. She herself was bound, he said, and with stronger ties than his; but she also, through him, could reach to light and life everlasting. He would take her to Hedeby, to the holy Ansgarius, and there, in that Christian city, the spell would be removed. But she must no longer sit in front of him on the horse, even if she went of her own free will. He dare not carry her like this.

"Thou must sit behind me, not before me; thy magic beauty has a power given by the Evil One which I dread. Yet I shall have victory through Christ!"

He knelt down and prayed humbly and earnestly. It seemed as if the quiet wood became a holy church consecrated by his worship. The birds began to sing as if they too were of this new congregation, and the fragrance of the wild flowers was like the ambrosial perfume of incense. The young priest recited the words of the Holy Writ: "The Dayspring from on high hath visited us. To give light to them that sit in darkness, and in the shadow of death, to guide their feet into the way of peace."

He spoke of the yearning of all nature for redemption, and while he spoke the horse which had carried them stood quietly by, only rustling among the bramble bushes, making the ripe, juicy fruit fall into little Helga's hands, as if inviting her to refresh herself. Patiently she allowed herself to be lifted onto the horse's back, and sat there like one in a trance, neither watching nor wondering. The Christian man bound together two branches in the shape of a cross, which he held aloft in his hand as he rode through the wood. The brushwood grew thicker and thicker, till at last it became a trackless wilderness. Bushes of the wild sloe blocked the way, and they had to ride around them. The bubbling springs turned to standing pools, and these they also had to ride around. They found strength and refreshment in the pure breezes of the forest, and no less a power in the tender words of faith and love spoken by the young priest in his fervent desire to lead this poor straying one into the way of light and love.

It is said that raindrops can wear a hollow in the hardest stone, and the waves of the sea can smooth and round the jagged rocks; and so did the dew of mercy, falling upon little Helga, soften all that was hard and smooth all that was rough in her. These effects were not yet to be seen. She did not even know that they had taken place, any more than the buried seed lying in the earth knows that the refreshing showers and the warm sunbeams will cause it to flourish and bloom.

As the mother's song unconsciously falls upon the child's heart, it stammers the words after her without understanding them. But later they crystallize into thoughts, and in time become clear. In this way the "Word" also worked here in the heart of Helga.

They rode out of the wood, over a heath, and again through trackless forests. Toward evening they met a band of robbers. "From where have you stolen this beautiful child?" they cried, stopping the horse and pulling down the two riders, for there were many of them.

The priest had no weapon but the knife which he had taken from little Helga, and with this he struck out right and left. One of the robbers raised his ax to strike him, but the Christian succeeded in springing to one side, or he would certainly have been hit. But the blade flew into the horse's neck, and the blood gushed forth. And the horse fell to the ground dead. Then little Helga, as if roused from a long deep trance, rushed forward and threw herself onto the gasping horse. The priest placed himself in front of her as a shield and defense. But one of the robbers swung his iron club with such force at his head that the blood and the brains were scattered about, and he fell dead upon the ground.

The robber seized little Helga by her white arms, but the sun was just going down, and as the last rays vanished she was changed into the form of a toad. A greenish-white mouth stretched half over her face. Her arms became thin and slimy; while her broad hands, with webbed fingers, spread themselves out like fans. The robbers in terror let her go, and she stood among them like a hideous monster. And, according to toad nature, she bounded away with leaps as high as herself, and disappeared in the thicket. Then the robbers perceived that this must be Loki's evil spirit or some other witchcraft, and they hurried away completely frightened.

The full moon had risen and was shining in all its splendor when poor little Helga, in the form of a toad, crept out of the thicket. She stopped by the body of the Christian priest and the dead horse. She looked at them with eyes which seemed to weep; and a sob came from the toad like that of a child bursting into tears. She threw herself down, first upon one, and then on the other; and brought water in her large, webbed, cup-like hand. She sprinkled them with it; but they were dead, and dead they must remain! This she understood. Soon wild animals would come and devour them; but no, that should never be. So she dug into the ground as deep as she could; for she wished to dig a grave for them.

She had nothing but the branch of a tree and her two hands, and she tore the web between her fingers till the blood ran. She soon saw that the task would be beyond her, so she fetched fresh water and washed the face of the dead man, and strewed fresh green leaves over it. She also brought large boughs to cover him, and scattered dried leaves between the branches. Then she brought the heaviest stones she could carry, and laid them over the dead body, filling up the spaces with moss. Now she thought the mound was strong and secure enough. The difficult task had taken the whole night; and the sun was just rising. And there stood little Helga in all her beauty with bleeding hands and maidenly tears for the first time on her blushing cheeks.

It was as in a transformation with two natures struggling within her. She trembled and glanced round as if she were just awaking from a troubled dream. She leaned for support against a slender beech, and at last climbed to the topmost branches like a cat and seated herself firmly upon them. She sat there for the whole livelong day, like a frightened squirrel in the solitude of the wood where all is still, and dead, as they say!

Dead—well, there flew a couple of butterflies whirling round and round each other, and close by were some anthills each with its hundreds of busy little creatures swarming to and fro. In the air danced countless midges, and swarm upon swarm of flies, ladybirds, dragonflies with golden wings, and other little winged creatures. The earthworm crept forth from the moist ground, and the moles—but except for them all was still and dead. When people say "dead" they don't really mean or understand what they say. No one noticed little Helga but a flock of jackdaws and they flew chattering round the tree where she sat. They hopped along the branch toward her, boldly inquisitive. But a glance from her eye was enough to drive them away. They could not understand her, though, any more than she could understand herself.

When the evening drew near and the sun began to sink, the approaching transformation aroused her to fresh exertion. She slipped down gently from the tree, and when the last sunbeam was extinguished she sat there once more, as the shriveled-up toad with her torn, webbed hands. But her eyes now shone with a new beauty which they had never possessed in all the pride of her loveliness. They were now the gentlest and tenderest maiden's eyes shining out of the face of the toad. They bore witness to the existence of deep feeling and a human heart. And the beauteous eyes overflowed with tears, weeping precious drops that lightened her heart.

The cross made of branches, the last work of him who now was dead and cold, still lay by the grave. Little Helga took it up; the thought came unconsciously. And she placed it between the stones which covered man and horse. At the sad memory her tears burst forth again, and in this mood she traced the same sign in the earth round the grave—and as she formed the sign of the cross, with both hands, the webbed skin fell away from her fingers like a torn glove. She washed her hands at the spring and gazed in astonishment at their delicate whiteness. Again she made the holy sign in the air, between herself and the dead man. Her lips trembled, her tongue moved, and the name which she had heard so often in her ride through the forest, rose to her lips, and she uttered the words "Jesus Christ."

The toad's skin fell away from her; and she was the beautiful young maiden, but her head bent wearily and her limbs required rest. She slept. But her sleep was short. She was awakened at midnight; and before her stood the prancing dead horse. Life shone from his eyes and his wounded neck. Close by his side appeared the murdered Christian priest, "more beautiful than Baldur," the Viking's wife might indeed have said, and he was surrounded by flames of fire.

There was such earnestness in his large, mild eyes, and such righteous judgment in his penetrating glance that they pierced into the remotest corners of her heart. Little Helga trembled, and every memory within her was awakened as if it had been the Day of Judgment. Every kindness which had ever been shown her, every loving word which had been said to her, came vividly before her. She now understood that it was love which had sustained her in those days of trial, through which all creatures made of dust and clay, with their soul and spirit, must wrestle and struggle. She acknowledged that she had only followed where she was called, and had done nothing for herself. All had been given to her. She bent now in lowly humility, full of shame, before Him who could read every impulse of her heart. And in that moment she felt the purifying flame of the Holy Spirit thrill through her soul.

"Thou daughter of earth!" said the Christian martyr, "out of the earth art thou come, from the earth shalt thou rise again! The sunlight within thee shall consciously return to its origin; not the beams of the actual sun, but those from God! No soul will be lost; things temporal are full of weariness, but eternity is life-giving. I come from the land of the dead; thou also must one day journey through the deep valleys to reach the radiant mountain summits where dwell grace and all perfection. I cannot lead thee to Hedeby for Christian baptism. First you must break the watery shield that covers the deep morass, and bring forth from its depths the living author of thy being and thy life. You must first carry out your vocation before your consecration can take place!"

Then he lifted her up onto the horse, and gave her a golden censer like those she had seen in the Viking's hall. A fragrant perfume arose from it, and the open wound on the martyr's forehead gleamed like a radiant diadem. He took the cross from the grave, holding it high above him, while they rode rapidly through the air across the murmuring woods, and over the heights where the mighty warriors of old lay buried, seated on their dead war horses. These strong men of war arose and rode out to the summits of the mounds. The broad golden circlets round their foreheads gleamed in the moonlight, and their cloaks fluttered in the wind. The great dragon hoarding his treasure raised his head to look at them, and whole hosts of dwarfs peeped forth from their hillocks, swarming with red, green, and blue lights, like sparks from the ashes of burned paper.

Away they flew over wood and heath, rivers and pools, up north toward the Wild Bog. They arrived here and hovered round in great circles. The martyr raised high the cross, it shone like gold, and his lips chanted the holy mass. Little Helga sang with him as a child joins in its mother's song. She swung the censer, and from it issued a fragrance of the altar so strong and so wonder-working that the reeds and rushes burst into blossom, and numberless flower stems shot up from the bottomless depths. Everything that had life within it lifted itself up and blossomed. The water lilies spread themselves over the surface of the pool like a carpet of woven flowers, and on this carpet lay a sleeping woman. She was young and beautiful. Little Helga fancied that she saw herself, her own picture mirrored in the quiet pool. It was her mother she saw, the wife of the Marsh King, the Princess from the river Nile.

The martyred priest commanded the sleeping woman to be

lifted up onto the horse, but the animal sank beneath the burden, as though it had no more substance than a winding-sheet floating on the wind. But the sign of the cross gave strength to the phantom, and all three rode on through the air to dry ground. Just then the cock crew from the Viking's hall, and the vision melted away in the mist, driven along by the wind, but mother and daughter stood side by side.

"Is it myself I see reflected in the deep water?" said the mother.

"Do I see myself mirrored in a bright shield?" said the daughter.

They approached and clasped each other heart to heart, the mother's heart beat the fastest, and she understood.

"My child! my own heart's blossom! my lotus out of the deep waters!" and she wept over her daughter. And her tears were a new baptism of love and life for little Helga. "I came hither in a swan's plumage, and here I threw it off," said the mother. "I sank down into the bog which closed around me. Some power always dragged me down, deeper and deeper. I felt the hand of sleep pressing upon my eyelids. I fell asleep, and I dreamed—I seemed to be again in the vast Egyptian Pyramid; but still before me stood the moving alder stump which had frightened me on the surface of the bog. I gazed at the fissures of the bark and they shone out in bright colors and turned to hieroglyphs. It was the mummy's wrappings I was looking at. The coverings burst asunder, and out of them walked the Mummy King of a thousand years ago, black as pitch, black as the shining wood snail or the slimy mud of the swamp. Whether it were the Mummy King or the Marsh King I knew not. He threw his arms around me, and I felt that I must die. When life came back to me I felt something warm upon my bosom; a little bird fluttering its wings and twittering. It flew from my bosom high up toward the heavy dark canopy, but a long green ribbon still bound it to me.

I heard and understood its notes of longing: 'Freedom! Sunshine! To the Father!' I remembered my own father in the sunlit land of my home, my life, and my love! and I loosened the ribbon and let it flutter away—home to my father. Since that hour I have dreamed no more. I must have slept a long and heavy sleep till this hour, when sweet music and fragrant odors awoke me and set me free."

Where did now the green ribbon flutter that bound the mother's heart to the wings of the bird? Only the stork had seen it. The ribbon was the green stem, the bow the gleaming flower which cradled the little baby, now grown up to her full beauty, and once more resting on her mother's breast. While they stood there pressed heart to heart the stork was wheeling above their heads in great circles. At length he flew away to his nest and brought back the swan plumages so long cherished there. He threw one over each of them. The feathers closed over them, and mother and daughter rose into the air as two white swans.

"Now let us talk!" said the father stork; "for we can understand each other's language—even if one bird has a different-shaped beak from the other. It is the most fortunate thing in the world that you appeared this evening. Tomorrow we should have been off, Mother and I and the young ones. We are going to fly southward. Yes, you may look at me! I am an old friend from the Nile, so is Mother too. Her heart is not as sharp as her beak! She always said that the Princess would take care of herself! I and the young ones carried the swan's plumage up here! How delighted I am, and how lucky it is that I am still here. As soon as the day dawns we will set off, a great company of storks. We will fly in front; you had better follow us and then you won't lose your way. And we will keep an eye out for you."

"And the lotus flower which I was to take with me," said the Egyptian Princess, "flies by my side in a swan's plumage.

I take the flower of my heart with me, and so the riddle is solved. Now for home! home!"

But Helga said she could not leave the Danish land without seeing her loving foster-mother, the Viking's wife, once more. For in Helga's memory there now rose up every happy recollection, every tender word and every tear her foster-mother had shed over her. And it almost seemed as if she loved this mother best.

"Yes, we must go to the Viking's hall," said the father stork. "Mother and the young ones are waiting for us there. How they will open their eyes and flap their wings! Mother doesn't say much. She is somewhat short and abrupt, but she means very well. Now I will make a great clattering to let them know we are coming!"

So he clattered with his beak, and he and the swans flew off to the Viking's hall.

Within they all lay in a deep sleep. The Viking's wife had gone to rest late, for she was in great anxiety about little Helga, who had not been seen for three days. She had disappeared with the Christian priest. She must have helped him get away, for her horse was missing from the stable.

By what power had this been brought to pass? The Viking's wife thought over all the many miracles which were said to have been performed by the "White Christ," and by those who believed in Him and followed Him. These thoughts took form in her dreams, and it seemed to her that she was still awake, sitting thoughtfully upon her bed while darkness reigned outside. A storm arose. She heard the rolling of the waves east and west of her from the North Sea, and from the waters of the Kattegat. According to her faith, the monstrous serpent, which encompassed the earth in the depths of the ocean, was trembling in convulsions from dread of "Ragnarok," the night of the gods. He personified the Day of Judgment when everything should pass away, includ-

ing the great gods themselves. The Gialler horn sounded, and away over the rainbow rode the gods, clad in steel to fight their last battle. Before them flew the shield maidens, the Valkyries, and the ranks were closed by the phantoms of the dead warriors. The atmosphere shone in the radiance of the Northern Lights, but in the end darkness conquered all.

It was a terrible hour, and in her dream little Helga sat close beside the frightened woman, crouching on the floor in the form of the hideous toad. She trembled and crept closer to her foster-mother who took her on her knee, and in her love pressed her to her bosom despite the hideous toad's skin. And the air resounded with the clashing of swords and clubs, and the whistling of arrows. It was as if a fierce hailstorm were passing over them and the hour had come when heaven and earth were to pass away, and the stars to fall. And everything would succumb to Surtur's fire—and yet a new earth and a new heaven would arise. Fields of corn would wave where the seas now rolled over the golden sands. The God whom none might name would reign, and to Him would ascend Baldur the mild, the loving, redeemed from the kingdom of the dead—he was coming! The Viking's wife saw him plainly, she knew his face—it was the face of the Christian priest, their prisoner.

"White Christ," she cried aloud, and as she named the name she pressed a kiss upon the forehead of the loathsome toad. The toad's skin fell away and before her stood little Helga in all the radiance of her beauty, gentle as she had never been before and with warm eyes gleaming. She kissed her foster-mother's hands, and blessed her for all the care and love she had shown in the days of her trial and misery. She thanked her for the thoughts she had instilled in her, and for naming the name which she now repeated, "White Christ!" Little Helga rose up like a great white swan and

spread her wings, with the rushing sound of a flock of birds of passage on the wing.

At the same moment, the Viking's wife was awakened by the rushing sound of wings outside. She knew it was the time when the storks took their flight, and it was these she heard. She wanted to see them once more and to bid them farewell, so she got up and went out on the balcony. She saw stork upon stork sitting on the roofs of the outbuildings round the courtyard, and flocks of them were flying round and round in great circles. Just in front of her, on the edge of the well where little Helga so often had frightened her with her wildness, sat two white swans, who gazed at her with their wise eyes. Then she remembered her dream, which still seemed quite real to her. She thought of little Helga in the form of a swan. She thought of the Christian priest, and suddenly a great joy arose in her heart. The swans flapped their wings and bent their heads as if to greet her, and the Viking's wife stretched out her arms toward them as if she understood all about it, and she smiled at them with tears in her eyes.

"We are not going to wait for the swans," said the mother stork; "if they want to travel with us they must come. We can't dawdle here till the plovers start! It is very nice to travel as we do, the whole family together, not like the chaffinches and the ruffs; with them, the males and females fly separately. It's hardly decent! And why are those swans flapping their wings like that?"

"Well, everyone flies in his own way," said the father stork. "The swans fly in an oblique line, the cranes in the form of a triangle, and the plovers in a curved line like a snake."

"Don't talk about snakes while we are flying up here," said the mother stork. "It puts desires into the young ones' heads which they can't gratify."

"Are those the high mountains I used to hear about?" asked Helga in the swan's plumage.

"Those are thunder clouds driving along beneath us," said her mother.

"What are those white clouds that rise so high?" again enquired Helga.

"Those are mountains covered with perpetual snows that you see yonder," said her mother, as they flew across the Alps down toward the blue Mediterranean.

"Africa's land! Egypt's strand!" sang the daughter of the Nile in her joy, as from far above in her swan's plumage, her eye fell upon the narrow waving yellow line, her birthplace. The other birds saw it too and hastened in their flight.

"I smell the Nile mud and the frogs," said the mother stork. "I am tingling all over. Now, you will have something nice to taste, and something to see too. There are the marabouts, the ibis, and the crane. They all belong to our family, but they are not nearly so handsome as we are. They are very stuck up, though, especially the ibis; they have been so spoiled by the Egyptians. They make mummies of him, and stuff him with spices. I would rather be stuffed with living frogs, and so would you, and so you shall be! Better have something in your crops while you are alive, than have a great fuss made over you after you are dead. That is my opinion, and I am always right."

"The storks have come back," was the cry in the great house on the Nile. Within the great hall the lord lay on his downy cushions covered with a leopard skin, scarcely alive, and yet not dead either, waiting and hoping for the lotus flower from the deep morass in the north.

Relatives and servants were standing round his couch, when two great white swans who had come with the storks flew into the hall. They threw off their dazzling plumage, and there stood two beautiful women as like each other as twin drops of dew. They bent over the pale withered old man, throwing back their long hair.

As little Helga bent over her grandfather, the color came back to his cheeks and new life returned to his limbs. The old man arose with health and energy renewed. His daughter and granddaughter clasped him in their arms, with a joyous morning greeting after the long and troubled night.

Joy reigned throughout the house and in the stork's nest too. But here the rejoicing was chiefly over the abundance of food, especially the swarms of frogs. And while the sages hastily sketched in the story of the two Princesses and the flower of healing, which brought such joy and blessing to the land, the parent storks told the same story in their own way to their family; but only after they had all satisfied their appetites. It would have been difficult to make them listen, when they had something better to do.

"Surely you will be given an appointment at last," whispered the mother stork. "It wouldn't be reasonable otherwise."

"Oh, what should I be made?" said the father stork, "and what have I done? Nothing at all!"

"You have done more than all the others! Without you and the young ones the two Princesses would never have seen Egypt again, nor would the old man have recovered his health. You will be made something. They will at least give you a doctor's degree, and our young ones will be born with the title, and their young ones after them. Why, you look like an Egyptian doctor already, at least in my eyes!"

And now the learned men and the sages set to work to propound the inner principle, as they called it, that lay at the root of the matter. "Love is the food of life," was their text. Then came the explanations. "The Princess was the warm sunbeam; she went down to the Marsh King, and from their meeting sprang forth the blossom."

"I can't exactly repeat the words," said the father stork.

He had been listening on the roof, and had now returned to the nest and wanted to tell them all about it. "What they said was so involved and so clever that not only were they given new rank, but presents too; even the head cook got a mark of distinction—most likely for the soup!"

"And what did you get?" asked the mother stork. "They shouldn't forget the most important person, and that is what you are! The sages have only cackled about it all. But your turn will come, no doubt!"

Late that night, when the whole happy household was wrapped in peaceful slumber, there was still one watcher. It was not father stork, although he stood up in the nest on one leg like a sentry asleep at his post. No, it was little Helga. She was watching, bending out over the balcony in the clear air, gazing at the shining stars, bigger and purer in their radiance than she had ever seen them in the north; and yet they were the same. She thought of the Viking's wife by the Wild Bog; she thought of her foster-mother's gentle eyes, and the tears she had shed over the poor toad child, who now stood in the bright starlight and delicious spring air by the waters of the Nile. She thought of the love in the heathen woman's breast, the love she had lavished on a miserable creature, who in human guise was a wild animal, and when in the form of an animal was hateful to the sight and to the touch. She looked at the shining stars, and remembered the dazzling light on the forehead of the martyred priest as he flew over moorland and forest. The tones of his voice came back to her, and words that he had said while she sat overwhelmed and crushed —words concerning the sublime source of love, the highest love embracing all generations of mankind. What was there that had not been won and achieved by this love?

Day and night little Helga was absorbed in the thought of her happiness. She entirely lost herself in the contemplation of it. She was like a child who turns hurriedly from the giver to examine the beautiful gifts. Happy she was indeed, and her happiness seemed ever growing; more might come, would come. She indulged in these thoughts, until she thought no more of the Giver. It was in the wantonness of youth that she sinned. Her eyes sparkled with pride, but suddenly she was roused from her vain dream. She heard a great clatter in the courtyard below, and, looking out, saw two great ostriches rushing hurriedly around in circles. Never before had she seen these great, heavy, clumsy birds, which looked as if their wings had been clipped, and the birds themselves looked as if they had been badly mistreated. She asked what had happened to them, and heard for the first time the legend the Egyptians tell about the ostrich.

Once, they say, the ostriches were a beautiful and glorious race of birds with large, strong wings. One evening the great birds of the forest said to it, "Brother, shall we tomorrow, God willing, go down to the river to drink?" And the ostrich answered, "I will!"

At the break of day, then, they flew off, first rising high in the air toward the sun, the eye of God. The ostrich flew, far in front of the other birds, in its pride flying higher and higher close up to the light. He trusted in his own strength, and not in that of the Giver. He would not say "God willing!" But the avenging angel drew back the veil from the flaming ocean of sunlight, and in a moment the wings of the proud bird were burned, and he sank miserably to the earth. Since that time the ostrich and his race have never been able to rise in the air. They can only fly terror-stricken along the ground, or round and round in narrow circles. It is a warning to mankind, reminding us in every thought and action to say "God willing!"

Helga thoughtfully and seriously bent her head and looked at the hunted ostrich, noticed its fear and its miserable pride at the sight of its own great shadow on the white moonlit wall.

Her thoughts grew graver and more earnest. A life so rich in joy had already been given to her; what more was to come? The best of all perhaps—"God willing!"

Early in the spring, when the storks were again about to take flight to the north, little Helga took off her gold bracelet, and, scratching her name on it, beckoned to father stork and put it round his neck. She told him to take it to the Viking's wife, who would see by it that her foster-daughter still lived, was happy, and had not forgotten her.

"It is a heavy thing to carry!" thought father stork, as it slipped around his neck. "But neither gold nor honor are to be thrown upon the highway! The stork brings good luck, they say up there!"

"You lay gold, and I lay eggs," said mother stork; "but you only lay once and I lay every year. And, no one appreciates us. I call it very mortifying!"

"One always has the consciousness of one's own worth, though, Mother!" said father stork.

"But you can't hang it on the outside," said mother stork. "It doesn't bring a fair wind or a full meal!" And they took their departure.

The little nightingale singing in the tamarind bushes was also going north soon. Helga had often heard it singing by the Wild Bog, so she decided to send a message by it too. She knew bird language from having worn a swan's plumage, and she had kept in practice by speaking to the storks and the swallows. The nightingale understood her quite well. She begged it to fly to the beechwood in Jutland, where she had made the grave of stones and branches. And she asked it to tell all the other birds to guard the grave and to sing over it. The nightingale flew away—and time flew away too.

In the autumn an eagle, perched on one of the Pyramids, saw a gorgeous train of heavily laden camels and men clad in armor riding fiery Arab steeds as white as silver with quivering red nostrils and flowing manes that reached to the ground. A royal prince from Arabia, as handsome as a prince should be, was arriving at the stately mansion where the storks' nest now stood empty. The storks were still in their northern home; but they would soon return now—nay, on the very day when the rejoicings were at their height they did return.

The rejoicings were over the bridal festivities, and little Helga was the bride clad in rich silk and many jewels. The bridegroom was the young Prince from Arabia, and they sat together at the upper end of the table between the mother and her grandfather.

But Helga was not looking at the bridegroom's handsome face round which his black beard curled, nor did she look into his fiery dark eyes which were fixed upon hers. She was gazing up at a brilliant twinkling star beaming in the heavens.

Just then there was a rustle of great wings in the air outside; the storks had come back. And the old couple, tired as they were and needing rest, flew straight down to the railing of the veranda. They knew nothing about the festivities. They had heard on the frontiers of the country that little Helga had had pictures of them painted on the wall, for they belonged to the story of her life.

"It was a nice thing for her to do," said father stork.

"It is the least she could do," said mother stork; "she could hardly do less."

When Helga saw them she rose from the table and went out onto the veranda to stroke their wings. The old storks bowed their heads and the very youngest ones watched and felt honored. And Helga looked up at the shining star which seemed to grow brighter and purer. Between herself and the star floated a form purer even than the air and therefore visible to her. It floated quite close to her and she saw that it was the martyred priest. He had come to her great festival too—come even from the heavenly kingdom.

"The glory and bliss yonder far outshines these earthly splendors," he said.

Little Helga prayed more earnestly and meekly than she had ever done before—prayed, that for one single moment she might gaze into the kingdom of heaven. Then she felt herself lifted up above the earth in a stream of sweet sounds and thoughts. The unearthly music was not only around her, it was within her. No words can express it.

"Now we must return; you will be missed," said the martyr.

"Only one more look," she pleaded; "only one short moment more."

"We must return to earth. The guests are departing."

"Only one look—the last."

Then little Helga was standing once again on the veranda, but all the torches outside were extinguished and the lights in the banqueting hall were out too. The storks were gone; no guests were to be seen; no bridegroom—all had vanished in those three short minutes.

A great dread seized upon Helga. She walked through the great empty hall into the next chamber where strange warriors were sleeping. She opened a side door which led into her own room, but instead she found herself in a garden which had never been there before. Red gleams were in the sky; dawn was approaching. Only three minutes in heaven, and a whole night on earth had passed away.

Then she saw the storks and she called to them in their own language. Father stork turned his head, listened, and came up to her.

"You speak our language," he said. "What do you want? Why do you come here, you strange woman?"

"It is I, it is Helga. Don't you know me? We were talking to each other in the veranda just three minutes ago."

"That is a mistake," said the stork; "you must have dreamed it."

"No, no," she said, and she reminded him of the Viking's stronghold, and the Wild Bog, and their journey together.

Father Stork blinked his eyes and said, "Why, that is a very old story. I believe it happened in the time of my great-great-grandmother. Yes, there certainly was a princess in Egypt who came from the Danish land, but she disappeared on her wedding night many hundred years ago. You may read all about it here, on the monument in the garden. There are storks and swans carved on it, and at the top you yourself, all in white marble."

And so it was: Helga understood all about it now and she fell upon her knees.

The sun burst forth, and as in former times when the toad's skin had fallen away before his beams and revealed the beautiful girl, so now in the baptism of light, a vision of beauty, brighter and purer than air—a ray of light—rose to the Father. The earthly body dropped away in dust—only a withered lotus flower lay where she had stood.

"Well, that is a new ending to the story," said father stork; "I hadn't expected that, but I like it very much."

"What will the young ones say about it?" asked mother stork.

"Ah, that is a very important matter," said father stork.

THE TRAVELING COMPANION

Poor John was very sad. His father was ill and dying. There was no one but the two in the little room, and the lamp had nearly burned out; for it was late in the night.

"You have been a good son, John," said the sick father. "And God will help you on in the world." As he spoke he looked at him, with mild, earnest eyes, drew a deep sigh, and died; yet it appeared as if he were still sleeping.

John wept bitterly. He had no one in the wide world now; no father, mother, brother, or sister. Poor John! he knelt down by the bed, kissed his dead father's hand, and wept many, many bitter tears. But at last his eyes closed, and he fell asleep with his head resting against the hard bedpost.

He dreamed a strange dream. He thought he saw the sun shining upon him, and his father was alive and well. He even heard him laughing as he used to do when he was very happy. A beautiful girl, with a golden crown on her head, and long, shining hair, gave him her hand; and his father said, "See what a bride you have won. She is the loveliest maiden on the whole earth." Then he awoke, and all the beautiful things vanished before his eyes, his father lay dead on the bed, and he was all alone. Poor John!

The week after, the dead man was buried. John walked behind the coffin which held his father, whom he so dearly loved, and would never again see. He heard the earth fall on the coffin lid, and watched it till only a corner remained in sight, and at last that also disappeared. He felt as if his heart would break with the weight of sorrow. Then those who stood round the grave sang a psalm, and the sweet, holy

"*The owl beat the drum, the crickets whistled, and the grasshoppers played the mouth organ. It was a very ridiculous ball.*" (Page 421) tones brought tears into his eyes, and this relieved him. The sun shone brightly down on the green trees, as if to say, "You must not be so sorrowful, John. See the beautiful blue sky above you? Your father is up there, and he prays to the loving Father of all, that you may do well in the future."

"I will always be good," said John, "and then I shall go to be with my father in heaven. What joy it will be when we see each other again! How much I shall have to tell him, and how many things he will be able to explain to me about the delights of heaven, and he will teach me as he once did on earth. Oh, what joy it will be!"

John pictured it all so clearly to himself, that he smiled even while the tears ran down his cheeks.

The little birds in the chestnut trees twittered, "Tweet, tweet." They were happy, even though they had seen the funeral. It seemed as if they knew that the dead man was now in heaven, and that he had wings much larger and more beautiful than their own; and that he was happy now, because he had been good here on earth, and they were glad of it. John saw them fly away out of the green trees into the wide world, and he longed to fly with them. But first he cut out a large wooden cross, to place on his father's grave; and when he brought it there in the evening, he found the grave decked out with gravel and flowers. Strangers had done this—they who had known and loved the good old father who was now dead.

Early the next morning, John packed up his little bundle of clothes, and placed all his money, fifty dollars and a few shillings, in his girdle. With this he determined to make his fortune in the world. But first he went into the churchyard and by his father's grave he said "Our Father"; and then added: "Farewell, dear father. I will always be a true and good man, and do thou ask the good God to make me good."

And as he passed through the fields, all the flowers looked

fresh and beautiful in the warm sunshine. And they nodded
in the wind, as if they wished to say, "Welcome to the greenwood; here all is fresh and bright."

Then John turned to have one more look at the old church
in which he had been christened in his infancy, and where his
father had taken him every Sunday to hear the service and
join in singing the psalms. As he looked at the old tower, he
saw the bell ringer standing at one of the narrow openings,
with his little pointed red cap on his head, shading his eyes
from the sun with his bent arm. John nodded farewell to him;
and the little ringer waved his red cap, laid his hand on his
heart, and kissed his hand to him a great many times, to show
that he felt kindly toward him, and wished him a prosperous
journey.

John went on, and he thought of all the wonderful things
he would see in the large, beautiful world, and he even found
himself farther away from home than ever he had been before.
He didn't even know the names of the places he passed
through, and could scarcely understand the language of the
people he met. He was far away in a strange land.

The first night he slept on a haystack, out in the fields, for
there was no other bed for him; but it seemed to him so nice
and comfortable that even a king needn't wish for better. The
field, the brook, the haystack, with the blue sky above, made
a beautiful bedroom. The green grass, with the little red and
white flowers, was the carpet; the elder bushes and the hedges
of wild roses looked like garlands on the walls. And for a
bath he could have the clear, fresh water of the brook; while
the rushes bowed their heads to him, to wish him good morning and good evening. The moon, like a large lamp, hung high
up in the blue ceiling, and he need have no fear of its setting
fire to his curtains. John slept here quite safely all night; and
when he awoke, the sun was up, and all the little birds were

singing round him, "Good morning! good morning! Are you not up yet?"

It was Sunday, and the bells were ringing for church. As the people went in, John followed them. He heard God's word, joined in singing the psalms, and listened to the preacher. It seemed to him as if he were in his own church, where he had been christened, and had sung the psalms with his father. Out in the churchyard there were several graves, and on some of them the grass had grown very high. John thought of his father's grave, which he knew at last would look like these, as he was not there to weed and care for it. So he set to work, pulled up the high grass, raised the wooden crosses which had fallen down, and replaced the wreaths which had been blown away, thinking all the time, "Perhaps someone is doing the same for my father's grave, since I am not there to do it."

Outside the churchyard door stood an old beggar, leaning on his crutch. John gave him his silver shillings, and then he continued his journey, feeling lighter and happier than ever. Toward evening, the weather became very stormy, and he hurried as quickly as he could to find shelter. It was quite dark by the time he reached a lonely little church which stood on a hill. "I will go in here," he said, "and sit down in a corner; for I am very tired, and want rest."

He went in, and seated himself. Then he folded his hands, and offered up his evening prayer, and was soon fast asleep and dreaming. Overhead the thunder rolled and the lightning flashed. When he awoke, it was still night; but the storm had ceased, and the moon shone in upon him through the windows. Then he saw an open coffin standing in the center of the church. It contained a dead man, waiting for burial. John was not at all timid; he had a good conscience, and he knew that the dead can never injure anyone. It is the living, wicked men who do harm to others. Two such wicked persons stood now by the dead man, who had been brought to the church to be buried. Their evil intentions were to throw the poor dead body outside the church door, and not allow him to rest in his coffin.

"Why do you do this?" asked John, when he saw what they were going to do. "It is very wicked. Leave him to rest in peace, in Christ's name."

"Bosh!" replied the two dreadful men. "He has cheated us. He owed us money which he could not pay, and now that he is dead we shall not get a penny. We mean to have our revenge, and let him lie like a dog outside the church door."

"I have fifty dollars," said John. "It is all I own in the world, but I will give it to you if you will promise me faithfully to leave the dead man in peace. I shall be able to get along without the money. I have strong and healthy limbs, and God will always help me."

"Why, of course," said the horrid men, "if you will pay his debt we will both promise not to touch him. You may depend upon that." And they took the money he offered them, laughed at him for his good nature, and went their way.

John laid the dead body back in the coffin, folded the hands, and departed; and went away contentedly through the great forest. All around him he could see the prettiest little elves dancing in the moonlight shining through the trees. They were not disturbed by his presence, for they knew he was good and harmless among men. It is only the wicked people who can never obtain a glimpse of the fairies.

Some of the elves were no taller than the breadth of a finger. They wore golden combs in their long yellow hair. They were rocking themselves two at a time on the large dewdrops which were sprinkled over the leaves and the high grass. Sometimes the dewdrops would roll away, and then they fell down between the stems of the long grass, and this caused a great deal of laughing and noise among the other little people.

It was charming to watch them at play. They sang songs, and John remembered that he had learned those same pretty songs when he was a little boy. Large speckled spiders, with silver crowns on their heads, were employed to spin suspension bridges and palaces from one hedge to another, and when the tiny drops fell upon them, they glittered in the moonlight like shining glass. All this went on till sunrise. Then the little elves crept into the flower buds, and the wind seized the bridges and palaces, and fluttered them in the air like cobwebs.

As John left the wood, a strong man's voice called after him, "Hallo, comrade, where are you traveling?"

"Into the wide world," he replied. "I am only a poor lad; I have neither father nor mother, but God will help me."

"I am going into the wide world also," replied the Stranger. "Shall we keep each other company?"

"With all my heart," said John. And so they went on together. They soon began to like each other very much, for they were both good men. But John found that the Stranger was much more clever than himself. He had traveled all over the world, and could describe almost everything. The sun was high in the heavens when they finally seated themselves under a large tree to eat their breakfast. And at the same moment an old woman came toward them.

She was very old and almost bent double. She leaned upon a stick and carried on her back a bundle of firewood, which she had collected in the forest. Her apron was tied round it, and John saw three great stems of fern and some willow twigs peeping out. Just as she came close to them, her foot slipped and she fell to the ground screaming loudly. Poor old woman, she had broken her leg! John proposed that they carry the old woman home to her cottage; but the Stranger opened his knapsack and took out a box, in which he said he had a salve that would quickly make her leg well and strong again, and she would be able to walk home by herself, as if her leg had never been broken. All that he would ask in return was the three fern stems which she carried in her apron.

"That is too high a price," said the old woman nodding her head quite strangely. She did not seem at all inclined to part with the fern stems. However, it was not very agreeable to lie there with a broken leg, so she finally gave them to him. And the power of the ointment was so great, that as soon as he rubbed her leg with it the old mother rose up and walked, better than she had done before. But then this wonderful ointment couldn't be bought at an apothecary's.

"What can you want with those three fern rods?" asked John of his fellow traveler.

"Oh, they will make excellent brooms," said he. "And, too, I like them because I am a whimsical fellow." Then they walked on together for a long distance.

"How dark the sky is becoming," said John; "and look at those thick, heavy clouds."

"Those aren't clouds," replied his fellow traveler. "They are mountains—large lofty mountains—when we are on top of them we shall be above the clouds, in the pure, free air. Believe me, it is delightful to climb so high. Tomorrow we shall be there." But the mountains were not as near as they appeared. They had to travel a whole day, and pass through black forests and piles of rock as large as a town before they reached them. The journey had been so fatiguing that John and his fellow traveler stopped to rest at a roadside inn, to gain strength for their journey on the morrow.

In the large public room of the inn a great many persons had assembled to see a comedy performed by dolls. The showman had just erected his little theater, and the people were sitting round the room to watch the performance. Right in front, in the very best place, sat a stout butcher, with a great bulldog, who seemed very much inclined to bite. He sat staring with all his eyes, and so indeed did everyone else in the room.

And then the play began. It was a pretty piece, with a king and queen in it. They sat on a beautiful throne, and had gold crowns on their heads. The trains to their dresses were very long, according to the fashion; while the prettiest of wooden dolls, with glass eyes and large moustaches, stood at the doors, and opened and shut them, that the fresh air might come into the room. It was a very pleasant play, not at all sad. But as the Queen stood up and walked across the stage, the great bulldog, who should have been held back by his master, made a spring forward, and caught the Queen's slender waist in his teeth. And she snapped in two! This was a very dreadful disaster.

The poor man, who was exhibiting the dolls, was very annoyed, and quite sad about his Queen. She was the prettiest doll he had, and the bulldog had broken her head and shoulders off. When all the people had gone away, the Stranger, who came with John, said that he could soon set her to rights. He brought out his box and rubbed the doll with some of the salve which had cured the old woman when she broke her leg. As soon as this was done the doll's back became quite right again. Her head and shoulders were fixed on, and she could even move her limbs herself. There was now no reason to pull the wires, for the doll acted just like a living creature, except that she could not speak. The man to whom the show belonged was delighted to have a doll who could dance by herself without being pulled by wires. None of the other dolls could do this.

During the night, when all the people at the inn had gone to bed, someone was heard sighing so deeply and painfully, and for so long a time, that everyone got up to see what could be the matter. The Showman went at once to his little theater and found that it came from the dolls. They all lay on the floor sighing piteously, and staring with their glass eyes. They all wanted to be rubbed with the ointment, so that, like the

Queen, they might be able to move by themselves. The Queen threw herself on her knees, took off her beautiful crown, and, holding it in her hand, cried, "Take this from me, but please rub my husband and his courtiers."

The poor man who owned the theater could scarcely keep from crying. He was so sorry that he could not help them. He immediately spoke to John's comrade, and promised him all the money he would get at the next evening's performance, if he would only rub the ointment on four or five of his dolls. But the fellow traveler said he did not want anything in return, except the sword which the Showman wore by his side. As soon as he received the sword he anointed six of the dolls with the ointment, and they were able immediately to dance so gracefully that all the living girls in the room could not help but join in the dance.

The coachman danced with the cook, and the waiters with the chambermaids, and all the strangers joined in. Even the tongs and the fire shovel gave it a try, but they fell down after the first jump. So it was a very merry night after all.

The next morning John and his companion left the inn to continue their journey through the great pine forests and over the high mountains. They arrived at last at such a great height that all the towns and villages lay beneath them, and the church steeples looked like little specks between the green trees. They could see for miles around, far away to places they had never visited, and John saw more of the beautiful world than he had ever known existed before. The sun shone brightly in the blue firmament above, and through the clear mountain air came the sound of the huntsman's horn. The soft, sweet notes brought tears to his eyes, and he could not help exclaiming, "How good and loving God is to give all this beauty and loveliness in the world to make us happy!"

His fellow traveler stood by with folded hands, gazing on the dark woods and the towns bathed in the warm sunshine.

At this moment sweet music sounded over their heads. They looked up, and discovered a large white swan hovering in the air, and singing as bird never sang before. But the song soon grew weaker and weaker, the bird's head drooped, and he sank slowly down, and lay dead at their feet.

"It is a beautiful bird," said the traveler, "and these large white wings are worth a great deal of money. I will take them with me. You see now that a sword will be very useful."

So with one blow, he cut off the wings of the dead swan, and carried them away with him.

They continued their journey over the mountains for many miles, till they reached a large city, containing hundreds of towers, that shone in the sunshine like silver. In the midst of the city stood a splendid marble palace, roofed with pure red gold. Here dwelt the King. John and his companion did not go into the town immediately. They stopped at an inn outside the town, to change their clothes; for they wished to appear respectable as they walked through the streets. The landlord told them that the King was a very good man, who never injured any one; but as to his daughter, "Heaven defend us!"

She was indeed a wicked Princess. She possessed beauty enough—no one could be more elegant or pretty than she. But what of that? She was a wicked witch; and because of her conduct many noble young princes had lost their lives. Anyone was at liberty to make her an offer—were he prince or beggar—it mattered not to her. She would ask him to guess three things which she had just thought of, and if he succeeded, he was to marry her, and be king over all the land when her father died. But if he could not guess these three things, then she ordered that he either be hanged or have his head cut off.

The old King, her father, was very grieved at her conduct. But he could not prevent her from being so wicked, because he had once said he would have nothing more to do with her lovers; she might do as she pleased. Each prince who came and tried the three guesses, to win and marry the Princess, had been unable to find them out, and had been hanged or beheaded. They had all been warned in time, and could have left her alone, but they didn't. The old King at last became so distressed at these dreadful circumstances, that for a whole day every year he and his soldiers knelt and prayed that the Princess might become good. But she continued to be as wicked as ever. The old women who drank brandy would color it black before they drank it, to show how they mourned. And what more could they do?

"What a horrible princess!" said John. "She ought to be flogged. If I were the old King, I would have her punished in some way."

Just then they heard the people outside shouting, "Hurrah!" They looked out, and saw the Princess passing by. And she was really so beautiful that everybody forgot her wickedness, and shouted, "Hurrah!" Twelve lovely maidens in white silk dresses, holding golden tulips in their hands, rode by her side on coal-black horses. The Princess herself had a snow-white steed, decked with diamonds and rubies. Her dress was of gold cloth, and the whip she held in her hand looked like a sunbeam. The golden crown on her head glittered like the stars of heaven, and her mantle was made of thousands of butterflies' wings sewn together. And she herself was the most beautiful of all.

When John saw her, his face became as red as a drop of blood, and he could scarcely utter a word. The Princess looked exactly like the beautiful lady with the golden crown, of whom he had dreamed on the night his father died. To him she appeared so lovely that he could not help loving her.

"It can't be true," he thought, "that she is really a wicked witch, who orders people to be hanged or beheaded, if they do not guess her thoughts. Everyone has permission to go and ask her hand, even the poorest beggar. I shall pay a visit to the palace," he said. "I must go. I cannot help myself."

Everyone advised him not to attempt it; for he would be sure to share the same fate as the rest. His fellow traveler also tried to persuade him against it. But John seemed quite sure of success. He brushed his shoes and his coat, washed his face and his hands, combed his soft flaxen hair, and then went out alone into the town, and walked to the palace.

"Come in," said the King, as John knocked at the door. John opened it, and the old King, in a dressing gown and embroidered slippers, came toward him. He had the crown on his head, carried his scepter in one hand, and the orb in the other. "Wait a bit," said he, and he placed the orb under his arm, so that he could offer the other hand to John. But when he found out that John was another suitor, he began to weep so violently that both the scepter and the orb fell to the floor, and he was obliged to wipe his eyes with his dressing gown. Poor old King!

"Let her alone," he said; "you will fare as badly as all the others. Come, I will show you." Then he led him out into the Princess's pleasure gardens, and there he saw a frightful sight. On every tree hung three or four princes, who had wooed his daughter, but had not been able to guess the riddles she gave them. Their skeletons rattled in every breeze, so that the terrified birds never dared to venture into the garden. The flowers were supported by human bones instead of stakes, and human skulls in the flowerpots grinned horribly. It was really a doleful garden for a princess. "Do you see all this?" said the old King. "Your fate will be the same as those who are here. Do not attempt it. You really make me very unhappy— I take these things to heart so very much."

John kissed the good old King's hand, and said he was sure it would be all right, for he was quite enchanted with the beautiful Princess. Then the Princess herself came riding into the palace yard with all her ladies, and he wished her "Good morning." She looked wonderfully fair and lovely when she offered her hand to John. And he loved her more than ever. How could she be a wicked witch, as all the people asserted? He accompanied her into the hall, and the little pages offered them gingerbread nuts and sweetmeats. But the old King was so unhappy he could eat nothing, and besides, gingerbread nuts were too hard for him to chew.

It was decided that John should come to the palace the next day to try and guess the first riddle. The judges and the counselors would be present. If he succeeded, he would have to come a second time; but if not, he would lose his life—and no one had ever been able to guess even one. However, John was not at all anxious about the result of his trial. On the contrary, he was very merry. He thought only of the beautiful Princess, and believed that in some way he would have help. But how he didn't know, and did not like to think about it. So he danced along the highroad and went back to the inn, where he had left his fellow traveler waiting for him. John could not refrain from telling him how gracious the Princess had been, and how beautiful she looked. He longed for the next day to come so he could go to the palace and try his luck at guessing the riddles. But his comrade shook his head, and looked very sad.

"I do so wish you to do well," said he. "We might have continued together much longer, and now I am likely to lose you; you poor dear John! I could shed tears, but I will not make you unhappy on the last night we may be together. We will be merry, really merry this evening. Tomorrow, after you are gone, I shall be able to weep undisturbed."

It was very quickly known among the people of the town that another suitor had arrived for the Princess, and there was great sorrow because of it. The theater remained closed, the women who sold sweetmeats tied crape round the sugar sticks, and the King and the priests were on their knees in the church. There was a great lamentation, for no one expected John to succeed any better than those who had been suitors before.

In the evening John's comrade prepared a large bowl of punch, and said, "Now let us be merry, and drink to the health of the Princess." But after drinking two glasses, John became so sleepy, that he could not possibly keep his eyes open, and fell fast asleep. His fellow traveler lifted him gently out of his chair, and laid him on the bed. As soon as it was quite dark, he took the two large wings which he had cut from the dead swan, and tied them firmly to his own shoulders. Then he put into his pocket the largest of the three fern stems which he had obtained from the old woman who had fallen and broken her leg. After this he opened the window, and flew away over the town, straight toward the palace, and seated himself in a corner, under the window which looked into the bedroom of the Princess.

The town was perfectly still as the clocks struck a quarter to twelve. Presently the window opened, and the Princess, who had large black wings on her shoulders, and a long white mantle, flew away over the city toward a high mountain. The fellow traveler, who had made himself invisible, so that she could not possibly see him, flew after her through the air, and whipped the Princess with his fern stem, and the blood came whenever he struck her. Ah, it was a strange flight through the air! The wind caught her mantle, so that it spread out on all sides, like the large sail of a ship, and the moon shone through it. "How it hails, to be sure!" said the Princess, at each blow she received from the stem; and it served her right to be whipped.

At last she reached the side of the mountain, and knocked on it. The mountain opened with a noise like the roll of thunder, and the Princess went in. The traveler followed her; no one could see him, as he had made himself invisible. They went through a long, wide passage. A thousand gleaming spiders ran here and there on the walls, making them glitter as if they were illuminated with fire.

Next they entered a large hall built of silver and gold. Large red and blue flowers shone on the walls. They looked like sunflowers in size. But no one could dare to pluck them, for the stems were hideous poisonous snakes, and the flowers had flames of fire, darting out of their jaws. Shining glow-worms covered the ceiling, and sky-blue bats flapped their transparent wings. Altogether the place had a frightful appearance. In the middle of the floor stood a throne supported by four skeleton horses, whose harness had been made by fiery-red spiders. The throne itself was made of milk-white glass, and the cushions were little black mice, each biting at the other's tail. Over it hung a canopy of rose-colored spider webs, spotted with the prettiest little green flies, sparkling like precious stones.

On the throne sat an old Magician with a crown on his ugly head, and a scepter in his hand. He kissed the Princess on the forehead, seated her by his side on the splendid throne, and then the music commenced. Great black grasshoppers played the mouth organ, and the owl struck herself on the body instead of a drum. It was altogether a ridiculous concert. Little black goblins with false lights in their caps danced about the hall; but no one could see the traveler. He had placed himself just behind the throne where he could see and hear everything.

The courtiers who came in afterward looked noble and grand; but anyone with common sense could see what they really were: broomsticks, with cabbages for heads. The Magician had given them life, and dressed them in embroidered robes. It answered very well, as they were only wanted for show anyway. After there had been a little dancing, the Princess told the Magician that she had a new suitor, and asked him what she should think of for the suitor to guess when he came to the castle the next morning.

"Listen to what I say," said the Magician. "You must choose something very easy: he is less likely to guess it then. Think of one of your shoes. He will never think of that. Then cut his head off; and mind you don't forget to bring his eyes with you tomorrow night, so I may eat them."

The Princess curtsied low, and said she would not forget the eyes.

Then the Magician opened the mountain and she flew home again. But the traveler followed and flogged her so much with the stem that she sighed quite deeply about the heavy hail-storm, and hurried to get back to her bedroom.

The traveler returned to the inn where John still slept, took off his wings and lay down on the bed, for he was very tired. Early in the morning John awoke, and when his fellow traveler got up, he said that he had had a very wonderful dream about the Princess and her shoe. He advised John to ask her if she had not thought of her shoe. Of course, the traveler had learned this from listening to the Magician in the mountain.

"I may as well say that as anything else," said John. "Perhaps your dream may come true. Still, I will say farewell, for if I guess wrong I shall never see you again."

Then they embraced each other, and John went into the town and walked to the palace. The great hall was full of people, and the judges sat in armchairs, with eider-down cushions to rest their heads upon, because they had so much to think of. The old King stood near, wiping his eyes with his white handkerchief. When the Princess entered, she looked even more beautiful than she had the day before. She greeted every one present most gracefully; but to John she gave her hand, and said, "Good morning to you."

Now came the time for John to guess what she was thinking of. And, oh, how kindly she looked at him as he began to speak. But when he uttered the single word *shoe*, she turned as pale as a ghost. All her wisdom could not help her, for he had guessed rightly. Oh, how pleased the old King was! It was quite amusing to see how he capered about. All the people clapped their hands, on his account and John's, who had guessed rightly the first time. His fellow traveler was glad also, when he heard how successful John had been. John folded his hands, and thanked God, who, he felt quite sure, would help him again; for he knew he had to guess twice more.

The next evening passed pleasantly like the one preceding. While John slept, his companion flew behind the Princess to the mountain, and flogged her even harder than before; this time he had taken two stems with him. No one saw him go in with her, and he heard all that was said. The Princess this time was to think of a glove, and he told John as if he had again heard it in a dream.

The next day, John was able to guess correctly the second time, and it caused great rejoicing at the palace. The whole court jumped about as they had seen the King do the day before. But the Princess lay on the sofa, and would not say a single word. All now depended on John. If he guessed rightly the third time, he would marry the Princess, and reign over the kingdom after the death of the old King. But if he failed, he would lose his life, and the Magician would have his beautiful blue eyes.

That evening John said his prayers and went to bed very early, and soon fell calmly asleep. His companion tied his wings to his shoulders, took three stems, and, with his sword at his side, flew to the palace. It was a very dark night, and so stormy that the tiles flew from the roofs of the houses, and the trees in the garden, upon which the skeletons hung, bent themselves like reeds before the wind. The lightning flashed, and the thunder rolled in one long-continued peal all night. The window of the castle opened, and the Princess flew out. She was as pale as death, but she laughed at the storm as if it were not bad enough. Her white mantle fluttered in the wind like a large sail, and the traveler flogged her with the three stems till the blood trickled down, and at last she could scarcely fly. She managed, however, to reach the mountain. "What a hailstorm!" she said, as she entered; "I have never been out in such weather as this."

"Yes, there may be too much of a good thing sometimes," said the Magician.

Then the Princess told him that John had guessed rightly the second time. And if he succeeded the next morning, he would win, and she could never come to the mountain again, or practice magic as she had done, and therefore she was very unhappy.

"I will find something for you to think of which he will never guess, unless he is a greater conjuror than myself," said the Magician. "But now let us be merry."

Then he took the Princess by both hands, and they danced with all the little goblins and jack-o'-lanterns in the room. The red spiders sprang here and there on the walls quite as merrily, and the flowers of fire looked as if they were throwing out sparks. The owl beat the drum, the crickets whistled, and the grasshoppers played the mouth organ. It was a very ridiculous ball. After they had danced a long while, the Princess had to go home, for fear she would be missed at the palace. The Magician offered to go with her, to keep her company on the way. They flew away through the bad weather, and the traveler followed them, and broke his three stems across their shoulders. The Magician had never been out in such a hailstorm as this. Just by the palace the Magician stopped to wish the Princess farewell, and to whisper in her ear, "Tomorrow think of my head."

But the traveler heard it, and just as the Princess slipped

through the window into her bedroom, and the Magician turned round to fly back to the mountain, he seized him by the long black beard, and with his saber cut off the wicked conjuror's head just behind his shoulders, and the Magician had not even seen who it was. He threw the body into the sea to the fishes, and, after dipping the head into the water, he tied it up in a silk handkerchief, took it with him to the inn, and then went to bed. The next morning he gave John the handkerchief, and told him not to untie it till the Princess asked him what she was thinking of. There were so many people in the great hall of the palace that they stood as thick as bunches of radishes. The council sat in their armchairs with the white cushions. The old King wore new robes. The golden crown and scepter had been polished up and he looked very smart. But the Princess was very pale, and wore a black dress as if she were going to a funeral.

"What have I thought of?" asked the Princess, of John. He immediately untied the handkerchief, and was himself quite frightened when he saw the head of the ugly Magician. Everyone shuddered, for it was terrible to look at. But the Princess sat like a statue and could not utter a single word. At length she rose and gave John her hand, for he had guessed rightly.

She looked at no one, but sighed deeply, and said, "You are my master now. This evening our marriage must take place."

"I am very much pleased to hear it," said the old King. "It is just what I wish."

Then all the people shouted "Hurrah!" The band played music in the street, the bells rang, and the cake-women took the black crape off the sugar sticks. There was universal joy. Three oxen, stuffed with ducks and chickens, were roasted whole in the marketplace, where everyone might help himself to a slice. The fountains spouted forth the most delicious wine, and whoever bought a penny loaf at the baker's received six large buns, full of raisins, as a present. In the evening the whole town was lit up. The soldiers fired off cannons, and the boys let off crackers. Everywhere there was eating, drinking, dancing and jumping! In the palace, the high-born gentlemen and the beautiful ladies danced with each other, and they could be heard at a great distance singing the following song—

> *Here are maidens, young and fair,*
> *Dancing in the summer air;*
> *Like to spinning wheels at play,*
> *Pretty maidens dance away—*
> *Dance the spring and summer through*
> *Till the sole falls from your shoe.*

But the Princess was still a witch, and she could not love John. His fellow traveler had thought of that, so he gave John three feathers out of the swan's wings, and a little bottle with a few drops in it. He told him to place a large bath full of water by the Princess's bed, and put the feathers and the drops into it. Then, at the moment she was about to get into bed, he must give her a little push, so she would fall into the water, and then he must dip her three times. This would destroy the power of the Magician, and she would be able to love him very much.

John did all that his companion told him to do. The Princess shrieked when he dipped her under the water the first time, and struggled under his hands in the form of a great black swan with fiery eyes. As she rose the second time from the water, the swan had become white, with a black ring round its neck. John allowed the water to close once more over the bird, and at the same time it changed into a most beautiful Princess. She was more lovely than ever before. She thanked him, her eyes sparkling with tears, for having broken the spell of the Magician.

The next day, the King and the whole court came to offer

their congratulations. They stayed till very late. Last of all came the traveling companion. He had his staff in his hand and his knapsack on his back. John kissed him many times and told him he must not go, he must remain with him, for he was the cause of all his good fortune. But the traveler shook his head, and said gently and kindly, "No. My time is up now. I have only paid my debt to you. Do you remember the dead man whom the bad people wished to throw out of his coffin? You gave all you possessed that he might rest in his grave. I am the dead man." And, as he said this, he vanished.

The wedding festivities lasted a whole month. John and his Princess loved each other dearly, and the old King lived to see many a happy day, when he took their little children on his knees and let them play with his scepter. And John became king over the whole country.

BOOBY HANS

OUT in the country lay an old manor house, and in it lived an old squire who had two sons who were twice as clever as they had any right to be. They were going to propose to the daughter of the King. They weren't afraid to, because she had announced that she was going to marry whoever could talk the best.

They spent eight days preparing themselves; for that was all the time they had. But they knew a lot of things beforehand, and that's always useful. One of them knew the whole Latin dictionary by heart and the town newspaper for three years both forward and backward. The other had acquainted himself with the laws of all the guilds and what every alderman should know. He could talk about state affairs, he thought; and besides that he could embroider suspenders, for he had a very delicate touch.

"I'll get the Princess!" both of them said, and then their father gave each of them a lovely horse. The one who knew the dictionary and the newspapers got a coal-black horse, and the one who knew about guilds and embroidery got a milk-white one, and then they rubbed the corners of the horses' mouths with fish oil to make them more supple. All the servants went down in the yard to see them get on their horses. And just then the third brother came. You see, there were really three, but nobody counted the last as a brother, because he wasn't a scholar like the other two. They just called him Booby Hans.

"Where are you going, all dressed up like that?" he asked.

"To the court, to win the Princess by talking! Haven't you heard what they are drumming about all through the country?"

And then they told him about it.

"Good gracious, I'd better go too, then!" said Booby Hans, and his brothers laughed at him and rode away.

"Father, let me have a horse!" shouted Booby Hans. "I feel just like getting married now. If she'll take me, then she'll take me! If she won't take me, then I'll have her anyway!"

"What nonsense," said the father, "I won't give any horse to you. You don't know how to talk! Your brothers are different; they're bright fellows!"

"If I can't have a horse," said Booby Hans, "then I'll take the goat. It's my own and it carries me very well!" And so he sat astride the goat, kicked his heels into its sides, and rushed away along the highroad. Whee! what speed! "Here I come!" said Booby Hans, and he sang till the noise went trailing after him.

The brothers were riding ahead very quietly. They weren't saying a word; they were thinking about all the good ideas they were going to have. Everything was going to be very clever.

"Hey, there, hello!" Booby Hans shouted. "Here I come! Look what I found on the road!" and he showed them a dead crow he had found.

"Booby!" they said, "what do you want with that?"

"I'll make a present of it to the Princess!"

"Oh, yes, do give it to her," they said, and laughed, and rode on.

"Hey there, hello! Here I come! Look what I found now. You don't find this on the road every day!"

And the brothers turned around to see what it was.

"Booby!" they said, "it's only an old wooden shoe with the uppers gone! Is the Princess going to get that too?"

"She is!" said Booby Hans, and the brothers laughed. They rode on far ahead.

"Hey there, hello! Here I am again!" shouted Booby Hans. "It's getting worse and worse now! Hey there! There never was anything like it!"

"What have you found now?" asked the brothers.

"Oh!" said Booby Hans, "I can hardly talk! How happy that Princess is going to be!"

"Pfui!" said the brothers, "it's nothing but mud that's been thrown up out of the ditch."

"That's what it is!" said Booby Hans. "And it's the very finest kind; you can hardly keep hold of it!" And so he filled his pockets.

The brothers rode on as fast as their horses would go, and they got there a whole hour ahead of him. They stopped at the city gate, and there every suitor was given a number. They

were all standing in line, six in every row and so close that
they couldn't move an arm. It was a good thing, too, or they
would have stabbed each other in the back just because one
stood in front of the other.

The rest of the people in the country were standing around
the castle, right up against the windows to watch the Princess
receive the suitors. As each one came into the room the
power of speech left him.

"No good!" said the Princess. "Get out!"

Now came the brother who knew the dictionary. But he
had clean forgotten it by standing in line so long, and the
floor creaked, and the ceiling was made of mirror glass, so
that he saw himself standing on his head. And three scriveners
and an alderman stood at every window and wrote down
everything that was said so that it could go right into the
newspaper and be sold for two cents on the corner. It was
terrible, and the stove was so hot that the pipe gleamed red.

"It's very hot in here," said the suitor.

"That's because my father is roasting cockerels today!"
said the Princess.

Boo! There he stood. He hadn't expected that kind of
speech. And he didn't have a word to say just when he
wanted so much to say something funny. Boo!

"No good!" said the Princess. "Get out!" And then he
had to leave. Now the second brother came.

"It's terribly hot in here," he said.

"Yes, we're roasting cockerels today!" said the Princess.

"What's—what?" he said, and all the scriveners wrote,
"What's—what?"

"No good!" said the Princess. "Get out!"

Then came Booby Hans on his goat. He rode right into
the room. "It's burning hot in here!" he said.

"That's because I'm roasting cockerels!" said the Princess.

"Isn't that nice!" said Booby Hans, "then I can get my crow roasted, I suppose."

"Certainly you can," said the Princess, "but have you anything to roast it in, because I haven't any pots or pans!"

"But I have!" said Booby Hans. "Here's a pot with tin nails!" And he pulled out the old wooden shoe and put the crow right in it.

"That will make a whole meal!" said the Princess. "But where do we get the gravy from?"

"I have that in my pocket!" said Booby Hans. "I have such a lot I can throw some of it away!" And he poured a little mud out of his pocket.

"That's what I like," said the Princess. "You can answer, and you can talk, and you're the man I want to marry! But do you know that every word we're saying and have said is being written down for tomorrow's newspaper? You see, there are three scriveners and an alderman standing by every window, and the alderman is the worst because he can't understand!" (She said that to scare him, and all the scriveners whinnied and dropped ink on the floor.)

"Oh, are they so grand?" said Booby Hans, "then the alderman will have to have the best!" And he turned his pockets inside out and threw the mud right in his face.

"That's what I like," said the Princess. "You can do that, and I'm going to learn!"

And so Booby Hans was King, and had a wife and a crown and sat on a throne, and we got that right out of the alderman's newspaper—and you can't depend on that.

THE WINDMILL

A WINDMILL stood upon the hill, proud to look at, and proud too.

"I am really not proud at all," it said. "But I am so enlightened without and within. I have sun and moon for my outward use, and for inward use too; and into the bargain I have tallow candles, train-oil lamps, and wax candles. I may very well say that I am enlightened. I am a thinking being, and so well constructed that it's quite delightful. I have a good windpipe in my chest, and I have four wings that are placed outside my head, just beneath my hat; the birds have only two wings, and have to carry them on their backs. I am a Dutchman by birth—that may be seen by my figure—a flying Dutchman. They are considered supernatural beings, I know, and yet I am quite natural. I have a gallery round my chest, and house room beneath it. That's where my thoughts dwell. My strongest thought, who rules and reigns, is called by the others 'The Man in the Mill.' He knows what he wants, and is lord over the meal and the bran. But he has his companion too, and she calls herself 'Mother.' She is the very heart of me. She does not run about stupidly and awkwardly, for she knows what she wants, she knows what she can do; she's as soft as a zephyr and as strong as a storm. She knows how to begin a thing carefully, and to have her own way. She is my soft temper, and the father is my hard one. They are two, and yet one; they each call the other 'My half.' They have some little boys, young thoughts, that can grow. The little ones keep everything in order.

"When, lately, in my wisdom, I let the father and the boys

examine my throat and the hole in my chest, to see what was going on there—for something in me was out of order, and it's well to examine oneself—the little ones made a tremendous noise. The youngest jumped up into my hat, and shouted so there that it tickled me. The little thoughts may grow; I know that very well. And out in the world thoughts come too, and not only of my kind, for as far as I can see I cannot discern anything like myself. But the wingless houses, whose throats make no noise, have thoughts too, and they come to my thoughts, and make love to them, as it is called. It's wonderful enough—yes, there are many wonderful things. Something has come over me, or into me—something has changed in the millwork. It seems as if the one half, the father, has altered. He has received a better temper, a more affectionate helpmate—so young and good, and yet the same, only growing more gentle and good through the course of time. What was bitter has passed away, and the whole is much more comfortable.

"The days go on, and the days come nearer and nearer to clearness and to joy. And then a day will come when it will be over with me; but not over altogether. I must be pulled down that I may be built up again. I shall cease, but yet I shall live on. To become quite a different being, and yet remain the same! That's difficult for me to understand, however enlightened I may be with sun, moon, stearine, train oil, and tallow. My old woodwork and my old brickwork will rise again from the dust!

"I will hope that I may keep my old thoughts, the father in the mill, and the mother, great ones and little ones—the family, I call them all, great and little, my *company of thoughts*, because I must, and cannot help it.

"And I must also remain 'myself,' with my throat in my chest, my wings on my head, the gallery round my body; or else I should not know myself. Nor would the others know me, and say, 'There's the mill on the hill, proud to look at, and yet not proud at all.' "

That is what the mill said. Indeed, it said much more, but that is the most important part.

And the days came, and the days went, and yesterday was the last day.

Then the mill caught fire. The flames rose up high, and beat out and in, and bit at the beams and planks, and ate them up. The mill fell, and nothing remained of it but a heap of ashes. The smoke drove across the scene of the conflagration, and the wind carried it away.

Whatever had been alive in the mill remained, and what had been gained by it has nothing to do with this story.

The miller's family—one soul, many thoughts, and yet only one—built a new, a splendid mill, which answered its purpose. It was quite like the old one, and people said, "Why, yonder is the mill on the hill, proud to look at!" But this mill was better arranged, more up to date than the last, so that progress might be made.

The old mill's beams had become wormeaten and spongy —they lay in dust and ashes. The body of the mill did not rise out of the dust as the people had believed it would do. They had taken it literally, and all things are *not* to be taken literally.

IN THE DUCK YARD

A DUCK arrived from Portugal. Some said she came from
Spain, but that's all the same. At any rate she was called the
Portuguese, and laid eggs, and was killed and cooked, and
that was *her* career. But the ducklings which crept forth from
her eggs were afterward also called Portuguese, and there is
something in that. Now, out of the whole family, there was
only one left in the duck yard—a yard to which the chickens
had access, and where the cock strutted about in a very aggres-
sive manner.

"He annoys me with his loud crowing!" observed the Portuguese Duck. "But he's a handsome bird, there's no deny-
ing that, though he is not a drake. He ought to moderate
his voice, but that's an art inseparable from polite education,
like that possessed by the little singing birds over in the lime
trees in the neighbor's garden. How charmingly they sing!
There's something quite pretty in their warbling. I call it
Portugal. If I only had such a little singing bird, I'd be a
mother to him, kind and good, for that's in my blood—my
Portuguese blood!"

And while she was still speaking, a little singing bird came
head over heels from the roof into the yard. The cat was behind him, but the bird escaped with a broken wing, and that's
how he came tumbling into the yard.

"That's just like the cat. She's a villain!" said the Portuguese Duck. "I remember her ways when I had children of
my own. That such a creature should be allowed to live, and
to wander about upon the roofs! I don't think they do such
things in Portugal!"

And she pitied the little Singing Bird. And the other ducks who were not of Portuguese descent pitied him too.

"Poor little creature!" they said, as one after another came up. "We certainly can't sing," they said, "but we have a sounding board, or something of the kind, within us. And we can feel that, even though we don't talk about it."

"But I can talk of it," said the Portuguese Duck. "And I'll do something for the little fellow, for that's my duty!" And she stepped into the water trough, and beat her wings upon the water so heartily that the little Singing Bird was almost drowned by the bath he got, but the Duck meant it kindly. "That's a good deed," she said. "The others may take example by it."

"Peep!" said the little Bird: one of his wings was broken, and he found it difficult to shake himself; but he quite understood that the bath was kindly intended. "You are very kindhearted, madam," he said; but he did not wish for a second bath.

"I have never thought about my heart," continued the Portuguese Duck, "but I know this much, that I love all my fellow creatures except the cat. Nobody can expect me to love her, for she ate up two of my ducklings. But please make yourself at home; you can at least make yourself comfortable. I myself am from a strange country, as you may see from my bearing and from my feathery dress. My drake is a native of these parts. He's not of my race; but for all that I'm not proud! If anyone here in the yard can understand you, I assure you that I am that person."

"She's quite full of Portulak," said a little common Duck, who was witty. And all the other common ducks considered the word *Portulak* quite a good joke, for it sounded like Portugal. And they nudged each other and said "Rapp!" It was too witty! And all the other ducks now began to notice the little Singing Bird.

"The Portuguese has certainly a greater command of language," they said. "For our part, we don't care to fill our beaks with such long words, but our sympathy is just as great. If we can't do anything for you, we will march about with you everywhere; and we think that is the best thing we can do."

"You have a lovely voice," said one of the oldest. "It must be a great satisfaction to be able to give as much pleasure as you are able to give. I certainly am no great judge of your song, and consequently I keep my beak shut. But even that is better than talking nonsense to you as others do."

"Don't plague him so," interrupted the Portuguese Duck. "He requires rest and nursing. My little Singing Bird, do you wish me to prepare another bath for you?"

"Oh, no! pray let me be dry!" was the little Bird's petition.

"The water cure is the only remedy for me when I am unwell," quoth the Portuguese. "Amusement is beneficial too. The neighboring fowls will soon come to pay their visit. There are two Cochin Chinese among them. They wear feathers on their legs, are well educated, and have been brought from afar. Consequently they stand higher than the others in my regard."

And the fowls came, and the Cock came. Today he was polite enough to abstain from being rude.

"You are a true singing bird," he said, "and you do as much with your little voice as can possibly be done with it. But you need a little more shrillness, so every listener may hear that you are a male."

The two Chinese stood quite enchanted with the appearance of the Singing Bird. He looked very rumpled after his bath, so that he seemed to them to have the appearance of a little Cochin China fowl.

"He's charming," they cried, and began a conversation with

him, speaking in whispers, and using the most aristocratic Chinese dialect.

"We are of your race," they continued. "The ducks, even the Portuguese, are swimming birds, as you cannot fail to have noticed. You do not know us yet; very few know us, or give themselves the trouble to make our acquaintance— not even the fowls, though we are born to occupy a higher grade on the ladder than most of them. But that does not disturb us. We quietly pursue our path amid the others, whose principles are certainly not ours. For we look at things on the favorable side, and speak only of what is good. Though it is difficult sometimes to find something when nothing exists. Except for us two and the Cock, there's no one in the whole poultry yard who is talented and polite at the same time. It cannot even be said of the inhabitants of the duck yard. We warn you, little Singing Bird: don't trust that one yonder with the short tail feathers, for she's cunning. The pied one there, with the crooked stripes on her wings, is a strife-seeker, and lets nobody have the last word, though she's always in the wrong. The fat duck yonder speaks evil of everyone, and that's against our principles. If we have nothing good to tell, we should hold our beaks. The Portuguese is the only one who has any education, and with whom one can associate, but she is passionate, and talks too much about Portugal."

"I wonder what those two Chinese are always whispering to one another about?" whispered one duck to her friend. "They annoy me—we have never spoken to them."

Now the Drake came up. He thought the little Singing Bird was a sparrow.

"Well, I don't understand the difference," he said; "and indeed it's all the same thing. He's only a plaything, and if one has them, why, one has them."

"Don't attach any value to what he says," the Portuguese whispered. "He's very respectable in business matters; and with him business takes precedence over everything. But now I shall lie down for a rest. One owes that to oneself, that one may be nice and fat when one is to be embalmed with apples and plums."

And accordingly she lay down in the sun, and winked with one eye. And she lay very comfortably, and she felt very comfortable, and she slept very comfortably.

The little Singing Bird busied himself with his broken wing. At last he lay down too, and pressed close to his protectress. The sun shone warm and bright, and he had found a very good place.

But the neighbor's fowls were awake. They went about scratching up the earth; and, to tell the truth, they had paid the visit simply and solely to find food for themselves. The Chinese were the first to leave the duck yard, and the other fowls soon followed them. The witty little Duck said of the Portuguese that the old lady was becoming a ducky dotard. At this the other ducks laughed and cackled aloud. "Ducky dotard," they whispered. "That's too witty!" and then they repeated the former joke about Portulak, and declared that it was vastly amusing. And then they lay down.

They had been lying asleep for some time, when suddenly something was thrown into the yard for them to eat. It came down with such a thwack, that the whole company started up from sleep and clapped their wings. The Portuguese awoke too, and threw herself over on the other side, pressing the little Singing Bird very hard as she did so.

"Peep!" he cried. "You trod very hard upon me, madam."

"Well, why do you lie in my way?" the Duck retorted. "You must not be so touchy. I have nerves of my own, but yet I never call out 'Peep!' "

"Don't be angry," said the little Bird. "The 'Peep' came out of my beak unawares."

The Portuguese did not listen to him, but began eating as

fast as she could, and had a good meal. When this was
ended, she lay down again. And then the little Bird came up.
He wanted to be amiable, and so he sang:

> *Tillee-lilly-lee,*
> *Of the good springtime*
> *I'll sing so fine*
> *As far away I flee.*

"Now I want to rest after my dinner," said the Portuguese.
"You must conform to the rules of the house while you're
here. I want to sleep now."

The little Singing Bird was quite taken aback, for he had
meant it kindly. When Madam afterward awoke, he stood before her again with a little corn that he had found, and laid
it at her feet. But since she had not slept well, she was naturally
in a very bad humor.

"Give that to a chicken!" she said. "And don't be always
standing in my way."

"Why are you angry with me?" replied the little Singing
Bird. "What have I done?"

"Done!" repeated the Portuguese Duck. "Your mode of
expression is not exactly genteel. A fact to which I must call
your attention."

"Yesterday it was sunshine here," said the little Bird. "But
today it's cloudy and the air is close."

"You don't know much about the weather, I fancy," retorted the Portuguese. "The day is not done yet. Don't stand
there looking so stupid."

"But you are looking at me just as the wicked eyes looked
when I fell into the yard yesterday."

"Impertinent creature!" exclaimed the Portuguese Duck,
"would you compare me with the cat, that beast of prey?
There's not a drop of malicious blood in me. I've taken your
part, and will teach you good manners."

And so saying, she bit off the Singing Bird's head, and he lay dead on the ground.

"Now, what's the meaning of this?" she said. "Could he not bear even that? Then certainly he was not made for this world. I've been like a mother to him, I know that, for I've a good heart."

Then the neighbor's Cock stuck his head into the yard, and crowed with steam-engine power.

"You'll kill me with your crowing!" she cried. "It's all your fault. He's lost his head, and I am very near losing mine."

"There's not much lying where he fell!" observed the Cock.

"Speak of him with respect," retorted the Portuguese Duck, "for he had song, manners, and education. He was affectionate and soft, and that's as good in animals as in your so-called human beings."

And all the ducks came crowding round the little dead Singing Bird. Ducks have strong passions, whether they feel envy or pity; and, as there was nothing here to envy, pity manifested itself, even in the two Chinese.

"We shall never get such a singing bird again. He was almost a Chinese," they whispered. They wept with a mighty clucking sound, and all the fowls clucked too, but the ducks went about with the redder eyes.

"We've hearts of our own," they said. "Nobody can deny that."

"Hearts!" repeated the Portuguese, "yes, that we have, almost as much as in Portugal."

"Let us think of getting something to satisfy our hunger," said the Drake, "for that's the most important point. If one of our toys is broken, why, we have plenty more!"

THE FIR TREE

FAR down in the forest, where the warm sun and the fresh air make a sweet resting place, there grew a pretty little fir tree. And yet it was not so happy—it wished so much to be tall like its companions, the pines and firs which grew around it. The sun shone, the soft air fluttered its leaves, and the little peasant children passed by, prattling merrily, but the fir tree paid no attention. Sometimes the children would bring a large basket of raspberries or strawberries, wreathed on a straw, and seat themselves near the fir tree and say, "Is this not a pretty little tree?" which made it feel more unhappy than before.

And yet all this while the tree grew a notch or a joint taller every year—for by the number of joints in the stem of a fir tree we can discover its age. Still, as it grew it complained, "Oh, how I wish I were as tall as the other trees. Then I would spread out my branches on every side, and my top would overlook the wide world. I should have the birds building their nests on my boughs, and when the wind blew, I should bow with stately dignity like my tall companions."

The tree was so discontented that it took no pleasure in the warm sunshine, the birds, or the rosy clouds that floated over it morning and evening. Sometimes in winter, when the snow lay white and glittering on the ground, a hare would come springing along and would jump right over the little tree, and then how mortified it would feel!

Two winters passed; and when the third arrived, the tree had grown so tall that the hare was obliged to run round it.

Yet it remained dissatisfied and would exclaim, "Oh, if I could but keep on growing tall and old! There is nothing else worth caring for in the world."

In the autumn, as usual, the woodcutters came and cut down several of the tallest trees. And the young fir tree, which was not grown to its full height, shuddered as the noble trees fell to the earth with a crash. After the branches were lopped off, the trunks looked so slender and bare that they could scarcely be recognized. Then they were placed upon wagons and drawn by horses out of the forest. "Where were they going? What would become of them?" The young fir tree wished very much to know. So in the spring, when the swallows and the storks came, it asked, "Do you know where those trees were taken? Did you meet them?"

The swallows knew nothing, but the stork, after a little reflection, nodded his head and said: "Yes, I think I do. I met several new ships when I flew from Egypt, and they had masts that smelled like fir. I think these must have been the trees. I assure you they were stately, very stately."

"Oh, how I wish I were tall enough to go on the sea," said the fir tree. "What is this sea, and what is it like?"

"It would take too much time to explain," said the stork, flying quickly away.

"Rejoice in thy youth," said the sunbeam. "Rejoice in thy fresh growth and the young life that is in thee." And the wind kissed the tree and the dew watered it with tears, but the fir tree paid no attention.

Christmas drew near and many young trees were cut down, some even smaller and younger than the fir tree, who enjoyed neither rest nor peace from longing to leave its forest home. These young trees, chosen for their beauty, kept their branches, but they too were laid on wagons and drawn by horses out of the forest.

"Where are they going?" asked the fir tree. "They are no taller than I am. Indeed, one is much shorter. And why are the branches not cut off? Where are they going?"

"We know. We know," sang the sparrows. "We have looked in at the windows of the houses in town, and we know what is done with them. They are dressed up in the most splendid manner. We have seen them standing in the middle of a warm room, and adorned with all sorts of beautiful things —honey cakes, gilded apples, playthings, and many hundreds of wax tapers."

"And then," asked the fir tree, trembling through all its branches, "and then what happens?"

"We did not see any more," said the sparrows. "But that was enough for us."

"I wonder whether anything so brilliant will ever happen to me," thought the fir tree. "It would be much better than crossing the sea. I long for it almost with pain. Oh, when will Christmas be here? I am now as tall and well grown as those which were taken away last year. Oh, that I were now laid on the wagon, or standing in the warm room, with all that brightness and splendor around me! Something better and more beautiful is to come after, or the trees would not be so decked out. Yes, what follows will be grander and more splendid. What can it be? I am weary with longing. I scarcely know how I feel."

"Rejoice with us," said the air and the sunlight. "Enjoy thine own bright life in the fresh air."

But the tree would not rejoice, though it grew taller every day. Winter and summer its dark green foliage might be seen in the forest, and passers-by would say, "What a beautiful tree!"

A short time before Christmas, the discontented fir tree was the first to fall. As the ax cut through the stem and divided the pith, the tree fell with a groan to the earth, conscious of pain and faintness, and it forgot all its anticipations of happiness in the sorrow of leaving its home in the forest. It knew that it should never again see its dear old companions, the trees, nor the little bushes and many-colored flowers that had grown by its side; perhaps not even the birds. Neither was the journey at all pleasant. The tree first recovered itself while being unpacked with several other trees in the courtyard of a house, and it heard a man say, "We want only one, and this is the prettiest."

Then two servants came in grand livery and carried the fir tree into a large and beautiful apartment. On the walls hung pictures and near the great stove stood great china vases, with lions on the lids. There were rocking chairs, silken sofas, and large tables covered with pictures, books, and playthings worth a great deal of money. At least, the children said so. The fir tree was placed in a large tub full of sand, but green baize hung all around it so that no one could see it was a tub, and it stood on a very handsome carpet. How the fir tree trembled! "What is going to happen to me now?"

Some young ladies came, and the servants helped them decorate the tree. On one branch they hung little bags cut out of colored paper, and each bag was filled with sweetmeats. From other branches hung gilded apples and walnuts as if they had grown there. And above and all around were hundreds of red, blue, and white tapers, which were fastened on the branches. Dolls exactly like real babies were placed under the green leaves—the tree had never seen such things before! And at the very top was fastened a glittering star made of tinsel. Oh, it was very beautiful!

"This evening," they all exclaimed, "how bright it will be!" "Oh, that the evening were here!" thought the tree. "And the tapers lighted! Then I shall know what else is going to happen. Will the trees of the forest come to see me? I wonder if the sparrows will peep in at the windows as they fly? Shall I grow faster here, and keep on all these ornaments during summer and winter?"

But guessing was of very little use. It made its bark ache, and this pain is as bad for a slender fir tree as a headache is for us. At last the tapers were lighted and then what a glistening blaze of light the tree presented! It trembled so with joy that one of the candles fell among the green branches and burned some of them. "Help! Help!" exclaimed the young ladies, but there was no danger, for they quickly extinguished the fire. After this the tree tried not to tremble, even though the fire frightened it. It was so anxious not to hurt any of the beautiful ornaments. Their brilliancy dazzled it. And now the folding doors were thrown open and a troop of children rushed in as if they intended to upset the tree. They were followed more slowly by their elders. For a moment the little ones stood silent with astonishment, and then they shouted for joy till the room rang, and they danced merrily round the tree, while one present after another was taken from it.

"What are they doing? What will happen next?" thought the fir. At last the candles burned down to the branches and were put out. Then the children received permission to plunder the tree.

They rushed upon it, till the branches cracked, and had it not been fastened with the glistening star to the ceiling, it would have been thrown down. The children danced about with their pretty toys, and no one noticed the tree except the children's maid, who came and peeped among the branches to see if an apple or a fig had been forgotten. "A story! A story!" cried the children, pulling a little fat man toward the tree.

"Now we shall be in the green shade," said the man, as he seated himself under it, "and the tree will have the pleasure of hearing also, but I shall tell only one story. What shall it be? Ivede-Avede? Or Humpty Dumpty, who fell downstairs but got up again, and at last married a princess?"

"Ivede-Avede," cried some. "Humpty Dumpty," cried others, and there was a fine shouting and crying out. The fir tree remained quite still and thought to itself, "Shall I have anything to do with all this?" But it had already amused them as much as they wished. Then the old man told them the story of Humpty Dumpty—how he fell downstairs, and was raised up again, and married a princess. And the children clapped their hands and cried, "Tell another! Tell another!" They wanted to hear the story of Ivede-Avede, but they had only Humpty Dumpty. After this the fir tree became quite silent and thoughtful. Never had the birds in the forest told such tales as Humpty Dumpty, who fell downstairs and yet married a princess.

"Ah, yes, so it happens in the world," thought the fir tree. It believed it all, because it was told by such a nice man. "Ah, well," it thought, "who knows? Perhaps I may fall down too, and marry a princess." And it looked forward joyfully to the next evening, expecting to be again decked out with lights and playthings, gold and fruit. "Tomorrow I will not tremble," it thought. "I will enjoy all my splendor, and I shall hear the story of Humpty Dumpty again, and perhaps Ivede-Avede." And the tree remained quiet and thoughtful all night. In the morning the servants and the housemaid came in.

"Now," thought the fir, "all my splendor is going to begin again." But they dragged it out of the room and upstairs to the garret and threw it on the floor in a dark corner where no daylight shone, and there they left it.

"What does this mean?" thought the tree. "What am I to do here? I can hear nothing in a place like this!" And it leaned against the wall and thought and thought.

It had time enough to think, for days and nights passed

and no one came near it, and when at last somebody did come, it was only to put away large boxes in a corner. So the tree was completely hidden from sight as if it had never existed. "It is winter now," thought the tree. "The ground is hard and covered with snow, so that people cannot plant me. I shall be sheltered here, I daresay, until spring comes. How thoughtful and kind everybody is to me! Still, I wish this place were not so dark and lonely, with not even a little hare to look at. How pleasant it was out in the forest when the snow lay on the ground. Then the hare would run by, yes, and jump over me too, although I did not like it then. Oh, it is terribly lonely here!"

"Squeak, squeak," said a little mouse, creeping cautiously toward the tree. Then came another, and they both sniffed at the fir tree and crept among the branches.

"Oh, it is very cold," said the mouse, "or else we should be comfortable here, shouldn't we, you old fir tree?"

"I am not old," said the fir tree. "There are many who are older than I am."

"Where do you come from and what do you know?" asked the mice, who were full of curiosity. "Have you seen the most beautiful places in the world, and can you tell us all about them? And have you been in the storeroom, where cheeses lie on the shelf and hams hang from the ceiling? One can run about on tallow candles there, and go in thin and come out fat."

"I know nothing of that place," said the fir tree. "But I know the wood where the sun shines and the birds sing." And then the tree told the little mice all about its youth. They had never heard such an account in their lives. After they had listened to it attentively, they said, "What a number of things you have seen! You must have been very happy."

"Happy?" exclaimed the fir tree. And then as it reflected upon what it had been telling them, it said, "Ah, yes. After all, those were happy days." But when it went on and told all about Christmas Eve, and how it had been dressed up with cakes and lights, the mice said, "How happy you must have been, you old fir tree!"

"I am not old at all," replied the tree. "I came from the forest only this winter. I am now checked in my growth."

"What splendid stories you can relate," said the little mice. And the next night four other mice came with them to hear what the tree had to tell. The more it talked, the more it remembered, and then it thought to itself, "Those were happy days, but they may come again. Humpty Dumpty fell downstairs, and yet he married the princess. Perhaps I may marry a princess too." And the fir tree thought of the pretty little birch tree that grew in the forest, which was to it a beautiful princess.

"Who is Humpty Dumpty?" asked the little mice, and then the tree told the whole story. It could remember every single word, and the little mice were so delighted with it that they were ready to jump to the top of the tree. The next night a great many more mice came, and on Sunday two rats came with them. But the rats said it was not a pretty story at all, and the little mice were very sorry, for it made them think less of it too.

"Do you know only one story?" asked the rats.

"Only one," replied the fir tree. "I heard it on the happiest evening in my life, but I did not know I was so happy at the time."

"We think it is a very miserable story," said the rats. "Don't you know any story about bacon or tallow in the storeroom?"

"No," replied the tree.

"Many thanks to you then," replied the rats, and they marched off.

The little mice also kept away after this, and the tree sighed and said: "It was very pleasant when the merry little

mice sat round me and listened while I talked. Now that is
all past too. However, I shall consider myself happy when
someone comes to take me out of this place." But would this
ever happen?

Yes, one morning people came to clear out the garret. The
boxes were packed away, and the tree was pulled out of the
corner and thrown roughly on the garret floor. Then the
servant dragged it out upon the staircase where the daylight
shone.

"Now life is beginning again," said the tree, rejoicing in
the sunshine and fresh air. It was carried downstairs and taken
into the courtyard so quickly that it forgot to think of itself,
and could only look about. There was so much to be seen!
The court was close to a garden, where everything looked
blooming. Fresh and fragrant roses hung over the little palings.
The linden trees were in blossom, while the swallows flew
here and there, crying, "Twit, twit, twit, my mate is coming."
But it was not the fir tree they meant.

"Now I shall live," cried the tree, joyfully spreading out
its branches. But alas, they were all withered and yellow, and
it lay in a corner among weeds and nettles. The star of gold
paper still stuck in the top of the tree and glittered in the
sunshine. In the same courtyard two of the merry children,
who had so happily danced round the tree at Christmas, were
playing. The youngest saw the gilded star and ran and pulled
it off the tree.

"Look what is sticking to the old ugly fir tree," said the
child, treading on the branches till they crackled under his
boots. And the tree saw all the fresh bright flowers in the
garden, and then looked at itself and wished it had remained
in the dark corner of the garret. It thought of its fresh youth

*" 'Who is Humpty Dumpty?' asked the little mice, and then the
tree told the whole story."*

in the forest, of the merry Christmas evening, and of the little mice who had listened to the story of Humpty Dumpty.

"Past! past!" said the old tree. "Oh, had I but enjoyed myself while I could have done so! Now it is too late."

Then a lad came and chopped the tree into small pieces, till a large bundle lay in a heap on the ground. The pieces were placed in a fire under the kettle, and they quickly blazed up brightly, while the tree sighed so deeply that each sigh was like a little pistol shot. Then the children, who were at play, came and seated themselves in front of the fire, and looked at it and cried, "Pop, pop." But at each "pop," which was a deep sigh, the tree was thinking of a summer day in the forest, or of some winter night there when the stars shone brightly, and of Christmas evening, and of Humpty Dumpty, the only story it had ever heard or knew how to relate—till at last it was consumed.

The boys still played in the garden, and the youngest wore on his breast the golden star with which the tree had been adorned during the happiest evening of its existence. Now all was past: the tree's life was past, and the story also—for all stories must come to an end.

THE FALSE COLLAR

THERE was once a fine gentleman, whose only belongings were a bootjack and a hair comb. But he had the finest false collars in the world; and it is about one of these collars that we are now about to hear.

It was so old, that it began to think of marriage. And it happened, that it came to be washed in company with a garter.

"Nay!" said the collar, "I never did see anything so slender and so fine, so soft and so neat. May I ask your name?"

"That I shall not tell you!" said the garter.

"Where do you live?" asked the collar.

But the garter was so bashful, so modest, and thought it was a strange question to answer.

"You are certainly a girdle," said the collar. "That is to say, an inside girdle. I see well that you are both for use and ornament, my dear young lady."

"I will thank you not to speak to me," said the garter. "I think I have not given the least occasion for it."

"Yes! when one is as handsome as you," said the collar, "that is occasion enough."

"Don't come so near me, I beg of you!" said the garter. "You look so much like those menfolks."

"I am also a fine gentleman," said the collar. "I have a bootjack and a hair comb."

But that was not true, for it was his master who had them. And he boasted.

"Don't come so near me," said the garter. "I am not accustomed to it."

"Prude!" exclaimed the collar; and then it was taken out of

the washtub. It was starched, hung over the back of a chair in the sunshine, and was then laid on the ironing-blanket. Next came the warm box iron. "Dear lady!" said the collar. "Dear widow lady! I feel quite hot. I am quite changed. I begin to unfold myself. You will burn a hole in me. Oh! I offer you my hand."

"Rag!" said the box iron; and went proudly over the collar. For she fancied she was a steam engine, that should go on the railroad and draw the wagons. "Rag!" said the box iron.

The collar was a little jagged at the edge, and so along came the long scissors to cut off the jagged part.

"Oh!" said the collar, "you are certainly the first opera dancer. How well you can stretch your legs out! It is the most graceful performance I have ever seen. No one can imitate you."

"I know it," said the scissors.

"You deserve to be a baroness," said the collar. "All that I have, is a fine gentleman, a bootjack, and a hair comb. If I only had the barony!"

"Do you seek my hand?" said the scissors. For she was angry; and, without more ado, she *cut him;* and then he was condemned.

"I shall now be obliged to ask the hair comb—It is surprising how well you preserve your teeth, Miss," said the collar. "Have you never thought of being betrothed?"

"Yes, of course! You may be sure of that," said the hair comb. "I *am* betrothed—to the bootjack!"

"Betrothed!" exclaimed the collar. Now there was no other to court, and so he despised it.

A long time had passed away; and the collar came into the rag chest at the paper mill. There was a large company of rags, the fine by themselves, and the coarse by themselves, just as it should be. They all had much to say, but the collar the most, for he was a real boaster.

"I have had such an immense number of sweethearts!" said the collar, "I could not be in peace! It is true, I was also a fine starched-up gentleman! I had both a bootjack and a hair comb, which I never used! You should have seen me then. You should have seen me when I lay down! I shall never forget my first love, she was a girdle, so fine, so soft, and so charming. She threw herself into a tub of water for my sake. There was also a widow, who became glowing hot, but I left her standing till she got black again. There was also the first opera dancer, she gave me this cut which I now go with, she was so ferocious! My own hair comb was in love with me; she lost all her teeth from the heartache. Yes, I have lived to see much of that sort of thing but I am extremely sorry for the garter—I mean the girdle—that went into the watertub. I have so much on my conscience; I want to become white paper!"

And it became so, all the rags were turned into white paper. But the collar came to be just this very piece of white paper we see here, and on which this story is printed; and that was because it boasted so terribly about things that had never happened to it. It would be well for us to beware, that we don't act in a similar manner, for we never know if we may not, in the course of time, also come into the rag chest, and be made into white paper. And then our whole life's history would be printed on it, even the most secret. And we would be obliged to run about and tell it ourselves, just like this collar.

THE COMET

Now the comet came with its shining nucleus and its nebulous tail. At the great castle they gazed at it, and from the poor shanty; the crowd in the street stared at it, and the solitary man, that went his way over the pathless heath. Everyone had his own thoughts. "Come and look at the vault of heaven; come out and look at the wonderful sight," they cried, and all hastened to look.

But inside the room there still sat a little boy and his mother. The tallow candle was burning, and the mother thought there was a moth in the light. The tallow formed in ragged edges around the candle, and ran down the sides. This, she believed, betokened that her son should die very soon—the shining little moth was turning toward him.

This was an old superstition in which she believed. The little boy was destined to live many years here on earth, and, indeed, lived to see the comet again, when it returned sixty years after.

The boy did not see the candlemoth in the light, and thought nothing of the comet, which then, for the first time in his life, looked brightly down from the skies. He sat quietly with an earthen dish before him. The dish was filled with soap water, in which he dipped the head of a clay pipe, and then he put the stem in his mouth, and made soap bubbles, big and small. They quivered and fluttered in their beautiful colors. They changed from yellow to red, from red to purple and blue; then they colored green, like the leaves when the sun is shining through them. "May God give thee many years to live here on earth, as many as the bubbles thou art blowing."

"So many, so many!" cried the little fellow. "I can never blow all the soap water into bubbles. There flies one year, there flies another!" cried he, when a new bubble broke loose from the pipe and flew off. Some of them flew into his eyes. They burned and smarted, and caused tears to flow. In every bubble he saw a picture of the future, glimmering and glittering.

"This is the time to see the comet!" exclaimed the neighbors. "Come out of doors, don't sit in the room."

And the mother took the boy by the hand. He had to lay the clay pipe aside, and leave his play with the soap bubbles. The comet was there.

And the boy saw the brilliant fireball, and the shining tail. Some said it was three yards long; others insisted it was several millions of yards long—only a slight difference.

Most of the people who had said that were dead and gone when the comet came again. But the little fellow, toward whom the candlemoth had been turned, of whom the mother thought, "He will die soon," he still lived, and had become old and white-haired. "White hairs are the flowers of old age," says the proverb; and he had a good many such flowers. He was now an old schoolmaster. The schoolchildren said that he was very wise, and knew so very much. He knew history, and geography, and all that was known about heaven and its stars.

"Everything comes again," said he. "Only pay attention to persons and events, and you will learn that they always return. There may be a hundred years between, or many hundred years, but then we shall have the same persons again, only in another coat, and in another country." And the schoolmaster told them about William Tell, who was compelled to shoot an apple from his son's head; but before he shot the arrow, he hid another one in his bosom, to shoot into the breast of the wicked Gesler. This took place in Switzerland.

But many years before that happened, the same event occurred in Denmark with Walraloke; he was also obliged to shoot an apple from his son's head, and he also hid an arrow in his bosom, to avenge the cruelty. And several thousand years before that, the same story was written down in Egypt. This is a story, and a true one; it came again, and will come again, like the comet, that returns, "flies away through space, stays away, but returns." And he spoke of the comet that was expected, the same comet that he had seen when he was a boy.

The schoolmaster knew what took place in the skies, but he did not forget history and geography. His garden was laid out in the shape of a map of Denmark. Here were herbs and flowers, which belong to different parts of the land.

"Fetch me herbs," said he, and they went to the bed that represented Laaland. "Fetch me buckwheat," and they went to Langeland. The beautiful blue gentian was found in Skagen. The shining Christ-thorn, at Silkeborg. Towns and cities were marked with images. Here stood St. Knud, with the dragon, which meant Odense; Absalon, with the bishop's staff, meant Sorö. The old boat with the oars was a sign that there stood Aarhuus. From the schoolmaster's garden you could learn the geography of Denmark. But one had to be instructed by him first, and that was a great pleasure.

Now the comet was expected again, and of that he spoke; and he told what people had said in the olden times, when it appeared last. They had said that a comet year was a good wine year, and that one could mix water with that wine, without its being detected. And that was why the merchants thought so much of a comet year.

The sky was overcast for two weeks; they could not see the comet, and yet it was there. The old schoolmaster sat in his little chamber adjoining the schoolroom. The old Bornholm clock of his grandfather's time stood in the corner; the heavy lead weights did neither ascend nor descend, the pendulum did not move. The little cuckoo, that used to come forward in past times to cuckoo the passing hours, had for many years ceased to do his duty. Everything was dumb and silent. The clock was out of order.

But near by the old clavichord, made in his father's time, still had a spark of life left. The strings could still ring. True, they were a little hoarse, but they could ring the melodies of a whole lifetime. With these, the old man remembered so much, both joyful and sorrowful, that had happened in the long series of years that had passed by since he, a little boy, saw the comet. And now, when that comet had come again, he remembered what his mother had said about the moth in the light. He remembered the beautiful soap bubbles that he blew, each of them representing a year of his life, as he had said, shining and sparkling in wonderful hues. He saw in them all his pleasures and sorrows, everything beautiful and sorrowful. He saw the child and its plays, the youth and his fancies, the whole world, in wavy brightness, opening before his gazing eyes. And in that sunlight he saw his future grow. These were the bubbles of coming time. Now, an old man, he heard from the clavichord's strings the melodies of passing time, mind's bubbles, with memory's variegated colors. And he heard his nurse's knitting song:

> *For sure no Amazone*
> *Did ever stockings knit.*

And then the strings sang the song the old papa of the house liked to sing to him, when he was a child:

> *In truth full many dangers*
> *Will grow up here below,*
> *For him, that yet is young,*
> *And doth not fully know.*

Now the melodies of the first ball were ringing the minuet and "Polonaise." The melancholy notes of the flute passed by; bubble after bubble they hurried on, very much like those that he blew with soap water, when a little boy.

His eyes were turned toward the window. A cloud in the sky was gliding by, and, as it passed, it revealed the comet to his gaze, the sparkling nucleus, the shining tail.

It seemed as if it had been only the evening of yesterday that he had seen that comet, and yet a whole eventful lifetime lay between that evening and this. Then he was a child, and looked through the bubbles into the future; now the bubbles pointed back in the past.

Once more he had a child's feeling and a child's trust. His eyes sparkled, and his hands sank down upon the keys. There came a sound like the breaking of a string.

"Come out and see!" shouted the neighbors. "The comet is here, and the sky is so clear; come out and look!"

The old schoolmaster answered not; he had gone where he would see more clearly. His soul was upon a journey far greater than the comet's, and into a wider space than the comet had to fly through.

And the comet was again seen from the rich castle, and from the poor shanty; the crowd in the street gazed at it, and the solitary man that walked through the pathless heath. But the schoolmaster's soul was seen by God, and the dear ones that had preceded him, and whom he so much longed for.

THE LEAPFROG

A FLEA, a grasshopper, and a leapfrog once wanted to see which could jump highest. And they invited the whole world, and everybody else besides who chose to come, to see the festival. Three famous jumpers were they, as everyone would say, when they all got together in the room.

"I will give my daughter to him who jumps highest," exclaimed the King. "For it is not so amusing when there is no prize to jump for."

The flea was the first to step forward. He had exquisite manners, and bowed to the company on all sides; for he had noble blood, and was, moreover, accustomed to the society of man alone; and that makes a great difference.

Then came the grasshopper. He was considerably heavier, but he was well mannered, and wore a green uniform, which he had by right of birth. He said, moreover, that he belonged to a very ancient Egyptian family, and that in the house where he was then he was thought much of. The fact was, he had just been brought out of the fields, and put in a pasteboard house, three stories high, all made of court cards with the colored side inward; and doors and windows cut out of the body of the Queen of Hearts. "I sing so well," said he, "that sixteen native grasshoppers who have chirped from infancy, and yet have no house of cards to live in, grew thinner than they were before for sheer vexation when they heard me sing."

It was thus that the flea and the grasshopper gave an account of themselves, and thought they were quite good enough to marry a princess.

The leapfrog said nothing. But people gave it as their

opinion that he therefore thought all the more. And when the house dog snuffed at him with his nose, he confessed the leapfrog was of good family. The old councilor, who had had three orders given him to make him hold his tongue, asserted that the leapfrog was a prophet; for one could see on his back if there would be a severe or mild winter, and that was something one could not see even on the back of the man who writes the almanac.

"I say nothing, it is true," exclaimed the King. "But I have my own opinion notwithstanding."

Now the trial was to take place. The flea jumped so high that nobody could see where he went to. So they all said he had not jumped at all; and that was dishonorable.

The grasshopper jumped only half as high. But he leaped into the King's face, who said that was ill-mannered.

The leapfrog stood still for a long time lost in thought. It was believed at last he would not jump at all.

"I only hope he is not unwell," said the house dog. When,

pop! he made a jump all on one side into the lap of the Princess, who was sitting on a little golden stool close by.

Hereupon the King said, "There is nothing above my daughter. Therefore, to bound up to her is the highest jump that can be made. For this, one must possess understanding, and the leapfrog has shown that he *has* understanding. He is brave and intellectual."

And so he won the Princess.

"It's all the same to me," said the Flea; "she may have the old leapfrog, for all I care. I jumped the highest; but in this world merit seldom meets its reward. A fine exterior is what people look at nowadays."

The flea then went into foreign service, where, it is said, he was killed.

The grasshopper sat outside on a green bank, and reflected on worldly things; and he said too, "Yes, a fine exterior is everything—a fine exterior is what people care about." And then he began chirping his peculiar melancholy song, from which we have taken this history; and which may, very possibly, be all untrue, although it does stand here printed in black and white.

GOOD-FOR-NOTHING

THE sheriff stood at the open window. He wore ruffles, and a dainty breastpin decorated the front of his shirt. He was neatly shaven, and a tiny little strip of sticking plaster covered the little cut he had given himself during the process. "Well, my little man?" quoth he.

The "little man" was no other than the laundress's son, who respectfully took off his cap in passing. His cap had a broken brim, and he could fold it and put it into his pocket on occasion. His clothes were poor, but clean, and very neatly mended, and he wore heavy wooden shoes. He stood still when the sheriff spoke, as respectfully as though he stood before the King.

"Ah, you're a good boy, a well-behaved boy!" said the sheriff. "And so your mother is washing down at the river; *she* isn't good for much. And you're going to her, I see. Ah, poor child!—well, you may go."

And the boy passed on, still holding his cap in his hand, while the wind tossed his waves of yellow hair to and fro. He went through the street, down a little alley to the brook, where his mother stood in the water, at her washing stool, beating the heavy linen. The water mill's sluices were opened, and the current was strong. The washing stool was nearly carried away by it, and the laundress had hard work to strive against it.

"I am very near taking a voyage," she said, "and it is so cold out in the water. For six hours have I been standing here. Have you anything for me?"—and the boy drew forth a phial, which his mother put to her lips. "Ah, that is as good

as warm meat, and it is not so dear. Oh, the water is so cold
—if only my strength will last me out to bring you up hon-
estly, my sweet child!"

At that moment an elderly woman approached, poorly
clad, blind in one eye, lame in one leg, and with her hair
brushed into one large curl to hide the blind eye—but in vain,
for the defect was only all the more conspicuous. This was
"Lame Maren," as the neighbors called her, a friend of the
washerwoman's. "Poor thing, slaving and toiling away in the
cold water! It is wrong that you should be called names"—
for Maren had overheard the sheriff speaking to the child
about his own mother—"wrong that your boy should be told
you are good-for-nothing."

"What! Did the sheriff really say that, child?" said the
laundress, and her lips quivered. "So you have a mother who
is good-for-nothing! Perhaps he is right, only he should not
say so to the child—but I must not complain, for good things
have come to me from that house."

"Why, yes, you were in service there once, when the
sheriff's parents were alive, many years ago. There is a grand
dinner at the sheriff's today," went on Maren. "It would have
been put off, though, if everything hadn't been prepared. I
heard it from the porter. News came in a letter, an hour ago,
that the sheriff's younger brother, at Copenhagen, is dead."

"Dead!" repeated the laundress, and she turned as white
as a corpse.

"What do you care about it?" said Maren. "To be sure, you
must have known him, since you served in the house."

"Is he dead? He was the best, the kindest of creatures! Indeed, there are not many like him," and the tears rolled down
her cheeks. "Oh, the world is turning round, I feel so ill!" and
she clung to the washing stool for support.

"You are ill, indeed!" cried Maren. "Take care, the stool
will overturn. I had better get you home at once."

"But the linen?"

"I will look after that—only lean on me. The boy can stay here and watch it till I come back and wash what is left. It is not much."

The poor laundress's limbs trembled under her. "I have stood too long in the cold water. I have had no food since yesterday. Oh, my poor child!" and she wept.

The boy cried too, as he sat alone beside the brook, watching the wet linen. Slowly the two women made their way up the little alley and through the street, past the sheriff's house. Just as she reached her humble home, the laundress fell down fainting on the paving stones. She was carried upstairs and put to bed. Kind Maren hastened to prepare a cup of warm ale—that was the best medicine in this case, she thought—and then went back to the brook and did the best she could with the linen.

In the evening she was again in the laundress's miserable room. She had begged from the sheriff's cook a few roasted potatoes and a little bit of bacon, for the sick woman. Maren and the boy feasted upon these, but the patient was satisfied enough with the smell of them—that, she declared, was very nourishing.

Supper over, the boy went to bed, lying crosswise at his mother's feet, with a coverlet made of old carpet ends, blue and red, sewed together.

The laundress now felt a little better. The warm ale had strengthened her, the smell of the meat done her good.

"Now, you good soul," said she to Maren, "I will tell you all about it, while the boy is asleep. And he already is. Look at him, how sweetly he looks with his eyes closed; he little thinks how his mother has suffered. May he never feel the same! Well, I was in service with the sheriff's parents when their youngest son, the student, came home. I was a wild young thing then, but honest—that I must say for myself. And the student was so pleasant and merry, a better youth never lived. He was a son of the house, I only a servant, but we became sweethearts—all in honor and honesty—and he told his mother that he loved me. She was like an angel in his eyes, so wise, kind, and loving! And he went away, but his gold ring of betrothal was on my finger. When he was really gone, my mistress called me in to speak to her; so grave, yet so kind she looked, so wisely she spoke, like an angel, indeed. She showed me what a gulf of difference in tastes, habits, and mind lay between her son and me. 'He sees you now to be good-hearted and pretty, but will you always be the same in his eyes? You have not been educated as he has been; you cannot rise to his level intellectually. I honor the poor,' she continued, 'and I know that in the kingdom of heaven many a poor man will sit in a higher seat than the rich. But that is no reason for breaking the ranks in this world, and you two, left to yourselves, would drive your carriage full tilt against all obstacles till it toppled over with you both. I know that a good honest handicraftsman, Erik, the glovemaker, has been your suitor. He is a widower without children, he is well off. Think whether you cannot be content with him.'

"Every word my mistress spoke went like a knife through my heart, but I knew she was right. I kissed her hand, and shed such bitter tears! But still bitterer tears came when I went into my chamber and lay upon my bed. Oh, the long, dreary night that followed! Our Lord alone knows what I suffered. Not till I went to church on Sunday did a light break upon my darkness. It seemed providential that as I came out of church I met Erik the glovemaker. There were no more doubts in my mind; he was a good man, and of my own rank. I went straight to him, took his hand, and asked, 'Are you still in the same mind toward me?'

" 'Yes, and I shall never feel otherwise,' he replied.

" 'Do you care to have a girl who likes and honors you, but does not love you?'

" 'I believe love will come,' he said, and so he took my hand. I went home to my mistress. I took out the gold ring that her son had given me, that I wore all day next to my heart, and on my finger in bed at night. I kissed it till my mouth bled, I gave it to my mistress, and said that next week the banns would be read for me and the glovemaker. My mistress took me in her arms and kissed me. She did not tell me I was good-for-nothing; I was good for something then, it seems, before I knew so much trouble. The wedding was at Candlemastide, and our first year all went well. My husband had apprentices, and you, Maren, helped me in the housework."

"Oh, and you were such a good mistress!" exclaimed Maren. "Never shall I forget how kind you and your husband were to me."

"Ah, you were with us during our good times! We had no children then. I never saw the student again—yes, once I saw him, but he did not see me. He came to his mother's funeral. I saw him standing by her grave, looking so sad, so ashy pale —but all for his mother's sake. When afterward his father died, he was abroad and did not come to the funeral. He hasn't been here since. He is a lawyer, that I know, and he has never married. But he thought no more of me, and had he seen me, he would certainly have never recognized me, as ugly as I am now. And it is right it should be so."

Then she went on to speak of the bitter days of adversity, when troubles had come upon them in a flood. They had five hundred rix-dollars, and as in their street a house could be bought for two hundred, it was considered a good investment to buy it, take it down, and build it anew. The house was bought. Masons and carpenters made an estimate that one thousand and twenty rix-dollars more would be required.

Erik arranged to borrow this sum from Copenhagen, but the ship that was to bring him the money was lost, and the money with it.

"It was just then that my sweet boy, who lies sleeping here, was born. Then his father fell sick; for three-quarters of a year I had to dress and undress him every day. We went on borrowing and borrowing. All our things had to be sold, one by one; at last Erik died. Since then I have toiled and moiled for the boy's sake, have gone out cleaning and washing, done coarse work or fine, whichever I could get. But I do everything worse and worse; my strength won't return any more. It is our Lord's will! He will take me away, and find better provision for my boy."

She fell asleep. In the morning she seemed better, and fancied she was strong enough to go to her work again. But no sooner did she feel the cold water than a shivering seized her. She felt about convulsively with her hands, tried to step forward, and fell down. Her head lay on the dry bank, but her feet were in the water of the brook, her wooden shoes were carried away by the stream. Here she was found by Maren.

A message had been taken to her lodging that the sheriff wanted her, had something to say to her. It was too late. The poor washerwoman was dead. The letter that had brought the sheriff news of his brother's death also gave an abstract of his will. Among other bequests he had left six hundred rix-dollars to the glovemaker's widow, who had formerly served his parents.

"There was some love nonsense between my brother and her," said the sheriff. "It is just as well she is out of the way. Now it will all come to the boy, and I shall apprentice him to honest folk who will make him a good workman." For whatever the sheriff might do, no matter how kind an action, he always spoke harshly and unkindly. Now he called the boy to him, promised to provide for him, and told him it was a good thing his mother was dead. She was good-for-nothing!

She was buried in the paupers' churchyard. Maren planted a little rose tree over the grave; and the boy stood by her side all the while.

"My darling mother!" he sighed, as the tears streamed down from his eyes. "It was not true that she was good-for-nothing!"

"No, indeed!" cried her old friend, looking up to heaven. "Let the world say she was good-for-nothing. Our Lord in His heavenly kingdom will not say so."

THE DAYS OF THE WEEK

"We will also have a good time for once," said the Days of the Week. "We will come together and have a feast."

But every one of the seven Days was so busy all the year round, that they hadn't a free moment left for their own enjoyment. They wanted to have a whole day to themselves, and such a day they get every four years in the intercalary day; this day is placed at the end of February, for the purpose of bringing order to the accounting of time.

And on this inserted day they decided to meet together, and hold their feast. February being the month of carnivals, they agreed to come together in carnival fashion, every one dressed according to his profession and destination. They would have the best things to eat, and drink the best wines, make speeches, and tell each other the most agreeable and most disagreeable things in unrestrained fellowship. The Norse heroes had a custom, in the good old times, of throwing the bones, which they had cleaned of all meat, at each other's heads. But the weekdays thought of throwing bombshells at each other with their mouths, in the form of scorching witticisms, that would be in keeping with innocent carnival amusements.

The twenty-ninth of February came in due time; and with it they assembled.

Sunday, foreman of the weekdays, came first, dressed in a black silk cloak. The pious people mistook the cloak for a minister's gown. The worldly minded, however, saw that he was dressed in domino for a frolic, and that the full-blown carnation, which he wore in his buttonhole, was nothing but a little red theater lantern, which said, "No more tickets: standing room only; hope you will enjoy yourself."

Monday, a young mechanic, a distant relative of Sunday, and much given to pleasures, came next. No sooner did he hear the military music of the parade, than he rushed out, saying, "I must go and hear Offenbach's music; it does not go to my head, neither to the heart: but it itches in the muscles of my legs. I must dance, and have a swing with the girls, get me a blue eye, and then sleep upon it. The next day I go to work with new vigor. Did you see the new moon of the week?"

Tuesday is Tyr's day, the day of strength. "Yes, that I am," said Tuesday. "I take hold of the work, fasten Mercury's wings to the merchant's boots, look after the factory, and see that the wheels are oiled, and turn easily. I also see to it that the tailor sits upon his table, and the street paver by his paving stones. I hold everybody to his business, and have an eye upon them all, and therefore I appear among you in a policeman's uniform, and my name is 'Politics day.' If this is a bad joke, then you may think of a better one every one of you."

"And now come I," said Wednesday. "I stand in the middle of the week; the Germans call me Mr. Midweek. I stand like a young clerk in a store, like a flower among the other honored days of the week. If we march up in file, then have I three days in front of me, and three days behind; they are my bodyguard. And I may with propriety say that I am the most prominent of all the days of the week."

And now Thursday came in, dressed up like a coppersmith, with a hammer and a copper kettle—token of his aristocratic descent. "I am of very high birth," said he. "In the northern countries I am named after Thor, the god of thunder. And in the south, after Jupiter, the god of lightning; these two understood how to thunder and lighten, and that has remained in the family."

And then he beat his copper kettle, and thus proved his high descent.

Friday was dressed up like a young girl, who called herself Freya, the goddess of beauty of the north. For variety's sake she called herself Venus; that depended altogether on the language of the country in which she appeared. She was of a quiet, cheerful character, she said; but this was the odd day of the leap year, which gives liberty to woman, so she may, according to an old custom, propose to the man she likes, without waiting for him to propose to her.

Last came Saturday, waddling along like an old housekeeper, with broom, dustpan, and other cleansing articles. Her favorit dish was beer soup, but she was not particularly anxious to have it put on the table on that festive occasion.

And thus the weekdays held a banquet, as I have described them; here they are, ready for family use as tableaus. Of course you may improve upon them. We only give them as vignettes for February, the only month that receives a day in addition.

WHAT THE OLD MAN DOES
IS ALWAYS RIGHT

I WILL tell you the story which was told to me when I was a little boy. Every time I think of the story, it seems to me to become more and more charming. For so it is with stories as it is with many people—they become better as they grow older.

I take it for granted that you have been in the country, and seen a very old farmhouse with a thatched roof, and mosses and small plants growing wild upon the thatch. There is a stork's nest on the summit of the gable; for we can't do without the stork. The walls of the house are sloping, and the windows are low, and only one of the latter is made so that it will open. The baking-oven sticks out of the wall like a little fat body. The elder tree hangs over the paling, and beneath its branches, at the foot of the paling, is a pool of water in which a few ducks are amusing themselves. There is a yard dog too, who barks at all comers.

Just such a farmhouse stood out in the country; and in this house dwelt an old couple—a peasant and his wife. Small as their property was, there was one article among it that they could do without—a horse, which made a living out of the grass it found by the side of the highroad. The old peasant rode into the town on this horse. And often his neighbors borrowed it from him, and rendered the old couple some service in return for the loan. But they thought it would be best if they sold the horse, or exchanged it for something that might be more useful to them. And what might this *something* be?

"You'll know that best, old man," said the wife. "It is fair day today, so ride into town, and get rid of the horse for money, or make a good exchange. Whichever you do will be right to me. Ride off to the fair."

And she fastened his neckerchief for him. She could do that better than he could; and she tied it in a double bow. She could do that very prettily. Then she brushed his hat round and round with the palm of her hand, and gave him a kiss. So he rode away upon the horse that was to be sold or bartered for something else. Yes, the old man knew what he was about.

The sun shone hotly down, and not a cloud was to be seen in the sky. The road was very dusty, for many people who were bound for the fair were driving, or riding, or walking upon it. There was no shelter anywhere from the sunbeams.

With them a man was trudging along, driving a cow to the fair. The cow was as beautiful a creature as any cow can be.

"She gives good milk, I'm sure," said the peasant. "That would be a very good exchange—the cow for the horse.

"Hallo, you there with the cow!" he said. "I tell you what —I fancy a horse costs more than a cow, but I don't care about that; a cow would be more useful to me. If you like, we'll exchange."

"To be sure I will," said the man; and they exchanged accordingly.

So that was settled, and the peasant might have turned back, for he had done the business he came to do. But since he had made up his mind to go to the fair, he decided to proceed, just to have a look at it. And so he went on to the town with his cow.

After a short time he overtook a man who was driving a sheep. It was a good fat sheep, with a fine fleece on its back.

"I should like to have that fellow," said our peasant to himself. "He would find plenty of grass by our palings, and in the winter we could keep him in the room with us. Perhaps it would be more practical to have a sheep instead of a cow. Shall we exchange?"

The man with the sheep was quite willing, and the bargain was struck. So our peasant went on in the highroad with his sheep.

Soon he overtook another man, who came into the road from a field, carrying a great goose under his arm.

"That's a heavy thing you have there. It has plenty of feathers and plenty of fat, and would look well tied to a string, or paddling in the water at our place. That would be something for my old woman. She could make all kinds of profit out of it. How often she has said, 'If we only had a goose!' Now, perhaps, she can have one; and, if possible, it shall be hers. Shall we exchange? I'll give you my sheep for your goose, and thank you into the bargain."

The other man hadn't the least objection. And so they exchanged, and our peasant became the proprietor of the goose.

By this time he was very near the town. The crowd on the highroad became greater and greater; and there was quite a crush of men and cattle. They walked in the road, and close by the palings. At the gate they even walked into the toll-man's potato field, where his own fowl was strutting about with a string to its leg, lest it should take fright at the crowd, and stray away, and be lost. This fowl had short tail-feathers, and winked with both its eyes, and looked very cunning. "Cluck, cluck!" said the fowl. What it thought when it said this I cannot tell you. But as soon as our good man saw it, he thought, "That's the finest fowl I've ever seen in my life! Why, it's finer than our parson's brood hen. On my word, I should like to have that fowl. A fowl can always find a grain or two, and can almost keep itself. I think it would be a good exchange if I could get that for my goose.

"Shall we exchange?" he asked the tolltaker.

"Exchange!" repeated the man; "well, that would not be a

bad thing." And so they exchanged; the tolltaker kept the goose, and the peasant carried away the fowl.

Now, he had done a good deal of business on his way to the fair, and he was hot and tired. He wanted something to eat, and a glass of brandy to drink. Soon he was in front of the inn. He was just about to step in, when the ostler came out, and they met at the door. The ostler was carrying a sack.

"What have you in that sack?" asked the peasant.

"Rotten apples," answered the ostler; "a whole sackful of them—enough to feed the pigs with."

"Why, that's a terrible waste! I should like to take them to my old woman at home. Last year the old tree by the turf-hole only bore a single apple, and we kept it in the cupboard till it was quite rotten and spoiled. 'It was always property,' my old woman said; but here she could see a quantity of prop-

erty—a whole sackful. Yes, I shall be glad to show them to her."

"What will you give me for the sackful?" asked the ostler.

"What will I give? I will give my fowl in exchange."

And he gave the fowl accordingly, and received the apples, which he carried into the guest room. He leaned the sack carefully by the stove, and then went to the table. But the stove was hot. He had not thought of that. Many guests were present—horse-dealers, ox-herders, and two Englishmen. The two Englishmen were so rich that their pockets bulged out with gold coins, and almost burst; and they could bet too, as you shall hear.

Hiss-s-s! hiss-s-s! What was that by the stove? The apples were beginning to roast!

"What is that?"

"Why, do you know—" said our peasant.

And he told the whole story of the horse that he had changed for a cow, and all the rest of it, down to the apples.

"Well, your old woman will give it to you good when you get home!" said one of the two Englishmen. "There will be a disturbance."

"What?—give me what?" said the peasant. "She will kiss me, and say, 'What the old man does is always right.' "

"Shall we wager?" said the Englishman. "We'll wager coined gold by the ton—a hundred pounds to the hundred-weight!"

"A bushel will be enough," replied the peasant. "I can only set the bushel of apples against it; and I'll throw myself and my old woman into the bargain—and I fancy that's piling up the measure."

"Done—taken!"

And the bet was made. The host's carriage came up. The Englishmen got in, and the peasant got in; and away they went! Soon they stopped before the peasant's farm.

"Good evening, old woman."

"Good evening, old man."

"I've made the exchange."

"Yes, you understand what you're about," said the woman. And she embraced him, and paid no attention to the strange guests, nor did she notice the sack.

"I got a cow in exchange for the horse," said he.

"Heaven be thanked!" said she. "What glorious milk we shall now have, and butter and cheese on the table! That was a most capital exchange!"

"Yes, but I changed the cow for a sheep."

"Ah, that's better still!" cried the wife. "You always think of everything. We have just enough pasture for a sheep. Ewe's milk and cheese, and woolen jackets and stockings! The cow cannot give those, and her hairs will only come off. How you think of everything!"

"But I changed away the sheep for a goose."

"Then this year we shall really have roast goose to eat, my dear old man. You are always thinking of something to give me pleasure. How charming that is! We can let the goose walk about with a string to her leg, and she'll grow fatter still before we roast her."

"But I gave away the goose for a fowl," said the man.

"A fowl? That *was* a good exchange!" replied the woman. "The fowl will lay eggs and hatch them, and we shall have chickens. We shall have a whole poultry yard! Oh, that's just what I was wishing for."

"Yes, but I exchanged the fowl for a sack of shriveled apples."

"What!—I must positively kiss you for that," exclaimed the wife. "My dear, good husband! Now I'll tell you something. Do you know, you had hardly left me this morning before I began thinking how I could give you something very nice this evening. I thought it should be pancakes with savory herbs. I had eggs, and bacon too; but I wanted herbs. So I went over to the schoolmaster's—they have herbs there, I know—but the schoolmistress is a mean woman, though she looks so sweet. I begged her to lend me a handful of herbs. 'Lend!' she answered me; 'nothing at all grows in our garden, not even a shriveled apple. I could not even lend you a shriveled apple, my dear woman.' But now I can lend *her* ten, or even a whole sackful. That I'm very glad of. That makes me laugh!" And with that she give him a resounding kiss.

"I like that!" exclaimed both the Englishmen together. "Always going downhill, and yet always merry! That's worth the money."

So they paid a hundredweight of gold to the peasant, who was not scolded, but kissed.

Yes, it always pays, when the wife sees and always asserts that her husband knows best, and that whatever he does is right.

You see, that is my story. I heard it when I was a child; and now you have heard it too, and know that "What the old man does is always right."

WHAT ONE CAN INVENT

THERE was once a young man who wanted to become a poet. He wanted to be a poet by the next Easter, so he might marry and live by poetizing. And that, he knew, merely consisted in having a knack for inventing. But then he never could invent! He was quite sure that he had been born too late. Every subject had been taken before he came into the world, and there was nothing left for him to write about!

"What happy mortals were those who were born a thousand years ago," he sighed, "for then it was an easy matter to become immortal! Even those who were born only a hundred years ago were enviable. Even at that time there was still something left to poetize about. But now all the subjects are worn threadbare, and there is no use in my trying to write the nap on them again!"

He thought and thought about it, till he grew quite thin and forlorn, poor fellow. No doctor could help him. There was only one who would be able to find the right remedy for him, and that was that wonderfully clever little old woman who lived in the little hut by the turnpike gate. She opened and shut it for all who passed that way. But she was wise and learned, and could open far more than the gate. She was much wiser than the doctor who drives in his carriage, and pays title taxes.

"I must go to her," said the young man. Her home was small and tidy, but tiresome to look at—not a tree, not a flower, grew anywhere near it. There was a beehive at the door—very useful! There was a little potato field—very useful! and a ditch with a blackthorn bush that had flowered,

and was bearing fruit—berries that draw your mouth together
if you eat them before the frost has nipped them.

"What a picture all this is of our unpoetic time," thought
the young man. At least here was a thought, a grain of gold
dust that he found at the door of the little old woman's cottage.

"Write that thought down," she said. "Crumbs are bread,
too. I know why you have come here. You cannot invent,
and yet you want to be a poet by next Easter!"

"Everything has been written about," he sighed. "Our time
is not like the olden time."

"No, it is not," said the old woman. "In the olden time
people like me, who knew many weighty secrets, and how
to cure by the help of wonderful herbs, were burned alive.
And in the olden time the poets went about with empty
stomachs and arms out at the elbows. Ours is a very good
time, the very best, much better than the olden time. Your
lack of invention all lies in your having no eyes to see, and
no ears to hear, and you do not say your prayers in the evening. There are any amount of things all around you that you
might poetize and write about. When you know *how* to write
stories, you can find it in the earth where it grows and sprouts;
you can dip into the running or the stagnant water, and you
will find it there. But first of all, you must understand the
way of doing it—must know how to catch a ray of sunshine.
Now, just try my spectacles, put my ear trumpet to your ear,
say your prayers, and do, for once, stop thinking of yourself."

That last request was almost more than he could fulfill—
more than even such a wonderful old woman ought to ask.

He got the spectacles and the ear trumpet, and was put out
into the middle of the potato field. Then she put a huge potato in his hand. Presently he seemed to hear sounds in the
potato, then came a song with words, a "story of everyday
life," in ten volumes—but ten hills will do as well.

What was it the potato sang? It sang about itself and its

ancestors, the arrival of the potato in Europe, and all it had had to suffer from suspicion and ill will before its value was recognized—before it was felt to be a much greater blessing than a lump of gold.

"We were distributed, by order of the King, at the court-house in every town. And a circular was issued, setting forth our value and great merits. But no one believed it. They hadn't the slightest idea how to plant us. One man dug a hole and threw his whole bushel of potatoes into it; another stuck them into the ground, one here, another there, and then waited for them to grow, and expected them to shoot up like trees that would bear potatoes, just as apple trees bear apples. Buds, and stems, and flowers, and watery fruit came up, but they all withered away, and no one thought of the real blessing, the potato, that lay hidden under it all, in the ground. Yes, we have suffered much and been tried—that is, our forefathers have, but it all comes right in the end. Now you know our story."

"That's enough," said the old woman. "Now look at the blackthorn."

"We, too," said the blackthorn, "have many relations in the land where the potatoes came from. A party of bold Norwegians from Norway steered their course westward through storm and fog till they came to an unknown country, where, under the ice and snow, they found herbs and grass, and bushes with blue-black berries on the vine—the blackthorn it was, whose berries ripen with the frost, and so do we. And that country they call 'Vineland,' and 'Greenland,' and 'Blackthorn Land.'"

"Why, that is quite a romantic story," said the young man.

"Now just follow me," said the little old woman, as she led him to the beehive. What life and movement there were! He looked in. There were bees standing in all the corridors, moving their wings like fans, so there would be plenty of fresh air all through that large honey factory; that was their department. Then there were the bees coming in from the outside, from the sunshine and the flowers; they had been born with baskets on their legs. They brought the dust of the flowers and emptied it out of their little leg baskets; then it was sorted and worked up into honey and wax. Some came, some went. The queen of the hive wanted to fly, but when she flew, then all the others must fly too, and the right time for that had not come yet. But fly she would, and then to prevent her doing so, they bit her majesty's wings off—so that she had to stay where she was.

"Now get up on the side of the ditch, where you can see all the townfolk going past," said the little old woman.

"Goodness! what an endless number of people," said the young man. "One story after another! I seem to hear such buzzing and singing, and now it all grows quite confused! I feel quite dizzy—I shall fall!"

"No, don't," said the old woman—"don't fall backward; just go forward, right into the crowd of people. Have eyes for all you see there, ears for all you hear, and above all, have a heart in it all! And before long you will be able to *invent*, and have thoughts for writing down. But before you go you must give me back my spectacles and my ear trumpet," and she took them both.

"Now I can't see anything," said the young man. "I don't even hear anything."

"In that case, it is quite impossible for you to be a poet by next Easter," said the old woman.

"But *when* shall I be a poet?" asked he.

"Neither by Easter nor by Whitsuntide! You have no knack at inventing," said she.

"But what must I do? To get my living is by poetizing?"

"That I will tell you. Write about those who have written. To hit their writing is to hit them. Don't let yourself be frightened. The more you do of such writing, the more you will earn, and you and your wife will be able to eat cake every day."

"What a trick *she* has at inventing," thought the young man, when he had thanked the old woman and bidden her good-by. And he did as she had told him. Finding he could not be a poet himself, invent, and have bright ideas that people would talk of, he took to handling—and rather roughly—all those who were poets.

All this the little old woman told me; she knows what one can invent!

"IT'S QUITE TRUE!"

"THAT is a terrible affair!" said a hen, and she said it in a quarter of the town where the occurrence had not happened. "That is a terrible affair in the poultry house. I cannot sleep alone tonight! It is quite fortunate that there are many of us on the roost together!" And she told a tale, at which the feathers of the other birds stood on end, and the cock's comb fell down flat. It's quite true!

But we will begin at the beginning; and the beginning begins in a poultry house in another part of the town. The sun went down, and the fowls jumped up on their perch to roost. There was a Hen, with white feathers and short legs, who laid her right number of eggs, and was a respectable hen in every way. As she flew up onto the roost she pecked herself with her beak, and a little feather fell out.

"There it goes!" said she. "The more I peck myself, the handsomer I grow!" And she said it quite merrily, for she was a joker among the hens, though, as I have said, she was very respectable. And then she went to sleep.

It was dark all around; hen sat by hen, but the one that sat next to the merry Hen did not sleep: she heard and she didn't hear, as one should do in this world if one wishes to live in quiet; but she could not refrain from telling it to her next neighbor.

"Did you hear what was said here just now? I name no names; but here is a hen who wants to peck her feathers out to look well. If I were a cock I should despise her."

And just above the hens sat the Owl, with her husband and her little owlets. The family had sharp ears, and they all heard every word that the neighboring hen had spoken. And they rolled their eyes, and the Mother Owl clapped her wings and said:

"Don't listen to it! But I suppose you heard what was said there? I heard it with my own ears, and one can hear a lot before one's ears fall off. There is one among the fowls who has completely forgotten what is becoming conduct in a hen and so she pulls out all her feathers, and then lets the Cock see her."

"*Prenez garde aux enfants,*" said the Father Owl. "That's not fit for the children to hear."

"I'll tell it to the neighbor owl. She's a very proper owl to associate with." And she flew away.

"Hoo! hoo! to-whoo!" they both screeched in front of the neighbor's dovecote to the doves within. "Have you heard it? Have you heard it? Hoo! hoo! There's a hen who has pulled out all her feathers for the sake of the cock. She'll die with cold, if she's not dead already."

"Coo! coo! Where, where?" cried the Doves.

"In the neighbor's poultry yard. I've as much as seen it myself. It's hardly proper to repeat the story. But it's quite true!"

"Believe it! believe every single word of it!" cooed the Doves, and they cooed down into their own poultry yard. "There's a hen, and some say there are two of them, that have plucked out all their feathers, that they may not look like the rest, and so may attract the cock's attention. That's a bold game, for one could catch cold and die of a fever. And now they are both dead."

"Wake up! wake up!" crowed the Cock, and he flew up onto the plank. His eyes were very heavy with sleep, but still he crowed. "Three hens have died of an unfortunate attachment to a cock. They have plucked out all their feathers. That's a terrible story. I won't keep it to myself. Let it travel farther."

"Let it travel farther!" piped the Bats. And the fowls clucked and the cocks crowed, "Let it go farther! let it go farther!" And so the story traveled from poultry yard to poultry yard, and at last came back to the place where it had started.

"Five fowls," it was told, "out of love for the Cock, have plucked out all their feathers to show which of them had become the thinnest; and then they pecked each other, and fell down dead, to the shame and disgrace of their families, and to the great loss of the proprietor."

The Hen who had lost the little loose feather of course did not recognize her own story again; and as she was a very respectable hen, she said:

"I despise those fowls; but there are many of that sort. One ought not to hush up such a thing, and I shall do what I can to see that the story gets into the papers, and then it will be spread over all the country. That will serve those fowls right, and their families too."

It was put into the newspaper; it was printed; and it's quite true—*that one little feather may swell till it becomes five fowls.*

THE BEETLE

THE Emperor's favorite horse was shod with gold. It had a golden shoe on each of its feet.

And why was this?

He was a beautiful creature, with delicate legs, bright intelligent eyes, and a mane that hung down his neck like a veil. He had carried his master through the fire and smoke of battle, and heard the bullets whistling around him. He had kicked, bitten, and taken part in the fight when the enemy advanced; and had sprung, with his master on his back, over the fallen foe. He had saved the crown of red gold, and the life of the Emperor, which was, of course, even more valuable than the red gold; and that is why the Emperor's horse had golden shoes.

And the Beetle came creeping forth.

"First the great ones," said he, "and then the little ones. But greatness is not the only thing that does it." And so saying, he stretched out his thin legs.

"And pray what do you want?" asked the Smith.

"Golden shoes," replied the Beetle.

"Why, you must be out of your senses!" cried the Smith. "Do you want to have golden shoes, too?"

"Golden shoes," replied the Beetle. "Am I not just as good as that big creature yonder, that is waited on, and brushed, and has meat and drink put before him? Don't I belong to the Imperial stable?"

"But just ask yourself, *why* is the horse to have golden shoes? Don't you understand that?" asked the Smith.

"Understand? I understand that it is a personal slight against myself," cried the Beetle. "It is done to annoy me, and therefore I am going into the world to seek my fortune."

"Go along!" said the Smith.

"You're a rude fellow!" cried the Beetle. And he went out of the stable, flew a little way, and soon afterward found himself in a beautiful flower garden, all fragrant with roses and lavender.

"Isn't it beautiful here?" asked one of the little Lady-birds that flew about, with delicate wings and red and black shields on their backs. "How sweet it is here—how beautiful it is!"

"I'm accustomed to better things," said the Beetle. "Do you call *this* beautiful? Why, there is not so much as a dungheap."

Then he went on, under the shadow of a great stack, and found a caterpillar crawling along.

"How beautiful the world is!" said the Caterpillar. "The sun is so warm, and everything so enjoyable! And when I go to sleep, and die, as they call it, I shall wake up as a butterfly, with beautiful wings to fly with."

"How conceited you are!" exclaimed the Beetle. "*You* fly about as a butterfly, indeed! I've come out of the stable of the Emperor, and no one there, not even the Emperor's favorite horse—who by the way wears my cast-off golden shoes—has any such idea. To have wings to fly! Why I can fly now." And he spread his wings and flew away. "I don't want to be annoyed, and yet I am annoyed," he said, as he flew off.

Soon afterward he fell down upon a great lawn. For a while he lay there and feigned slumber; at last he fell asleep in earnest.

Suddenly a shower of rain came pattering from the clouds. The Beetle woke up at the noise, and wanted to escape into the earth, but could not. He was tumbled over and over. Sometimes he was swimming on his stomach, sometimes on his back, and as for flying, that was out of the question. He doubted whether he could escape from this place with his life. He therefore remained where he was.

When the rain had let up just a little, and the Beetle had rubbed the water out of his eyes, he saw something gleaming. It was linen that had been placed there to bleach. He managed to make his way up to it, and crept into a fold of the damp linen. Certainly this place was not as comfortable to lie in as the warm stable. But there was no better to be had, and therefore he remained lying there for a whole day and a whole night, and all that time the rain came down. Toward morning he crept forth. He was very irritated over the climate.

On the linen two frogs were sitting. Their bright eyes absolutely gleamed with pleasure.

"Wonderful weather this!" one of them cried. "How refreshing! And the linen keeps the water together so beautifully. My hind legs seem to quiver as if I were going to swim."

"I should like to know," said the second, "if the swallow, who flies so far round in her many journeys in foreign lands, ever meets with a better climate than this. What delicious dampness! It is really as if one were lying in a wet ditch. Whoever does not rejoice in this certainly does not love his fatherland."

"Have you been in the Emperor's stable?" asked the Beetle. "There the dampness is warm and refreshing. That's the climate for me; but I cannot take it with me on my journey. Is there never a muck heap here in the garden, where a person of rank, like myself, can feel himself at home, and take up his quarters?"

But the frogs either did not or would not understand him.

"I never ask a question twice!" said the Beetle, after he had already asked this one three times without receiving any answer.

Then he went a little farther, and stumbled against a fragment of pottery, that certainly should not have been lying there; but since it was, it gave a good shelter against wind and weather. Here dwelt several families of earwigs. And they did not require much, only sociality. The female members of the community were full of the purest maternal affection, and accordingly each one considered her own child the most beautiful and clever of all.

"Our son has engaged himself," said one mother. "Dear, innocent boy! His greatest hope is that he may creep one day into a clergyman's ear. It's very artless and lovable, that; and being engaged will keep him steady. What joy for a mother!"

"Our son," said another mother, "had scarcely crept out of the egg, when he was already off on his travels. He's all life and spirits; he'll run his horns off! What joy that is for a mother! Is it not so, Mr. Beetle?" for she knew the stranger by his horny coat.

"You are both quite right," said he; so they begged him to walk in—that is to say, to come as far as he could under the bit of pottery.

"Now, you can also see *my* little earwig," observed a third mother and a fourth. "They are lovely little things, and highly amusing. They are never ill-behaved, except when they are uncomfortable in their insides; and, unfortunately, one is very subject to that at their age."

Thus each mother spoke of her baby. And the babies talked among themselves, and made use of the little nippers they have in their tails to nip at the beard of the Beetle.

"Yes, they are always busy about something, the little rogues!" said the mothers; and they quite beamed with maternal pride. But the Beetle felt bored by it, and therefore he inquired how far it was to the nearest muck heap.

"That is quite a ways out in the big world, on the other side of the ditch," answered an Earwig. "I hope none of my children will go so far, for it would be the death of me."

"But *I* shall try to get so far," said the Beetle. He went off without taking formal leave; for that is considered the polite thing to do. And by the ditch he met several friends—beetles, all of them.

"Here we live," they said. "We are very comfortable here. Might we ask you to step down into this rich mud? You must be fatigued after your journey."

"Certainly," replied the Beetle. "I have been exposed to the rain, and have had to lie upon linen, and cleanliness is a thing that greatly exhausts me. I also have pains in one of my wings, from sitting in a draft under a fragment of pottery. It is really quite refreshing to be among one's companions once more."

"Perhaps you come from a muck heap?" observed the oldest of them.

"Indeed, I come from a much higher place," replied the Beetle. "I came from the Emperor's stable, where I was born with golden shoes on my feet. I am traveling on a secret mission. You must not ask me any questions, for I can't betray my secret."

With this the Beetle stepped down into the rich mud. There sat three young maiden Beetles; and they tittered, because they did not know what to say.

"Not one of them is engaged yet," said their mother. And the Beetle maidens tittered again, this time from embarrassment.

"I have never seen greater beauties even in the royal stables," exclaimed the Beetle, resting himself.

"Don't spoil my girls," said the mother. "And don't talk to them, please, unless you have serious intentions. But of course your intentions are serious, and therefore I give you my blessing."

"Hurrah!" cried all the other Beetles together; and our friend was engaged. Immediately after the betrothal came the marriage, for there was no reason for delay.

The following day passed pleasantly, and the next in tolerable comfort. But on the third it was time to think of food for the wife, and perhaps for children.

"I have allowed myself to be taken in," said our Beetle to himself. "And now there's nothing to do, but to take *them* in, in turn."

So said, so done. Away he went, and he stayed away all day, and all night; and his wife sat there, a forsaken widow.

"Oh," said the other Beetles, "this fellow whom we received into our family is nothing more than a complete vagabond. He has gone away and left his wife a burden upon our hands."

"Well, then, she shall be unmarried again, and sit here among my daughters," said the mother. "Fie on the villain who forsook her!"

In the meantime, the Beetle had been journeying on, and had sailed across the ditch on a cabbage leaf. In the morning two persons came to the ditch. When they saw him, they took him up, and turned him over. They looked very learned, especially one of them—a boy.

"Allah sees the black beetle in the black stone and in the black rock. Isn't that written in the Koran?" Then he translated the Beetle's name into Latin, and enlarged upon the creature's nature and history. The second person, an older scholar, voted for carrying him home. He said they wanted just such good specimens. This seemed an uncivil speech to our Beetle, and in consequence he flew suddenly out of the speaker's hand. As he now had dry wings, he flew quite a distance, until he reached a hotbed, where a sash of the glass roof stood open. He quietly slipped in and buried himself in the warm earth.

"Very comfortable it is here," said he.

Soon after he went to sleep, and dreamed that the Emperor's favorite horse had fallen, and had given him his golden shoes, with the promise that he should have two more.

That was all very charming. When the Beetle woke up, he crept forth and looked around him. What splendor there was in the hothouse! In the background great palm trees grew up on high; the sun made them look transparent. And beneath them what a luxuriance of green, and of beaming flowers, red as fire, yellow as amber, and white as fresh-fallen snow!

"This is an incomparable plenty of plants," cried the Beetle. "How good they will taste when they are decayed! A capital storeroom this! There must certainly be relations of mine living here. I will just see if I can find anyone with whom I may associate. I'm proud, cetrainly, and I'm proud of being so."

And so he prowled about in the earth, and thought what a pleasant dream that was about the dying horse, and the golden shoes he had inherited.

Suddenly, a hand seized the Beetle, and pressed him, and turned him round and round.

The gardener's little son and a companion had come to the hotbed, and spied the Beetle; and they wanted to have their fun with him. First, he was wrapped in a vine leaf, and then put into a warm trousers pocket. He cribbled and crabbled about in there with all his might; but he got a good pressing from the boy's hand for this, which was a hint to him to keep quiet. Then the boy went rapidly toward the great lake that lay at the end of the garden. Here the Beetle was put in an old broken wooden shoe, on which a little stick was placed upright for a mast, and to this mast the Beetle was bound with a woolen thread. Now he was a sailor, and had to sail away.

The lake was not very large, but to the Beetle it seemed like an ocean. He was so astonished at its extent, that he fell over on his back, and kicked out with his legs.

The little ship sailed away. The current of the water seized it. But whenever it went too far from the shore, one of the boys turned up his trousers and went in after it, and brought it back to the land. But after a while, just when it had gone merrily out again, the two boys were called away, and very harshly, so that they hurried to obey; and they ran away from the lake, and left the little ship to its fate. It drove away from the shore, farther and farther into the open sea. It was terrible for the Beetle, for he could not get away because he was tied to the mast.

Then a fly came and paid him a visit.

"What beautiful weather!" said the Fly. "I'll rest here, and sun myself. You've an agreeable time of it."

"You speak without knowing the facts," replied the Beetle. "Don't you see that I'm a prisoner?"

"Ah! but I'm not a prisoner," observed the Fly; and he flew away accordingly.

"Well, now I know the world," said the Beetle to himself. "It is an abominable world. I'm the only honest person in it. First, they refuse me my golden shoes; then I have to lie on wet linen, and stand in the draft. And to crown it all, they fasten a wife upon me. Then, when I've taken a quick step out into the world, and found out how one can have it there, and how I wished to have it, one of these human boys comes and ties me up, and leaves me to the mercy of the wild waves, while the Emperor's favorite horse prances about proudly in golden shoes. That is what annoys me more than anything. But one must not look for sympathy in this world! My career has been very interesting; but what's the use of that, if nobody knows it? The world does not deserve to be made acquainted with my history, for it ought to have given me golden

shoes. When the Emperor's horse was shod, I stretched out my feet to be shod too. If I had received golden shoes, I should have become an ornament to the stable. Now, the stable has lost me, and the world has lost me too. It is all over!"

But all was not over yet. A boat, in which there were a few young girls, came rowing up.

"Look, there is an old wooden shoe sailing along," said one of the girls.

"There's a little creature bound fast to it," said another.

The boat came quite close to our Beetle's ship, and the young girls fished him out of the water. One of them drew a small pair of scissors from her pocket, and cut the woolen thread, without hurting the Beetle. And when she stepped on shore, she put him down on the grass.

"Creep, creep—fly, fly—if you can," she said. "Liberty is a splendid thing."

And the Beetle flew up, and straight through the open window of a great building. There he sank down, tired and exhausted, and right on the mane of the Emperor's favorite horse. He stood in the stable when he was at home, and the

Beetle did also. The Beetle clung fast to the mane, and sat there a short time to recover himself.

"Here I am sitting on the Emperor's favorite horse—sitting on him, just like the Emperor himself!" he cried. "But what was I saying? Yes, now I remember. That's a good thought, and quite correct. The smith asked me if I didn't know why the golden shoes were given to the horse. Now I'm quite clear about the answer. They must have been given to the horse on *my* account."

And now the Beetle had put himself in a good temper again.

"Traveling expands the mind in a rare way," said he.

The sun's rays came streaming into the stable, and shone upon him, and made the place lively and bright.

"The world is not so bad, upon the whole," said the Beetle; "but one must learn how to take things as they come."

THE STRANGE GALOSHES

I

A Beginning

In a house in Copenhagen, not far from the King's New Market, a company—a very large company—had assembled. They had received invitations to an evening party there. One half of the company already sat at the card tables; the other half awaited the result of the hostess's question, "What shall we do now?" They had progressed so far, and the entertainment began to take some degree of animation. Among other subjects the conversation turned upon the Middle Ages. Some considered that period much more interesting than our own times. Councilor Knap defended this view so zealously that the lady of the house went over at once to his side; and both loudly exclaimed against Oersted's treatise in the Almanac on old and modern times, in which the chief advantage is given to our own day. The Councilor considered the times of the Danish King Hans * as the noblest and happiest age.

While the conversation takes this turn, only interrupted for a moment by the arrival of a newspaper, which contains nothing worth reading, we will wander into the vestibule, where the cloaks, sticks, and galoshes had found a place.

Here sat two maids—an old one and a young one. One would have thought they had come to escort their mistresses home; but, on looking at them more closely, the observer could see that they were not ordinary servants. Their shapes were too graceful for that, their complexions too delicate, and the cut

* A.D. 1482–1513.

of their dresses too uncommon. They were two fairies. The younger was not Fortune, but lady's maid to one of her ladies of the bedchamber, who carry about the more trifling gifts of Fortune. The elder one looked somewhat more gloomy —she was Care, who always goes herself in her own exalted person to perform her business. For thus she knows that it is well done.

They were telling each other where they had been that day. The messenger of Fortune had transacted only a few unimportant affairs—as, for instance, she had preserved a new bonnet from a shower of rain, had procured for an honest man a bow from a titled nobody, and so on; but what she had still to tell was something quite extraordinary.

"I can likewise tell," said she, "that today is my birthday. And in honor of it a pair of galoshes has been entrusted to me. I am to bring them to the human race. These galoshes have a special property and every one who puts them on is at once transported to the time and place in which he likes best to be—every wish in reference to time, place, and circumstance is at once fulfilled. And so for once man can be happy here below!"

"Believe me," said Care, "he will be very unhappy, and will bless the moment when he can get rid of the galoshes again."

"What are you thinking of?" retorted the other. "Now I shall put them at the door. Somebody will take them by mistake, and become the happy one!"

You see, that was the dialogue they held.

II

What Happened to the Councilor

It was late. Councilor Knap, lost in contemplation of the times of King Hans, wished to get home; and fate willed that instead of his own galoshes he should put on those of Fortune, and thus went out into East Street. But by the power of the galoshes he had been put back three hundred years—into the days of King Hans; and therefore he put his foot into mud and mire, because in those days there was not any pavement.

"Why, this is horrible—how dirty it is here!" said the Councilor. "The good pavement is gone, and all the lamps are put out."

The moon did not yet stand high enough to give much light, and the air was very thick, so that all objects seemed to melt together in the darkness. At the next corner a lamp hung before a picture of the Madonna, but the light it gave was as good as none. He noticed it only when he stood just under it, then his eyes fell upon the painted figure.

"That is probably a museum of art," thought he, "where they have forgotten to take down the sign."

A couple of men in the costume of those past days went by him.

"How they look!" he said. "They must come from a masquerade."

Suddenly there was a sound of drums and fifes, and torches gleamed brightly. The Councilor started. And now he saw a strange procession go past. First came a whole troop of drummers, beating their instruments very dexterously. They were followed by men-at-arms, with longbows and crossbows. The chief man in the procession was a clerical lord. The astonished Councilor asked what was the meaning of this, and who the man might be.

"That is the Bishop of Zealand."

"What in the world has happened to the Bishop?" said the Councilor, with a sigh, shaking his head. "This can not possibly be the Bishop!"

Ruminating on this, and without looking to the right or to the left, the Councilor went through East Street, and over the Highbridge Place. The bridge which led to the Palace Square was not to be found. He saw the shore of a shallow water, and at length encountered two people, who sat in a boat.

"Do you wish to be ferried over to the Holm, sir?" they asked.

"To the Holm!" repeated the Councilor, who did not know, you see, in what period he was. "I want to go to Christian's Haven and to Little Turf Street."

The men stared at him.

"Pray tell me where the bridge is?" said he. "It is shameful that no lanterns are lighted here; and it is as muddy, too, as if one were walking in a marsh." But the longer he talked with the boatmen the less he could understand them. "I don't understand your Bornholm talk," he cried, angrily, and turned his back upon them. He could not find the bridge, nor was there any paling. "It is quite scandalous how things look here!" he said—never had he thought his own times so miserable as this evening. "I think it will be best if I take a cab," thought he. But where were the cabs?—not one was to be seen. "I shall have to go back to the King's New Market, where there are many carriages standing, otherwise I shall never get as far as Christian's Haven."

Now he went toward East Street, and had almost gone through it when the moon burst forth.

"What in the world have they been erecting here!" he exclaimed, when he saw the East Gate, which in those days stood at the end of East Street.

In the meantime, however, he found a passage open, and through this he came out upon our New Market; but it was a broad meadow. Single bushes stood there, and across the meadow ran a great canal or stream. A few miserable wooden booths for Dutch skippers were erected on the opposite shore.

"Either I behold a Fata Morgana, or I am tipsy," sighed the Councilor. "What can that be? What can that be?"

He turned back in the full persuasion that he must be ill. In walking up the street he looked more closely at the houses; most of them were built of laths, and many were only thatched with straw.

"No, I don't feel well at all!" he lamented. "And yet I only drank one glass of punch! But I cannot stand that; and besides, it was very foolish to give us punch and warm salmon. I shall mention that to our hostess—the agent's lady. Suppose I go back, and say how I feel? But that looks ridiculous, and it is doubtful if they will still be up."

He looked for the house, but could not find it.

"That is dreadful!" he cried; "I don't know East Street again. Not one shop is to be seen; old, miserable, tumbledown huts are all I see, as if I were at Roeskilde or Ringstedt. Oh, I am ill! It's no use to make a fuss. But where in all the world is the agent's house? It is no longer the same. People are still up within. I certainly must be ill!"

He now reached a half-open door, where the light shone through a chink. It was a tavern of that time—a kind of beer house. The room had the appearance of a Dutch wineshop. A number of people, consisting of seamen, citizens of Copenhagen, and a few scholars, sat in deep conversation over their jugs, and paid little attention to the newcomer.

"I beg pardon," said the Councilor to the hostess, "but I feel very unwell; would you let them get me a fly to go to Christian's Haven?"

The woman looked at him and shook her head; then she spoke to him in German.

The Councilor now supposed that she did not understand Danish, so he repeated his wish in the German language. This, and his costume, convinced the woman that he was a foreigner. She soon understood that he felt unwell, and therefore brought him a jug of water. It certainly tasted a little of sea water, though it had been taken from the spring outside.

The Councilor leaned his head on his hand, drew a deep

breath, and thought of all the strange things that were happening about him.

"Is that today's number of the *Day?*" he said quite mechanically, for he saw that the woman was putting away a large sheet of paper.

She did not understand what he meant, but handed him the paper: it was a woodcut representing a strange appearance in the air which had been seen in the city of Cologne.

"That is very old!" said the Councilor, who became quite cheerful at the sight of this antiquity. "How did you come by this strange paper? That is very interesting, although the whole thing is a fable. Nowadays these appearances are explained to be Northern Lights that have been seen. They probably arise from electricity."

Those who sat nearest to him and heard his speech, looked at him in surprise, and one of them rose, took off his hat respectfully, and said with a very grave face, "You must certainly be a very learned man, sir!"

"Oh, no!" replied the Councilor; "I can only say a word or two about things one ought to understand."

"*Modestia* is a beautiful virtue," said the man. "Moreover, I must say to your speech, '*mihi secus videtur*'; yet I will gladly suspend my *judicium*."

"May I ask with whom I have the pleasure of speaking?" asked the Councilor.

"I am a bachelor of theology," replied the man.

This answer sufficed for the Councilor; the title corresponded with the garb.

"Certainly," he thought, "this must be an old village schoolmaster, a queer character, such as one finds sometimes over in Jutland."

"This is certainly not a *locus docendi*," began the man; "but I beg you to take the trouble to speak. You are doubtless well read in the ancients?"

"Oh, yes," replied the Councilor. "I am fond of reading useful old books; and am fond of the modern ones, too, with the exception of the *Everyday Stories*, of which we have enough, in all conscience."

"*Everyday Stories?*" said the Bachelor, inquiringly.

"Yes, I mean the new romances we have now."

"Oh!" said the man, with a smile, "they are very witty, and are much read at court. The King is especially partial to the romance by Messieurs Iffven and Gaudian, which talks about King Arthur and his Knights of the Round Table. He has jested about it with his noble lords." *

"That I have certainly not yet read," said the Councilor: "that must be quite a new book published by Heiberg."

"No," retorted the man, "it is not published by Heiberg, but by Godfrey von Gehmen." †

"Indeed! is he the author?" asked the Councilor. "That is a very old name: wasn't that the name of about the first printer who appeared in Denmark?"

"Why, he *is* our first printer," replied the man.

So far it had gone well. But now one of the men began to speak of a pestilence which he said had been raging a few years ago; he meant the plague of 1484. The Councilor supposed that he meant the cholera, and so the conversation went on tolerably. The Freebooters' War of 1490 was so recent that it could not escape mention. The English pirates had taken ships from the very wharves, said the man; and the Councilor, who was well acquainted with the events of 1801, joined in manfully against the English. The rest of the talk,

* Holberg relates in his *Stories of Denmark's Kings* that one day when King Hans had been reading in the *Romance of King Arthur*, he said in jest to his boon companion, Otto Rud, whom he loved very much: "These Knights, Iffven and Gaudian, whom I find in this book, must have been wonderful knights, such as one does not find nowadays"; whereupon Otto Rud replied: "If there were such a champion as King Arthur, then you would find many knights like Iffven and Gaudian."

† The first printer and publisher in Denmark, under King Hans.

however, did not pass so well. Every moment there was a contradiction. The good Bachelor was terribly ignorant, and the simplest assertion of the Councilor seemed too bold or too fantastic. They looked at each other, and when it became too bad, the Bachelor spoke Latin, in the hope that he would be better understood. But it was of no use.

"How are you now?" asked the Hostess, and she plucked the Councilor by the sleeve.

Now his memory came back; in the course of the conversation he had forgotten everything that had happened.

"Good heavens! where am I?" he said, and he felt dizzy when he thought of it.

"We'll drink claret, mead, and Bremen beer," cried one of the guests, "and you shall drink with us."

Two girls came in. One of them had on a cap of two colors. They poured out drink and bowed. The Councilor felt a cold shudder running all down his back. "What's that? What's that?" he cried; but he was obliged to drink with them. They took possession of the good man quite politely. He was in despair, and when one said that he was tipsy he felt not the slightest doubt regarding the truth of the statement, and only begged them to procure him a droshky. Now they thought he was speaking Muscovite.

Never had he been in such rude, vulgar company.

"One would think the country was falling back into heathenism," was his reflection. "This is the most terrible moment of my life."

But at the same time the idea occurred to him to bend down under the table, and then to creep to the door. He did so; but just as he had reached the entry the others discovered his intention. They seized him by the feet. And now the galoshes, to his great good fortune, came off, and—the whole enchantment vanished.

The Councilor saw quite plainly, in front of him, a lamp

burning, and behind it a great building. Everything looked familiar and splendid. It was East Street, as we know it now. He lay with his legs turned toward a porch, and opposite him sat the watchman asleep.

"Good heavens! Have I been lying here in the street dreaming?" he exclaimed. "Yes, this is East Street, sure enough! How splendidly bright and gay! It is terrible what an effect that one glass of punch must have had on me!"

Two minutes afterward he was sitting in a fly, which drove him out to Christian's Haven. He thought of the terror and anxiety he had undergone, and praised from his heart the happy present, our own time, which, with all its shortcomings, was far better than the period in which he had been placed a short time before.

III

The Watchman's Adventures

"On my word, yonder lies a pair of galoshes!" said the watchman. "They must certainly belong to the lieutenant who lives upstairs. They are lying close to the door."

The honest man would gladly have rung the bell and delivered them, for upstairs there was a light still burning; but he did not wish to disturb the other people in the house, and so he let it alone.

"It must be very warm to have a pair of these things on," said he. "How nice and soft the leather is!" They fitted his feet very well. "How droll it is in the world! Now, he might lie down in his warm bed, and yet he does not! There he is, pacing up and down the room. He is a happy man! He has neither wife nor children, and every evening he is at a party. Oh, I wish I were he; then I should be a happy man!"

As he uttered the wish, the galoshes he had put on produced

their effect, and the watchman was transported into the body and being of the lieutenant. He stood up in the room, and held a little pink paper in his fingers, on which there was a poem— a poem written by the lieutenant himself. For who is there who has not, once in his life, had a poetic moment? And at such a moment, if one writes down one's thoughts, there is poetry.

O, WERE I RICH!

"O, were I rich!" Such was my wish, yea such,
When hardly three feet high, I longed for much.
O, were I rich! an officer were I,
With sword, and uniform, and plume so high.
And the time came—an officer was I!
But yet I grew not rich. Alas, poor me!
Have pity Thou, who all man's wants dost see.

I sat one evening sunk in dreams of bliss,
A maid of seven years old gave me a kiss.
I at that time was rich in poesy
And tales of old, though poor as poor could be;
But all she asked for was this poesy.
Then was I rich, but not in gold, poor me!
As Thou dost know, who all men's hearts canst see.

O, were I rich! Oft asked I for this boon.
The child grew up to womanhood full soon.
She is so pretty, clever, and so kind;
O, did she know what's hidden in my mind—
A tale of old. Would she to me were kind!
But I'm condemned to silence; O, poor me!
As Thou dost know, who all men's hearts canst see.

O, were I rich in calm and peace of mind,
My grief you then would not here written find!
O thou, to whom I do my heart devote,
O, read this page of glad days now remote,
A dark, dark tale, which I to night devote!
Dark is the future now. Alas, poor me!
Have pity Thou, who all men's pains dost see.

Yes, people write poetry when they are in love; but a prudent man does not print such poems. The lieutenant was in love—and poor—that's a triangle, or, so to speak, the half of a broken square of happiness. The lieutenant felt that very keenly, and so he laid his head against the window frame and sighed a deep sigh.

"The poor watchman in the street yonder is far happier than I. He does not know what I call want. He has a home, a wife and children, who weep at his sorrow, and rejoice at his joy. Oh! I should be happier than I am, if I could change my being for his, and pass through life with his humble desires and hopes. Yes, he is happier than I!"

In that same moment the watchman became a watchman again. For through the power of the galoshes of Fortune, he had assumed the personality of the lieutenant: but then we know he felt far less content, and preferred to be just what he had despised a short time before. So the watchman became a watchman again.

"That was an ugly dream," said he, "but droll enough. It seemed to me that I was the lieutenant up yonder, and that it was not pleasant at all. I was without the wife and the boys, who are now ready to half stifle me with kisses."

He sat down again and nodded. The dream would not go quite out of his thoughts. He had the galoshes still on his feet. A falling star glided down along the horizon.

"There went one," said he, "but for all that, there are

enough left. I should like to look at those things a little nearer, especially the moon, for that won't vanish under one's hands. The student for whom my wife washes says that when we die we fly from one star to another. That's not true, but it would be very nice. If I could only make a little spring up there, then my body might lie here on the stairs for all I care."

Now, there are certain assertions we should be very cautious of making in this world, but doubly careful when we have galoshes of Fortune on our feet. Just hear what happened to the watchman.

So far as we are concerned, we all understand the rapidity of dispatch by steam; we have tried it either in railways or in steamers across the sea. But this speed is as the crawling of the sloth, or the march of the snail in comparison with the swiftness with which light travels. That flies nineteen million times quicker. Death is an electric shock we receive in our hearts, and on the wings of electricity the liberated soul flies away. The sunlight requires eight minutes and a few seconds for a journey of more than ninety-five millions of miles. On the wings of electric power the soul requires only a few moments to accomplish the same flight. The space between the orbs of the universe is, for her, not greater than, for us, the distances between the houses of our friends dwelling in the same town, and even living close together. Yet this electric shock costs us the life of the body here below, unless, like the watchman, we have the magic galoshes on.

In a few seconds the watchman had traversed the distance of two hundred and sixty thousand miles to the moon, which body, as we know, consists of a much lighter material than that of our earth, and is, as we should say, soft as new-fallen snow. He found himself on one of the many ring mountains with which we are familiar from Dr. Mâdler's great map of the moon. Within the ring, a great bowl-shaped hollow went down to the depth of a couple of miles. At the base of the hollow lay a town, of whose appearance we can only form an idea by pouring the white of an egg into a glass of water. The substance here was just as soft as egg white, and formed similar towers, and cupolas, and terraces like sails, transparent and floating in the thin air. Our earth hung over his head like a great dark red ball.

He immediately became aware of a number of beings, who were certainly what we call "men," but their appearance was very different from ours. A far more correct imagination than that of the pseudo-Herschel* had created them. If they had been put up in a row and painted, one would have said, "That's a beautiful arabesque!" They also had a language, but no one could expect that the soul of the watchman should understand it. But the watchman's soul did understand it, for our souls have far greater abilities than we suppose. Doesn't its wonderful dramatic talent show itself in our dreams? Then every one of our acquaintances appears, speaking in his own character, and with his own voice, in a way that not one of us could imitate in our waking hours. How does our soul bring back to us people of whom we have not thought for many years? Suddenly they come into our souls, with their smallest peculiarities about them. In fact it is a fearful thing, that memory which our souls possess. It can reproduce every sin, every bad thought. And then, it may be asked, shall we be able to give an account of every idle word that has been in our hearts and on our lips?

Thus the watchman's soul understood the language of the people in the moon very well. They disputed about this earth, and doubted if it could be inhabited. The air, they asserted, must be too thick for a sensible moon man to live there. They

* This relates to a book published some years ago in Germany, and said to be by Herschel, which contained a description of the moon and its inhabitants, written with such a semblance of truth that many were deceived by the imposture.

considered that the moon alone was peopled; for that, they said, was the real body in which the old-world people dwelt. They also talked of politics.

But let us go down to the East Street, and see how it fared with the body of the watchman.

He sat lifeless upon the stairs. His pike had fallen out of his hand, and his eyes stared up at the moon, which his honest body was wandering about.

"What time is it, watchman?" asked a passer-by. But the man who didn't answer was the watchman. Then the passers-by tweaked him quite gently by the nose, and then he lost his balance. There lay the body stretched out at full length—the man was dead. All his comrades were very much frightened: dead he was, and dead he remained. It was reported, and it was discussed, and in the morning the body was carried out to the hospital.

That would be a pretty jest for the soul if it should chance to come back, and probably seek its body in the East Street, and not find it! Most likely it would go first to the police and afterward to the address office, that inquiries might be made from thence respecting the missing goods; and then it would wander out to the hospital. But we may console ourselves with the idea that the soul is most clever when it acts upon its own account; it is the body that makes it stupid.

As we have said, the watchman's body was taken to the hospital, and brought into the washroom; and naturally enough, the first thing they did there was to pull off the galoshes; and then the soul had to come back. It took its way directly into the body, and in a few seconds there was life in the man. He declared that this had been the most terrible night of his life. He would not have such feelings again, not for a shilling; but now it was past and over.

The same day he was allowed to leave; but the galoshes remained at the hospital.

IV

A Great Moment; A Very Unusual Journey

EVERYONE who belongs to Copenhagen knows the look of the entrance to the Frederick's Hospital in Copenhagen. But as, perhaps, a few will read this story who do not belong to Copenhagen, it becomes necessary to give a short description of it.

The hospital is separated from the street, by a high railing, in which the thick iron rails stand so far apart that certain very thin inmates are said to have squeezed between them, and thus paid their little visits outside the premises. The part of the body most difficult to get through was the head; and here, as it often happens in the world, small heads were the most fortunate. This will be sufficient as an introduction.

One of the young volunteers, of whom one could say that only in one sense had he a great head, had the watch that evening. The rain was pouring down. But in spite of this obstacle he wanted to go out, for a quarter of an hour. It was needless, he thought, to tell the porter of his wish, especially if he could slip through between the rails. There lay the galoshes which the watchman had forgotten. It never occurred to him in the least that they were galoshes of Fortune. They would do him very good service in this rainy weather, and he pulled them on. Now the question was whether he could squeeze through the bars. Till now he had never tried it. There he stood.

"I wish to goodness I had my head outside!" cried he. And immediately, though his head was very thick and big, it glided easily and quickly through. The galoshes must have understood it well; but now the body was to slip through also, and that could not be done.

"I'm too fat," said he. "I thought my head was the thickest. I shan't get through."

Now he wanted to pull his head back quickly, but he could not manage it. He could move his neck, but that was all. His first feeling was one of anger, and then his spirit sank down to zero. The galoshes of Fortune had placed him in this terrible condition, and, unfortunately, it never occurred to him to wish himself free. No: instead of wishing, he only strove, and could not stir from the spot. The rain poured down; and not a creature was to be seen in the street. He could not reach the gate bell, and how was he to get loose? He foresaw that he would have to remain here until the morning, and then they would have to send for a blacksmith, to file through the iron bars. But such a business is not to be done quickly. The entire charity school would be there; the whole sailors' quarter close by would come up and see him standing in the pillory; and a fine crowd there would be.

"Hu!" he cried, "the blood's rising to my head, and I shall go mad! Yes, I'm going mad! If I were free, most likely it would pass over."

That's what he ought to have said at first. The very moment he had uttered the thought his head was free. He rushed in, quite dazed with the fright the galoshes of Fortune had given him. But we must not think the whole affair was over; there was much worse to come.

The night passed away, and the following day too, and nobody sent for the galoshes. In the evening a display of oratory was to take place in an amateur theater in a distant street. The house was crammed; and among the audience was the volunteer from the hospital, who appeared to have forgotten his adventure of the previous evening. He had the galoshes on, for they had not been sent for; and as it was dirty in the streets, they might do him good service. A new piece was recited: it was called *My Aunt's Spectacles*. These were spectacles which, when worn in a great assembly of people, made all those present look like cards, and one could prophesy from the cards all that would happen in the coming year.

The idea struck him; he would have liked to possess just such a pair of spectacles. If they were used rightly, they would perhaps enable the wearer to look into people's hearts; and that, he thought, would be more interesting than to see what was going to happen in the next year. Future events would be known in good time; but people's thoughts never.

"Now I'll look at the row of ladies and gentlemen on the first bench; if one could look directly into their hearts! Yes, it would be like a hollow, a sort of shop. How my eyes would wander about in that shop! In every lady's yonder, I should doubtless find a great milliner's warehouse. With this one here, the shop is empty, but it would do no harm to have it cleaned out. But would there really be such shops? Ah, yes!" he continued, sighing, "I know one in which all the goods are first-rate, but there's a servant in it already; and that's the only drawback in the whole heart! From one and another the word would be 'Please to step in!' Oh, that I might only step in, like a neat little thought, and slip through their hearts!"

That was the word of command for the galoshes. The volunteer shriveled up, and began to take a very remarkable journey through the hearts of the first row of spectators. The first heart through which he passed was that of a lady; but he immediately fancied himself in the Orthopedic Institute, in the room where the plaster casts of deformed limbs are kept hanging against the walls. The only difference was, that these casts were formed in the Institute when the patients came in, but here in the heart they were formed and preserved after the good persons had gone away. For they were casts of female friends, whose bodily and mental faults were preserved here.

Quickly he had passed into another female heart. But this

seemed to him like a great holy church; the white dove of innocence fluttered over the high altar. Gladly would he have sunk down on his knees; but he was obliged to go away into the next heart. Still, however, he heard the tones of the organ, and it seemed to him that he himself had become another and a better man. He felt himself not unworthy to enter into the next sanctuary, which showed itself in the form of a poor garret, containing a sick mother. But through the window the warm sun streamed in, and two sky-blue birds sang full of childlike joy, while the sick mother prayed for a blessing on her daughter.

Now he crept on his hands and knees through an overfilled butcher's shop. There was meat, and nothing but meat, wherever he went. It was the heart of a rich, respectable man, whose name is certainly to be found in the address book.

Now he was in the heart of this man's wife; this heart was an old dilapidated pigeon house. The husband's portrait was used as a mere weathercock; it stood in connection with the doors, and these doors opened and shut, as the husband turned.

Then he came into a cabinet of mirrors, such as we find in the castle of Rosenburg; but the mirrors magnified to a great degree. In the middle of the floor, sitting, like a Grand Lama, was the insignificant *I* of the proprietor, astonished in the contemplation of his own greatness.

Then he fancied himself transported into a narrow needle-case full of pointed needles; and he thought, "This must decidedly be the heart of an old maid!" But that was not the case. It was a young officer, wearing several orders, and of whom one said, "He's a man of intellect and heart."

Quite confused was the poor volunteer when he emerged from the heart of the last person in the first row. He could not arrange his thoughts, and fancied it must be his powerful imagination which had run away with him.

"Gracious powers!" he sighed, "I must certainly have a

great tendency to go mad. It is also unconscionably hot in here; the blood is rising to my head!"

And now he remembered the great event of the last evening, how his head had been caught between the iron rails of the hospital.

"That's where I must have caught it," thought he. "I must do something at once. A Russian bath might be very good. I wish I were lying on the highest board in the bathhouse." *

And so there he lay on the highest board in the steambath; but he was lying there in all his clothes, in boots and galoshes, and the hot drops from the ceiling were falling on his face.

"Hi!" he cried, and jumped down to take a plunge bath.

The attendant uttered a loud cry on seeing a person there with all his clothes on. The volunteer had, however, enough presence of mind to whisper to him, "It's for a wager!" But the first thing he did when he got into his own room was to put a big plaster on the nape of his neck, and another on his back, that they might draw out his madness.

Next morning he had a very sore back; and that was all he got from the galoshes of Fortune.

V

The Transformation of the Copying Clerk

THE watchman, whom we surely have not yet forgotten, in the meantime thought of the galoshes, which he had found and brought to the hospital. He took them away; but as neither the lieutenant nor anyone in the street would own them, they were taken to the police office.

"They look exactly like my own galoshes," said one of the

---

* In these Russian (vapor) baths the person extends himself on a bank or form, and as he gets accustomed to the heat, moves to another higher up toward the ceiling, where, of course, the steam is warmest. In this manner, he ascends gradually to the highest.

copying gentlemen,* as he looked at the unowned articles and put them beside his own. "More than a shoemaker's eye is required to distinguish them from one another."

"Mr. Copying Clerk," said a servant, coming in with some papers.

The copying clerk turned and spoke to the man. When he had done this, he turned to look at the galoshes again. He was in great doubt if the right-hand or the left-hand pair belonged to him.

"It must be those that are wet," he thought. Now here he thought wrong, for these were the galoshes of Fortune; but why shouldn't the police be mistaken sometimes? He put them on, thrust his papers into his pocket, and put a few manuscripts under his arm, for they were to be read at home, and abstracts to be taken from them. But now it was Sunday morning, and the weather was fine. "A walk to Fredericksburg would do me good," said he; and he went out accordingly.

There could not be a quieter, steadier person than this young man. We grant him his little walk with all our hearts; it will certainly do him good after so much sitting. At first he only walked like a vegetating creature, so the galoshes had no opportunity of displaying their magic power.

In the avenue he met an acquaintance, one of our younger poets, who told him that he was going to start, next day, on a summer trip.

"Are you going away again already?" asked the copying clerk. "What a happy, free man you are! You can fly wherever you like; we others have a chain to our foot."

"But it is fastened to the bread tree!" replied the poet. "You need not be anxious for the morrow; and when you grow old you get a pension."

* As on the Continent in all law and police practices nothing is verbal, but any circumstance, however trifling, is reduced to writing, the labor, as well as the number of papers that thus accumulate, is enormous. In a police office, consequently, we find copying clerks among many other scribes of various denominations, of which, it seems, our hero was one.

"But you are better off, after all," said the copying clerk. "It must be a pleasure to sit and write poetry. Everybody says agreeable things to you, and then you are your own master. Ah, you should just try it, poring over the frivolous affairs in the court."

The poet shook his head; the copying clerk shook his head also. Each retained his own opinion; and thus they parted.

"They are a strange race, these poets!" thought the copying clerk. "I should like to try and enter into such a nature—to become a poet myself. I am certain I should not write such complaining verses as the rest. What a splendid spring day for a poet! The air is so remarkably clear, the clouds are so beautiful, and the green smells so sweet. For many years I have not felt as I feel at this moment."

We already notice that he has become a poet. To point this out would, in most cases, be what the Germans call "mawkish." It is a foolish fancy to imagine a poet different from other people, for among the latter there may be natures more poetical than those of many an acknowledged poet. The difference is only that the poet has a better spiritual memory. His ears hold fast the feeling and the idea until they are embodied clearly and firmly in words; and the others cannot do that. But the transition from an everyday nature to that of a poet is always a transition, and as such it must be noticed in the copying clerk.

"What glorious fragrance!" he cried. "How it reminds me of the violets at Aunt Laura's! Yes, that was when I was a little boy. I have not thought of that for a long time. The good old lady! She lies yonder by the canal. She always had a twig or a couple of green shoots in the water, let the winter be as severe as it might. The violets bloomed, while I had to put warm farthings against the frozen windowpanes to make peepholes. That was a pretty view. Out in the canal the ships were frozen in, and deserted by the whole crew; a screaming crow was the only living creature left. Then when the spring breezes blew, it all became lively. The ice was sawn asunder amid shouting and cheers, the ships were tarred and rigged, and then they sailed away to strange lands. I remained here, and must always remain, and sit at the police office, and let others take passports for abroad. That's my fate. Oh, yes!" and he sighed deeply.

Suddenly he paused. "Good Heaven! what is come to me? I never thought or felt as I do now. It must be the spring air; it is just as dizzying as it is charming!" He felt in his pockets for his papers. "These will give me something else to think of," said he, and let his eyes wander over the first lead. There he read: " 'Dame Sigbirth; an original tragedy in five acts.' What is that? And it is my own hand. Have I written this tragedy? 'The Intrigue on the Promenade; or the Day of Penance—Vaudeville.' But where did I get that from? It must have been put into my pocket. Here is a letter. Yes, it is from the manager of the theater; the pieces are rejected, and the letter is not at all politely worded. H'm! h'm!" said the copying clerk, and he sat down upon a bench. His thoughts were elastic; his head was quite soft. Involuntarily he grasped one of the nearest flowers; it was a common little daisy. What the botanists require several lectures to explain to us, this flower told in a minute. It told the glory of its birth; it told of the strength of the sunlight, which spread out the delicate leaves and made them give out fragrance. Then he thought of the battles of life, which likewise awaken feelings in our breasts. Air and light are the lovers of the flower, but light is the favored one. Toward the light it turned, and only when the light vanished could the flower roll her leaves together and sleep in the embrace of the air.

"It is light that adorns me!" said the flower.

"But the air allows you to breathe," whispered the poet's voice.

Just by him stood a boy, knocking with his stick upon the

marshy ground. The drops of water spurted up among the green twigs, and the copying clerk thought of the millions of infusoria which were cast up on high with the drops, which was the same to them, in proportion to their size, as it would be to us if we were hurled high over the region of clouds. And the copying clerk thought of this, and of the great change which had taken place within him; he smiled. "I sleep and dream! It is wonderful, though, how naturally one can dream, and yet know all the time that it is a dream. I should like to be able to remember it all clearly tomorrow when I wake. I seem to myself quite unusually excited. What a clear appreciation I have of everything, and how free I feel! But I am certain that if I remember anything of it tomorrow, it will be nonsense. That has often been so with me before. It is so with all the clever famous things one says and hears in dreams, as with the money of the elves under the earth. When one receives it, it is rich and beautiful, but looked at by daylight, it is nothing but stones and dried leaves. Ah!" he sighed, quite plaintively, and gazed at the chirping birds, as they sprang merrily from bough to bough, "they are much better off than I. Flying is a noble art. Happy he who is born with wings. Yes, if I could change myself into anything, it should be into a lark."

In a moment his coattails and sleeves grew together and formed wings; his clothes became feathers, and his galoshes claws. He noticed it quite plainly, and laughed inwardly. "Well, now I can see that I am dreaming, but so wildly I have never dreamed before." And he flew up into the green boughs and sang; but there was no poetry in the song, for the poetic nature was gone. The galoshes, like everyone who wishes to do any business thoroughly, could only do one thing at a time. He wished to be a poet, and he became one. Then he wished to be a little bird, and, in changing thus, the first peculiarity was lost.

"That is charming!" he said. "In the daytime I sit in the

police office among the driest of law papers; at night, I can dream that I am flying about like a lark in the Fredericksburg Garden. One could really write quite a popular comedy upon it."

Now he flew down into the grass, turned his head in every direction, and beat with his beak upon the bending stalks of grass, which, in proportion to his size, seemed to him as long as palm branches of northern Africa.

It was only for a moment, and then all around him it became like the blackest night. It seemed to him that some immense substance was cast over him. It was a great cap, which a sailor boy threw over the bird. A hand came in and seized the copying clerk by the back and wings in a way that made him whistle. In his first terror he cried aloud, "The impudent rascal! I am copying clerk at the police office!" But that sounded to the boy only like "Peep! peep!" and he tapped the bird on the beak and wandered on with him.

In the alley, the boy met with two other boys, who belonged to the educated classes, socially speaking. But according to abilities, they ranked in the lowest class in the school. They bought the bird for a few Danish skillings; and so the copying clerk was carried back to Copenhagen.

"It's a good thing that I am dreaming," he said, "or I should become really angry. First I was a poet, and now I'm a lark! Yes, it must have been the poetic nature which transformed me into that little creature. It is a miserable state of things, especially when one falls into the hands of boys. I should like to know what the end of it will be."

The boys carried him into a very elegant room. A stout, smiling lady received them. But she was not at all gratified to see the common field bird, as she called the lark, coming in too. Only for one day she would consent to it; but they must put the bird in the empty cage which stood by the window.

"Perhaps that will please Polly," she added, and laughed at

a great parrot, swinging himself proudly in his ring in the handsome brass cage.

"It's Polly's birthday," she said simply, "so the little field bird shall congratulate him."

Polly did not answer a single word; he only swung proudly to and fro. But a pretty canary, who had been brought here last summer out of his warm, fragrant fatherland, began to sing loudly.

"Screamer!" said the lady; and she threw a white handkerchief over the cage.

"Peep, peep!" sighed he. "Here's a terrible snowstorm." And thus sighing, he was silent.

The copying clerk, or, as the lady called him, the field bird, was placed in a little cage close to the canary, and not far from the parrot. The only human words which Polly could say, and which often sounded very comically, were *"Come, let's be men, now!"* Everything else that he screamed out was just as unintelligible as the song of the canary, except to the copying clerk, who was now also a bird, and who understood his comrades very well.

"I flew under the green palm tree and the blossoming almond tree!" sang the canary. "I flew with my brothers and sisters over the beautiful flowers and over the bright sea, where the plants waved in the depths. I also saw many beautiful parrots, who told the merriest stories."

"Those were wild birds," replied the parrot. "They had no education. Let us be men now! Why don't you laugh? If the lady and all the strangers could laugh at it, so can you. It is a great fault to have no taste for what is pleasant. No, let us be men now."

"Do you remember the pretty girls who danced under the tents spread out beneath the blooming trees? Do you remember the sweet fruits, and the cooling juice in the wild plants?"

"Oh, yes!" replied the parrot; "but here I am far better off.

I have good care and genteel treatment. I know I've a good head, and I don't ask for more. Let us be men now. You are what they call a poetic soul. I have thorough knowledge and wit. You have genius, but no prudence. You mount up into those high natural notes of yours, and then you get covered up. That is never done to me; no, no, for I cost them a little more. I make an impression with my beak, and can cast wit and humor round me. Come, let us be men!"

"Oh, my poor blooming fatherland!" sang the canary. "I will praise thy dark-green trees and thy quiet bays, where the branches kiss the clear watery mirror. I'll sing of the joy of all my shining brothers and sisters, where the plants grow by the desert springs and the cactus grows."

"Now, pray leave off these dismal tones," cried the parrot. "Sing something at which one can laugh! Laughter is the sign of the highest mental development. Can a dog or a horse laugh? No; they can cry; but laughter—that is given to men alone. Ho, ho, ho!" screamed Polly, and finished the jest with "Let us be men now."

"You little gray northern bird," said the canary; "so you have also become a prisoner. It is certainly cold in your woods, but still liberty is there. Fly out! they have forgotten to close your cage. The upper window is open. Fly, fly!"

Instinctively the copying clerk obeyed, and flew forth from his prison. At the same moment the half-opened door of the next room creaked, and stealthily, with fierce sparkling eyes, the house cat crept in, and chased after him. The canary fluttered in its cage, the parrot flapped its wings, and cried "Let us be men now." The copying clerk felt mortally afraid, and flew through the window, away over the houses and streets; and at last he was obliged to rest a little.

The house opposite had a homelike look; one of the windows stood open, and he flew in. It was his own room. He perched upon the table.

"Let us be men now," he broke out, involuntarily imitating the parrot; and in the same moment he was restored to the form of the copying clerk. But he was perching on the table.

"Heaven preserve me!" he cried. "How could I have come here and fallen so soundly asleep? It was an unquiet dream, too, that I had. The whole thing was great nonsense."

VI

The Best That the Galoshes Brought

On the following day, quite early in the morning, as the clerk still lay in bed, there came a tapping at his door. It was his neighbor who lodged on the same floor, a young theologian; and he came in.

"Lend me your galoshes," said he. "It is very wet in the garden, but the sun shines gloriously, and I should like to smoke a pipe down there."

He put on the galoshes, and was soon in the garden, which contained a plum tree and an apple tree. Even a little garden like this is highly prized in the midst of great cities.

The theologian wandered up and down the path; it was only six o'clock, and a post horn sounded out in the street.

"Oh, traveling, traveling!" he cried out, "that's the greatest happiness in all the world. That's the highest goal of my wishes. Then this disquietude that I feel would be stilled. But it would have to be far away. I should like to see beautiful Switzerland, to travel through Italy, to—"

Yes, it was a good thing that the galoshes took effect immediately, for he might have gone too far even for himself, and for us too. He was traveling; he was in the midst of Switzerland, packed tightly with eight others in the interior of a diligence. He had a headache and a weary feeling in his neck, and his feet had gone to sleep, for they were swollen by the heavy boots he had on. He was hovering in a state between sleeping and waking. In his right-hand pocket he had his letter of credit, in his left-hand pocket his passport, and a few louis d'or were sewn into a little bag he wore on his breast. Whenever he dozed off, he dreamed he had lost one or other of these possessions; and then he would start up in a feverish way, and the first movement his hand made was to describe a triangle from left to right, and toward his breast, to feel whether he still possessed them or not. Umbrellas, hats, and walking sticks swung in the net over him, and almost took away the prospect, which was impressive enough. He glanced out at it, and his heart sang what one poet at least, whom we know, has sung in Switzerland, but has not yet printed:

> *'Tis a prospect as fine as heart can desire,*
> *Before me Mont Blanc the rough:*
> *'Tis pleasant to tarry here and admire,*
> *If only you've money enough.*

Great, grave, and dark was all nature around him. The pine-woods looked like little mosses upon the high rocks, whose summits were lost in cloudy mists; and then it began to snow, and the wind blew cold.

"Hu!" he sighed; "if we were only on the other side of the Alps, then it would be summer, and I should have got money on my letter of credit. My anxiety about this prevents me from enjoying Switzerland. Oh, if I were only at the other side!"

And then he was on the other side, in the midst of Italy, between Florence and Rome. The lake Thrasymene lay spread out in the evening light, like flaming gold among the dark-blue hills. Here, where Hannibal beat Flaminus, the grapevines held each other by their green fingers. Pretty, half-naked children were keeping a herd of coal-black pigs under a clump of fragrant laurels by the wayside. If we could reproduce this scene accurately, all would cry, "Glorious Italy!" But neither the theologian nor any of his traveling companions in the carriage of the vetturino thought this.

Poisonous flies and gnats flew into the carriage by the thousands. In vain they beat the air frantically with a myrtle branch —the flies stung them, nevertheless. There was not one person in the carriage whose face was not swollen and covered with stings. The poor horses looked miserable, the flies tormented them woefully. It mended the matter only for a moment when the coachman dismounted and scraped them clean of the insects that sat upon them in great swarms. Now the sun sank down; at once an icy coldness pervaded all nature; it was like the cold air of a funeral vault after the sultry summer day. And all around the hills and clouds put on that remarkable green tone which we notice in some old pictures, and consider unnatural unless we have ourselves witnessed a similar play of color. It was a glorious spectacle; but the stomachs of all were empty and their bodies exhausted, and every wish of the heart turned toward a resting place for the night. But how could that be won? To find this resting place all eyes were turned more eagerly to the road than toward the beauties of nature.

The way now led through an olive wood; he could have fancied himself passing between knotty willow trunks at home. Here, by the solitary inn, a dozen crippled beggars had taken up their positions. The quickest among them looked, to quote an expression of Marryat's, like the eldest son of Famine, who had just come of age. The others were either blind or had withered legs so that they crept about on their hands, and some had withered arms with fingerless hands. This was misery in rags indeed. *"Eccellenza, miserabili!"* they sighed, and stretched forth their diseased limbs. The hostess herself, in untidy hair, and dressed in a dirty blouse, received her guests. The doors were tied up with string; the floor of the room was of brick, and half of it was grubbed up. Bats flew about under the roof, and oh! the smell within—

"Yes, lay the table down in the stable," said one of the travelers. "There, at least, one knows what one is breathing."

The windows were opened, so that a little fresh air might find its way in; but quicker than the air came the withered arms and the continual whining, "*Miserabili, Eccellenza!*" On the walls were many inscriptions; half of them were spiteful toward "*La bella Italia.*"

The supper was served. It consisted of a watery soup, seasoned with pepper and rancid oil. This last dainty played a big part in the salad dressing. Musty eggs and roasted cockscombs were the best dishes. Even the wine had a strange taste —it was a dreadful mixture.

At night the boxes were placed against the doors. One of the travelers kept watch while the rest slept. The theologian was the sentry. Oh, how close it was in there! The heat oppressed him, the gnats buzzed and stung, and the *miserabili* outside moaned in their dreams.

"Yes, traveling would be all very well," said the theologian, "if one had no body. If the body could rest, and the mind fly! Wherever I go, I find a want that oppresses my heart. It is something better than the present moment that I desire. Yes, something better—the best; but what is that, and where is it? In my own heart I know very well what I want. I want to attain to a happy goal, the happiest of all."

And so soon as the word was spoken he found himself at home. The long white curtains hung down from the windows, and in the middle of the room stood a black coffin: in this he was lying in the quiet sleep of death; his wish was fulfilled— his body was at rest, and his spirit roaming. "Esteem no man happy who is not yet in his grave," were the words of Solon; here their force was proved anew.

Every corpse is a sphinx of immortality. The sphinx here also, in the black sarcophagus, answered, what the living man had laid down two days before:

Thou strong, stern Death! Thy silence waketh fear;
Thou leavest mold'ring gravestones for thy traces.
Shall not the soul see Jacob's ladder here?
No resurrection type but churchyard grasses?
The deepest woes escape the world's dull eye:
Thou that alone on duty's path hast sped,
Heavier those duties on thy heart would lie
Than lies the earth now on thy coffined head.

Two forms were moving to and fro in the room. We know them both. They were the Fairy of Care and the Ambassadress of Fortune. They bent down over the dead man.

"Do you see?" said Care. "What happiness have your galoshes brought to men?"

"They have, at least, brought a permanent benefit to him who slumbers here," replied Fortune.

"Oh, no!" said Care. "He went away by himself; he was not summoned. His spirit was not strong enough to lift the treasures which he had been destined to lift. I will do him a favor."

And she drew the galoshes from his feet. Then the sleep of death was ended, and the awakened man raised himself up. The Fairy of Care vanished, and with her the galoshes disappeared too; doubtless she looked upon them as her property.

OLE SHUT-EYE

In the whole world there is nobody who knows so many stories as Ole Shut-Eye. He can tell such wonderful ones!

As evening comes on, when the children still sit nicely at table or on their stools, then comes Ole Shut-Eye. He comes up the stairs very softly, for he walks in his stocking feet. He opens the door noiselessly, and *st!* he squirts sweet milk in the children's eyes, a small, small stream, but enough to prevent them from keeping their eyes open. And then they cannot see him. He creeps among them, and blows softly upon their necks, and this makes their heads heavy. Oh, yes, but it doesn't hurt them, for Ole Shut-Eye is very fond of the children. He only wants them to be quiet. And quiet they're not until they are taken to bed. Then they must be quiet so he can tell them his stories.

When the children sleep, Ole Shut-Eye sits down upon their bed. He is well dressed. His coat is of silk, but it is impossible to say of what color, for it shines red, green, and blue, as he turns. Under each arm he carries an umbrella. The one with pictures he spreads over the good children, and then they dream all night the most glorious stories. But on his other umbrella nothing at all is painted, and this he spreads over the naughty children, and they sleep in a dull way, and when they awake in the morning they have not dreamed of anything.

Now we shall hear how Ole Shut-Eye came, every evening through one whole week, to a little boy named Hjalmar. And we shall hear what he told him. There are seven stories, for there are seven days in the week.

Monday

"LISTEN," said Ole Shut-Eye in the evening, when he had put Hjalmar to bed. "Now I'll begin."

And all the flowers in the flowerpots became great trees, stretching out their long branches under the ceiling of the room and along the walls, so that the whole room looked like a lovely bower. And all the twigs were covered with flowers, and each flower was more beautiful than a rose, and smelled so sweet that one wanted to eat it. It was sweeter than jam. The fruit gleamed like gold, and there were cakes bursting with raisins. It was splendid. But at the same time a terrible wail sounded from the table drawer, where Hjalmar's schoolbook lay.

"Whatever can that be?" said Ole Shut-Eye. And he went to the table, and opened the drawer. It was the slate, suffering from convulsions. A wrong number had got into the sum, and it was nearly falling in pieces. The slate pencil tugged and jumped at its string, as if it had been a little dog who wanted to help the sum; but it could not. And then there was a great lamentation in Hjalmar's copybook; it was terrible to hear. On each page the great letters stood in a row, one underneath the other, and each had a little one at its side. That was the copy. And next to them were a few more letters which thought they looked just like the first. And Hjalmar had written them. But they lay down as if they had tumbled over the pencil lines on which they were to stand.

"See, this is how you should hold yourselves," said the Copy. "Look, sloping in this way, with a powerful swing!"

"Oh, we would be very glad to do that," replied Hjalmar's Letters, "but we cannot. We are too weakly."

"Then you must take medicine," said Ole Shut-Eye.

"Oh, no," cried they. And they immediately stood up so gracefully that it was beautiful to behold.

"Yes, now we cannot tell any stories," said Ole Shut-Eye. "Now I must exercise them. One, two! one, two!" and so he exercised the Letters. And they stood quite slender, and as beautiful as any copy could be. But when Ole Shut-Eye went away, and Hjalmar looked at them the next morning, they were as weak and miserable as ever.

Tuesday

As soon as Hjalmar was in bed, Ole Shut-Eye touched all the articles of furniture in the room with his little magic gun, and they immediately began to talk together. Each one spoke of itself, with the exception of the spittoon, who stood silent, and was vexed that they should be so vain as to speak and think only of themselves, without any regard for him. He, who stood so modestly in the corner for everyone's use.

Over the chest of drawers hung a great picture in a gilt frame—it was a landscape. Inside one could see large old trees, flowers in the grass, and a broad river which flowed round about a forest, past many castles, and far out into the wide ocean.

Ole Shut-Eye touched the painting with his magic gun, and the birds began to sing, the branches of the trees stirred, and the clouds began to move across it; one could see their shadows glide over the landscape.

Now Ole Shut-Eye lifted little Hjalmar up to the frame, and put the boy's feet into the picture, just in the high grass. And there he stood; and the sun shone upon him through the branches of the trees. He ran to the water, and seated himself in a little boat which lay there. It was painted red and white, the sails gleamed like silver, and six swans, each with a gold circlet round its neck, and a bright blue star on its forehead,

drew the boat past the great wood, where the trees tell of
robbers and witches, and the flowers tell of the graceful little
elves, and of what the butterflies have told them.

Gorgeous fishes, with scales like silver and gold, swam after
their boat. Sometimes they gave a spring, so that it splashed in
the water. And birds, blue and red, little and great, flew after
them in two long rows. The gnats danced, and the cockchafers
said, "Boom! boom!" They all wanted to follow Hjalmar,
and each one had a story to tell.

That was a pleasure voyage. Sometimes the forest was thick
and dark, sometimes like a glorious garden full of sunlight
and flowers. And there were great palaces of glass and of
marble. On the balconies stood princesses, and these were all
little girls whom Hjalmar knew well; he had already played
with them. Each one stretched forth her hand, and held out
the prettiest sugar heart that ever a cake-woman could sell.
And Hjalmar took hold of each sugar heart as he passed by,
and the Princess held fast, so that each of them got a piece—
she the smaller share, and Hjalmar the larger. At each palace
little princes stood sentry. They shouldered golden swords,
and caused raisins and tin soldiers to shower down. One could
see that they were real princes.

Sometimes Hjalmar sailed through forests, sometimes
through great halls, or through the midst of a town. He also
came to the town where his nurse lived. She had carried him
in her arms when he was a little boy, and she had always been
so kind to him. She nodded and beckoned, and sang the pretty
verse she had made up herself and sent it to Hjalmar—

> *I think of you, so oft, so oft,*
> *My own Hjalmar, ever dear;*
> *I've kissed your little lips so soft,*
> *Your forehead and your cheeks so clear.*
> *I heard you utter your first word,*
> *Then was I forced to say farewell;*

Now will I trust you to our Lord,
A good boy here, an angel there to dwell.

And all the birds sang too, the flowers danced on their stalks, and the old trees nodded, just as if Ole Shut-Eye had been telling stories to *them*.

Wednesday

How the rain was streaming down outside! Hjalmar could hear it in his sleep. And when Ole Shut-Eye opened a window, the water stood up to the windowsill. There was quite a lake outside, and a noble ship lay close to the house.

"If you will sail with me, little Hjalmar," said Ole Shut-Eye, "you can voyage tonight to foreign climes, and be back again tomorrow."

And Hjalmar suddenly stood in his Sunday clothes upon the glorious ship, and immediately the weather became fine, and they sailed through the streets and steered round by the church; and now everything was one great wild ocean. They sailed on until land was no longer to be seen. And they saw a number of storks, who also came from their home, and were traveling toward the hot countries. These storks flew in a row, one behind the other, and they had already flown far—far! One of them was so weary that his wings would scarcely carry him farther. He was the very last in the row, and soon fell a great way behind the rest. At last he sank, with outspread wings, deeper and deeper; he gave a few more strokes with his pinions, but it was of no use. Now he touched the rigging of the ship with his feet, then he glided down from the sail, and—bump!—he stood upon the deck.

The cabin boy took him and put him into the hen coop with the fowls, ducks, and the turkeys; and the poor stork stood among them quite embarrassed.

"Just look at the fellow!" said all the fowls.

And the turkey cock swelled himself up as much as ever he could, and asked the stork who he was. And the ducks walked backward and quacked to each other, "Quackery! quackery!"

And the stork told them of hot Africa, of the pyramids, and of the ostrich, which runs like a wild horse through the desert. But the ducks did not understand what he said, and they said to one another,

"We're all of the same opinion, namely, that he's stupid."

"Yes, certainly he's stupid," said the turkey cock; and he gobbled.

Then the stork was silent, and thought of his Africa.

"Those are wonderful thin legs of yours," said the turkey cock. "Pray, how much do they cost a yard?"

"Quack! quack! quack!" grinned all the ducks. But the stork pretended not to hear them.

"You may as well laugh too," said the turkey cock to him, "for that was very wittily said. Or was it, perhaps, too clever for you? Yes, yes, he isn't very penetrating. Let us continue to be interesting among ourselves."

And then he gobbled, and the ducks quacked, "Gick! gack! gick! gack!" It was terrible how they made fun among themselves.

Hjalmar went to the hen coop, opened the back door, and called to the stork. And the stork hopped out to him on the deck. He had rested, and it seemed as if he nodded to Hjalmar, to thank him. Then he spread his wings, and flew away to the warm countries, but the fowls clucked, and the ducks quacked, and the turkey cock became fiery red in the face.

"Tomorrow we shall make songs about you," said Hjalmar. And so saying he awoke, and was lying in his linen bed. It was a wonderful journey that Ole Shut-Eye had made him take that night.

Thursday

"I TELL you what," said Ole Shut-Eye, "you must not be frightened. Here you shall see a little mouse," and he held out his hand with the pretty little creature in it. "It has come to invite you to a wedding. There are two little mice here who are going to enter into the marriage state tonight. They live under the floor of your mother's store closet. It is said to be a charming dwelling place!"

"But how can I get through the little mouse hole in the floor?" asked Hjalmar.

"Let me manage that," said Ole Shut-Eye. "I will make you small."

And he touched Hjalmar with his magic gun, and the boy began to shrink and shrink, until he was no longer than a finger.

"Now you may borrow the uniform of a tin soldier. I think it would fit you, and it looks good to wear a uniform when one is in society."

"Yes, certainly," said Hjalmar.

And in a moment he was dressed like the smartest of tin soldiers.

"Will your honor be kind enough to take a seat in your mamma's thimble?" asked the mouse. "Then I shall have the honor of drawing you."

"Will the young lady really take so much trouble?" cried Hjalmar.

And so they drove to the mouse's wedding. First they came into a long passage beneath the boards. It was just high enough for the thimble to drive through. The whole passage was lit up with rotten wood.

"Isn't there a delicious smell here?" observed the mouse.

"The entire road has been greased with bacon rinds. There can be nothing more exquisite."

Now they came into the festive hall. On the right hand stood all the little lady mice. And they whispered and giggled as if they were making fun of each other. On the left stood all the gentlemen mice, stroking their whiskers with their forepaws. And in the center of the hall the bridegroom and bride were standing in a hollow cheese rind, kissing each other terribly before all the guests. For this was the betrothal, and the marriage was to follow immediately.

More and more strangers kept flocking in. One mouse nearly trod another to death. The happy couple had stationed themselves in the doorway, so that one could neither come in nor go out. Like the passage, the room had been greased with bacon rinds, and that was the entire banquet. But for dessert a pea was produced. In it a mouse, belonging to the family, had bitten the name of the betrothed pair—that is to say, the first letter of the name; and that was something quite out of the ordinary.

All the mice said it was a beautiful wedding, and that the entertainment had been very agreeable. Then Hjalmar drove home again. He had been obliged to crawl, to make himself little, and to put on a tin soldier's uniform, but he had really been in grand company.

Friday

"It is wonderful how many grown-up people there are who would be glad to have me!" said Ole Shut-Eye. "Especially those who have done something wrong. 'Good little Ole,' they say to me, 'we cannot close our eyes, and so we lie all night and see our evil deeds, which sit on the bedstead like ugly little goblins, and throw hot water over us. Won't you come and drive them away, so that we may have a good sleep?' And then they sigh deeply—'We would really be glad to pay for it. Good night, Ole—the money lies on the windowsill.' But I do nothing for money," said Ole Shut-Eye.

"What shall we do this evening?" asked Hjalmar.

"I don't know if you care to go to another wedding tonight. It is a different kind than yesterday's. Your sister's big doll, that looks like a man, and is called Hermann, is going to marry the doll Bertha. Moreover, it is the dolls' birthday, and therefore they will receive very many presents."

"Yes, I know that," replied Hjalmar. "Whenever the dolls want new clothes, my sister lets them have their birthday or celebrate a wedding. It has certainly happened a hundred times already."

"Yes, but tonight is the hundred and first wedding; and

when number one hundred and one is past, it is all over. And that is why it will be so splendid. Just look!"

And Hjalmar looked at the table. There stood the little cardboard house with the windows lit up, and in front of it all the tin soldiers were presenting arms. The bride and bridegroom sat quite thoughtful, and with good reason, on the floor, leaning against a leg of the table. And Ole Shut-Eye, dressed up in the grandmother's black gown, married them to each other. When the ceremony was over, all the pieces of furniture struck up the following beautiful song, which the Pencil had written for them. It was sung to the melody of the soldiers' tattoo—

> *Let the song swell like the rushing wind,*
> *In honor of those who this day are joined,*
> *Although they stand here stiff and blind,*
> *Because they are both of a leathery kind.*
> *Hurrah! hurrah! though they're deaf and blind,*
> *Let the song swell like the rushing wind.*

And now they received their presents—but they refused to accept provisions of any kind, for they intended to live on love.

"Shall we now go into a summer lodging, or start on a journey?" asked the bridegroom.

And the swallow, who was a great traveler, and the old yard Hen, who had brought up five broods of chickens, were consulted on the subject. And the swallow told of the beautiful warm climate, where the grapes hang in ripe, heavy clusters, where the air is mild, and the mountains glow with colors that are unknown here.

"But you haven't got our brown cabbage there!" objected the Hen. "I was once in the country, with my children, in a summer that lasted five weeks. There was a sandpit, in which we could walk about and scratch. And we had the *entrée* to a garden where brown cabbage grew. It was so hot there that one could scarcely breathe. And we don't have all the poisonous animals that infest these warm countries of yours, and we are free from robbers. He is a villain who does not consider our country the most beautiful—he certainly does not deserve to be here!" And then the Hen wept, and went on, "I have also traveled. I rode in a coop for more than twelve miles; and there is no pleasure at all in traveling!"

"Yes, the Hen is a sensible woman!" said Bertha, the doll. "I don't think much of traveling among mountains, for you only have to go up, and then down again. No, we will go into the sandpit beyond the gate, and walk about in the cabbage garden."

And so it was settled.

Saturday

"AM I to hear some stories now?" asked little Hjalmar, as soon as Ole Shut-Eye had sent him to sleep.

"This evening we have no time for that," replied Ole Shut-Eye. And he spread his finest umbrella over the lad. "Only look at these Chinese!"

And the whole umbrella looked like a great china dish, with blue trees and pointed bridges, with little Chinese upon them, who stood there nodding their heads.

"We must have the whole world prettily decked out for tomorrow morning," said Ole Shut-Eye, "for that will be a holiday—it will be Sunday. I will go to the church steeples to see that the little church goblins are polishing the bells, so they may sound sweetly. I will go out into the field, and see if the breezes are blowing the dust from the grass and leaves. And, what is the greatest work of all? I will bring down all the stars, to polish them. I take them in my apron; but first each one must be numbered, and the holes in which they are placed up there must be numbered likewise, so that they can go back in the same grooves again. Otherwise they would not sit fast, and we would have too many shooting stars, for one after another would fall down."

"Hark ye! Do you know, Mr. Ole Shut-Eye," said an old Portrait which hung on the wall where Hjalmar slept, "I am Hjalmar's great-grandfather? I thank you for telling the boy stories; but you must not confuse his ideas. The stars cannot come down and be polished! The stars are world-orbs, just like our own earth, and that is what's good about them."

"I thank you, old great-grandfather," said Ole Shut-Eye, "I thank you! You are the head of the family. You are the ancestral head. But I am older than you! I am an old heathen. The Romans and Greeks called me the Dream God! I have been in the noblest houses, and am admitted there still! I know how to act with great people and with small! Now you may tell your own story!" and Ole Shut-Eye took his umbrella, and went away.

"Well, well! Can't one even give an opinion nowadays?" grumbled the old Portrait. And Hjalmar awoke.

Sunday

"Good evening!" said Ole Shut-Eye. Hjalmar nodded, and then ran and turned his great-grandfather's Portrait against the wall, so it would not interrupt them, as it had done yesterday.

"Now you must tell me stories—about the five green peas that lived in one shell, and about the cock's foot that paid court to the hen's foot, and of the darning needle who gave herself such airs because she thought herself a working needle."

"That may be too much of a good thing!" said Ole Shut-Eye. "You know that I prefer showing you something. I will show you my own brother. His name, like mine, is Ole Shut-

Eye, but he never comes to anyone more than once. And he takes him to whom he comes upon his horse, and tells him stories. He knows only two. One of these is so exceedingly beautiful that no one in the world can imagine it, and the other so horrible that it cannot be described."

And then Ole Shut-Eye lifted little Hjalmar up to the window, and said:

"There you will see my brother, the other Ole Shut-Eye. They also call him Death! Do you see, he does not look so terrible as they make him in the picture books, where he is only a skeleton. No, that is silver embroidery that he has on his coat; that is a splendid hussar's uniform; a mantle of black velvet flies behind him over the horse. See how he gallops along!"

And Hjalmar saw how this Ole Shut-Eye rode away, and took young people as well as old upon his horse. Some of them he put before him, and some behind. But he always asked first, "How do you stand in the mark book?" "Well," they all replied. "Yes, let me see it myself," he said. And then each one had to show him the book. And those who had "very well" and "remarkably well" written in their books, were placed in front of his horse, and a lovely story was told to them. While those who had "middling" or "tolerably well," had to sit up behind, and hear a very terrible story indeed. They trembled and wept, and wanted to jump off the horse, but this they could not do, for they had all grown fast to it.

"But Death is a most splendid Ole Shut-Eye," said Hjalmar. "I am not afraid of him!"

"Nor need you be," replied Ole Shut-Eye. "Just see that you have a good mark book!"

"Yes, that is improving!" muttered great-grandfather's Portrait. "It is of some use giving one's opinion." And now he was satisfied.

That is the story of Ole Shut-Eye, you see. And now he may tell you more himself, this evening!

AN AFTERWORD
BY CLIFTON FADIMAN

Hans Christian Andersen wrote many more fairy tales like the ones you have just read. But the fairy tale he lived was as wonderful as any of them. In fact it *was* one of them: *The Ugly Duckling*.

Hans was born in 1805 in the little Danish town of Odense. His father (whom he lost at eleven) was a poor shoemaker, his mother took in washing, his grandfather was not entirely right in the head, his education was scrappy—and he himself was gawky, lanky, awkward, with a thin, high voice: a real Ugly Duckling. Yet once, during his boyhood, an old woman (she might have been a wise witch from one of his own stories) predicted that "one day the whole of Odense will be illuminated for him."

The prophecy came true. In time Hans became the friend of kings and one of the most famous men in Europe. Of certain fairy tales he said: "They become better as they grow older." And this was true of his own life. Even his appearance changed. A famous painter said of him, "One was accustomed to call him ugly but, in later life, his head became beautiful." The Ugly Duckling had indeed changed into a Swan.

And it all came about because of these fairy tales, some of them based on old Danish folk legends, others invented by him—and, believe me, it's very hard to invent a *new* fairy tale. They have been loved for a hundred years and more; they have been translated into over forty languages; some of them, such as *The Ugly Duckling* and *The Emperor's New Clothes*, are referred to in ordinary conversation every day.

But what makes them different from other excellent fairy tales, like those collected by the Brothers Grimm? Two things, I think.

The first is that Andersen put so much of his own life into them. We feel a *person* behind the stories. *The Ugly Duckling* is Andersen himself. *The Red Shoes* goes back to an episode in his own life. The Tin Soldier who loved the Ballerina was himself: Andersen fell in love with a beautiful actress but failed to win her. And a story like *Aunty* is filled with his own lifelong love of the theater.

The second thing that makes these tales the best of their kind ever written is the way in which he makes everything come alive: toys, flowers, animals, darning needles, china ornaments, snowmen. Not only people, but the whole world talks, moves, dances, makes jokes, suffers, rejoices. Andersen makes you believe, as he so often says, that "this is a true story."

I am much older than you. But I think I got as much pleasure in re-reading these lovely tales as you did in reading them, perhaps for the first time. I felt in them a wisdom, and often a sadness, that I didn't feel when I was a child. And that is why Andersen keeps his magic for young and old.

About the author

HANS CHRISTIAN ANDERSEN

Hans Christian Andersen was born in 1805 in Odense, Denmark. His father was a poor shoemaker and could hardly give his son the bare essentials. However, since he had always wanted to be a scholar himself, he faithfully read the classics to his son. After his father's death, Hans' mother remarried and, as a washerwoman, she continued to support him. Proud and vain, ashamed of his poverty, Hans dropped out of-school, burying himself instead in the colorful world of his imagination and his homemade puppet theater.

At fourteen, he went to Copenhagen and made a nuisance of himself to the prominent men in the art world. He sang, danced, quoted his own writings—even when they did not wish to see or hear him. He was ignored for the most part, but finally received a small pension through the aid of several interested people. He published his first book, *The Ghost at Palnatoke's Grave*, and then went on to school at Slagelse and Elsinore. In 1833, the king gave him a pension which allowed him to travel. He arrived in Rome in October of 1834, and early in 1835 he received his first critical acclaim with the publication of *The Improvisator*. This was followed a few months later by the first volume of his *Fairy Tales*. The fairy tales were not popular at first. But in the following years, as more of them were published, his fame grew. He was lionized in all of Europe and numbered among his friends Charles Dickens and Jenny Lind. He died in his home near Copenhagen in August of 1875.

About the artist

LAWRENCE BEALL SMITH

Lawrence Beall Smith is renowned for his painting of children and as a portrait artist of great distinction. It is understandable therefore that he has been sought by publishers for book illustration. His work in this area includes another Macmillan Classic, *Rebecca of Sunnybrook Farm*, and *The Jungle of Tonza Mara* (Macmillan, 1963).

Mr. Smith was born in Washington, D.C., and was graduated from the University of Chicago. He received his art training at the Chicago Art Institute and under Hopkinson and Zimmerman in Boston.

During World War II, he was an artist correspondent covering the Normandy invasion and Army medical activities in England and France.

His work hangs in the permanent collections of many museums including Harvard University, Addison Gallery of American Art in Andover, the John Herron Art Institute, Indianapolis, and the Encyclopædia Britannica Collection.

Mr. Smith lives with his wife and three children in Cross River, New York.

THE MACMILLAN CLASSICS • These handsome new editions of thirty-five landmarks in American and world literature offer children, teenagers, and parents a distinguished home library of fine reading. Young readers will find Clifton Fadiman's warm and informal discussion of each book a rewarding "afterword." The distinctive illustrations, by some of today's finest artists, catch the individual tone and character of each book. ৯

LITTLE MEN
BY LOUISA MAY ALCOTT
ILLUSTRATED BY PAUL HOGARTH

LITTLE WOMEN
BY LOUISA MAY ALCOTT
ILLUSTRATED BY BETTY FRASER

ANDERSEN'S FAIRY TALES
BY HANS CHRISTIAN
ANDERSEN
ILLUSTRATED BY
LAWRENCE BEALL SMITH

**EAST OF THE SUN AND
WEST OF THE MOON
AND OTHER TALES**
Collected by P. C. ASBJORNSEN
and JORGEN E. MOE
ILLUSTRATED BY TOM VROMAN

PRIDE AND PREJUDICE
BY JANE AUSTEN
ILLUSTRATED BY BERNARDA BRYSON

THE WIZARD OF OZ
BY L. FRANK BAUM
ILLUSTRATED BY W. W. DENSLOW

JANE EYRE
BY CHARLOTTE BRONTE
ILLUSTRATED BY ATI FORBERG

WUTHERING HEIGHTS
BY EMILY BRONTE
ILLUSTRATED BY BERNARDA BRYSON

**ALICE'S ADVENTURES
IN WONDERLAND
AND THROUGH
THE LOOKING-GLASS**
BY LEWIS CARROLL
ILLUSTRATED BY SIR JOHN TENNIEL

**THE AENEID FOR
BOYS AND GIRLS**
Retold by ALFRED J. CHURCH
ILLUSTRATED BY EUGENE KARLIN

**THE ADVENTURES
OF PINOCCHIO**
BY C. COLLODI
ILLUSTRATED BY NAIAD EINSEL

**THE RED BADGE
OF COURAGE**
BY STEPHEN CRANE
ILLUSTRATED BY HERSCHEL LEVIT

ROBINSON CRUSOE
BY DANIEL DEFOE
ILLUSTRATED BY
FEDERICO CASTELLON

A CHRISTMAS CAROL
BY CHARLES DICKENS
ILLUSTRATED BY JOHN GROTH

DAVID COPPERFIELD
BY CHARLES DICKENS
ILLUSTRATED BY N. M. BODECKER

A TALE OF TWO CITIES
BY CHARLES DICKENS
ILLUSTRATED BY
RICHARD M. POWERS

**TALES OF
SHERLOCK HOLMES**
BY SIR ARTHUR
CONAN DOYLE
ILLUSTRATED BY
HARVEY DINNERSTEIN

THE THREE MUSKETEERS
BY ALEXANDRE DUMAS
ILLUSTRATED BY
JAMES DAUGHERTY

GRIMMS' FAIRY TALES
BY THE BROTHERS GRIMM
ILLUSTRATED BY ARNOLD ROTH

**RIP VAN WINKLE AND
THE LEGEND OF
SLEEPY HOLLOW**
BY WASHINGTON IRVING
ILLUSTRATED BY DAVID LEVINE

**TALES
FROM SHAKESPEARE**
BY CHARLES AND MARY LAMB
ILLUSTRATED BY
RICHARD M. POWERS

THE CALL OF THE WILD
BY JACK LONDON
ILLUSTRATED BY KAREL KEZER

KING ARTHUR
Stories from Sir Thomas Malory's
Morte d'Arthur
Retold by MARY MacLEOD
ILLUSTRATED BY HERSCHEL LEVIT

MOBY DICK
BY HERMAN MELVILLE
ILLUSTRATED BY ROBERT SHORE

**TALES AND POEMS OF
EDGAR ALLAN POE**
ILLUSTRATED BY RUSSELL HOBAN

BLACK BEAUTY
BY ANNA SEWELL
ILLUSTRATED BY JOHN GROTH

**FIVE
LITTLE PEPPERS**
BY MARGARET SIDNEY
ILLUSTRATED BY
ANNA MARIE MAGAGNA

HEIDI
BY JOHANNA SPYRI
ILLUSTRATED BY GRETA ELGAARD

ENGLISH FAIRY TALES
Retold by FLORA ANNIE STEEL
ILLUSTRATED BY
ARTHUR RACKHAM

TREASURE ISLAND
BY ROBERT LOUIS
STEVENSON
ILLUSTRATED BY JOHN FALTER

GULLIVER'S TRAVELS
BY JONATHAN SWIFT
Retold by PADRAIC COLUM
ILLUSTRATED BY WILLY POGANY

**THE ADVENTURES OF
HUCKLEBERRY FINN**
BY MARK TWAIN
ILLUSTRATED BY JOHN FALTER

**THE ADVENTURES OF
TOM SAWYER**
BY MARK TWAIN
ILLUSTRATED BY JOHN FALTER

**TWENTY THOUSAND
LEAGUES UNDER
THE SEA**
BY JULES VERNE
ILLUSTRATED BY CHARLES MOLINA

**REBECCA OF
SUNNYBROOK FARM**
BY KATE DOUGLAS WIGGIN
ILLUSTRATED BY
LAWRENCE BEALL SMITH